Praise for *The Black Crescent*

'Master storyteller Jane Johnson takes the reader on **a fascinating journey** through one man's extraordinary life, adventures, and self-discoveries, with an irresistible cat by his side. A **unique, captivating tale** that held me spellbound throughout.'

> **GENEVIEVE GRAHAM**, #1 bestselling author of *Bluebird*
> and *The Forgotten Home Child*

'I was enraptured from the first to the last page. Hamou is such a fascinating character—a decent man, trapped in extraordinary times. This is **a riveting novel**.'

> **ROBERTA RICH**, bestselling author of *The Jazz Club Spy*

'A hugely **enjoyable and unusual** historical novel.'

> **RACHEL HORE**, bestselling author of *A Beautiful Spy* and
> *The Love Child*

'[A] marvellous novel, **evocative, powerful, and transportive**, and Hamou is a wonderful protagonist, full of empathy and curiosity about people. I loved it and felt I had been steeped in Morocco.'

> **ELIZABETH CHADWICK**, bestselling author of
> *The King's Jewel* and *A Marriage of Lions*

'[A] compelling narrative.'

> ***The Times***

'I loved *The Black Crescent*. It put me so **vividly** into the landscape and character of the people, it was as though I had been there.'

> **BARBARA ERSKINE**, bestselling author of
> *The Dream Weavers* and *The Ghost Tree*

'A **vivid** novel with fascinating characters that will linger in one's thoughts long after the final page. **Highly recommended**.'

> ***The Historical Novels Review***

The Black Crescent

JANE JOHNSON

Published by Simon & Schuster

New York   London   Toronto   Sydney   New Delhi

SIMON &
SCHUSTER
CANADA

A Division of Simon & Schuster, LLC
166 King Street East, Suite 300
Toronto, Ontario M5A 1J3

First published in the United Kingdom in 2023 by Head of Zeus Ltd, part of Bloomsbury Publishing Plc

This Simon & Schuster Canada edition March 2024

SIMON & SCHUSTER CANADA and colophon are registered trademarks of Simon & Schuster, LLC

Simon & Schuster: Celebrating 100 Years of Publishing in 2024

For information about special discounts for bulk purchases, please contact Simon & Schuster Special Sales at 1-800-268-3216 or CustomerService@simonandschuster.ca.

Manufactured in the United States of America

10 9 8 7 6 5 4 3 2 1

Library and Archives Canada Cataloguing in Publication
Title: The black crescent / Jane Johnson.
Names: Johnson, Jane, 1960- author.
Description: Simon & Schuster Canada edition.
Identifiers: Canadiana (print) 20230218326 | Canadiana (ebook) 20230218369 |
ISBN 9781668017500 (softcover) | ISBN 9781668017524 (EPUB
Classification: LCC PR6060.O357 B53 2024 | DDC 823/.914—dc23

ISBN 978-1-6680-1750-0
ISBN 978-1-6680-1752-4 (ebook)

For Abdel, whose book this is

I

TIZIANE
ANTI-ATLAS MOUNTAINS OF MOROCCO

June 1939

Even though many things had changed, some things never changed. Hamou Badi walked along the alley, past the sacks of couscous and flour, dried mussels, almonds, chickpeas and lentils that the tradesmen weighed out in their big brass balances, past the *hammam* with its chimney streaming woodsmoke into the clear blue sky, past the knot of gossiping black-robed women, and all the way, the scents and smells of the village chased him and wrapped him in their familiarity. His younger cousin Moha trailed him, the milk churn bumping against his leg.

They were on their way to fetch the milk from Taba Tôt at the farm. This was Hamou's task most mornings, one he never relished, for Taba Tôt scared the living daylights out of him. Today was worse than usual because of Moha's constant string of irritating questions.

'Why does everyone ride donkeys here? Don't you have any cars?'

'Why are there so many dogs running around? Doesn't anyone own them?'

'Can't we just go to a shop for our milk like normal people?'

Hamou had given up answering with anything more than a grunt because no matter how many questions he answered there were always more. He turned on Moha now. 'Look, just shut up, all right? If you chatter on at Taba Tôt she'll put the evil eye on you and probably on me as well.'

Moha laughed. 'The evil eye! You'll be telling me she commands djinns next.'

Hamou reddened. Of course Taba Tôt communed with djinns, everyone knew that.

The great house rose up before them like a cliff, arrow-slit windows in its walls of rosy *pisé*, an iron-studded door wide enough to give entrance to two horsemen riding abreast, crenellations around its roof: a miniature kasbah. The queue for the milk from the farm attached to the great house already reached back around the corner.

Hamou let out an exasperated sigh. If he hadn't been saddled with his slow-legged cousin, a city boy raised in far-off Casablanca, he'd already have been on his way home, milk and all. Now he would have to endure not only the long queue and Taba Tôt's rising temper, but also his mother's impatience at having to wait for the milk. He did try, from the lofty heights of his eleven years, to feel charitably towards the younger boy – after all, it couldn't be easy being eight years old with his mother so sick that he'd been sent off on a seven-hundred-kilometre bus ride all alone from Casablanca to Marrakech, from Marrakech to Agadir to Tiznit, then up through the mountains here to Tiziane, a world away from everything and everyone he knew – but there was something about Moha that drove deep any charitable instincts he might have had. It wasn't just the incessant questions or his slowness that roused his fury but the younger boy's refusal to defer to him in anything. He'd even had the gall to mock Hamou's *djellaba* this morning. 'You're going out in that raggedy thing?'

Hamou had looked down at his striped camel-wool robe, bewildered. It was what most people wore here. Certainly, it wasn't new – it had been passed down from his older brothers as they grew out of it, and maybe to them by his father, and to his father by his grandfather – but that just meant it was of good quality, to last so long. But now Moha had mentioned it he had started to notice details: moth holes; frayed cuffs; dirt along the hem; and always the distinct aroma of the original animal of which he had believed only he was aware. Moha wore a plain navy djellaba over his Casa street clothes, including a pair of smart lace-up shoes rather than the yellow leather *babouches* typically worn here. Hamou took satisfaction from the despoliation of these shoes – a day and a half of Tiziane dust had already taken a toll.

They joined the back of the queue behind Anir Oulhaj and Iza Moussaoui. The girl turned to regard them with interest. 'Who's this, Hamou?'

Hamou raised a shoulder dismissively. 'My little cousin Moha.'

Iza grinned at Moha. 'Isn't he cute?'

'Not really,' said Hamou.

'Where are you from?' Iza asked Moha. 'The valley? One of the mountain villages?'

Moha bridled. 'I'm not a yokel. I'm from Casa.'

Now it was Anir's turn to be curious. 'Have you seen USM play?'

'What's USM?'

'Union Sportive Casa – the football club,' Hamou said in disbelief. 'Everyone knows that.'

'I don't like football.'

'You can't be serious!' The boys regarded Moha as if he was of another species. Football was everything!

But Iza's grin widened. 'What do you like, Moha?'

'School,' Moha declared after brief consideration. 'I like school.'

The queue shuffled forward as the boys digested this. School meant interminable hours of Qur'anic verses copied out on their wooden tablets, learning passages by rote, getting whacked by Sidi Belqassim's stick for writing with your left hand. 'School? Who likes school? No one likes school.'

'I do. I'm going to run a company, like Papa.' He used the French word rather than the local word '*baab*'. 'What are you going to do?'

'Me?' Anir had never given it a thought. Then he grinned. 'I'm going to be a public assassin, like Slimane Chafari.'

Moha stared at him. 'There's no such thing.'

'Is so. Isn't there, Hamou?'

Hamou nodded. Chafari was a figure of local legend, a rebel and freedom fighter. 'He gets paid for killing people,' he told his cousin cheerfully. He paused. 'Perhaps I'll save up and get him to kill you.'

Iza and Anir laughed loudly, but Moha frowned.

'Anyway,' Anir said, 'who wants to run a company? Sitting on your arse in an office isn't a job for a free man.' The very word for their people – the Amazigh – meant 'free men'. It was what defined them as a race, distinct from the Arabs, and of course from the French occupiers. It was the first principle they learned.

Now it was Moha's turn to laugh. 'Free? You Berbers are funny. Look around.'

A pair of uniformed men were coming down the street, kepis on their heads, rifles slung over the back of their khaki jackets, ammunition belts bulging. Hamou glanced towards the soldiers, then away. 'So?'

'So, you'd better get used to not being "free men". That's all in the past.'

Anir squared his shoulders. 'We will never give in to the French. The nationalists will see them off.' Anir's uncles had left the region to join up with Bennacer ou Saïd's forces in the High Atlas, launching raids on the French in Marrakech.

As for Moha, Hamou thought he had a nerve thinking he was any better than the Amazigh: his mother was Hamou's father's sister!

When the soldiers approached, Hamou and Anir studied the ground. It didn't do to attract attention. Even though the policy was to govern with a light hand, some individuals liked to throw their weight around.

'*Bonjour, messieurs!*' Moha piped up.

'Shut up, you idiot!' Hamou hissed, but it was too late: the soldiers were coming over.

'What's your name?'

You never gave them your name. Hamou quickly trod on his cousin's smart shoe.

'Ow! Moha bin Salim, *monsieur*.'

The soldier ruffled his hair. 'What impeccable manners. Setting an example to the rest of these ruffians, eh?' He reached into his pocket and drew out a sweet, which he gave to Moha. 'You see?' he said to Hamou and Anir. 'If you're nice to us, we'll be nice to you.' The pair moved on.

Hamou and Anir exchanged dark glances. Moha put down the milk churn, unwrapped his bonbon and sucked loudly on it for the whole time it took them to reach the gate.

The smell of the farm assailed Hamou long before he came to it: cow dung and chicken shit, but also fresh bread and the hot stones in the clay oven in which it was baked, the pungent lanolin scent of the sheep, and the spicy soup kept simmering all day in the firepot to feed the workers. And closer still, the scent of Taba Tôt herself, a wave of musk and incense and orange blossom. Wholesome enough, but underlain by the smell of blood: it was said that Taba Tôt carried out the practice of butchering the farm's livestock.

The complex aromas made Hamou's innards turn over, remembering the pinches on his arms, the clips around the head, the painful pokes in the ribs Taba Tôt had given him over the years. She took a particular interest in him, one he didn't understand. Even as he had grown taller and stronger, she seemed to get no less massy or terrifying, which must be further evidence of the magic she wielded.

There she was now, in front of the big iron-bound door of the house's strongroom – ladling milk out of the copper vat into the pail of Fatima bent Habiba, whose thin little arm shook as she tried to hold the bucket steady under its growing weight. When the housekeeper straightened from her task you could take in the full size of her – as big as a bull, encased in an embroidered black robe pinned with a jewelled fibula. Strands of amber beads, each as large as a baby's fist, garlanded her neck and five massive iron keys lay upon her chest as a symbol of her power and authority.

Taba Tôt was the stuff of shared nightmares for all the village children, who told tale after tale of her butcheries and also of her occasional disorientating kindnesses. But Moha just gazed at her in wonder, without a trace of fear, which won him a degree of grudging respect from Hamou.

'*Yalla!*' she boomed. 'Come on!'

It was as if the stones of the house itself had spoken. She took a step towards the next child and chickens flurried out of her way, trying to avoid being turned into escalopes by those huge feet in their garish red booties.

Hamou watched the child answer the summons smartly, running up the path to pay his respects and have his milk churn filled. Then it was Anir's turn. Anir, in his haste to obey Taba Tôt's summons, failed to see a fat brown hen, got his feet caught up with it and hit the ground with an ill-considered curse. The hen tottered off in a zigzag run, shedding feathers. At once Taba Tôt was upon him, belabouring his shoulders and back with the ladle, her silver bracelets rattling on her wrists with every strike. She had never liked Anir, who had a tendency to answer back, and to make such an error was a gift to her temper. Anir, who revered the brave Amazigh warriors in the tales, tried to take his punishment like a man, but by the time he came back, Hamou could see the tearstains on his cheeks. He said nothing, but Moha stared.

Now it was Iza's turn. She kept her head down, kissed Taba Tôt's hand, waited patiently till her pail was full, then walked carefully with it back to the gate.

Hamou's heart started to race. 'Give me the churn,' he said brusquely to Moha. 'You can wait here.'

But Moha's knuckles whitened on the wooden handle. 'I want to meet Taba Tôt.'

There was no time for argument; the housekeeper was beckoning impatiently.

'Good luck,' Iza whispered in passing. 'She's in a rotten mood.'

'Who is this young person?' Taba Tôt demanded without a word of greeting or any of the niceties that were customary in Tiziane, where, by the time you left anyone you'd randomly encountered in the street, you'd be fully apprised of the well-being of every member of their family, down to their sheep and chickens.

Hamou opened his mouth to reply, but he was too slow. Moha was already gabbling about being called Mohamed really and visiting from Casablanca to stay with his cousins because his mother was ill and was complimenting her on the heaps of jewellery she wore. Taba Tôt preened, then patted Moha's head. 'You could learn a lot about manners from this one,' she said, addressing Hamou.

Hamou glared at Moha as the housekeeper turned to fill up the churn, but Moha just smiled.

'And how is your esteemed mother, *Lalla* Saïda?' Taba Tôt enquired.

'She's well, *alhamdullilah*,' Hamou replied formally, but once more Moha cut in.

'She isn't well, really. She was complaining about her hands aching and kept rubbing her joints.'

Taba Tôt's bloodshot eyes bulged as if the upwelling of thoughts behind them was exerting physical pressure. 'Are her knuckles swollen?'

'Yes, and a bit red,' said Moha.

Hamou felt irrational fury. She was *his* mother, not a subject for public discussion. '*Yam'mi*'s waiting for the milk. Let's go,' he said roughly to Moha.

7

Taba Tôt's big hand grabbed his shoulder as he turned to leave. He could feel the meaty weight of it, the power in her fingers, and smell the heart-stopping whiff of her animal-scent. He stopped dead. 'Wait here,' she rumbled. 'Do not move a muscle.' She swayed with slow grace back to the storeroom and disappeared inside.

'Now we're going to be even later,' Hamou groaned. 'Why couldn't you keep your mouth shut?'

But his cousin assumed the serene expression of the righteous and said nothing.

At last, Taba Tôt shuffled back outside, stopping to exchange words with a tall, thin man dressed top to toe in sun-faded black cotton, with a long, forked mattock balanced on his shoulder. It was Taba Tôt's husband, Da Bassim the gardener, with whom Hamou and his gang had tangled on various occasions after ravaging the grapevines. Hamou looked away, not wanting to attract his attention, especially while he was carrying that wicked-looking implement. Impatient faces regarded him accusingly from the queue: this delay was making all of them late.

Taba Tôt's shadow fell over him. She carried a small clay pot, but when Hamou reached out to take it, she held on to his hand and did not let go. '*You* will carry the milk,' she decreed severely. 'This child is not your servant.'

As she turned her head to address Moha, sunlight flashed on the slave rings she wore in her long ears. She pressed the little jar into the boy's hands. 'This is for Lalla Saïda,' she told him. 'Tell her Taba Tôt says to rub it into her hands morning and night. A little lavender oil will make it smell better.'

'Yes, *madame*.' Moha offered her the French honorific and her grin widened so that you could almost see the pretty girl she might once have been.

Now Taba Tôt turned her attention back to Hamou, turning over the hand she held on to. She scrutinised his palm and traced the perfect horizontal line that ran across the centre from one side to the other. 'Our little *zouhry*,' she said quietly.

It was a word Hamou had heard whispered before, from his mother, from his aunts. He didn't really know what it meant, only that up to last year, when he had turned ten, his mother had kept him beside her far more than he would have liked, saying he must be careful, not talk to strangers, not wander far, and always wear mittens, even in the summer. On his tenth birthday, she had given thanks to God for preserving him. 'Now you are truly mine,' she had said. 'Now you are safe.'

'You have the luck. You have *baraka*,' Taba Tôt said. 'It makes you strong, it makes you a good person. Honour your mother and your father, for she is a fine woman, and he is a brave man, and they and the djinns made you as you are.'

Hamou frowned. His father was a trader, gone almost all the time. It was hard to consider him brave, though desert travel was hard and no doubt dangerous.

Taba Tôt leaned closer. 'They do say a zouhry is always able to find treasure in the world.' She grinned, showing the wide gap between her front teeth. 'Now, run along with your little cousin. Be kind to him and try to listen to the good angel on your shoulder and not the devil.' At last, she released him.

Hamou resisted the voice of the good angel. He jammed the lid onto the churn with more violence than was required, then turned to go.

'We'll have to take a shortcut,' he told the boy, walking out onto the street with exaggerated speed. 'So just keep up, right?'

Instead of returning along the alley that led back the easier, longer way they had come, through the centre of the village, past the hammam, the stalls and the market square and the bridge, he headed towards the river and the palm grove. The river was filled with water only in the rainy season. At this time of year, it was as dry as dust, though further up towards the plateau there were still pools where the women could do the laundry. In spring, the air would be loud with the croaking of frogs and feral dogs would stand on rocks in the middle of the flow to snatch them out of the running water.

Hamou wriggled through the gap in the orchard wall, knowing that Da Bassim was safely engaged at the farm, and made his way quickly between the orange trees, their orbs of fruit hanging like bright jewels amongst the dark, glossy leaves. Usually, he would stop to scrump a few, but there was no time for that now. He turned and beckoned Moha to catch up: the boy was staring around, large-eyed, as if he had no idea where fruit came from.

Hamou threaded between the grapevines he and his friends often raided, till he reached the far side of the orchard where the fig trees grew. Here, you could wedge yourself between the fig tree and the wall to make an easy ascent. Hefting the churn onto his shoulder and then to a ledge near the top of the wall, Hamou climbed up nimbly. Astride the sun-warmed stones, he retrieved the churn, then reached a hand down to his young cousin, who was staring up uncertainly.

'Haven't you ever climbed a wall before?'

Moha shook his head.

'What on earth do you do all day in the city?'

Moha took his hand and scrabbled inelegantly with his slippery modern shoes till he reached the top of the wall. 'What I'm told, mostly.' He looked gloomily down at the scratches and dust now marring his footwear.

Life in Casa sounded unbearably dull to Hamou. He climbed down the other side and rocked the churn off its perch and into his arms. 'Oof!' He left Moha to make his own way down: if he couldn't jump off a wall, what hope was there for him?

Striking out towards the *oued*, he made a beeline for home, only a few hundred yards away from here, across the dry riverbed, through the palm grove, and over the road that led in from the valley. He knew Moha would have difficulty negotiating the rocky sides, but the sun was beating down and he was hot and irritable, the handle was digging into his hand, his arms ached, and he could just imagine the tongue-lashing he was going to get when he finally made it back to the house.

Behind him, he heard the thud of the boy jumping down from the wall and the scuff of his feet in the dust on the other side. Hamou headed for the point in the oued which offered an easier descent, wrestled the milk churn through the notch with him and padded through the deep drift of sand and fallen palm branches lining the riverbed.

The other side was trickier, but by now he just didn't care whether Moha managed to follow him or not. No one ever really got lost in Tiziane – everyone knew everyone else, and a stray child would soon be located and returned to safety.

Even, he thought with a sudden shot of discomfort, by a French soldier. He imagined his mother's fury if a uniformed man knocked at the door of the family house. No, that wouldn't do at all. He turned back to look for his cousin, but the boy was nowhere to be seen. He called out his name. No reply. Overhead, a crow gave out a cry and took off with a rattle of feathers.

Hamou set the milk churn against the bole of a tree and ran along the bank until at last he spotted a flash of colour down in the riverbed. He ran towards it, but even before he got there he could see – and smell – that whatever it was, it was not his cousin Moha.

There he was, standing at the lip of the oued, staring down uncertainly. Hamou sighed. Did the boy not know how to jump? 'Come on, I'll catch you.'

His cousin havered, then launched himself with more power than Hamou had been expecting, bowling him over. Moha got up and carefully dusted down his clothes, then turned around.

'What are you doing?'

Hamou had crawled to the bank and was investigating something caught up in the roots of the palm trees there. The flash of colour turned out to be a bundle of cloth that appeared to have been stuffed in under the bank. He wondered what could be inside it. Had someone wrapped valuable items inside the cloth and buried it there? Perhaps Taba Tôt was right: perhaps he did have a gift for finding treasure! He pulled a piece of the cloth away and a scorpion scuttled into the sunlight, its feet whisking across the sand, pincers raised in angry defence.

He barely noticed it, for he had realised something bigger and more important, and the understanding of this swelled in his throat and chest.

The bundle was not treasure.

In a catastrophic tumble of cloth and dry earth, the rags and their contents fell from their resting place onto the floor of the dry riverbed, sending up a cloud of dust. When it settled, Hamou glimpsed a ghastly face, and he turned away to retch.

It was the first time he had ever seen a corpse.

But it would not be the last.

2

CASABLANCA, MOROCCO

April 1955

Hamou Badi watched the big black Citröen bump its way out of the dirt road and cruise slowly past him to the junction, where it turned onto the Boulevard Mazagan, its headlights carving twin channels through the thick night air. He wondered what business the occupants of such a vehicle should have in the poor backstreets of the Derb Ghrallef, though he had his suspicions. Continuing along the Rue Géricault, he stopped at the stall on the corner to purchase five Anfas, his small and only luxury, and stashed them carefully away in his jacket pocket to smoke later. Crossing the next alley, he disturbed a pair of cats squaring up to one another with backs arched and teeth bared, their weird eyes reflecting the moonlight like the headlights of the French car. So intent were they on their private war that they barely registered his presence. At night, the city belonged to them: humans had no place here. He walked on.

'Good evening, Hamou Badi.'

Hamou looked down. 'Oh, hello, Didi.'

The young man squatted with his back against the wall, his withered arm balanced on top of the blanket that swathed his knees, palm up – a shockingly pale pink – as a silent prompt. Quashing a brief spasm of regret, Hamou took out two of the five cigarettes and placed them on the upturned palm.

Didi's grin gleamed white in the darkness. '*Shokran, sidi!*'

Hamou could see from here that there was a single light on at the house in which he rented his room, up on the second floor. It was late: most of the occupants would be settling down for the night or already asleep. With a wave to the beggar, he walked quickly on and tried to open the front door. As usual, the key stuck in the faulty lock. Tempting though it might be to swear or rattle the door, he patiently withdrew the key, then replaced it, jiggling it till he felt it slide home. The hinges squealed, but still he made the effort to close the iron door behind him as quietly as he could, guiding it with the flat of his hand, went softly up the stairs and let himself into his small apartment at the top of the building. The flick of a switch filled the bare room with light as stark as a shout. Even after all these years in the city, Hamou found himself marvelling at the miracle of electricity. Back in Tiziane, only French houses boasted such amenities.

Hamou took the cigarettes from his pocket and placed them on the table, then lit the little butane stove and put the kettle on to make tea. While he waited for it to boil, he removed his uniform jacket, smoothed the fabric, rebuttoned it so that it would hang properly, and returned it to the wardrobe. Despite the heat during the day and the mugginess of the evening, his shirt would do for another day, he decided. Stripping off the rest of his clothing, he poured a little of the warmed water into a bowl and washed himself, his movements as neat as those of the prowling cats.

He was just pulling a cotton djellaba over his head when he heard a quiet metallic scrape against the floor outside his door. His ears quested after the sounds, heart rate quickening; then came the sound of retreating footsteps, and he breathed out.

Opening the door, he looked out into the darkness. At his feet lay a tray covered with a chequered tea-cloth which did little to muffle aromas that made his treacherous stomach rumble. He retrieved the tray, feeling both pleased and guilty. His neighbour's food was always perfectly spiced and richly sauced but with every mouthful he would be reminded of his mother's warning:

'Watch out for those Arab women, my son. They'll be dying to get their claws into you, to drag you in for their daughters like mountain lions bringing down a gazelle for their cubs.' His mother had a colourful turn of phrase. 'Don't get yourself into awkward situations, you hear me? Let them lay obligations upon you and they'll have you. I know their schemes!' He knew she knew their schemes, for they were her own. Despite his mother's warnings, he was already obliged to the Chadlis. And hungry. He set the tray down, made a pot of mint tea and settled himself at the table. The cloth hid a clay tajine, a small round loaf and a slice of iced cake. When he lifted the lid of the cooking pot, he was overcome by a cloud of fragrant steam freighted with the scents of preserved lemon, garlic, saffron and chicken, and his mouth ran with water.

Before long, he had scraped every sliver of caramelised onion from the base of the tajine, pressed every crumb of bread and then cake with a finger and licked it clean. Replete, his being teetered on the edge of perfect happiness that could be completed only by smoking a cigarette on the roof terrace.

Putting off that final treat, he washed the tajine and the plate, wiped and dried them and the tray, folded the cloth, and padded down to his neighbour's door, laying them down beside the neat row of outdoor shoes that indicated the family was at home. The shoes were clean, but cheap: Rachid Chadli was a carpenter, with a family to support. Again, Hamou felt guilt tug at him.

Returning to his room, he poured himself a glass of mint tea, retrieved his cigarettes and matches and slipped up to the roof terrace, a space that during the day was the realm of women, but was neutral territory after dark.

Leaning on the parapet, he gazed out into the Casablanca night, feeling the cooling air caress his skin, listening to the distant howl of dogs. Tiny pinprick lights in the darkness picked out the extent of the *bidonville*, the shantytown in the wasteland to the south. The man who had owned this big parcel of land in the Derb Ghrallef had encouraged Moroccans to come and live here, to build whatever structures and homes they could afford. The French had tried to construct a wide road through the middle of the land, but each night the Moroccan homes crept over it a little more, a few centimetres of concrete block here, a few iron stakes there, until the road was obliterated, and the French gave up the project as a bad job, just as a farmer abandons the wildest corner of a field as not being worth the effort. Now there was barely a metre of unoccupied space, and where there was, chickens pecked and scratched and scrawny goats and sheep roamed, foraging through the rubbish for scraps. Hamou preferred these anarchic spaces to the regimented cleanliness of the French quarters, with their manicured parks and wide boulevards. They reminded him of Tiziane, before his father died and he'd come to Casa to earn money to send home to his family.

If you'd told the eleven-year-old Hamou that within a few years he'd be living in Casablanca, fostered by his cousin Moha's family, sent to a French school to learn to read and write and calculate, and then be training to join the French-run police service, he'd have been aghast. He was Hamou Badi – gangleader, fruit-stealer, unhobbler of donkeys, catapult-maker and general promoter of chaos – and he resented the French who occupied his country with a passion. And now here he was, paid to keep order for the very regime he had so disliked. French money was sent home to his mother; French money paid for his rent, his cigarettes, his visits to the cinema; for his tea, his food, his clothes, his newspapers and his radio: everything that made life worth living.

Despite this, his decision to join the police service had a kind of logic to it, ever since he had come upon the body of that poor woman bundled in under the dry riverbank. No one had ever found out who had killed her and hidden her body. He had found it hard to comprehend that such a terrible crime – the murder of another human being – could go unpunished. The idea that the killer was still walking the earth, free to laugh with his friends, eat his Friday couscous, maybe even kill again, was inexplicable. And so, when given the choice between the civil service and the Sûreté, he had chosen the latter. To make an imperfect world a little better, act by act. To listen to the good angel on his shoulder. Or that was what he had then, in his naivety, believed. Now, he was less sure. Right and wrong blurred into one another, or changed places altogether, depending on your perspective, and the paths you took through life, which you thought were clear and true, turned out to be winding and treacherous.

Hamou took out one of the remaining Anfas, lit it, took a deep draw that made the tip glow like a firefly, and pondered the ways of the world.

How could it be right that Didi should be forced to live on the street with just a blanket to his name, or that so many people had to live squeezed together in flimsy shacks made from banged-together squares of old oil drums, under roofs of corrugated iron, which were like ovens by day and cold as caves by night, eking out a pittance in the sardine factories at the docks, while barely a mile away the French lived in fancy white buildings, drove gleaming limousines and made fortunes out of the resources they dug out of someone else's country?

He took another drag on the cigarette, feeling the familiar acrid vapour scorch his windpipe, and blew the smoke out into the night air, where it hazed the scene before him like a filmy curtain. Of course, modern life was not straightforward. Today, he had paid out of his own pocket for a *petit taxi* to take a boy with an ankle he had broken playing football in the street to get it attended to at the hospital, as well as the sum he'd need to pay the doctors. It would leave Hamou short till he was paid, but it was worth it to know the lad wouldn't end up begging on crutches for the rest of his life: it was not so long ago he too had been barefoot and kicking a rag-and-string football around. Back at the *commissariat central*, he'd had to fill in form after form to process a man charged with distributing anti-colonial propaganda, while the defendant had glared accusingly at him from beneath bushy white eyebrows that reminded him of his grandfather. No, life was not simple.

Hamou turned his thoughts to Zina, the young woman who lived downstairs: Samira and Rachid's eldest daughter who worked as a nurse at the local hospital. He had not seen her for a couple of days because of the change in his shift pattern and it had cast a pall over him. There was something about the sharpness of her regard and the grace of her movements that lifted his heart. That was all it was, he told himself, the appreciation of natural beauty, as you might appreciate the scent and form of a perfect rose, without any intent to pick it.

He finished his cigarette, managed not to light a second one, stubbed it out on the parapet, brushed the soot away, and took the butt downstairs with him so as to leave no trace behind.

3

Hamou slept through the call to prayer, but that was not unusual; working shifts upset the natural rhythms of life. He had writhed and dreamed, woken, fallen back to sleep at dawn, and had woken again sharply some hours later in panic, sure he was late for work. Then he remembered that he was not on duty again until the afternoon and the adrenalin receded, leaving him feeling weak, and then ravenous.

He decided to make his way to Nabil's café in the Maarif, then on to the market to buy supplies. He couldn't go on being fed by the carpenter's wife. And on his way out, he should knock on their door and say thank you for last night's tajine and explain that his shifts were all over the place this week and so it would be best that he fend for himself. Even this was cowardly. A stronger man would say briskly, *Now look here, Lalla Chadli, I can't go on taking advantage of your kindness. Please don't prepare any more meals for me. No, I won't discuss it further: you have already been far too kind.* Yes, that was what he should say, what he *would* say.

But as he crept down the stairs, he found himself quickening his pace as he passed the Chadlis' door, telling himself that he would formulate a better response, *after fortifying myself with breakfast and strong coffee, and returning with my groceries, may God be my witness.*

Rather than walk up the Boulevard Mazagan, with its many

lanes of traffic, he crossed deeper into the local *quartier* and took one of the smaller streets. He liked to see real people living real lives: women coming out at the sound of the Javel man's musical bicycle horn to buy their litres of bleach; boys running home from the bakery with warm loaves hugged to their chests; carpenters sawing and hammering and covering the alleys with wood-dust and shavings; the old man on the corner making running repairs to bicycles and scooters.

Taking the Rue de Cluny, he came out onto the Mazagan, a dividing line between Africa and Europe, an interzone where ancient and modern, poor and rich, Muslim and Christian, met and mingled, and waited his moment between the streams of buses and cars, petit taxis, bikes and donkey carts, before running to the central island and waiting to complete the crossing. Already the sun was hot on the top of his head, the shadows on the ground sharp and black. The air was full of diesel and dust, and, as he started to cross, dodging a cart piled high with crates of oranges, a flight of pigeons burst up from a roof opposite as if alarmed by the sound of a shot no one else could hear.

Hamou made for the Rue de Jura, quieter now than it would be later in the day, when the crowds turned out to eat, to drink and to promenade in their best clothes, or to go to one of the three cinemas there. What a revelation such places had been to him when he'd first moved to Casa. He'd hardly been able to drag his eyes away from the French women in their flared skirts and high heels, their graceful, silk-stockinged calves, and the nipped-in waists that accentuated the shape of their bodies, instead of swathing and obscuring them like the modest black *tamelhafts* women wore back home. He could hardly stop thinking about them amid the haze of their perfume. Women! They were so beautiful, sashaying down the street with their fashionable handbags over their arms, their scarlet smiles, the seductive anonymity of their sunglasses, their abundant hairstyles in brown and black and blonde, so brazenly displayed. He had watched them licking their ice creams like cats – neat and greedy, aware of his attention, enjoying their power over him. Thankfully, he was more used to them now, and where once his head had been turned, now his eyes skated over them: they were just foreigners, and not for him.

As a rookie, he had been posted here occasionally; it had been one of the easier beats to patrol and he had known most of the café and restaurant owners by name and had been happy to accept a coffee here, a cigarette there, a chat, even a full meal. But last year the French had deposed the sultan and exiled him first to Corsica and then to Madagascar – Madagascar of all places! – and the mood had changed, on both sides. The Moroccans were more hostile to his uniform and role; they no longer exchanged gossip with him or welcomed him inside, and, just as his mother had warned him about 'Arab women', his bosses warned him against accepting favours. Unless he could gain information that way, they added with a wink. But Hamou had no interest in informing on his own people: he was no *chkam*.

Nabil's was an old-fashioned place tucked away on a side street. It was rare that foreigners came in here: they had their pick of the smarter, brighter establishments on the Jura, places that were neutral ground, where no one would stare at you or slap your cup down aggressively so that half the contents spilled. It lay in the shade in the mornings and the interior looked dark, half-asleep. Hamou pushed open the door and stepped inside, his eyes taking a few seconds to adjust to the change of light.

There was his cousin Moha in his usual corner. Moha shared a small apartment with one of his brothers above a shop just down the road and his family apartment was a few streets deeper into the quartier. His cousin was in conversation with a couple of other men, one of whom Hamou recognised as Omar Belhaj, who worked alongside him in the family import business. He was a plump fellow with a lugubrious appearance that could transform instantly into childish delight at scurrilous tales or terrible jokes. Hamou liked him: he was easy company. The other man had his back to him but turned when Hamou pulled out the spare chair beside him. There was a sudden, startled silence, then Moha leapt up and embraced him. 'My cousin, Hamou Badi!' he declared to the third man, whom he named as Ahmed Choukri.

Hamou held out a hand to the stranger, before realising he wasn't fully a stranger. He knew his face from somewhere, they had met before, though he couldn't quite place where, and the man gave no sign of knowing him.

'*As salaam aleikum*,' the man growled, his mouth hidden behind the dark briar of his beard.

The waiter brought coffee and water for Hamou, took his order for croissants and confiture and refilled the other men's cups.

'Aren't you eating?' Hamou enquired, taking in the table empty of plates, empty of everything but a half-full ashtray.

Omar waved a hand. 'Already eaten. Though…' He beckoned the waiter back and ordered two *pains au chocolat*. 'Can't let you eat alone.'

'I don't believe we've met, Hamou Badi,' Ahmed said, as if saying this made it so. 'What do you do?'

Hamou saw a pained expression cross his cousin's face before Moha answered the question for him. 'Hamou works for the Sûreté. Somebody's got to, right?'

Hamou laughed, a little nervously. But Ahmed did not laugh. 'Maybe you could be of use to us,' he said thoughtfully.

'I doubt it: I'm in a very lowly position,' Hamou said. 'Paperwork mainly.'

Ahmed said nothing, but Hamou felt his eyes on him as they talked.

The waiter returned with the patisserie and Hamou picked up one of the croissants and bit into the warm, buttery pastry with sensuous delight. One thing you could thank the French for, he thought, but did not say.

Moha turned the conversation to the subject of his father's

health and now Hamou felt guilty at not having asked before he started eating. 'Cousin Yasmine came last night and rubbed his legs with that herbal stuff she makes – smells like shit, but he's convinced it helps...'

And all at once, Hamou was back in Tiziane, watching Mimouna rubbing Taba Tôt's foul-smelling ointment into his mother's arthritic hands while his little sister Sofia moaned that the odour stung her nose.

'You should get him to the hospital,' he said to Moha. 'They have proper doctors there.'

'French doctors.' Ahmed spat out the words. 'They're poisoning us all little by little with all their chemicals in the water, and their foreign medicines. Who knows what's in that stuff? They're plotting to weaken us so that we accept Ben Arafa as our sultan and stop making trouble.'

Hamou tried not to snort. Ahmed was one of those who saw conspiracy and nefarious plots everywhere, was he? Not everything the protectorate did was evil, even if removing the sultan was wrong and they kept order with a heavier hand than was sometimes necessary. 'The chemicals in the water make it safer to drink,' he pointed out quietly.

'Besides,' said Omar, 'who knows what's in Yasmine's ointment? It wouldn't surprise me if she boils up cats' testicles and babies' hands.'

Moha laughed. 'Certainly smells like it.' He pulled a packet out of the breast pocket of his djellaba and lit himself a cigarette before offering the packet around. Omar took one, but Hamou took out his Anfas.

'Well, at least you smoke Moroccan,' Ahmed said grimly. He tapped a finger on Moha's Gitanes. 'Putting money in French pockets, shame on you, brother.'

Moha blew nonchalant smoke rings into the air. 'The French own all the tobacco companies. It's just marketing.'

'You should stop smoking altogether,' Ahmed said fiercely. 'It's a political act.'

'That's what the Istiqlal say,' Omar said, his plump mouth downturned. 'They say it's un-Islamic, or unhealthy, or something.'

The Istiqlal were the Independence Party. For years they'd concentrated on the political enlightenment and education of the common man, which was all very laudable, but since the sultan had been so recklessly deposed, their attitudes had hardened and now they were determined to make the French restore the sultan to his throne and force them into some form of power-sharing. Before things had got so heated, Hamou had gone to a couple of meetings and had even helped some of the lads with their reading, but the atmosphere was a lot more fervid now. There had been beatings in dark alleys, plots, murders of those suspected of spying for the French, even an assassination attempt on the life of the *préfet*, and the French had of course retaliated, sending squads of their special forces into the bidonvilles and backstreets, pulling suspected nationalists in for questioning, referring to them openly now as 'terrorists'. Six had been executed only weeks before. It was turning into a bitter, underground civil war.

'I advise you to be careful how you spend your money,' Ahmed said. He turned his dark gaze upon Hamou. 'And where you get that money from. Battle lines are being drawn up and soon you'll have to decide which side you're on. Better choose the right one or...' He drew a finger across his throat, then got up, pushing back his chair so hard that its feet scraped on the tiled floor and heads all around the café turned. 'See *you* later,' he said meaningfully to Moha and Omar.

'Sorry,' Moha said after the café door closed again. 'He can be intense, Ahmed, but he's all right really. Comes from Salé, and you know what they're like. He's one of Hicham's friends more than mine.'

Hicham was Moha's youngest brother, a young firebrand of nineteen. Moha was twenty-three, Hamou twenty-six. It was funny, he thought, how that age difference no longer mattered, when as children it had seemed an unbridgeable gap. But everything had changed since then: he was a minor functionary in the police service, and Moha was a big wheel, practically running an international business – tea and cotton from Egypt, onions and dates from Algeria. The world had turned upside-down.

'*Wachha*,' Hamou said. 'It's OK. Takes all sorts, right?'

Omar grinned. 'You're a good fellow, Hamou Badi, whatever anyone else says.'

Hamou wasn't sure how to take that. Were people other than Ahmed talking about him? Was he on someone's list? A shiver ran down his spine.

He ran his errands in the market and took his purchases back to the apartment. But his courage failed him when it came to knocking on Samira Chadli's door and asking her not to cook for him any longer. The encounter with the young nationalist had left him feeling out of sorts. He had to pull himself together and get himself to the commissariat to see what his duties were for the day.

4

In the days running up to Ramadan, Hamou found himself walking the beat around Mers Sultan Nord. This largely Moroccan quarter lay beyond the big hospital and the affluent European area, which was full of smart restaurants, cafés and shops bordering onto the huge Mers Sultan roundabout, the convergence of a spiderweb of the city's arterial roads.

The covered market just off the Rue de Londres was particularly busy during the day with housewives out buying cereal, spices, cones of sugar, dates, honey, flour, couscous, almonds, rosewater and orange essence – all the staples they would need to cook up treats for the evening feast. Preparing food during a fast was a particular kind of masochistic pleasure: the aromas of cooking in the day, imagining the flavours on the tongue, looking but not tasting, sharpening the hunger. Rather like watching all the pretty young women go by in their best clothes, Hamou thought.

He moved among the crowds, enjoying the festive air. Stall-owners handed dates and orange segments to children, gave free bunches of herbs to shoppers, and everyone laughed and exchanged pleasantries, and no one complained about being bumped by baskets or when the boys sent for more supplies bulldozed their laden trolleys through the narrow aisles shouting '*Balak, balak!*' No one glared at his uniform or fell silent at his approach: he was just one more ant in the anthill, and for the first time in months he felt he was a part of this city, of his people, rather than a *braani*, an outsider looking in.

But his sense of well-being was not destined to last.

At around six o'clock on the eve of Ramadan, Hamou joined dozens of other men queueing to enter the hammam close to his home, each armed with towels and soap and long, rough knotted cloths for scrubbing the skin. The changing room was crammed, everyone bumping elbows and knees as they wrestled off djellabas and fought to find a space to stow their things on the long shelves above the wooden benches.

The first chamber – the hot room – was packed with bodies visible only as indistinct shapes in the steam, like a congregation of djinns. It was impossible to find a spot in which to sit down, so Hamou got his buckets of water and passed into the second chamber. Having no wife, he did not feel the same pressing need to steam from his person the traces of sexual congress (if only), to scour body and soul clean of bodily intimacy, to purify himself for the fast. But the second chamber was equally rammed, and the noise was overwhelming as shouts for more hot water, for soap, for back-scrubbing, mingled with shouted greetings and general merriment. Usually, Hamou preferred quiet time in the hammam, during hours when there were few other customers, when he could laze at his leisure on the hot floor after work, feeling the warmth seep into every pore of his skin, feeling the tensions of the week drip out of him along with the scurf and suds down the central drain. But there was something about this noisy, near-naked experience of men together that reminded him of being swept along in the crowds at the Stade Philip, watching football. He could lose his individuality and personal frustrations in the shared fervour and excitement of the throng, his lonely, singular Hamou-ness submerged in the tide of humanity, so that he would leave feeling at once buoyed up and reinvigorated.

The hammam reduced you to your essential being. Dressed only in your undershorts, you became no more than a bag of skin and bones, nerves and blood, an animal at the waterhole. Beggars and property kings, grocers and governors, sinners and saints: it made no difference here, where all the money or power in the world could not buy you an extra centimetre of space. The anonymity was a welcome escape.

A man passed Hamou his exfoliating net and turned his back to him, and Hamou enthusiastically scrubbed away, making the man's skin glow pink, then turned to receive the same treatment, and found himself suddenly nose to nose with Ahmed Choukri, his cousin's nationalist friend.

Hamou started to greet the man from Salé, but Ahmed thrust his face at him. 'My brother Abdelkrim was taken by the police last night!' he roared, punctuating his words with a straight finger jabbed so hard into Hamou's chest that it left livid marks. 'He's in a cell at the commissariat and they won't let us see him. He's probably dead by now.'

Hamou tried to push him away, but the press of bodies was too thick. 'It's nothing to do with me!'

Ahmed turned to address those around him. 'This fucker works for the Sûreté: he's a chkam.'

Hamou protested, but his words were drowned out as others joined Ahmed in their recriminations.

'Traitor!'

'Working for the bastard French!'

'They'll kill us all!'

The man who had been scrubbing his back slung the netting around Hamou's throat and held him choked.

'Turncoat!'

'Informer!'

The knotted rag tightened and Hamou clawed at it desperately.

Just as black stars dotted his vision, there was a surge of movement, and someone shouldered Ahmed aside. 'Leave him alone! He's a decent man, not a snitch.'

It was Didi, the beggar from the corner of his street, who shoved away the man who was garrotting him, and with him was his neighbour, the carpenter Rachid Chadli. 'Leave him be! Call yourself Muslims? You should be ashamed, on the eve of Ramadan, harassing this man.'

Those who had been threatening now looked away, then backed off, returning to their ablutions. The beggar and the carpenter accompanied Hamou back to the changing room, leaving a ripple of discontent and confusion in their wake. Outside on the street, where it was barely any cooler than inside the bathhouse, Hamou leaned up against the wall, getting his bearings.

'Are you all right?' The carpenter was solicitous.

Hamou nodded. 'A bit shocked, is all.'

'I'm not surprised. Tempers are running high.' Chadli sighed.

'I didn't know about Ahmed's brother.'

Didi laughed. 'Where have you been, under a stone? The specials did a sweep. There were Citröens everywhere, like locusts.'

It was a bit much, having a beggar ribbing him about his ignorance. 'I had a day off,' he said defensively. He'd spent the day with his aunt Jamila, helping her carry purchases from the market in the Maarif, including a new mattress to accommodate family who were coming in from the *bled*.

'They arrested over a dozen last night. Members of the Black Hand.'

Hamou had heard about the Black Hand. They had sprung up out of the shantytowns during the past year, taking more direct action than the official independence party. They had a lot of grass roots support: people were becoming impatient, convinced that the Istiqlal were making deals with the French. It was rumoured that there were more extreme splinter groups too, for whom even the Black Hand were not sufficiently direct.

The carpenter looked uncomfortable. 'Best not to talk about such things out on the open street,' he said. 'Let's go back to the house.'

'I was going to go to the mosque...' Hamou started.

'I'm sure we all were, but maybe it's best to make our prayers at home tonight.'

They made their way back along the Rue Géricault. At the junction, Didi took his usual place on the corner, but Rachid Chadli caught him by his good arm. 'Not tonight, Didi. Tonight, you share our family couscous.'

'*Habibi*, I have brought company!' the carpenter called from the door, as Hamou and Didi removed their footwear and laid them by the wall. There was a brief, murmured conversation within and then Rachid Chadli returned to usher them into the guest salon.

Didi gazed around at the unaccustomed splendour of his surroundings as if committing every detail to memory, at the green-brocade cushions lining three sides of the room, the tribal rug and the low, round wooden table set in the middle of it, the framed portrait of the sultan on the wall, and sighed. 'This is a palace, my friend,' he declared, offering the carpenter his wide, white smile.

'May God continue to be kind to us,' said Rachid Chadli. '*Inshallah*.'

Hamou was reminded sharply of his mother's salon, identical in all but hue, except for the books on a shelf, and the radiogram he had taken with him on the bus on his last visit. He had shown her how to work it and found a station that played traditional music as well as the interminable news bulletins. She had been enchanted, but he knew that unless he was there she would never turn it on, as if to do so would wear out its newness. Like the salon, it was kept for best, used only for the most important visitors.

The carpenter moved the table to one side so that they had room to kneel, and they made their prayers, overly conscious of each other's presence. After they had finished, he moved the table back into place and they sat down around it, cross-legged, as Samira Chadli bustled in with a bowl, a copper kettle full of hot water and an embroidered towel. They all washed their hands. Hamou saw her glance rest for a moment on the beggar's withered arm, then flick away.

Didi sniffed his skin. 'Roses,' he said with wonder.

The carpenter's wife smiled. 'Yes, roses. From the market.'

Didi watched her depart, and he blinked rapidly, then rubbed his good hand across his eyes, and Hamou realised he was overwhelmed to be treated as a valued guest.

'The meal smells wonderful,' Hamou said politely, and then quickly, as if this might be construed as reopening her invitation to supply him with constant streams of food, added, 'A special treat.'

'You are always welcome to share our food, Hamou Badi. As you know, we regard you as one of the family.'

Hamou sighed inwardly and his chest tightened as if he found himself in the coils of a constricting snake. On cue, in came Zina, bearing an enormous platter heaped with couscous. When she set it down and the fragrant steam cleared, Didi craned his neck, taking in the intricate patterning of the orange pumpkin and carrot, the slices of courgette and aubergine laid in vertical stripes down the yellow pyramid, the caramelised onion and tiny turnips and garlic and chickpeas, the golden globules of fat gilding the rich red sauce; but all Hamou could look at was Zina, in her lovely robe of turquoise cotton, her heart-shaped face framed by a white headscarf tied with the fringes hanging to either side, her sparkling eyes accentuated with kohl; but she kept her gaze averted until she had placed the dish on the table and straightened up. Then she stared at him, gave a single unsmiling nod of acknowledgement, turned and left.

He could not read that gesture. Was it friendly or unfriendly? Maybe a little hostile? They had had so little recent contact that he could not tell, and he had no experience with women within the domestic sphere. Perhaps she resented his invasion into their private dinner or was aware of her mother's manoeuvrings and was embarrassed by them; perhaps it was a concession of fellow feeling; perhaps something else entirely. The connection felt unnerving, intense, and an uncomfortable and not very godly jolt of heat shot through him even as the carpenter gave thanks for the food, and they all said, '*Bismillah.*'

Didi looked down at his withered arm, then up at his hostess. 'Forgive me, lalla, God has not granted me the use of my right hand and I do not wish to dishonour your kindness.'

She leaned across and patted his shoulder. 'My son, he gave you a hand that is both left and right for you. Now eat.' Then she followed Zina to take her repast in the kitchen.

After mint tea and little almond cakes that melted like nectar on the tongue, the men sat back, replete. Already, the altercation in the hammam was beginning to feel to Hamou like a bad dream, slipping out of focus, the edges tattering away.

'I do not like to boast, but my daughter is a superb cook,' the carpenter said, patting his stomach; and Hamou realised that all this time it had been food made by Zina's skilful hands that he had been eating. Perhaps that explained the effect she had on him.

'She is a goddess,' said Didi. 'That was the best meal I ever ate, and that is neither compliment nor lie.'

When it was time to leave, Hamou got to his feet and thanked Rachid for his hospitality and he and Didi made their way to the door. While they were retrieving their shoes, Samira Chadli glided into view, silent and nimble despite her bulk.

'*Ramadan mubarak*, Hamou,' she said. 'You will, I hope, join us regularly for *iftar* throughout the holy month. It will be our honour, and a great pleasure, especially for Zina.'

Oh no. Hamou could hear his mother's voice in his head, but still his blood thumped and he felt colour rise up his neck. He touched his hand to his heart and bowed his head deferentially. 'It is very kind of you, but my work shifts during Ramadan tend to be unpredictable and I would not want to hold up the breaking of your fast.' He hesitated, then added, 'But I'm sure Didi here—'

The door was closed before he could even finish the sentence. Hamou and Didi exchanged glances and the beggar laughed loudly. 'Oh my man,' he managed at last. 'You are in big trouble.'

Hamou knew it.

5

A Letter from Tiziane

Alhamdulillah. Inshallah that my letter reaches the safety of your hands.

Azul, my son.

I send you our blessings. All is well with me and the girls, with Mimi the cat, also with our goats and sheep, but I regret to say that a jackal took my favourite chicken, Timimt, leaving nothing but feathers behind. This is a sad loss for me, and Izum the cockerel is miserable and will not come out of the coop or go about his business. I looked him over, but he appears unharmed other than for the droop of his wattle. I think Izum is ashamed that he was unable to protect her, and even some scrambled egg with Taba Tôt's cream has not revived him. I worry that we shall be forced to eat him, which would be a pity, for he has been a good fellow.

Thank you for your kind and thoughtful gifts. Your sisters were excited to receive so much chocolate and would have eaten it all at once had I not managed to confiscate it. I reminded them of your uncle Omar's problems with his teeth, and the next day I invited him for tea to show us where the dentist had just removed two of them – this was not the French dentist in the town, mind you, but our new travelling dentist whom they call Moussa Toothman. He sets up his tent in the weekly souk and works with pliers. Omar told them how his cries frightened the donkeys so they broke their pickets and stampeded down the valley road, although I am not sure how true this is. You know your uncle's stories. Mimouna was so shocked that she declared she would eat chocolate no more. So, I beg you, my son, not to send chocolate again, unless it is for your poor old mother.

All is well in the village, though there is word that Sidi Abdesalam's beautiful voice is losing its power, so the calls to prayer are less forceful than they might be, but we are managing as best we can, for we are very fond of our *muezzin*.

The news of the week is that the Bensaleh girl is marrying the teacher's son. I wish you had let me speak for you to her parents. She is a fine, strapping girl and will give him many children. We must talk about this the next time you visit Tiziane. A woman needs grandchildren, and I am not getting any younger, you know.

And do not fall for the wiles of those city women. I am sure they are very smart with their French perfumes and lipsticks but remember that they are no better than djinns disguised as women! I have not raised you all these years, kept you safe from fortune-hunters and charlatans, for you to throw yourself away on one of these painted *tadgalin*. (I apologised for my choice of words to Sidi Malik, who is writing this letter for me, but, my son, I cannot state this strongly enough.)

To ensure that you are safe, I am sending you, along with a new pair of babouches made specially for you by Mouloud the shoemaker (using your old ones as a pattern), your grandfather's amulet. I have had it repaired and cleaned and the *fkih*, Sidi Daoud, has filled it with baraka: a mixture of *kbrit*, alum crystals and harmala seeds. Wearing this will, I promise you, keep you safe from those who would do you harm. The sulphur will speak to the djinns, the alum to the angels, and the rue will protect from the evil eye. I know you will say that you do not believe in such nonsense and that you cannot wear such a thing under your uniform, but I am your mother and closer to you than your own skin. You are particularly at risk during the holy month, which is why I handed this package to Mehdi, the only bus driver I trust, to deliver direct to you.

Peace be upon you, my son. Write to your poor old mother again soon, and remember her and your sisters, and also, if you can, the cockerel, in your Ramadan prayers.

Your loving mother.

This was signed with a dark, inky thumbprint: his mother always insisted on doing this, rather than have the public letter writer sign her name for her, so that Hamou would know the letter was genuine. Every time he saw the thumbprint he smiled – at her ferocity, at her paranoia, at the fact that she had touched this piece of paper with her own hands.

He read it again, frowning at the mention of his mother's wish to matchmake, glad that Lina Bensaleh was off the market. Then he unwrapped the babouches. They were huge. Shucking off his old slippers, he slid his feet into them, and laughed out loud. Far, far too big for him now. When he had first left Tiziane, he had spent so much of his youth running around barefoot that he had grown a false sole as thick as the thickest shoe leather, that spread beyond the normal contours of his feet, and had been unable to squeeze them into regulation police boots. Now that false sole had vanished, leaving his feet bony and neat. Even if he stuffed newspaper into them, the acid yellow babouches would still be too big. He might match them for size against Rachid Chadli's shoes left outside the family's door and offer them to the carpenter instead. Or maybe that would be insulting, suggesting that he had noticed that Rachid's footwear needed replacing. He would give them to Didi instead.

He peeled back the piece of cotton that enfolded the other

package to reveal a heavy square of silver, hinged at the bottom and with a little clasp at the top, suspended from a thong of twisted leather. Markings had been engraved all over the amulet's outward surface – sharp little arrows and triangles designed to put out the evil eye. He remembered how as a baby he had been fascinated by it when his grandfather had leaned down to him, the light making the silver sparkle; how he'd tried to grab it and been reprimanded, because it was valuable and old, a family heirloom.

Hamou closed his fingers over the amulet and felt tears prick his eyes. He missed the old man. He missed his mother. He missed his dead father. He missed his sisters. He missed the animals. He missed Tiziane. But there was no way he was going to wear this thing. He lived in Casablanca, the shining white city of the future, not a remote mountain village with both feet in the past. He wrapped it back up in the scrap of fabric and put it carefully away in a drawer.

6

May 1955

Hamou stood in the doorway of the grocer's on the Rue de Strasbourg, watching the passers-by. Absent-mindedly, he patted the breast pocket of his uniform jacket, and found it empty. To avoid temptation during Ramadan, he had left his cigarettes in his room.

It was mid-afternoon and so hot that his clothes were sticking to him. This morning, an inversion layer of cloud had hung over the city, trapping the heat and fumes so that each breath he took felt heavy with diesel and cooking fat. Flies were everywhere. During lulls in the traffic, Hamou could hear the low, steady buzz of them like a giant motor, as if the energy they generated was secretly powering the city.

He watched a dark-skinned man striding away down the street, his white cotton robe billowing. Moroccans knew how to dress for this sort of weather, and it didn't involve thick serge. But to remove your uniform jacket while you were on duty was prohibited. Yet another French oppression of body and soul.

The shop doorway in which he stood belonged to a business that had been boarded up. Last week it had been firebombed because the rumour had gone round that the merchant who owned it was a collaborator. Scorch marks showed all around the door and the smell of char was still discernible. Quite why he had been sent to patrol an area that had already been hit by the militants, he didn't know. He suspected it was just to make it look as if the police were doing something. No one appeared to be taking any notice of him, anyway.

He watched a group of men strolling past, laughing and smoking, shirtsleeves rolled up. They wore sunglasses and their hair was slicked back in the foreign fashion, but despite this and the cigarettes he knew they were Moroccans playing at being sophisticated Frenchmen and for a moment was pierced by envy, before the emotion was transmuted to a stab of shame for their transgression and his own brief yearning.

The holy month was dragging its feet. It was an especially warm May, and the days were punishingly long, the sun often not setting till nearly nine in the evening, hard to bear when you started your day with an early shift. His tongue felt dry and swollen. He reached into his pocket and took out the item he had put there this morning: a river pebble from Tiziane, a grey oval about the size of a small partridge egg, polished smooth by the tumble of winter water that ran down into the village from the Djebel Kest. He wished that he could be back in the cool of one of those mountain ravines where the waterfalls never ran dry, listening to birdsong in the palms, to the baas of the foraging goats and the women singing as they washed their linen in the pools; away from the dusty-dry city that was so gripped by political tensions. He popped the pebble in his mouth – an old Tuareg trick his father had taught him for keeping thirst at bay in the desert – and sucked on it. Within seconds, he felt some relief from tormenting thoughts of water and cigarettes, if not from outer discord.

Tempers were frayed because of conspiracies, arrests and disappearances, suspicions of complicity, of bribe-taking and dirty deals done not just in dark corners but in glittering palaces. Every day brought some new atrocity, or the rumour of an atrocity. A policeman had been shot near the central market – just up there towards the port – where a year and a half ago Mohammed Zerqtouni had ridden a bicycle carrying a bomb right into the crowd of shoppers and detonated the device and had somehow escaped the hail of bullets that rained down on him, only to die from taking a cyanide capsule on his way to the commissariat six months later when the police finally caught up with him. The timing of the bombing had been deliberate. The French had taken the sultan away on the holy day of Eid, so the nationalists had chosen an equally symbolic day – Christmas Eve – for their reprisal. Nineteen dead, including women and children.

Hamou had felt ill when he heard about it, for the death of innocents, for the merciless violence of the deed, and for the perceived need for it. Things had quietened for a while as the Sûreté cracked down, but over the course of the last six months the atmosphere had become ever more febrile. Fights broke out everywhere over the slightest matter. Just in the past few days, Hamou had stopped a fight between brawling kif-dealers, adjudicated a disagreement between a woman and a date-seller who the woman claimed had placed his thumb on the scales, and saved a pickpocket being beaten to death by vengeful shoppers. Everything felt balanced on a knife's edge.

It did not help that the Europeans gave little thought to those observing the fast. They were out in the streets, laughing, smoking, strolling; sitting outside the cafés with their bottles of beer and their baguettes filled with ham and cheese. Two women, arms linked so that from a distance they appeared to be some exotic hybrid creature, sauntered towards him in their summer dresses, their bare arms glowing like old ivory. They were eating ice creams from the gelateria on the corner; one laughed as hers started to drip and dipped her head to lap at her hand. They stopped right in front of him, dabbing at their ice creams with their tongues, giggling with pleasure, so close that he could smell the vanilla, their soapy perfumes, and their sweat. His pebble clacked painfully against his teeth, the hard-won saliva gushing suddenly in his mouth, and then they had passed by into the sunshine beyond.

He stepped out into the light and walked in the opposite

direction, passing the gelateria with his head averted, towards the main road, where buses and trucks surged past donkey carts and mules drawing carriages in which courting couples sat holding hands or even scandalously kissing for all the world to see. Hamou thought about Zina, and the look she had given him when he and Didi the beggar had come to the apartment. That hard, level stare that he had been unable to interpret. Since then, he had seen her pegging out washing on the line on the roof terrace and had admired the tidy efficiency with which she addressed the task, not stopping even for a moment to look out over the wall or even at him: focused, and precise, she had accomplished the task swiftly, and within minutes as he idled there, trespassing, really, in her space, looking out over the world passing below, he saw her walking quickly across the road with a basket over her arm. He had wondered where she was going – the local souk was in the other direction – but really it was none of his business.

As he reached the junction, a horse-drawn dray came clattering past, laden with crates of Stork beer from the Brasseries du Maroc factory. Right in the middle of Ramadan, as if this were not a Muslim country at all but just an extension of France's colonial empire. Which of course was what they had been reduced to. Even as he was marvelling over the insult of this, a *mobilette* came puttering up behind him and a voice called out, 'Hamou Badi!'

He turned to see Ismail the Cockroach, one of the department's runners. A rat-faced man in his sixties, Ismail spent his days zipping around the city streets carrying messages, spying on everyone's comings and goings; another pair of snooping eyes for the administration. Hamou did not like or trust the man: he had seen him taking money from dubious characters and yet he had no hesitation in snitching on people like Hamou for taking a longer than usual coffee break, or for being just a little bit too friendly with stallholders in the course of his duties. Ismail had a knack for covering even the most innocent action or phrase in enough shit to land you in trouble with the higher-ups. Hence his nickname.

Ismail set the scooter on its kickstand and scuttled over to Hamou, who had stopped in his tracks, waiting, the wet pebble transferred back into his trouser pocket.

'What is it?'

No pleasantries between them, no Ramadan greeting.

'You're to report to the commissariat immediately.'

Hamou felt a chill run through him. Had someone told tales on him? He racked his memory for any misdemeanour he might have inadvertently committed and came up empty. 'Why?'

But the man was already back on his scooter and beckoning Hamou to follow. 'Just get on, now.'

From its entrance on the Boulevard Jean Courtin, where it was tucked away between leafy plane trees and the Lycée des Jeunes Filles, the commissariat central appeared elegant and innocuous. Beside its double doors, potted hibiscus and jasmine rambled in profusion, their flowers bright against the whitewash. But Hamou knew that behind this façade, the building enlarged suddenly to surround huge courtyards, around and beneath which lay hundreds of offices, cells, and interrogation chambers, a secret world within a world. He had often thought it was the perfect symbol for the French administration itself: outwardly urbane and civilised, masking far worse.

He watched the Cockroach ride off on another errand, and went in. Dozens of people milled around the locals' reception desk – women in *haiks* and djellabas, shouting children, harassed-looking men, and an old fellow with a bandaged head; at the French desk, two or three Europeans waited in an orderly queue. All around the walls were travel posters depicting an idealised Morocco that existed only in French minds: pristine images of kasbahs and arched doorways, proclaiming 'Morocco Land of Great Tourism', or picturesque robed figures, camels and mules passing the famous Koutoubia Mosque. As if you were entering some sort of charming fantasyland rather than the infamous central police station.

The man behind the Moroccan desk saw Hamou and waved him to approach, simultaneously hitting the reception bell over and over, its tinny ding cutting through the hubbub. Almost at once a scrawny adolescent appeared at Hamou's side. 'Take Officer Badi down to Room 125!' the receptionist bellowed, and the boy took Hamou by the sleeve and towed him through the crowd.

They passed the muster room where Hamou and the others gathered each day to check which duties they had been assigned and carried on down an apparently endless corridor lined with closed doors which finally led to a steep flight of steps. At the bottom of this, the boy led him along another corridor, which turned back on itself. They met a number of uniformed men coming towards them at speed. Hamou recognised some of the officers, but there was no time to exchange words. The one bringing up the rear, Sabir – a fellow Soussi – raised a hand in greeting and made a woeful face at Hamou; but then he was gone, leaving Hamou's gut tight with anxiety.

'Do you know what's going on?' he asked his guide, but the boy just shook his head and quickened his pace.

Some of the doors they passed were open. Hamou glimpsed desks piled with paperwork and occasionally a functionary at work – on the telephone, at a typewriter, stamping documents. The overweening complexities of French bureaucracy had been a revelation to Hamou when he had come to Casablanca: there were documents for everything – to register births and marriages, to confirm your identity, place of residence and work, to license a vehicle, even down to the feeblest little mobilette; to register your crimes, small and large. He had never seen so much paper. In Tiziane, it was a rare commodity, and the local authorities were still adjusting to the French system even after all this time. There, everyone knew everyone else and an official kept the register of births, deaths and marriages, each entry signed with thumbprints. Here, the French never used just one piece of paper when ten would do.

By the time they reached their destination, Hamou was completely disorientated. He hoped the boy would wait for him to guide him back to reception. If he were allowed to leave at all. It was cooler here, and he could hear distant cries: they must be near the detainment cells. The thought of that deepened the chill.

The boy stopped at a door, rapped, then opened it and let Hamou pass beyond. Inside were five other officers, two seated, three standing. Hamou knew two of the three – Driss Talbi, a lantern-jawed fellow with whom he had studied at the academy, and Saleh Zaoui, whom he did not like at all. But at least it appeared he was not being singled out for some unknown or special punishment. He took his cap off and joined the other men.

'Ah, Badi, excellent,' said one of the seated men, looking up from his notes. The three white bands on his uniform marked him out as a captain, but not one Hamou had seen before; the man seated beside him was the superintendent, Emile Fouquet.

'You have been selected for special duties,' the Frenchman enunciated. 'From tomorrow you will report for firearms training. We've been watching you closely and consider you to be sufficiently trustworthy officers that we may have confidence in you to uphold the law in this country diligently and to defend the state from those who would seek to destroy it.' His dark regard rested on Hamou for a second. He looked faintly amused.

Hamou's glance slid sideways to the others who had been singled out for this training. To a man they appeared pleased and proud at this promotion. He tried to align his features to match theirs, but inside his thoughts ran riot. He was to be given a gun, and trained how to use it, on his own people. He wanted to turn and walk out – to run – down the endless corridors, up the stairs, and out of this vast, oppressive building. Out onto the streets, out of this French-built, French-run city, all the way back to the mountains, to the haven of Tiziane. But of course, he did not. He stayed rooted until the officers finished speaking and he snapped a salute along with the rest of them.

The boy escorted them all back up to the muster room. They had been given the rest of the day off, a sort of gift, so that they could be 'rested and alert' for training tomorrow. 'You will need to learn a lot in a short time,' was the explanation. And then they had signed papers affirming their change of duties – so many sheets of paper that Hamou skimmed the closely typed script, by the end of which he had no idea what the words meant, or whether it represented language at all. Seeing the small photograph of himself on the front page had come as a shock. He looked more a child than a man in it, his mountain heritage clear in the narrow bones of his face, his deep-set eyes, his wary expression. And there was his name in foreign script, printed out in full: MOHAMMED BEN M'BAREK BEN ALI, followed by the names of his parents and his place of birth. Under his father's name someone had handwritten in tiny italics the word 'deceased'. His mother's address, the signature of Caid Hajj Abdullah, the administrative endorsement from the préfet in Tiznit, the regional capital; his address in Casablanca, in the Derb Ghrallef; his landlord's name and address; his qualifications and date of matriculation from the academy... the pages went on and on, documenting his life from birth to this very moment, it seemed; repeated in triplicate, signed and stamped and dated.

Mohammed ben M'barek ben Ali. Mohammed, the son of M'barek, the son of Ali. It was not how he thought of himself at all. Everyone called him Hamou Badi.

He walked out into reception and ploughed through the jostle of complainants, pushed through the doors and was assailed by the scent of jasmine.

7

It was gone six and Hamou was off duty. He could go to the hammam, to the mosque, then home. But his nerves were still jangling, and if he went back to his room, he knew he'd never have the strength of will to resist the cigarettes he had left there until the sun went down. How easily he could visualise pocketing them and fleeing up to the roof terrace to let the telltale smoke trail innocently away into the early evening air. And returning to the hammam after his previous experience was not enticing.

He had avoided eating with the Chadlis during Ramadan, but they had without fail left him a tray bearing soup, dates and little cakes every night. Often, he came back after dark, having eaten with friends or in the street, to find the tray there outside his door; then he would slip out with it to Didi on the corner, waiting until he scraped the bowl empty before creeping back in and leaving the cleaned tray and utensils outside the carpenter's door. He felt guilty about passing the family's generosity on to someone else, but still he had not grasped the lion by the throat and asked Samira Chadli not to leave food out for him. *I will do it tonight,* he told himself, yet again. *It is Ramadan, and I must not lie, even to myself.*

He would sweeten his words with a gift. *Chebakia.* Yes! Even as his mind framed the word, his memory was filled with the taste of them: the sweetness of the honey, the nutty sesame, the rosewater, the sticky caramel, the crunch of the pastry. It would be a perfect gift. And then he remembered that time last year when he and his friend Hassan had wandered the medina and found an amazing baker tucked away in the labyrinth of winding streets who made pyramids of the sweet pastries piled on platters of silver board to take home for iftar. Those pyramids had left him and Hassan gasping with laughter at such sheer greedy folly: 'Imagine getting that home on the bus!'

Now it was all Hamou could think of. The delight of the Chadlis when he brought in such a grand offering. Surely his gentle batting away of Samira Chadli's merciless offers of food would go easier with such a honeyed treat? Saliva flooded his mouth. The chebakia would not come cheap, but he was about to be awarded a small pay rise...

All at once the sweet taste in his imagination soured; he was getting a pay rise for being trusted by the occupiers of his country with a gun. He imagined the horrified look on Zina's face if he turned up at the house armed with a pistol. But of course, that wouldn't happen: you didn't get to take your gun home.

He pushed the thought away. He was a policeman. He upheld the law. He protected the weak. He tried to do good in the world. He would go and buy the chebakia.

The medina – the ancient heart of the original city of Anfa on which Casablanca had been founded – was just over a mile away, towards the port. The air was heavy with accumulated heat and fumes. He stepped into Lyautey Park and stood at the public fountain, splashing his face with cool water. He took off his jacket and his cap, stuffed the latter into the pocket of the former, which he tucked under his arm, and watched the little birds swoop in and out of the trees. How he would like a garden, he thought suddenly. A place where he could grow flowers and fruit and where running water would fall from a tiled fountain and run in rilled channels through a courtyard fringed by roses.

But what an absurd idea. Only rich people had gardens: not a lowly Berber policeman living in a rented room in the Derb Ghrallef.

He quickened his pace, passing the vast white edifice of the Cathedral of the Sacred Heart with its twin towers and soaring arches, an immense art deco structure into which you could surely fit every mosque in the city. It was, he thought, at once inspiring and oppressive. You had to admire the vision and focus that had brought such a strikingly modern building into existence, but to smack it down right in the middle of a Muslim city was an act of provocation, a forceful statement of power.

As he came out onto the Avenue de Général Moinier, it struck Hamou that there was less traffic on the road than he would have expected at such an hour, when everyone would normally be headed home to join their families. But the usual roar and rush of vehicles had been replaced by a distant rumble, like thunder rolling in from over the sea. By the time he reached the greenery of Louis Gentil Park, the noise had intensified: less a rumble now than the angry buzzing of a disturbed swarm of bees. Every step he took towards the old town clarified the sound until he could almost make out individual voices, and as he emerged onto the junction to the south of the Place de France, he could see the source of the hubbub. A huge crowd was advancing on the square from the north, blocking the traffic in all directions, leaving buses and cars stranded and engulfed. They swept past the *tour de l'horloge*, the old clock tower, towards the Excelsior Hotel and the Café de France, where police had gathered, for now just lounging against the wall, watching the marchers' approach.

Hamou turned left, intending to head for the Bab Marrakech, the gate into the medina, but now another mob was heading into the square down the Boulevard de 2e Tirailleurs, blocking his way, pictures of the exiled sultan held above their heads.

For a moment a wave of tiredness and irritation swept over him. All he wanted was to slip into the old city, locate the baker, buy the chebakia and present it to Zina's mother. He stepped out into the trafficless square. If he hurried... But within moments he was surrounded by the protestors. All around him shouts rang out:

'Return our sultan!'

'Morocco for Moroccans!'

'Get the French out!'

He was jostled, swept along. People grinned at him, as if he had joined the march of his own accord. Someone clapped him on the back; someone else passed him a flyer. Hamou smiled and stuffed it in his pocket. Someone started to sing one of the nationalist songs:

The birds are calling to us in the night
They call in the tongue they share with us
Telling us that their land is our land,
From the sea over the mountains to the far desert
We are free but you are not free
Fly with us! cry the birds. Take wing!
Join together to chase the jackals away…

It was an old tribal folk song, repurposed to fit the Istiqlal cause. Hamou knew the words and he felt an urge to join in as more and more voices took up the tune, but there was something obstinate in him that just wouldn't let him do it.

As the song ended, the muezzin's call to the Maghrib prayer sounded from a minaret on the other side of the medina wall. A second voice joined the first in melodious counterpoint, from a mosque further away inside the old city walls. The two muezzins sang so that the blended notes shivered in the air, the sound so beautiful that Hamou felt struck to the heart. He gazed at the faces surrounding him and saw that others were reacting to the *adhan*, their expressions smoothing, their eyes dreamy.

But if he had thought their anger and determination would dissipate at the end of the call to prayer, he was very wrong. The flags waved more boldly than ever, so that one furled itself briefly around his head. The flag-bearer laughed and disentangled him, holding the pole even higher and crying: 'Give us back our king! No sultan, no work!'

A woman in a headscarf and a mouth veil brandished a portrait of the deposed sultan. Hamou looked up into the solemn face beneath the pointed hood of the white djellaba, the dark eyes gazing sorrowfully out from beneath heavy, dark brows as if the sultan were disappointed in what he saw; as if to say, 'Hamou Badi, why aren't you singing and chanting my name with your countrymen?'

He had, of course, been sorry when the French had sent the sultan and his family away. It seemed demeaning, impossible, seeing them on the black and white newsreel at the cinema leaving the Royal Palace and boarding a fleet of buses to take them to the airport and thence to exile. His aunt – Moha's mother, his father's sister – had wept. 'What have we become? God has cursed us.'

Hamou himself had little feeling one way or the other. The sultan was as far from him as the Shah of Iran or the Emperor of Japan. He understood that, for many, Ben Youssef was next to God, was their bulwark against the enemy and everything they stood for: the theft of their land and its resources, of their labour, from which only the Europeans seemed to profit. And yet the French had brought medicine and clinics and education to their country, roads and railways, electricity and drainage and new agricultural systems that improved productivity. But they had also brought unrest and despotism and a great deal of unfairness, since all the best land had somehow been taken out of tribal hands and distributed to the most bullying colonists who treated the locals as cheap labour at best, beggars at worst.

But there were also opportunities for those who entered and engaged with the system. Hamou had believed his teachers at the lycée when they told him, 'You're a bright lad: you'll go far,' and had taken the opportunities that had been offered. He had taken from the French the money that kept his mother comfortable in her house, bought her a sheep at Eid, paid for his sisters' clothes and tiny luxuries. The contradictions made his head hurt.

Making a greater effort now, he shouldered his way through the crowd, but it was getting ever more impenetrable. He was pushed up against something solid and had to scramble up and over it to avoid losing his balance. The scent of roses filled his nose and he realised he was standing in the flowerbeds that adorned the centre of the square. From his slightly elevated position he could see that police reinforcements had arrived at the south of the Place de France and were advancing, which was why the crowd was getting so squeezed. If they continued to press, things were going to get nasty.

'Sorry, pardon me,' he said, angling himself between a line of protesters.

Someone pushed him, but there was nowhere to fall, so he stumbled on, a man catching his arm to keep him upright with a 'Careful, brother.'

Another bottleneck had formed around one of the becalmed buses which had been taken over by a group of women giving out dates and almonds and milk, by which Hamou ascertained that the fast was broken. One of the women thrust her basket at him and called, 'Help yourself, my son. Bless you for all you are doing!'

It seemed rude to refuse, so Hamou took a handful of dates, eating one at once and putting the others in his pocket. The sweetness of the fruit and the gesture was so overwhelming that it brought tears to his eyes. 'Shokran, lalla,' he said, and passed around the side of the bus, and back into the throng. He tried to press on again towards the medina but the crowd began to surge backwards and he was carried along as if on a tide, away from his goal. Soon it became obvious that there was no point in resisting, and he let himself go with the flow. There was a lot of shouting – not just the demonstrators' chants and songs and support for the sultan – but orders in French and once, causing an ever greater surge, a volley of bullets fired into the air, so close that his ears rang. Even as he fled with the rest of the crowd some part of his brain was thinking that the very next day he too would be learning to fire warning shots over such people – people who had held him up, stopped him falling, called him brother, called him son; gave him dates.

In the end, exhausted, Hamou found himself up near the docks in the falling dark. The protesters had dispersed, and he was alone and on the wrong side of the medina. A chill permeated his shirt, which was soaked in his own sweat. He could smell it: a rank note of fear as well as of effort. Hamou put his jacket back on and jammed his cap down on his head. A miracle that he hadn't lost them in the mêlée.

He came down a street near the Avenue Delcasse and found a group of boys gathered in a circle, jeering and shouting insults. He caught the words 'whore' and 'bastard' and every so often one of them would break the circle and dash in, like dogs baiting a wild boar.

Armoured by his uniform, Hamou approached them. 'Hey!' he shouted. He thought they might be torturing a feral cat or some other creature by the noises he could hear.

The boys looked up, shouted a warning, then scattered into the darkness, leaving their prey on the ground. Hamou ran over, to find a small shape rolled into a ball, a child in a rough brown djellaba lying still, arms over his head and knees drawn up to protect his soft parts. He was gripped by horror. Was the child dead? Had he just witnessed a murder? *Please, God, no*, he prayed. He knelt in the dust and laid a hand on the boy's back and was hugely relieved when he felt him cringe away from his touch.

'You're safe,' he said in Arabic. '*Mezian.*' But when the child did not respond, he repeated the phrase in Tachelhit. '*Youda, youda.*'

Slowly, the child uncurled, sniffling mightily. Hamou helped him sit up and was struck by the sight of a beautiful heart-shaped face, though the huge, dark eyes were full of tears.

'What's your name?' Hamou asked. He wiped the street dirt gently away from the boy's cheeks and checked him over for damage. 'I am Hamou.'

But this kindness just seemed to break something inside the child, and he started to cry, great sobs wracking his tiny body. Hamou looked around for some woman – any woman – to help him, but the street was deserted. Everyone was indoors, enjoying their *harira* soup, their dates and milk and spicy tajines… and chebakia. Damn.

He looked to the sky as if for inspiration. The moon gleamed down. It was waning – Eid was next week – but it was full enough. He took the crumpled flyer out of his pocket and smoothed it out. The black and white portrait of the sultan gazed up at him, a little amused.

'Hey, little one, do you want to see the sultan in the moon?'

The child's sobs became staccato, and he frowned, puzzled. '*Na'am.*'

Hamou held the picture out to him. 'Look at his face. Look hard.'

At last, wonderfully, the boy stopped crying. He held the piece of paper close to his nose and stared and stared, and after a minute, Hamou took the flyer away and directed the child's gaze upwards. 'Now, look at the moon and tell me if you can see him.'

The boy sniffed his snot back loudly, then cried out, 'Yes, yes! I see him! The sultan is in the moon!' He turned to Hamou, ecstatic. 'He's really up there!'

'He's looking down at you,' Hamou said solemnly. His friends had played the same optical trick on him last year. 'Now tell me your name and where you live, and I will take you home.'

The boy's lower lip began to quiver and Hamou felt despair sweep over him again. Despair and a certain light-headedness. Nothing had passed his lips – except the single date the woman on the bus had given him – since two that morning.

'S-S-S-Sofiane,' the child managed at last.

'Good,' Hamou said encouragingly. 'Sofiane, where do you live?'

The lip trembled harder: then Sofiane mastered himself. '*Zhlih*,' he lisped.

'You're lost?' Hamou's heart sank. 'Can you at least tell me the quarter where you live? Which *derb*? Which way did you come?'

Sofiane stared around uncertainly. 'It's dark.'

There was no denying that. 'It is.' Hamou tried for patience. 'Were you near your house when those boys found you?'

The child shook his head. 'I was with Yam'mi.'

His mother: that was something, at least. 'Were you heading home?'

The boy nodded. 'But then all these people came and there was a lot of noise and pushing and shouting and the boys were there and my yam'mi, my yam'mi, she...' Tears welled.

'Come on, little man,' Hamou said briskly. 'She what?'

'She let go my hand. And I didn't see her any more.' The tears spilled and fell, tracking pink runnels through the dirt on his face.

'I think you got caught up in the same demonstration as I did,' Hamou said, wiping Sofiane's face again. He dug in his pocket and brought out one of the dates the woman had given him. 'Here, have this.'

The boy stuffed it in his mouth and chewed greedily.

'Come on, give me your hand and we'll head back in that direction and maybe that will jog your memory.'

Sofiane nodded, then glanced back up at the moon. His face fell. 'The sultan, he's gone.'

8

Hamou walked with the child back towards the Place de France. After his delight about the sultan in the moon, Sofiane had become silent and withdrawn again, even when Hamou squeezed his hand and gave him a reassuring smile. They stood on the pavement at the junction and stared out into the resumed crawl and honk of vehicles. No sign remained of the demonstration except a scatter of flyers fluttering in the wake of the passing cars like wounded pigeons. They crossed the first two lanes and waited in the space between the elevated flowerbeds for a gap in the traffic.

How surreal, Hamou thought, *just an hour ago – less – I was standing here, crushing roses underfoot, trapped in the crowd, with my own colleagues shooting over our heads.* Now, it was as if none of this had happened.

'Which way now?' he asked the boy as they reached the other side, but Sofiane turned doleful eyes up to him.

'Don't know.'

Exhaustion and hunger began to crush Hamou like a fist. 'Do you live near the medina, or inside the walls?' he managed at last.

Sofiane's pout was back, and he looked down at his feet. Hamou had the awful feeling that he was going to have to walk the boy all the way to the commissariat and hand him in like lost property till someone came to claim him. But the idea of the lad told to sit quietly in a corner for the night seemed unbearable, and so he pressed on, trusting that chance would repay a good deed.

A stream of people was issuing out of the medina, all in their best clothes: men in robes and skullcaps, women in their brightest headscarves and djellabas. Floral patterns clashed with stripes, yellow with pink, green with orange. As they made their way through the arch, Hamou realised they were coming out of the old mosque after the last prayer. In a highly ungodly fashion, his guts – which did not give two figs for prayer – protested loudly that it had only been fed a couple of dates all day, and as soon as he thought that, he was assailed by the honeyed scent of toasting peanuts and his stomach clenched painfully again.

A couple was approaching them, not just in the flow of people, but with purpose. 'What are you doing with that boy?' the woman asked pugnaciously, taking in Sofiane's tearstained cheeks, the dirt on his clothes, the flowering bruises. 'Surely he's far too young to have committed any crime?'

The husband looked embarrassed at his wife's challenge and Hamou adopted an official tone. 'The child was found wandering over near Delcasse. I'm trying to locate his mother.'

The woman bent to examine Sofiane more closely, but the boy turned away from her scrutiny, burying his face in Hamou's trouser leg in a strangely touching gesture.

'I think,' the husband said cautiously, 'he might be Aicha Ghazaal's boy. It's Sofiane, isn't it? Hello?' But the child would not look at him.

His wife gave her husband a hard stare, then dragged him away.

'Your mother's name is Aicha, is it?' Hamou asked the child. 'And you live in the old medina?'

'Yeth,' the boy lisped. 'In Bousbir.'

The cogs in Hamou's mind whirled and clicked into place. 'The old Bousbir?'

Sofiane nodded.

In the twenties, the French had constructed a new quarter of the city away from the ancient centre, to cater to a particular type of tourist. It looked like a film set of Morocco as conceived through European eyes: all elegant white arches and colonnades, potted palms and fountains in paved courtyards, tumbles of bougainvillea, wafting incense. There were cinemas and high-class restaurants, attractive boutiques and even its own police station, where Hamou had been posted for a few weeks last year. At first, he had been enchanted by the new Bousbir, as they called it, as if to give it the name of the old red-light district would erase the existence – maybe even the memory – of the original. It looked so clean and smart, so... sanitised.

And after a while he realised that was exactly what it was: a sanitised version of old Morocco for the safe delight of tourists and gawkers. Somewhere they could stroll and eat and enjoy the flavour of what they saw as an exotic country, without the danger of being mugged in a dark alley; where they could select and fuck one of the imprisoned women who were dressed and perfumed and presented like odalisques in a painting, like the courtesans from a harem in *The Thousand and One Nights*. It was all fantasy – for the visitors – and hard labour for the workers, for precious little in return except a bit of cash to go back into the pockets of the occupiers and the business owners.

By the end of his secondment there, Hamou had felt sick at heart; when the Istiqlal had forced the closure of the new Bousbir earlier that year, a small, resentful, native part of him had rejoiced. No more exploitation of the poor by the powerful. But of course, that was a naive view, and he knew it: when the new Bousbir had been closed down, where did those women go? The oldest profession in the world did not simply come to a halt because a group of professors and politicians deemed it unworthy of their idea of a modern Morocco – it went back into the shadows. Back into the ancient heart of the city, the old medina. Back to the original Bousbir.

That was why those boys had been taunting poor Sofiane.

That was why they had used those ugly words. His grip tightened on the child's hand. 'Come on, son. We'll have you safely home soon.'

Even so, the medina was huge, and the Bousbir a labyrinth. Although he had the mother's name and her profession, finding her would still be like finding a single ant in an ants' nest. But he was a policeman, and it was his duty.

He towed Sofiane through the promenaders. All around there was a festive air. People were happy after breaking their fast and making their prayers and successfully negotiating another day of Ramadan. The perfume sellers were doing good business: incense hazed the darkening air – amber and musk, frankincense and roses. Little groups of women gathered around the stalls, cupping their hands over the fragrant vapours, fanning the scents towards their friends. Hamou thought about approaching them to see if any of them knew the boy's mother, but to his untrained eye they looked like respectable matrons with their daughters, and his courage failed him. He passed them by. Likewise, the women browsing the jewellery shops, cooing over the glittering array of gold and silver ornaments. And anyway, the Bousbir was further in, away from the mosques and the high-end vendors.

They pushed their way through the crowd browsing fabrics and clothing and emerged into a square with a public fountain at which people queued with their buckets and children ran and shouted. Several boys were kicking a rag football around. A couple of them watched Hamou's approach warily. One said something to the rest of the group, and they suddenly scattered, shrieking with pretend terror and with laughter, and Hamou was reminded piercingly of his childhood in Tiziane, caught stealing fruit from the lord's garden, breaking the vines as he fled. How he missed the mountains: the clean air, the sense of space and freedom; the caps of cloud in the early morning; the deep red of the rock walls in the evening light. He missed being in a place where he knew everyone else and where the violence and politics fuelling such tensions here in the city were far, far away.

Sofiane tugged his hand, recalling him from his reverie. 'There's Lalla Mariam.'

Hamou saw a little old lady bent almost double by a deformation of the spine, shuffling along the dusty street with a baguette under her arm.

'Excuse me, lalla!'

The old woman's eyes were heavily kohled, the angle of her cocked head reminiscent of a crow eyeing up carrion. 'Is that young Sofiane?'

Hamou felt his mood lift by a degree. 'Yes,' he said quickly to the old woman. 'Can you show me where he lives?'

'I can, but it won't help you.'

Hamou gritted his teeth against a hasty reply. 'Why not, lalla?'

'Because there's no one home.'

'His mother…?'

'Working.' The old woman regarded him beadily.

Hamou took a deep breath. 'Might I leave the boy with you until she's finished her… work?'

Lalla Mariam huffed. 'I should think not. I have enough to do without taking in strays.'

Unhelpful. 'Might you at least show me where the lady is working?' Hamou found it almost inconceivable that the boy's mother should have continued her work despite having mislaid her child, but who was he to judge?

The old lady grunted. 'Oh, all right then. I suppose it is Ramadan and I am nearing the time when my deeds will be tallied.'

Hamou took the shopping basket from her and followed at a painfully slow pace through the narrow streets, where a constant stream of neighbours and a river of relatives kept annoyingly greeting her so that they had to stop to exchange pleasantries and explain the presence of the policeman and the boy. Given the explanation, they smiled at Hamou and tousled Sofiane's hair.

Exhaustion and hunger were gnawing at him. The temptation

to simply drop both the basket and the boy's hand and make a run for the food stalls was almost overwhelming. After all, the child would be safe now, even if the crone was an annoying old baggage. But the police had a bad enough name at the best of times, so he smiled and nodded and waited.

By now they were deep inside the medina. The houses had become older and more dilapidated, plaster fallen from the walls had left deep scars behind; long ochre shutters hung askew, or had lost louvres, and doors were rusted. Here there was little lamplight and the scent of incense had been replaced by an ammonial whiff.

At last, they came out into a scruffy courtyard in which men chatted and smoked, or sat on benches, as if waiting for something. They were all European in appearance and looked utterly out of place, though they seemed at ease.

The old woman spat in the dirt. 'She's in there.' She indicated a house with torches burning outside. 'I'm not passing any more time in this place.' And, wrenching the basket back from Hamou, she scuttled back the way she had come.

The waiting clients regarded Hamou with no curiosity. Policemen weren't a threat or a problem to them. The women for the most part operated under licence and anyway, there would be officers inside, smoking kif, taking their own pleasure.

Not Hamou. He squared his shoulders and marched up to the door, dragging Sofiane behind him.

'Hey! There's a queue!' one of the men complained.

'I'm not here as a customer.' He banged on the door with the flat of his hand. 'Open up!' He could hear shouting inside, and someone – a woman – crying. He turned the large, ornate doorknob, and the door swung open.

The hallway was lit with flickering lanterns and the air was thick with the smell of hashish and sex. As he stepped inside, a wide woman bustled into view, her frown suggestive of a grim familiarity with dealing with intruders. She flicked her fingers at Hamou as if banishing him, along with djinns and other evil influences. 'Out, out!' she screeched, and her gold earrings rattled. Then she looked down and saw the child and her expression changed. 'Oh, Sofiane!' She knelt and crushed the boy against her. 'Well, that's a relief.' She looked up at Hamou. 'His wretched mother has been completely useless to me ever since they brought her back without him, crying as if the world had come to an end.'

It *was* a relief. Hamou turned to go.

'Not so fast.' The madam pushed Sofiane back at Hamou. 'Just wait here.'

She disappeared down the corridor to the room from which the wailing issued and emerged a moment later followed by a small woman whose mascara streaked her face, and a tall man in an expensive suit. The crying woman at once launched herself at Sofiane, hugging him and kissing his face over and over, and Hamou was assailed by her scent: a rich, deep musk, overlain with roses.

'I thought I'd never see you again!' She brushed the boy's hair back and exclaimed at the bruises and dirt. 'Oh, my poor baby boy! What did they do to you?'

She gazed up at Hamou and he was at once struck by her delicate beauty, the clean lines of her face, the lambent brown eyes. Taking a corner of her veil, she rubbed the streaks of smeared cosmetic away, then wiped her hand on her robe and extended it to Hamou, who took it gingerly. It felt tiny in his grasp, fragile but full of determined life, like a small bird.

'God bless you for bringing my son back to me.' She turned his hand over and made to kiss it, but then recoiled.

'Baraka,' Aicha whispered, tilting his palm for a better view. 'The mark of the treasure-finder. So that is how you found my boy.' Her fingernail traced the straight line that ran from one side of his palm to the other and Hamou shivered. 'God has blessed me indeed today. A zouhry found my child.'

Then she laid her lips carefully upon the line in his palm as if the luck it contained might somehow transfer itself to her. The touch of her mouth sent a flash of heat through him. He pulled his hand away, and turned to leave.

'You have been so kind, so good, sidi. But I have one more favour to beg of you.'

Those eyes. A circle of green-gold rimmed the brown iris, and Hamou thought suddenly of the river stones at his favourite spot back home, where he had fished for frogspawn while dragonflies darted in blue streaks overhead and crested larks soared, charging the air with their ecstatic songs.

'Whatever I can do, *okhti*.'

His use of the honorific 'sister' widened her beguiling smile. She was probably younger than he was. The realisation of what her life had, and still, entailed came crushingly upon him. 'Anything,' he offered, foolishly.

'Please, officer, this is no place for a child, as I'm sure you understand. And I have work to do...' She glanced back at the suited man, now lounging against the doorframe, watching the scene through hooded eyes.

A foreigner, was all Hamou thought then, and a rich one. A foreigner, watching a scene play out in a culture and language he did not understand, watching with a sort of hunger that filled Hamou with both shame and envy.

'Please would you take Sofiane away for an hour with you? That's all I ask. And would you perhaps buy him something to eat? I will pay you back, I promise, when you return.'

Despite everything – the inconvenience, the lateness of the hour, his unfulfilled mission – Hamou said yes, and was rewarded by the warmth of Aicha's regard, which bathed him all the way to the food stalls near the public fountain.

9

Hamou and Sofiane wolfed down chicken *brochettes* and spicy potato cakes and felt like new men. They wandered the medina hand in hand like father and son, dodging the beggars and the trolleymen, Sofiane exclaiming over the camel's head hanging outside the butcher's store and the piles of chicken feet the women used to make stock. Hamou rather enjoyed their tour of the market, pointing out to the boy the artistry with which the vendors displayed their gravity-defying pyramids of spice – deep red paprika, golden turmeric, fawn ginger, special mixes for couscous and fish and tajines; green olives, black olives and glistening lemons preserved in salt. 'They make these displays every day from scratch,' he said to Sofiane. 'Can you imagine the skill and patience that takes?'

The child's gaze was one of such awe that the stallholder selected some plump green olives and offered them to him with a gap-toothed grin.

Sofiane popped one in his mouth uncertainly, chewed briefly, then turned and spat it into the dirt, before turning an outraged face up at the adults as if they had played a cruel trick on him. 'That was horrid!'

Hamou and the stallholder laughed.

'Your son does not yet have a very discerning palate.'

'Oh, he is not...' Hamou decided to say no more. He wished the shopkeeper a good Ramadan and walked on.

They still had time to kill, so he allowed Sofiane to lead him to where a woman sold rabbits, docile and flop-eared, and let him pet them for a minute or two, while he and the woman exchanged an understanding grimace. The animals were destined for the pot.

They kept walking until the smell of ordure was gradually replaced by that of herbs and perfumes. A group of women had gathered at a stall garlanded with perforated brass lanterns that scattered lozenges of golden light over the wares, and Sofiane pulled Hamou towards them, exclaiming excitedly, 'Al Attar does magic!'

Hamou snorted. The medina was full of charlatans who sold love potions and fertility philtres; spells and ointments to enhance beauty and hold back the years. They concocted unlikely recipes involving hard-to-come-by ingredients – the scales of dragons, the shit of whales, the eyelashes of an albino mouse, the whiskers of a sterile tomcat. Hamou had seen them all – and not just in Casa. Back home in Tiziane the travelling tinkers would spread their blankets in the market square and offer their dried truffles and ginseng and saffron, argan butter and scarabs crushed in egg yolks: all guaranteed to have couples 'climbing the curtains'. Hamou and Anir, worming their way through the pack of local men, had been puzzled by this phrase: 'Why would you want to climb the curtains?'

'It's to make your prick stiff,' a man beside them said and everyone had laughed.

'Mine gets stiff all the time,' Anir said, and Hamou had nodded. At thirteen who needed an aphrodisiac? They looked around the audience in pity – at the baker and the muezzin's son; at the butcher and the mechanic. How sad it was that half the village needed to buy bizarre potions to feel vigorous.

Even so, Hamou allowed the boy to lead him over to the crowded stall.

'Look! He has chameleons!' Sofiane gazed in fascination at the cage of weird reptiles with their independent eyes and their question-mark tails. He poked a finger between the bars and one of the beasts inched across the cage and curled a long, scaly claw possessively around it.

Lamplight danced in the boy's eyes as he turned to Hamou. 'Can I have him?'

'I don't think your mother would thank me for that!'

'But I would look after him!' Sofiane protested. 'I would find him everything he needs, and he would be my friend.'

Hamou knew what the chameleons were for. The credulous bought them for the purposes of augury, or to add their meat and bones to meals to feed to a straying husband. 'Their bite is fatal,' he told the boy: an old superstition.

But Sofiane was stroking the creature. 'Look! He likes me.'

And indeed, the chameleon's clawed hand had now encircled the boy's finger and pulses of rose-gold rippled its scaly flank, as if colour were the language with which it communicated.

'I am sure we could come to a mutually satisfactory price for the creature.' The stallholder, a wizened man in a crocheted skullcap, had materialised suddenly behind the cage. Between the beasts and the bars, his bright eyes bored into Hamou. 'For the son of an officer of the law, I will make a very good price.'

Hamou shook his head. 'No, thank you. And he's not mine, I'm just watching him for a friend.'

Al Attar stretched his neck for a better view. 'Ah, it's young Sofiane, the Gazelle's lad,' he said with a half smile. 'I see.'

Hamou felt himself colour. Of course, the stallholder knew the boy: Sofiane had mentioned him by name. No doubt his mother came here often for whatever herbs and treatments she required to ward off pregnancy and disease. In the new Bousbir there had, belatedly, been a modern pharmacy, but the old ways ruled in the medina.

'Please don't let us distract you from your clients,' Hamou said, looking towards the women pawing the wares and chattering about their possible applications.

For a moment, the stallholder hesitated, as if fearing to lose other sales, but as he turned away, Sofiane piped up in a high voice that cut through the noise. 'Hamou is a zouhry!'

Al Attar's attention snapped back to Hamou, who went hot, then cold. 'A zouhry?'

On the other side of the stall murmurs arose and women echoed the word between themselves. A tangible excitement filled the air.

Hamou pulled Sofiane away from the chameleon cage. 'We must go back now. Your mother will be wondering where you are.'

But a crowd had started to coalesce around them. The stallkeeper slipped between the cages and baskets of henna and crystals, crows' wings and animal skulls, and gripped Hamou's free hand, turning it up into the light of one of the hanging lanterns. Gold scattered across Hamou's palm, and Al Attar smiled widely. 'He is!' he announced. 'This man does indeed bear the symbol of the zouhry!' He turned to Hamou. 'Put out your tongue, sir. Let me see if the djinns have truly marked you as one of their own.'

Hamou clamped his mouth shut. He was in some sort of nightmare. 'Please,' he whispered through gritted teeth. 'Don't do this. We have to leave.'

'All in good time!' Al Attar had spotted a fine opportunity. He raised his voice again. 'Who here knows the legend of the zouhry?'

Several voices were raised in affirmation; still more clamoured for the herbman to 'Tell us! Tell us!'

'Some say that originally,' Al Attar declaimed, 'the zouhry was of the people of the djinns – peace be upon them – a baby whom they left in place of the human child they stole for their own realm. Some say, though,' and here he lowered his voice theatrically, 'that sometimes a woman lies down with a djinn—' and when Hamou started to protest he added quickly, 'but often unknowingly: for when a husband forgets to invoke the name of

Allah before he lies down with his wife, a djinn may slip between them and join them in their pleasure.'

There were gasps of thrilled outrage from the gathered women.

'And the offspring thus conceived is born nine months later – or maybe less, for djinn babies mature faster than their human counterparts. A zouhry is much prized, for they can move between worlds. They can divine water even in the desert; they can locate and bear away the long-buried treasure of the djinns and not incur their wrath; and they carry great luck, great baraka. You can tell a true zouhry by three things.' He raised Hamou's hand out towards his audience, which was increasing by the moment, and indicated the perfectly horizontal line that ran from one edge of the palm to the other, and the women exhaled as one. 'You see? The line of the zouhry. He has no other. No discernible lifeline or heart line. He does not need them, for he is half-djinn, a creature of smokeless fire encased in human skin! Also: see the brightness of his eyes—'

Hamou tried to wrench himself free, but the herbman dug a sharp thumbnail into an excruciatingly tender spot at his wrist and instead of breaking free, he let out a yelp of pain. Quicker than a striking cobra, Al Attar caught the end of his tongue and pulled on it hard. 'You see?' he declared triumphantly. 'He has their mark upon his tongue, too! A vertical line that bisects his tongue from root to tip, marking him as half and half: half man, half djinn!'

'For god's sake, let me go!' Hamou tried to say, but it came out as gibberish, and with a laugh, the herbman released his tongue, wiping his fingers on his robe. Even Sofiane was laughing at his discomfiture, and this enraged Hamou.

'I am not a bloody djinn! I can't locate treasure, I can't divine water or perform magic. That's all rubbish. I'm just a policeman, trying to do my job.'

'He found me when I was lost,' Sofiane said loudly. 'He has baraka.'

67

The auspicious word was repeated over and over, and the crowd pressed tighter. For the second time that day, Hamou feared he might be crushed.

'Stand back!' Al Attar ordered. 'Give the zouhry some air.' As if his voice commanded them, the women fell back. He whispered to Hamou, 'We've made a good show, but I beg your forbearance for a few minutes more. I will make it worth your while.'

What could he do? Hamou could see that to assert his role as an officer of the law, or to manhandle the herbman would at the least cause a scene and probably prolong the torture. He sighed. 'Oh, all right, get it over with. You may as well fully humiliate me.'

'Nonsense, lad. They think you're magic.' Al Attar winked. Then he turned to the women. 'For your pleasure and protection, ladies, I will have the zouhry here bless some crystals for you. He will imbue them with his baraka and you may take one home with you for a very reasonable price.'

He named an eyewatering sum and a woman cried, 'Too much!' The protest was taken up by those around her.

The herbman regarded these dissenters. 'Too much? Too much to guarantee yourself and your loved ones the best of health and luck? Too much, to be able to touch the crystal to your daughter's brow and ensure she has the babies she craves? Too much, to ward off the evil eye your envious cousin has placed upon you? Too much, to prevent your husband from looking upon another woman with lust in his mind? Too much, to ensure he will always please you so that your cries wake the neighbours? I am a humble man,' he touched a hand sincerely to his heart, 'but I would pay a dozen times this price to guarantee such blessings upon my family.' He paused, watching their expressions slowly change as they calculated how they might skimp on other household items in order to be able to afford a crystal charged with the magic of a zouhry. 'And remember,' he finished with a flourish, 'it's Ramadan, so the blessings thus conferred will be doubled in their effect!'

This seemed to do the trick. Two women pushed their way to the front and selected the largest crystals in the basket, and the herbman took them and made Hamou press them between his palms while Al Attar muttered extravagant prayers over them, then busily took their money. One after another, they came, some daring to touch Hamou for extra luck, and if they could not reach him, they touched Sofiane – for a zouhry's son must surely carry his father's magic, mustn't he?

'Will you meet me by the central fountain tomorrow?' one homely-looking woman asked Hamou. 'You must share our iftar. My daughter will be there. You could perhaps touch her with your power, maybe lie with her—'

Hamou recoiled. 'No, no! There's nothing special about me. I'm just an ordinary man.'

She made a face but bought a crystal anyway.

At last, the herbman's basket of crystals was empty and his money-satchel and even his pockets bulged with notes and coins, and the crowd dispersed. In the dappled lantern light, Al Attar looked less wizened than he had at first appeared. He called and two boys appeared as if from nowhere and began to pack away the stall, removing the baskets and crates and cages into a shuttered building behind the stall. One by one, the herbman extinguished the hanging lanterns, snuffing out each candle between wetted fingers so that they did not smoke. Then he beckoned Hamou and Sofiane to follow him into the interior of the building, where the boy at once located the chameleons in their cage and reacquainted himself with his scaly friend.

Hamou slumped, exhausted, onto the banquette against the back wall. He just needed a moment to regain his energy: he felt as if the herbman had somehow drained his essence into those damned crystals.

Al Attar emptied the contents of his satchel and pockets onto a bone-inlaid table and took swift, expert account of his takings. Then he made a roll of notes and held them out to Hamou. 'Your percentage. I said I would make it worth your while.'

Hamou shook his head. 'I can't take money made from cheating people.'

Al Attar laughed. 'More fool you. Do you intend to remain a junior member of the Sûreté all your life?'

That hit home, but even so, Hamou was resolute. 'I can't take it. And now, I must get the boy back to his mother.' The hour, according to his watch, was very nearly up.

'Ah yes, the mother,' the herbman said, rolling the word judiciously around his mouth. 'The exquisite Aicha. Such a pity that such a lovely creature should have to labour hour after hour upon her back for the grunting pleasure of infidels.'

Hamou looked quickly towards Sofiane, but he gave no sign of having heard the herbman's crude words, still engrossed by the chameleons. 'Yes, it's awful that anyone should be forced to earn a living in such a manner.' *The exquisite Aicha.* Yes, she was indeed exquisite. He caught this thought by the tail and pulled it back. It had nothing to do with her beauty, he told himself fiercely, remembering the sermon the man from the Istiqlal had delivered at the meeting he had attended last year. The speaker had decried prostitution wholesale, saying that it was not the fact that sex was traded for money that was a specific problem, but that it epitomised the oppression of the poor by the rich, exposing the gulf in their society that the occupiers had forced upon Morocco: 'They are shafting us all!'

He heard himself say, 'I will take the money. Not for myself—'

Al Attar closed Hamou's fist over the bundle of notes. 'Of course not,' he cooed. 'I could tell at once that you were a good man, even before your secret was revealed.'

What secret? Hamou wondered, in some panic before he realised that the herbman meant the ridiculous lines on his hands. He shook his head. What a mad day it had been.

'I would beg one more favour,' Al Attar said softly.

Almost exactly the same words Aicha had used when asking him to take Sofiane.

'What?' Hamou asked, tiredness making him brusque. He tucked the notes into his inside breast pocket, where they deformed his uniform jacket like some cancerous growth.

'Let me take a little of your blood,' the herbman coaxed, his eyes gleaming.

Hamou was revolted. 'What? No!'

'Just one or two vials. Then I can do some proper magic. It's been a while...'

Hamou realised with a jolt that Al Attar really believed in this zouhry nonsense. He had not for an instant considered that the man might be genuine in his credo, and he still resisted the possibility. Al Attar had all the bravado and the patter of the market-square charlatans – but what if there was some small kernel of truth at the heart of the bluster? After all, his mother had believed people might try to abduct or hurt him when he was a child because of the marks on his hands. And his mother was no fool... But then, if any grain of this superstition was true, why *was* he pounding the beat on a meagre wage on behalf of the French instead of hunting treasure and making himself a rich man?

Exhaustion really was making him lose his mind. He laughed quietly to himself. 'No,' he said to the herbman. 'No, you can't have my blood, I need every drop.' He paused. 'Besides, I'm not going to be further complicit in your tricks. Good Ramadan to you.' He got to his feet, detached Sofiane from the chameleons' cage, and swiftly left the building.

The streets had emptied out. Shops were dark, windows louvred, storefronts shuttered. So that, Hamou thought, feeling defeated, was the end of his mission to buy the chebakia. He walked quickly, his mind racing ahead, as Sofiane chattered on and on, explaining that it really would be all right for him to own a chameleon and that he was sure his mother wouldn't mind, and perhaps Hamou could come back tomorrow and buy him one?

After a couple of wrong turns, Hamou managed to navigate

them back towards the square where the brothel was located. There were no customers lounging around outside now, just a pair of stray dogs trotting down one of the alleys, their nails clicking on the concrete, and a feral cat slinking into, then out of, the pool of light shed by a single street lamp. Overhead, the three-quarter moon shone down, and Hamou smiled to himself, remembering the trick that had won the child's confidence. In a way, he was no better than Al Attar.

Just as they emerged into the square, the brothel's door opened and a tall, well-dressed figure stepped out, adjusting his hat, patting his pockets in a gesture Hamou knew well. He felt a sharp desire for a cigarette himself, but the Derb Ghrallef felt an immensely long way away, in another world. He comforted himself that there would surely be a tobacco cart operating somewhere between the medina and his home.

The man looked up as the child and policeman came into view and Hamou realised it was Aicha's foreign client. He gave him a brief nod of acknowledgement but the man advanced across the square, his hand extended.

'I owe you much thanks, sir,' he said in bad French, and pumped Hamou's hand vigorously. 'I have had an evening marvellous because of you. I couldn't – you know – when she was so distressed. But then – bam! – you arrive with her lost boy...' He bent and laid a hand on Sofiane's springy curls. 'Well, what a night.' He grinned broadly. 'I love your city.'

Hamou muttered that he was just doing his duty, but the man would have none of it.

'No, I know it's your Ramadan and you should be home at your family to celebrate. Here...' He reached into his pocket and for a moment Hamou feared he was about to press money on him – since everyone else appeared to be doing that tonight – but all the man offered him was a small, rectangular card. 'You ever want a beer... no, of course not... Or a good meal at one of the expensive hotels, you call me, right? In fact, if you ever need anything at all! Officer...?'

'Mohammed ben M'barek. But I prefer simply Hamou. Hamou Badi.'

The foreigner repeated his name as if committing it to memory, then tipped his hat and strode confidently off into the darkness. He was probably a regular. Hamou thought about throwing the card away but not wanting to add to the strewn rubbish, instead stuffed it into his trouser pocket. When he looked up again, the light was flooding out of the brothel's front door and there was Aicha, demure in headscarf and djellaba, with a basket over her arm, like a housewife heading to the market. Sofiane shouted, 'Yam'mi!' and hurtled into her arms.

Hamou turned to go, then remembered the object pressing against his breastbone. He felt suddenly awkward about his decision to take the herbman's money and could feel anxieties starting to rise, so before he could examine them too closely, he dug out the bundle of notes and thrust it unceremoniously at Aicha. 'For you, and the boy.'

For a long moment she stared down at it uncomprehending; then she looked up at him, her expression of shock almost erased by one of resignation. 'Of course, come with me,' she said flatly, and began to lead him back into the building.

Hamou's face flamed. 'Oh. No, oh no! That's not what I meant at all. The money is for you and for Sofiane. To live on. To pay for your food and bills, not…'

The relief in her eyes made his heart clench. But calculation and need sharpened her features, and she tucked the bundle away in the depths of her robe, then turned a professional smile upon him. 'Of course. Well, you must visit us any time. We are at your service.'

It had been wrong to take the money from the charlatan: Hamou regretted it now. How stupid he had been to think it was a gift to be lightly given and lightly received. Money represented a transaction to a working woman like Aicha, and brought with it heavy expectations. To change the subject, he said quickly, 'I came to the medina to find chebakia for my neighbours, but then...' He spread his hands. 'And now everywhere is shut. Do you happen to know...?'

Aicha seized the olive branch. 'The baker will open for me. Come.'

He followed her through the maze of alleys, while Sofiane ran between them, laughing and singing, happy to be out so late, until Aicha stopped at a shuttered house and rapped sharply on a door. 'Babrahim, it is me, Aicha Soussi!'

In the long silence that followed, Hamou stared at her. 'You're from the Souss?' Her accent was not his own.

'Yes. I was born in one of the almond villages.'

He knew this string of villages. They lay a few miles from Tiziane, further down the valley beneath the Djebel Kest, the tall red mountain range that dominated the landscape. The knowledge rendered him speechless. It made him both ecstatic and uncomfortable, as if he had found a long-lost cousin, and then discovered her profession.

Aicha knocked again, more loudly, and Hamou was saved from further embarrassment by the sound of feet on the other side of the door, the clank of bolts and a face peering out at him. 'Is there a fire? An earthquake? Has war broken out? It had better be something momentous to excuse rousing an old man from his sleep!' Then the baker's gaze fell upon Aicha and he opened the door wider, the candle-lantern in his hand lending a bloom of golden light to his white beard and nightcap.

Hamou spread his hands wide. 'I am sorry to disturb your rest, sidi—'

Aicha cut him off. 'Babrahim, darling Babrahim, it breaks my tender heart to wake you, but I have a very good reason.' And she told the baker how Sofiane had been wrenched away from her in the crowd, emphasising her tears and terror, and how Hamou had rescued her boy and come far out of his way to bring him back to her. 'All he wants is to take some chebakia home to his neighbours, and yours is the best in Casa, so how could I insult you – or him – by taking him anywhere else?'

The baker's face became a touch less lugubrious, and he gave a defeated sigh. 'Wait here,' he said grumpily.

'I feel terrible about waking him,' Hamou said as the baker moved away from them.

Aicha shrugged. 'He'll be boasting about it all over the medina tomorrow. Woken at midnight by a member of the Sûreté because he makes the best chebakia in the city and nothing else would do. He'll probably write a sign to advertise it tomorrow.'

A little further up the alley, a metal grille grated upwards to reveal the baker's shopfront and its mouthwatering displays of patisserie, and Babrahim beckoned them over and indicated a gleaming tower of sticky oval pastries scattered liberally with sesame seeds, piled tier upon diminishing tier. 'This do?'

Hamou hesitated: it was enormous. But Aicha had no qualms. 'Perfect,' she declared. She presented her back to the men, then turned to Babrahim with a fan of notes in her hand.

'No!' cried Hamou, and thrust his own wallet towards the baker.

Babrahim's eyes glittered greedily from one to the other, but then he shook his head. 'Save your money. It's Ramadan.'

There was no arguing with him. As the baker bustled into his shop to extricate the pyramid from the display, Hamou said quietly, 'I have no idea how I'll get it home.'

Aicha grinned, then put two fingers to her mouth and issued the sort of fluting whistle the boys back home used to communicate with one another in the hills. A moment later a sleepy-eyed lad stuck his head around the door at the back of the shop.

'Zak, fetch your scooter!' Aicha commanded imperiously. 'This officer needs a lift back to... Where did you say you lived?'

He hadn't. 'Derb Ghrallef.'

Zak looked woeful: that was a long way.

'Never mind,' Hamou said. 'I'm sure I can find a taxi.'

'Not at this hour you won't. Give me two minutes.' Zak gazed at Aicha with sheep's eyes before disappearing back into the house, and Hamou began to understand a degree of the dynamic at work here.

Zak returned wheeling a dusty scooter that looked as if it had seen better days, and Hamou and the chebakia were settled precariously on the back behind the baker's son. Hamou clung on and tried to protect his precious cargo.

Babrahim chuckled. 'Don't worry, my honey-sugar mix glues them together like *zellij*: you'll need to put some effort in to pull them apart. But when you do…' He put his bunched fingers to his lips, then flared them out. '*Imim!*' The Tachelhit word for 'delicious'.

Hamou grinned and wished him goodnight in the same dialect, but before he could say farewell to Aicha, or give Sofiane the topmost chebakia as he had planned, the scooter shot forward and he had to use every muscle in his body to stay safely on board as Zak hurtled through the dark alleys of the medina, past startled cats and prowling dogs, past the *nafar* with his long brass trumpet balanced on his shoulder as he stood propped against a palm tree, smoking a cigarette, waiting for the time to sound his horn for the breaking of the fast before dawn; through the smells of spice and incense; through layers of history, and out of the Bab Marrakech into another world altogether, where car headlights and sodium lamps made a false day of the night.

IO

A *Letter from Tiziane*

Alhamdulillah.

Azul, my son.

All is well with me and your sisters, with your uncle and aunt and your cousins, with Mimi the cat, also with our goats and sheep, but I am afraid that we have had to eat poor Izum, and that since then the chickens have not been laying, for I do not think they like his replacement, Agulez (I have named him Wolf in the hope that will keep the jackals at bay), even though he struts like a little sultan around his palace.

And talking of strutting little roosters, we have a new French commandant to replace Landerneau. (Sidi Malik would like to note here that these are my words, not his own.) The whole village was put to work before his arrival – you have never seen such hubbub: people running here and there with paint pots and ladders, smartening up the old houses, sweeping the streets (though the dust returns miraculously overnight), trees planted where there were no trees before. And given our water shortages, very miserable they look too. They must chat to one another at night. I can imagine the Lemon Tree asking the Orange, 'Where have you come from?' and the Orange Tree replying, 'From Agadir, where I could feel the sea breeze on my leaves.'

'Ah, Agadir, you were lucky.'

'How about you?'

'All the way from Marrakech.'

My poor sheep and goats were confined to their paddock for three days so that they would not stray and inconvenience the great man and his retinue. I half expected some *chausch* to come knocking, demanding that we bind up Agulez's beak to prevent him from crowing at too early an hour, lest he wake the commandant's wife!

I have to tell you, son, for I know how fond of animals you are, that they rounded up all the feral dogs, luring them with meat, and they all mysteriously disappeared overnight. I am sure the authorities thought this a fine solution to the nuisance of their barking and such, but as with all ill-thought-out decisions, it had unforeseen repercussions. The roundabouts and verges on the way into the village were all dug up and planted with geraniums and marigolds. They made a beautiful display ready for the arrival of the commandant, but the night after the feral dogs were taken away there was a great invasion of wild boars from the mountains and they rooted up all the new plants! They must have thought a tasty banquet had been laid out for them, for they devoured every leaf and blossom, leaving it all looking worse than it had before. What a panic!

The governor summoned the *pasha,* and the pasha summoned the *caid,* and the caid summoned the chief *mokhazni* and told him to sort it out, or he would be dishonourably dismissed. New flowers were ordered and planted and a man with a shotgun stationed at each flowerbed to see the beasts off. No one slept for nights before the commandant arrived, I can tell you, for the noise of the shots fired and the wild boar rampaging around the streets.

At least Commandant Martinot (that is his name) is now installed and the flowers have been left to fend for themselves, and the sheep and goats have finished off what the boars started. But really, what a to-do!

As I mentioned earlier, we have a shortage of water and some of the wells have failed, but as ever the people of Tiziane have rallied around and made sure everyone has the water they need, especially the old and infirm. Youngsters have been dispatched with buckets and milk churns to fill at the deeper wells and distribute where needed.

I saw Madame Martinot yesterday in the souk. I dare say many will regard her as very elegant, with her curled yellow hair and her dress so tightly fitted, but I think she resembles a wasp. And you know what I think of wasps, son.

I exhort you once more not to get involved with any unsuitable women. I have some irons in the fire here, which I shall remove for inspection upon your return when you are next on leave and are able to visit your loving mother and sisters.

Eid Mubarak, my son.

II

So now he was firearms trained. On the bus back into the centre of the city after a long day of being shouted at, of tensed muscles, fumbling with mechanisms and squinting down sights, settling the butt of the rifle into his shoulder, Hamou sat with his ears still ringing, despite the wads of cotton he had been given to protect his hearing, and it sounded as if somewhere outside the bus the whole world was screaming.

It wasn't as if he hadn't fired a gun before. On the granite plains above Tiziane he had gone many times with his uncle Omar to shoot rabbits and rock squirrels, though his uncle's *bouchfar* was antique compared to the sleek modern weapons the French instructors taught them to use. He vividly remembered, as the smell of the chemical propellant at the firing range filled his nostrils, how he had watched his uncle melting lead to make his own ammunition over a burner set on the kitchen table, much to his aunt's annoyance, and the pungent smell of the molten metal. He remembered how the gun had leapt and kicked in his hands when he had discharged it, the first time almost knocking him over. He rarely hit anything – that old blunderbuss was accurate only in the hands of an expert when it came to shooting anything smaller than a boulder – but the power he had felt at holding even such a theoretical deliverer of destruction in his hands had been a thrill.

Hamou had felt none of that power during the day's

instruction. The sole point of such training was to ready them to use the guns to control crowds and ultimately to shoot their countrymen. He wasn't prepared to shoot another human being. He'd found it hard enough to despatch the wounded mountain hare he had once shot. Seeing the pain and fear in the animal's huge eyes had sent such a tremor of empathy through him that he'd had to hand back the rock his uncle had given him for the gruesome task. 'I just can't do it. Sorry.' And he'd turned his face away before Omar could see his tears.

He had been so ashamed then, of being a coward, a baby; unmanly. But Uncle Omar had placed a hand on his shoulder as they walked back to the village. 'You're a good lad, Hamou. God made us all – animals and people. We must honour each life.' Then he had laughed and swung the dead hare up by its hind legs. 'We shall honour this one by eating every scrap of it.'

The other policemen on the bus were talking loudly – probably because like him they were half-deafened – laughing and bragging about the points they had scored and the number of targets they had hit. They had all passed the course, and Hamou had surprised himself, and everyone who knew him, by ending up in the top five marksmen. In their breast pockets they carried the folded papers, all duly signed and stamped, to prove their qualification. It was a step up the ladder: greater responsibility, greater trust from the regime, and of course more pay. Even so, Hamou felt uncomfortable.

He turned his thoughts aside from work and considered with some pleasure the pyramid of chebakia, miraculously transported without breakage from the medina last night and now on the table in his apartment, covered with a piece of cloth to keep the flies off. He imagined handing the platter to Zina and seeing the amazement and gratitude in her eyes. Then he remembered that his plan had been not to elicit gratitude but to pay a debt, and to sweeten his words as he begged mother and daughter to stop feeding him and thus adding to his obligation. Spurning the Chadlis' food would mean that he would have to become self-sufficient. He'd better purchase some provisions on his way back.

The bus came to a halt at the corner of the Rue du Commandant Lamy and they all piled off, but instead of taking his usual route home, Hamou headed for the big souk at the Place du Marché. It being near the end of the working day, there was quite a crowd buying ingredients for the evening meal. The very thought of food made Hamou's stomach gripe. At the training ground they had been offered a substantial lunch of chicken casserole, vegetables, bread and fruit, as if they were somewhere other than Morocco during Ramadan. Hamou had been surprised, and indeed rather shocked, that a number of his fellow officers had partaken. It wasn't even as if he was devout, but it felt wrong, a betrayal, not only of his religion and culture, but also somehow of his country.

He made up for it now by revelling in the sights and smells of the market: the colourful displays of fruit and vegetables, the aroma of freshly baked bread, the stalls selling kebabs and treats that could be wrapped and taken home for later. That was what he would do, Hamou thought. He'd buy a few sticks of spiced lamb, some bread, some oranges to squeeze for juice, some *taibouhari* in a cone of paper to eat on the roof terrace when he went up for a cigarette later. He could imagine the crunch of the fried chickpeas between his teeth, the momentary resistance of their spiced shells, the sudden surrender, the smokiness of the paprika and cumin on his tongue. Saliva collected in his mouth, and he had to swallow. Why was the anticipation of food so powerful? He felt like storming the snack vendor's stall and burying his face in the goods like a cow at a trough.

Mastering himself, he stood at the edge of the market square, leaning against the pillar of the baker's shop, and watched the people making their purchases: harried men with their overalls covered in the dirt of their professions, coming from building sites, from the fish-canning factories or from the docks; women towing howling children behind them, stately matrons in multicoloured djellabas, austere wives in full *niqab*. And then he saw her.

Zina Chadli. Standing in the midst of the flow of shoppers, looking over their heads, searching. It was not just her striking looks that caught his attention but something about the intensity of her questing gaze. Why was she here? There were other markets much closer to the Derb Ghrallef, and women did not generally travel so far from home to fetch the daily shopping. He watched her dip a shoulder and weave a path through the crowd towards a stall piled with watermelons, and found his own feet moving to follow her. Why he did this he couldn't explain even to himself. Sheer curiosity, perhaps. Attraction, certainly, but there was something wary in her movements, something watchful about how she turned her head quickly, scanning the people around her. He found himself moving stealthily, placing himself behind bulkier shoppers, at the corner of the tall orange juice dispenser, to observe her unseen. He watched Zina say something to the melon seller, and how something passed between them – some flash of recognition or intimacy – and he felt a sharp, shaming jolt of jealousy. Could it be that she was involved with this insignificant-looking man? He found himself scrutinising the stallholder with growing dislike; a young man, a little overweight, going thin on top. Not much of a catch, as his mother would say. Perhaps he was a cousin. But there was nothing in the man's unfamiliar, blunt features that offered him consolation.

The watermelon man served another customer, picking one of the huge green melons off the top of the pile and settling it in the woman's shopping bag, before returning his attention to Zina. He looked around shiftily, Hamou thought, then bent and picked out a melon from underneath the cart. No money changed hands between them. Zina took the melon in her basket, then turned away, and Hamou saw her arrange the rest of her purchases over the top of it, which struck him as odd, although it was an entirely practical thing to do, given the weight of the melon.

Now, she threaded a passage between the rows of stalls, walking as fast as the crowd would allow. Hamou followed at a distance, all thoughts of spiced chickpeas and kebabs vanishing.

'Balak!' cried a man pushing a trolley piled with crates of squawking chickens, and Hamou was forced to leap out of the way. By the time he got to the end of the market square, there was no sign of Zina. He scanned the Rue de Zürich, the junction with the Rue de Faucilles, but he could not see her anywhere. He stood there for a time in case she reappeared at one of the side streets, but it seemed that she had vanished. Eventually, he turned and walked back into the souk and made his half-hearted purchases: his appetite had faded. But why shouldn't Zina visit a different market to her usual haunts? Maybe she had been visiting relatives in that quarter. Even so, unreasonable dread tugged at him.

Back at his apartment, Hamou stared at the shrouded chebakia: a monumental folly in the light of day. Sighing, he removed the cloth, hoisted up the platter and took it gingerly down the stairs to the Chadlis' door, where he rapped loudly. He heard the clatter of crockery, then the door opened a crack and Samira peered out, looking fearful. Then she saw it was only Hamou and flung the door wide. He looked past her down the corridor, but there was no sign of Zina. Hefting his gift, he thrust the pyramid at Samira. 'For you. And the family. Obviously. As thanks for all your generous hospitality. I'll be eating with my cousins in the Maarif from now on: I'll never hear the end of it from my aunt otherwise, you know how it is.' This all came out in a gabbling torrent, and from Samira's blank expression he feared she hadn't understood a word. But then she clucked her tongue and took the chebakia.

'Family is very important. It's good to see a young man with proper values. But how will we eat all this? You must at least come in for iftar tonight to help us out!'

Hamou raised his palms in defence. 'No, honestly, I've

promised my aunt: she'll be expecting me.' And with a bow, he backed away and fled upstairs.

Damn. Now he was either going to have to creep around in his apartment, pretending he wasn't there, or he would have to go out again. He felt exhausted, strung out, and very, very hungry. The idea of having to buy street food and hang around locally was unappealing, especially after the incident at the hammam. With a sigh, he washed, changed into a clean robe, gathered what little was left of his energy and left the building. Better make the lie a truth.

'Hamou! Alhamdullilah! Where have you been all this time, the moon?'

Hamou smiled wanly as his uncle Salim enveloped him in a bear hug, after which he was engulfed by a tide of cousins, male and female, adult and child; and lastly Moha, who stood propped against the hallway wall, watching on sardonically.

'Good evening, Officer Badi!' He snapped a salute and burst out laughing at Hamou's dismayed expression. 'I know, I know, you're off duty and don't even want to think about work.' He threw an arm around his cousin's neck and dragged him into the salon.

The atmosphere was convivial and loud with chatter. Wonderful smells emanated from the kitchen. Hamou made himself comfortable in the elegant room with its smart furniture and velvet drapes, the gold-framed portrait of the deposed sultan in pride of place; a smaller one of his cousin, the puppet sultan Mohammed Ben Arafa, shoved off to the side in a cheap wooden frame. He watched his cousins Ali and Tahar discussing with some seriousness a problem that had arisen that day with some poor-quality flour; their wives, Khadija and Naima, resplendent in their holiday kohl and painted nails visible through their peep-toe high-heeled French shoes, silver bangles rattling as they gesticulated and giggled; the little girls and boys scrabbling over some painted wooden toys, Moha's youngest brother, Hicham, joining in. This was his Casa family and yet he hardly ever saw them, and he didn't really understand why, because wasn't it lovely to be here, accepted for just being plain old Hamou Badi in his embroidered Soussi robe, sitting here amongst people he knew and loved, with music playing and the air thick with apple-flavoured hookah smoke and incense and laughter?

He spent a while drifting in and out of this sense of belonging, sometimes in the thick of the joking and gossip, sometimes at a remove as some turn of the conversation threw him out of the flow and reminded him of his dual identity as a member of this clan who were all so bound up in the joint enterprise of their business of import and export, the busy comings and goings of stock, the bookkeeping and payments, the management of staff and customers and premises; but also as a member of the Sûreté, working for the colonisers, and now licensed to carry and use a lethal weapon.

'You must come to us for Eid next week,' Aunt Jamila pressed at the end of the evening, the shape of her eyes and the cast of her brows reminding him sharply of his lost father, her brother. 'Promise me that you will.'

'I will,' said Hamou, feeling a hardness in his throat.

He always came to celebrate the end of Ramadan with his Casa family. He had lived here in this apartment when he had first come to the city, gone to the lycée around the corner with Moha and his younger brothers. He had slept on a pallet in the main room surrounded by the rest of them: he was familiar with every different timbre of their snores and snuffles. Over the years Moha and he had at first grown close, then drifted in different directions, exchanging their previous positions. It amused Hamou to think what a tearaway he had been back in Tiziane, and how they had regarded him as a little ruffian when he'd arrived in the city scruffy and defiant and determined not to show how scared he was by being plunged into the centre of this big, white, modern European city. Then, Moha had been the example held up to all: polite, clever, well-behaved, excelling at school, conforming to all the rules. At some point they had met in the middle as Hamou had come to the uncomfortable understanding that a contrarian attitude merely served to strew self-devised obstacles in his path; while at the same time Moha had started to emulate his older cousin, becoming increasingly troublesome, getting into fights and espousing unwinnable causes. These diverging trajectories had seen Hamou enrol in the police force and Moha cutting corners and doing dubious deals as he worked in his father's business, forging questionable connections, but somehow bringing more money in. He had a talent for seeing and seizing opportunities and had gradually become influential in the Maarif.

Replete and happy, Hamou walked the couple of miles between his uncle's apartment and the Derb Ghrallef. It was balmy and the traffic on the Mazagan was light. Another Ramadan was almost completed and next month he would be able to send his mother and sisters more money than usual and maybe a few little luxuries as well. But not chocolate. He realised he had no idea what else they would like, indeed what any woman might want. Maybe he should ask his aunt or one of his cousin's wives. Or Zina Chadli. She was a smart, modern young woman who made money of her own from working at the local hospital. She would know.

It was with this pleasant thought that he jiggled his key in the lock of the apartment building, and let himself in. It was too nice a night to spend sitting inside, listening to the radio, so Hamou took his cigarettes and matches and went up to the roof terrace to smoke beneath the stars.

Above, the Guide had risen and he could make out the faintly twinkling constellation of the Sky Sisters. He took a deep draw on his cigarette and felt any remaining tension drain out of him. It was good to know how to handle a firearm, right? It had been pleasing to discover that he had a sharp eye and a steady hand. Next time he went home to Tiziane he would be able to show off to Uncle Omar. Then his optimism faded. Omar was older now and walked with a stick: how quickly time took its toll on the frail human body.

He finished his cigarette and ground out the butt, picked it up and took it with him to throw away in his own bin. When he reached the door down from the terrace, he paused, his attention caught by a smell, a note of lingering sweetness, and then a sound.

Flies, buzzing, the sound amplified by the iron of the latched-back door and the crook of space behind it. Curious, he unlatched the door, being careful not to let it swing back and leave him locked out up here, and let the moonlight fall on the crevice, revealing a pile of what appeared to be discarded slices of fruit, and a spiral of annoyed flies, disturbed in their feasting. Perhaps the Chadlis had come up here to share their dessert in the cooler environs of the terrace?

Hamou bent and picked up a big chunk, turned it over in his hands. Watermelon. Some odd mark marred the smooth green shell. He played a fingertip over it and felt the sharp edge, as if it had been carved. How strange.

Feeling foolish in his curiosity, he relatched the terrace door and took the hacked wedge of fruit over to the parapet. Angling it into the moonlight didn't enlighten the hole, or Hamou, so he lit a match to examine it better.

In the flare of the flame, the shape leapt into relief. Someone had cut the shape of a small crescent moon into this melon. Why? Hamou's brain supplied the answer instantly: to mark it out from the others.

His whole body broke out in gooseflesh.

He went back to the mound of discarded fruit and carried it out into the open, fitting the pieces together like a child's puzzle, then turning them flesh side out. The melon had been cleanly cut into four uneven pieces, and the softest flesh and pips in the middle scooped out. Into what remained of the red flesh he made out – lighting match after match in a sort of compulsive frenzy – the indistinct impression where an object had been pressed into the fruit. He looked from one section of melon to the next, holding the shape in his head, until he knew with awful certainty what he was looking at. Someone, for some reason, had concealed a handgun in this melon, much like the pistol he had been using on the range this very day. And someone had carved the mark of the violent dissident splinter group into the skin of the fruit, so that it could be identified.

The Black Crescent, so extreme that they had all but wiped out the Black Hand and blatantly assassinated figures in the French regime.

He remembered how the melon seller in the market earlier had not taken a fruit from the top of his display as he had for the previous customer, but had reached beneath his cart to select the melon for Zina Chadli, how she had concealed it in her basket, and hurried away.

Here was the melon, or what was left of it. But where was the gun?

Were the Chadlis members of the Black Crescent? That seemed absurd. But here was their mark, on the fruit he had seen Zina take with his own eyes.

Hamou's head swam. He carefully carried the pieces of melon shell and dumped them behind the terrace door again. His hands were shaking, his heart thudding. He reached for his cigarette packet. Just one more, to calm his nerves. Propped against the parapet, he stared out into the darkness, taking in the roads, the European sectors, and at the edge of his view the pinpricks of light in the local bidonville, and beyond deeper darkness. In the street below, a pair of feral dogs flowed through the shadows and disappeared into the alley where the butcher's bins stood.

He took a long last draw on his cigarette and saw a figure down below, coming out of the shared front door. At once he knew it was Zina Chadli. His back prickled. Then he stamped the cigarette butt underfoot, for the first time ever not stopping to retrieve it or the little pile of spent matches, and went hurtling down the stairs and out onto the street before he was even consciously aware of his own intent.

Zina had almost reached the corner – not the end of the street that led towards the Mazagan, but in the opposite direction, towards the shantytown. Even though she wore a dark, shapeless djellaba with the hood drawn up he knew it was her by the way she moved, her stride measured and purposeful. In one hand, a basket with a cloth over the contents, just like any housewife carrying treats to the family. Was the gun in that basket?

No cover now: he had reached the extent of the built-up section of the Derb Ghrallef. Beyond lay the bidonville, the place where the poorest of the poor fetched up. The place where the most desperate, and possibly the most dangerous, lived.

He watched Zina go in.

12

November 1952

It was a Sunday, for Hamou a rare day off. He joined Moha for a late lunch in their usual café in the Maarif and was surprised when instead of lingering for further tea and cigarettes, Moha suddenly leapt to his feet and said, 'There's something I need to do on the other side of town. Fancy a drive?'

'Sure.' Hamou had nothing else to do and the idea of returning to his chilly new apartment was less than appealing.

They walked down the street a little way and Hamou was surprised when Moha stopped beside a gleaming ivory-coloured automobile with long, elegant lines and colour-coordinated hubcaps. Hamou gave a low whistle. 'Who did you steal this from?' For how else did a twenty-year-old lay hands on such a vehicle?

His cousin grinned. 'She's a beauty, isn't she? A 170s Cabriolet, last year's model. Someone owed me a favour.'

'It must have been a very big favour.'

'Oh, believe me, it was!'

Moha rolled down the soft top and ushered Hamou into the passenger seat and they sailed off through the light traffic on Casablanca's wide boulevards, with the wind on their faces and envious eyes turned upon them at every junction. They drove east along the Avenue de la République, through the Place Mirabeau and south of the Roches Noires into the industrial area. Hamou had never been this far east in the city before, had no idea that

the bounds of Casa stretched so far. The environs they passed
through became increasingly grim, and when Moha took a right
that carried them up onto a high overpass he was given a view of
warehouses, abattoirs and factories, scrubland and serried ranks
of railway lines heading south and east.

'Where are we going?' he asked nervously, feeling as if they
were crossing out of the known world into a wasteland. 'Don't
we need a permit to come this far out of the city? What if we're
stopped by the police? Won't they think you've stolen this
car?'

Moha chuckled. 'Relax, cousin. You're letting your peasant
roots show!'

Hamou seethed quietly. To be reminded that he was still
regarded as an inferior country cousin was galling.

'At least tell me where we're going?'

'Tin Can City. The Carrières centrales. I have some business
there.'

Hamou stiffened. The Carrières centrales was the biggest
shantytown in Casablanca about which he had heard only
terrible things. That the people were as rough as rats. That it
was a hotbed of terrorists. That the women would poison you
as soon as look at you and the men garotte you, then stuff
your balls in your mouth. Those who offered these unnerving
observations were all Francophone officers – if not actually
French, then drafted in from other parts of the French-speaking
world, like Yaya and Alphonse – or fellow Moroccans who
had thrown their lot in with the colonists. And surely a great
deal of fear underlaid the exaggerated claims, the sneering and
condescension, and also a good deal of underestimation. Hamou
began to wonder whether Moha had asked him to accompany
him that day as moral support, or as muscle. Or maybe his
cousin was just showing off – not just the smart, expensive car,
but also his greater worldliness, his understanding of the layers
of the giant onion in which they lived.

Moha parked the car beside a modern concrete housing block

and waited half a minute until a group of little boys came running to surround them, gasping in admiration over the vehicle. He picked the two biggest among them and beckoned them aside. 'One *rial* now and four when we get back, all right? Make sure there isn't a scratch on it, or this gentleman here will track you down and take you to the cells in the Derb Moulay Cherif.' He dropped Hamou a wink.

They crossed the road and followed the long wall to an opening where some burly men lounged, smoking cheap cigarettes. The men chatted with Moha so familiarly that it seemed they knew one another, which Hamou found odd, till he realised the Carrières must provide a rich pool of willing workers – those who like Hamou had come to the city in search of better fortunes, and unlike Hamou had found themselves further reduced. One of the men held out his hand to clasp Moha's and the pair shook. Hamou's sharp eyes caught a glimpse of the small denomination banknote that passed from his cousin to the other man. After this transaction, it seemed they were 'permitted' to enter the bidonville.

Moha walked confidently between rows of shacks where lines of washing flapped in the breeze, each dwelling erected close to the next, rickety structures cobbled together out of panels hammered out of old oilcans and roofed with corrugated iron or pieces of tarpaulin. In summer, Hamou thought, they must be like ovens; in winter, like refrigerated units.

As they walked, dodging fast-walking housewives swathed in scarves, boys carrying trays of loaves on their heads, hundreds of foraging sheep and goats, he took in more details: communal clay ovens blackened by char, very much like the ones back home; tiny patches of cultivated ground where herbs and flowers grew; battered water containers; drainage channels dug in neat lines; wastepipes welded together out of the same tin can fragments as the shanties.

'The public fountain is a mile away,' Moha said, 'but when the weather's particularly hot or the fountain runs dry, the French authorities will drop off a big bowser of water if they deem local behaviour good enough to deserve such support.'

Hamou was shocked: as they said back home, '*aman iman*': water is life.

They passed a square in which maybe fifty children sat listening to a storyteller or teacher, and a row of shanty-shops. It being November, the sun was faint and the temperature low; the air was full of the scent of charcoal braziers, burning both wood and dried animal dung. Here, people had brought with them the country ways. They could eke a living out of practically nothing – and many of them had to.

In a clearing a few hundred yards into the bidonville, Moha stopped and gave a whistle, and within moments three men materialised as if out of nowhere. The first man strode ahead to greet Moha formally. He was tall and dark-skinned, with long limbs, a sharply boned face and a salient nose, and his hair sprang out from his head in a riot of springy black curls. He wore a southern robe. Hamou wondered if he had desert heritage. The other two were more heavy-set and did not give their names.

Hamou was introduced merely as Moha's cousin.

'Come.' The tall man told them his name was Brahim Keita.

Moha and Hamou followed Brahim to a larger than usual residence made out of the same oilcan panels but with a faded awning extending the living area to the fore. Someone had made a great effort to beautify this simple dwelling: tins that had contained tomatoes or cooking oil had been repurposed as plant pots and even at this time of the year the geraniums and jasmine in them were still flowering. A reed mat covered the ground beneath the awning; cushions were arrayed all around.

Brahim called out, and a woman appeared at the door of the shack, wiping her hands on her apron. She had striking blue eyes and her skin was the colour of milky coffee. Big silver hoops hung from her ears and bracelets jangled on her arms as she removed the apron and modestly pulled a corner of a spotless blue robe up over her head.

'My wife, Biba,' Brahim declared proudly. 'Tea, my love, for our guests, if you wouldn't mind.'

Biba grinned at him, then stepped back inside, returning a minute later with a round red metal teapot which she placed upon the brazier, after wafting the coals to life with a piece of cardboard. Behind her, an elderly woman in a black-and-orange haik shuffled out bearing a platter of pastries. Everyone took a seat and Brahim withdrew an embroidered pouch and a long, intricately carved reed pipe from some hidden pocket. With clever fingers, he pushed a little of the leaf from the pouch into the bowl of the pipe, lit it and passed it to Hamou. Hamou saw Moha shoot him a questioning look. He smiled genially back at his cousin. It was a bit old-fashioned to smoke tobacco this way, but he'd seen old men do it in the marketplace back home. He took the pipe from Brahim, took a deep draw on it, and felt the fumes hot in the back of his throat, then searing down his windpipe and flaring out across the expanse of his chest cavity. A powerful aroma enveloped him, making his eyes water. The ends of his toes started to tingle. And then he began to cough and cough.

Brahim said, 'I don't think he's played golf in the desert before!' and everyone laughed.

Hamou was seized by a shock of memory – out behind the clinic in Tiziane, smoking his first cigarette with a group of older boys he'd been trying to impress. Not even a full cigarette, but the half-smoked, discarded butt of a Kebir. Even stale, it was horrible, harsh and tarry. He'd inhaled too deeply and spent the next twenty minutes hacking his lungs up while they too had laughed at him. After that, he'd gone to a quiet place where he could practise without an audience. Smoking was a skill to be acquired: a move along the road to being a man. One day he would apply similar principles to the skill of holding off his own orgasm while bringing a woman to climax – but that was still a long way in his future.

Moha took two quick puffs on the pipe before passing it back to Brahim, who, with an expert flick of the wrist, expelled the ball of spent kif into one of the tin ashtrays like a little golf ball, and Hamou understood the meaning of the phrase he had used earlier. Distantly, as if in another room, he felt himself blush, but at the same time found himself so pleasantly dissociated from his own thoughts that he didn't really care if he had been gauche.

As the pipe did the rounds, he helped himself from the plate of pastries and munched contentedly, pausing only to watch with a sort of stupefied delight as the old lady rummaged under her skirts, pulled from her boot a longer, larger, more extravagantly decorated pipe of her own, and filled it with a substantial bolus.

Afternoon slid into the evening in a bit of a haze for Hamou and when, after a lot of talk about politics and other matters he found it impossible to focus on, they got up to leave, it felt as if his legs belonged to someone else.

Moha teased him relentlessly on the drive back and it had taken some days for Hamou to put two and two together – Brahim and his associates did indeed work with Moha in his family's import business. And he had a pretty good idea exactly what it was they helped him to import. He wondered, given the amount of money that must be involved in such an operation, why Brahim opted to live in the shantytown, and realised there were probably many reasons, not least among which were camouflage and a sense of belonging. He'd come away impressed and touched by the welcome he'd received in the Carrières centrales; by the cooperative way of living – the sharing of amenities, the community spirit, the refusal to be hammered down by the inequities of French-imposed society. When he went back to his new apartment that night, which he had regarded as a step up, he felt a little sad and displaced. Not that he wanted to live in a corrugated iron shack in the bidonville, crossing legal lines and risking everything to scratch a living, but he missed his home, and being around people he knew. He even missed living with Moha and his family, despite the squabbles, the noise, the impossibility of privacy. Anyway, Moha didn't live at home any more. Moha drove a Mercedes-Benz Cabriolet and, in all likelihood, traded in hashish. Really, given the career path he had chosen, Hamou knew he ought to cut all ties with his cousin, but the thought of setting himself adrift and alone in this big city was chilling indeed, and he had put it from his mind.

Just under a month after his trip into the bidonville Hamou came out of college one evening to find his aunt Jamila waiting for him outside. She rained kisses down upon him, much to Hamou's embarrassment. Yaya and Alphonse, passing, had sniggered. 'Isn't she a bit old for you, Hamou Badi?'

Hamou made a rude gesture towards them, then apologised to his aunt. He took her by the arm and walked her quickly away. 'What is it, *amti*?'

'It's Moha.' She hadn't seen him for a week, no one had. 'He's not even eating!' she wailed. She had been going to his home and leaving a tajine and some cakes outside his door after persuading the concierge to let her in, but always they had been left untouched. 'What if he's lying dead inside?'

'Did you call out to him?'

'Yes, and he shouted, "Go away!"'

Hamou, unable to help himself, grinned. 'Well, he's not dead then, amti.'

'But that was two days ago. Please, Hamou, you're closer to him than his own brothers. Would you go to see him? Maybe he'll open his door to you.'

Hamou had had plans that evening to go and see *Les Diaboliques* at the cinema in the Habous, the new medina. Alphonse had told him it was about a woman and her husband's mistress who conspired to murder the man, and it sounded intriguing. He had wondered if he could solve the mystery before it fully played out on the screen. But that little treat would have to wait. He sighed. 'Of course, amti.'

The concierge of the flats was an elderly man from Hamou's region. He had a face like a dried walnut, with a corrugation of lines that flowed into his short white beard.

'*Timinciwin*, Qarim.' Hamou wished him a good evening in their own dialect and the old man beamed and wished blessings on Hamou and his family.

'It's one of my family I've come to see,' Hamou said. 'Moha bin Salim.'

The old man clicked his tongue and looked upwards. 'Up there.'

'His mother is convinced he's dead.'

Omar laughed, showing yellow tooth stumps. 'Mothers, eh? I've heard the water is still flushing in his bathroom. He has one of those newfangled French things in there.'

'A toilet?'

Omar rolled his eyes as if this were the height of decadence. 'I don't know what's wrong with the old ways. It makes some racket. The Widow keeps complaining.'

Hamou had encountered The Widow, a diminutive Arab woman with severe features. He commiserated with Omar, then went up the stairs.

Not even a strip of light showed beneath Moha's door. Hamou knocked and waited. A listening silence followed, a silence full of awareness and tension, but he could smell his cousin inside. He just could. 'Moha, it's me, Hamou. I'm alone.' He heard a stirring but the door still did not open. He could feel his cousin's presence mere inches away, as if they breathed in synchronicity. 'Moha?'

'Why are you here, Hamou?' The voice was as scratchy as a rusty gate-hinge.

'Amti Jamila asked me to check on you.'

'I don't believe you. Did they send you to bring me in? I've heard what happens to prisoners they take to the commissariat.'

'What? No! Of course not. I came because everyone's so worried about you.'

A long silence. Then Moha said, 'Well, you can tell them you've spoken to me. I just want to be left alone.'

'I've brought gazelle horns and cigarettes. I'll leave them outside if you don't want to see me, but it's sad to eat gazelle horns on your own. I could make some tea...'

The silence felt more considering. Then bolts scraped and the door opened a crack. Inside, the apartment was dark, and the air smelled close and sickly. 'Are you hurt?'

A small noise escaped Moha. Then the door opened wider and a hand grabbed Hamou's arm and pulled him inside. The door closed again with a bang, and Moha shot the bolts. It took Hamou's eyes a few moments to adjust to the semi-darkness. The place – usually obsessively orderly and clean – was a tip. He could smell old blood and a sort of rancid-sweet smell on top of that. Alarmed, Hamou walked to the window and flung back the shutters. Light flooded in, making Moha blink and cry out. Hamou also cried out...

His cousin's face was dark and puffy with bruises, his left arm hung in a makeshift sling patched with brown stains. 'Heavens, Moha, what happened to you? Who did this?' His thoughts drifted once more to the bidonville, the illicit drugs, the turbaned man and his burly 'cousins'. 'Was it Brahim?'

Moha's expression crumpled and then he started to cry. Horrified, Hamou guided his younger cousin to the couch and sat him down, then ran to the kitchen and fetched a glass of water and an ashtray. He set both on the round table in front of Moha, brought out the cigarettes, his matches and the bag of pastries and placed them down too.

'Brahim,' Moha sobbed.

Hamou felt a deep rage building within him. 'I'll kill him for this,' he swore, feeling suddenly protective towards his younger relation.

Moha stopped sobbing abruptly and stared at Hamou. 'What?'

Hamou set his jaw. Where he came from, injury to a friend or relative required payment in kind, or worse. 'I will kill Brahim for doing this to you!'

'He didn't do this... It was Brahim... who died.'

It took a long time to get the story out of him, and by the end of it Hamou rather wished he hadn't. He'd heard something about the events of the past few days, of course, but from a different point of view. He knew there had been a political assassination by the French in Tunis – a man called Ferhat Hached. The Tunisian nationalist movement he represented was affiliated with the struggle for independence in Morocco, and so the Moroccan workers' party, the UGSCM, the communists and the Istiqlal had called for a general strike. Boniface, the Resident General, had condemned the strike and vowed to prevent it. But none of this explained the injury to his cousin or Brahim's death, so he pressed Moha for the details.

'The regime sent out their people into the Carrières centrales, to pass the word that the strike was forbidden. They told the butchers and the grocers that if they didn't open their shops as usual, their shops would be torn down. A big group of residents got into a fight with the guards they sent in, then marched out and surrounded the police station at the Derb Moulay Cherif, shouted and threw stones to make their protest. And what did those bastards do?' He stared at Hamou, wide-eyed. 'They shot them. There was a running battle. Many were wounded, many killed. Including... Brahim.'

Hamou remembered the laughter and warmth of the evening he had passed in the heart of the tin-can city; the tall man's bonhomie; his pretty wife, Biba; his kif-smoking old mother; his brood of now-fatherless children; and he felt ashamed at thinking Brahim might have done violence to his cousin. But even so, it was hard to believe the authorities could have shot him just for shouting or throwing a stone, and he said so.

Moha stared at him. 'They hate us, the French. Especially, they hate the poor. Hate and fear them. There are so many, and so close to their nice houses and shops. And they know they are in the wrong, occupying this country. People don't want them here, taking all the good things, leaving nothing for the rest of us. They've come into our house like thieves in the night and we're supposed to thank them for stealing our possessions!'

Hamou thought about Moha's fine car and usually fancy clothes, and it didn't seem that clear-cut to him. He could enumerate the good things the French had done for Morocco but he knew there was no point in rehearsing such arguments right now. Instead, he said, 'It sounds as if things got out of hand and they were trying to restore order.'

'Order? The French aren't interested in restoring order! All they want is an excuse to murder us, they look for every opportunity.'

'Murder's a harsh word,' Hamou said quietly.

'Murder's a harsh death.'

Hamou fell silent. Then he said, 'My colleague Yaya told me two European women were abducted by communists, dragged into the bidonville and raped and had their throats cut...' Even as he said it, he knew it sounded wrong.

'For God's sake, Hamou, you've been there. You've seen the people. Do you think they're murderers and rapists and communists? Why do you think I took you with me?'

Hamou admitted he had wondered why.

'To show you another side of the city. Real poverty, but real community. People who live on the edge because that's where the French have pushed them: to the edge of existence. To show you why we are resisting.'

'Desperate people do desperate things,' Hamou started, but Moha cut him off. 'When we were kids, you hated the French, but here you are, becoming one of them. I can't believe you of all people are falling for their propaganda. It's what they do, spread false news, to rile people up, make them angry and malleable. How else can they justify their brutality? Look: I went to Brahim's funeral – the funeral of all those that were shot and killed at the Derb Moulay Cherif. Thousands of us went. We walked all the way to the cemetery near Ben M'sik. It was peaceful. It was respectful; it was a real statement of togetherness and protest. And you know what? On the way back they ambushed us. Boniface sent in the *goums* and armoured cars. They shot at the cortège. Can you believe that? They mowed down peaceful mourners. Is that the action of a benevolent power? Is it?'

Hamou stared at his hands. All he'd heard was that there'd been 'trouble' on the road to Mediouna, that a mob had tried to invade the French quarters of the city and had killed and beaten any Europeans they encountered. There had been no talk of a cortège, of funerals or mourners.

'How do you think I got like this? I got beaten up, then one of the goums shot me.' Moha made a sound like a bark. 'Yes, that's right, a fucking Berber in a French army uniform. Laughed, then shot me. If I hadn't dodged, I'd have been as dead as Brahim.'

'My god,' Hamou said, trying to take this in. 'They shot you?'

'The bullet went straight through the muscle. I'll live. Maybe.' Moha laughed hollowly. 'Though I'm not sure I even want to. Not in this world.' He hung his head and his mouth began to tremble.

'I'll make us some tea.' Hamou felt a great need to clear his thoughts. He wanted to believe there was truth on both sides, but he could not defend the shooting of unarmed Moroccans; he could not accept the death of Brahim or the wounding of Moha, his little cousin, whom he had known for over a decade as a bit of a mouse, in no way a thug, a rioter, or a communist. Moha couldn't land a punch or wrestle an opponent to the ground. As a boy he'd just run away from fights.

I must get him out of here, he thought as he boiled the water for tea, digging in Moha's sparsely stocked cupboards for tea-leaves and sugar. *He needs that wound tended to.* But who could he take Moha to? Aunt Jamila would have conniptions, and Moha's sisters would probably faint at the sight of a bullet hole. You couldn't just show up at the hospital, either: all admissions and treatments were fully documented and the police would be asking questions, seeking out rioters and troublemakers. They would arrest Moha if they found out he had taken a bullet.

And then the solution came to him.

It took a good deal of persuasion to get Moha to agree to leave his rooms. Hamou had helped his cousin to wash, got him into clean clothes. They left under the cover of darkness and made the twenty-minute walk down through the Maarif to the Derb Ghrallef, keeping to the backstreets, Moha's wounded arm hidden beneath a draped overcoat.

He had knocked on the Chadlis' door and carefully, delicately, diplomatically explained the situation to Samira, leaving it unsaid but perfectly clear that his cousin had sustained a severe wound 'while mourning the death of a friend'. Samira's face had clouded and for a moment Hamou had thought she would turn them away, wanting no trouble, but no.

Zina had tended to Moha, barely saying a word other than, 'This will probably hurt.' She sewed up and dressed the wound with unsparing practicality, not even pausing when Moha flinched or cried out. Even Samira Chadli, whom Hamou had taken to be a rather histrionic woman, had been quiet and grim-faced throughout, except for one exclamation that had stayed with Hamou: 'Bastard French!'

He thought he must have misheard.

13

May 1955

Now, Hamou watched Zina disappear into the Derb Ghrallef bidonville. Two and a half years had passed since he had last set foot in one of the tin-can cities and this slum was a lot smaller and closer to home than the Carrières centrales. But even so, he hesitated to follow her inside. He knew no one who lived here – at least he didn't think he did. People who worked all over the city as cleaners and factory workers, as bus drivers and teachers, nurses and care workers, secretaries and concierges, shop staff and waiters often lived in these shacks, putting on meticulously cleaned and folded clothing early each morning before taking a bus across the city to keep the rich world turning. But there were other types here too – as a policeman, Hamou knew that only too well – people to whom Hamou was the enemy and who might recognise him by sight because that was their job. He would have passed them on the street without even realising they were watching him and reporting back to their employers. Police – even off duty, were not welcome here, unless unofficially and under the protection of family hospitality.

He havered outside the shantytown. Things could escalate quickly if you were caught in the wrong place at the wrong time. But concern for Zina took hold of him and he suddenly found himself walking quickly after her.

Eid was just a few days away and there were few signs of

life evident beyond a few flickering candle lanterns and the light of campfires in the distance. The tin-shack shopfronts were shuttered, the shopkeepers gone home to eat and sleep. It was almost midnight: people had work the next day. The most observant would be getting up before dawn to eat an early breakfast before the sunrise call to prayer.

Hamou scanned the dark alley and caught a flicker of movement towards the end of it. Zina, about to turn the corner? He picked up his pace till he nearly collided with two men coming out of an unseen junction. Averting his face, he mumbled apologies, but one of the men kept staring at him and when he made to continue, he stepped in front of Hamou, barring his way. 'You look lost... officer.'

Hamou tried not to show his dismay. 'I'm looking for a friend.'

'Sure you're not looking for a suspect?'

'No, not at all. Just a friend.'

The man moved his hand slowly out of his pocket to show the blade of a knife glinting in the moonlight. Menace hung in the air between them.

Hamou thought fast. The entrance wasn't far behind him. Could he turn and outrun them?

'Hey, my man!'

All three turned towards the newcomer.

It was Didi, the beggar from the street corner near Hamou's apartment. His new yellow babouches glowed in the darkness.

'Didi!' Hamou had never felt so glad to see anyone in his life.

The beggar threw his withered arm around Hamou's shoulders. 'Peace be with you, my friend. Come on, we'll be late!' He showed his teeth to the other men. 'We're invited to eat with my mother!'

The knife-man scoffed. 'You haven't got a mother!'

Didi roared with laughter. 'It's true: I'm a wonder of nature!' Somehow, he had managed to manoeuvre Hamou onto his other side, away from the two men. 'Come and join us, lads – there will be lemon cake and almond pastries.'

'Don't bother with them,' the taller man growled to the knife-bearer. 'A beggar and a chkam. They're nothing. Come on.'

And they walked on, the knife-man throwing a filthy look back over his shoulder as they passed.

'Thank you, Didi.'

'Are you mad, coming in here after dark? What did you think you were doing?'

'I was looking for a friend,' Hamou said, giving Didi the half-truth.

'I know exactly what you were doing. I followed you. Indeed, I followed both of you, so I know who you're following. I just don't know why.'

'To be honest,' said Hamou, 'neither do I.' He shot the beggar a look. 'I'm worried about her, Didi.'

'That one can take care of herself, I'd say. I'm sure she doesn't need you to keep an eye on her. Especially not here.'

Hamou said nothing, could think of nothing to say.

'Come away,' Didi said. 'You can give me a smoke or two to thank me for rescuing you.'

Hamou laughed. 'I'd have been fine.'

'I don't think so.'

In the darkness, the beggar's face was visible only by the sheen of his eyes. 'You know, Hamou, you stand with a foot in two worlds that are moving further apart by the day. Sooner or later, you'll have to come down on one side or the other or you'll find yourself falling between them.'

'That's a bit deep, Didi.' Hamou remembered Moha's friend Ahmed the nationalist saying something very similar to him in Nabil's café. Did he really stand on the opposite side to Zina? He was supposed to maintain law and order, but she was carrying a gun that was surely on its way into terrorist hands. He took out his packet of Anfas and pressed it into the beggar's hand. 'I'll see you in a little while,' he promised.

Didi shook his head sadly. 'She won't thank you for whatever it is you think you're doing.'

'When did you get so wise about women?'

The beggar grinned, his teeth shockingly white in the darkness. 'Hamou, it's not that I got wise, it's that you got stupid.' And with that he was gone into the night.

Hamou walked quickly around the corner and down the alley that Zina had taken, but she had disappeared into the heart of the bidonville. After a number of dead ends and false trails, he had no choice but to retrace his steps. He scanned the streets outside the slum, but there was no sign of Didi either. He tapped his pocket, then sighed, remembering he had given the last of his cigarettes to the beggar. Damn. There would be a shop open on the way back towards his apartment. He could go that way, buy another packet and wait to intercept Zina there. But no, he couldn't, not under the streetlamps where they would be too visible: scandalously, a man and a single woman together after dark.

He would wait here for a little while, he decided, and if she didn't reappear, he would go home. It was entirely possible that he had imagined the shape of the firearm within the bits of melon skin – who in their right mind would conceal a gun in such a bizarre manner?

But no matter how he might try to rationalise his suspicions away, always his mind came circling back to how the melon had not been taken off the top of the seller's display, but carefully selected from beneath the cart; and how the little crescent had been incised into the peel – a symbol deliberately cut by human hands.

The Black Crescent.

First, there had been the Istiqlal. Earnest, intellectual, political in their opposition to the French regime, steadfast in their support for the sultan. He had been to meetings. The meetings had been rather dull, peppered with austere directives about self-improvement and the good of the many, about education and enfranchisement. Of course, these were all good and necessary things. But the progress made towards even these abstract goals seemed so slow as to be non-existent; let alone the matter of getting the French to return their sultan from exile and negotiate for power-sharing and eventual independence. It had not surprised Hamou when dissident splinter groups had formed, impatient with the mouse strikes and passive opposition, the diplomacy and determined reasonableness of the Istiqlal. Indeed, he admitted to a reluctant admiration for some of these operatives, who risked their lives to oppose the regime: their actions were direct and sometimes heroic. But when it came to violent political assassinations, he shied away. Such bloodshed did not sit well with him, especially when innocents were caught up in these actions. The bombing of the Central Market on Christmas Eve in 1953 had really shocked him. Nineteen people dead, and hardly any of them directly involved with the regime. Were such means justifiable in obtaining Morocco's freedom? Could you rebuild a country on such bloody foundations?

He looked up into the starry heavens, as if the answer might be written there, but if they were it was in no language he could decode. The yearning for a cigarette came up on him again and he recognised it for what it was: the need for comfort, a way to make his tense muscles relax and his troubling thoughts slide away into familiar rituals.

Oh well, he would buy another packet soon enough.

He listened to the sounds of the night – the chirr of insects, a lone bird singing, distant music – women's voices raised high in a traditional song from the mountains – it sounded tinny and attenuated: a radio, rather than live musicians? He bent his attention on trying to make out the melody, when there was a sudden scuffle, followed by a shriek so close by it made his ears hurt. Hamou, all senses on overdrive, ran towards the sound, only to have a pair of feral cats shoot past him, hissing and spitting.

He turned to watch them skid into the next alley, and when he looked back it was to see Zina Chadli appearing at the corner of the shuttered shops. They stared at one another and when she opened her mouth to scream he launched himself at her – for both their sakes, he told himself in that shocking moment of illicit contact, feeling her hot breath on his palm, her full lips crushed against his fingers, her body pressed against his own.

'Please, please,' he kept saying as she squirmed in his hold. 'Please don't make a noise.' Her strength and her panic was disturbing: it was like wrestling a giant serpent.

Then she twisted free of him and was opening her mouth – but not to scream—

'No!' he cried.

How did he know what she intended? When he looked back on that moment, he still had no conscious idea. It was an instant of pure instinct, pure horror, but somehow, he was sure. He caught hold of the hand she raised to her mouth, twisted her wrist till she mewed, forced her fingers apart until he heard something drop to the ground.

'No!' Zina fell to her knees, scrabbling for the lost item, but it was Hamou who found it first.

He pocketed the item that confirmed all his worst fears. Zina stayed where she was, kneeling on the hard-packed earth, breathing heavily. Then she pushed herself to her feet and stood facing Hamou.

'Was it the melon shell? What an idiot I was to leave it up there.'

'Yes,' Hamou said, 'and the fact that you've come back without the basket. I saw you buy that melon, you know, in the big souk at the Place du Marché.'

He felt her expression shift as if the air between them had changed shape.

'How long have you been following me? They said you were a spy, but I didn't believe them. More fool me.'

Hamou was insulted. 'Who said that?'

'You think I will give you names? Why do you think I tried to take the cyanide?'

So, it was just what he had thought. Hamou felt the cold

settling in his stomach, seeping through his limbs, weighing down his soul. 'But to kill yourself, Zina. That's a terrible thing. Why would you try to do that?'

She stared away from him into the night. 'You wouldn't understand.'

Hamou felt wounded. 'I love my country. My people.'

'You? You take French coin. You wear their uniform.'

'I uphold the law. I don't kill people.'

'You will.'

He didn't know what to say to that. Would he kill on behalf of the French? The idea seemed ludicrous, but here he was, qualified to use a firearm in their service. He frowned deeply, feeling a quicksand of uncertainty surround him.

It was Zina who broke the silence. 'So, what are you going to do about me?' she asked defiantly.

That really was the question. He had not thought things all the way through. Was he Hamou Badi, officer in the Sûreté, or Hamou Badi, whose cousin Moha's gunshot wound Zina had attended to and never said a word about?

She held out her hands to him, goading. 'Go on. Take me in. You can do what you want with me, you and your French masters. I will never give up our people. They are fighting to free us from our oppressors, to restore our sultan and our pride, everything that makes us Moroccans.'

So passionate, so proud, so imperious. Hamou felt dwarfed by her courage. She was like Tin Hinan, who walked out into the Sahara during the time of the Romans to found a new tribe of people; like the warrior Queen Kahina, who led the Amazigh against the invading Arabs.

He stepped back, put his hands up as if in surrender. 'I am truly sorry that I followed you, that I frightened you so much that you tried to kill yourself. I couldn't forgive myself if you had.'

'You? *You* didn't frighten me.' She was scornful. 'Give me back my cyanide pill.'

Hamou was shocked. 'What? No.'

'If you're not going to arrest me, I'm not going to take it. But you think I was going to kill myself out of fear?' She laughed bitterly. 'We are given the pill to protect the others in our circle. It's what I've sworn to do: to God and the sultan and our country.'

To expect someone to kill themselves like this seemed very wrong to Hamou. In Islam, suicide was forbidden. 'Zina, I can't give it back to you. I just can't.'

'Then you place us all in danger and make yourself our enemy.'

And she pushed past him and walked swiftly away, leaving Hamou stranded. He wanted to run after her, to do... what? To apologise? To return the capsule to her? He didn't know. Indecision rooted him to the earth, not just between two political worlds but between his own fears and desires.

Fear, that he had made himself an enemy of the Black Crescent.

Desire: the thing that had made him tremble was that all he had really wanted to do was not to arrest, but to kiss Zina Chadli.

14

Hamou was still on duty. It was Eid and he had had to work all night, and still had to process this pickpocket, who was pretending to know no Arabic, no Tamazight, nor even any French. He should have been at mosque with his cousins, wearing his best clothes, making his ablutions, observing the time-honoured rituals to mark the end of Ramadan, before going home with them to eat. Instead, he was in a stuffy office at the commissariat, faced by a pile of uncompleted forms and the recalcitrant young man sitting opposite him, still in handcuffs, staring at the ceiling and refusing to speak.

'Look,' Hamou said reasonably in French, trying to hide his impatience. 'This attitude won't get you anywhere. If you cooperate, we can both get out of here more quickly. I'm sure you have better things to do.'

The young man closed his eyes as if feigning sleep. Another officer might have given him a slap at this point, but it wasn't really Hamou's style. 'You know that to be out without your ID is an offence in itself?' He and Jules had searched the suspect and found nothing on him except a packet of black tobacco, some rolling papers and the money he had stolen from the old lady on her way to the covered market. No identification at all, no house keys even. He wore a cheap watch, European slacks, and a worn linen shirt with sweat patches under the armpits.

'It's Eid, you know,' he said at last. 'I should be with my family.

How would you like it if I pointlessly delayed you on Christmas Day?'

The young man opened his eyes and smiled meanly. Hamou took the pouch of tobacco, and began to slowly pour the contents into his wastepaper bin.

'Hey! That's mine. You can't do that!' In French, with a strong Spanish accent.

Hamou stopped pouring and regarded the prisoner steadily. 'Come on, man: name, address, fingerprints. We have three witnesses to the theft' – statements that he still had to complete before he could sign off – 'and if we don't get the paperwork done, you're going in one of the cells *down there.*' He pointed downwards.

The pickpocket lifted a shoulder in a half shrug. 'I've got nowhere else to be.'

Hamou sighed. Now he would have to go and ask the custody officer to book the creep in and Martin had already made it clear this morning that they were understaffed because of Eid, and not to lock up anyone unless it was a matter of dire necessity. Another man would probably just have taken the money off the thief and turned him loose. But Hamou was not that man. Justice needed to be done and be seen to be done. And the bundle of notes needed to be returned to the old woman, who had wept when he'd explained that even though he'd detained the pickpocket he had to log the money in as evidence. 'You're just like the rest of them, even though you're one of us!' she had wailed. 'You pretend to help, but all you do is rob us in a uniform.'

It distressed Hamou to think this was what people thought about the police. He ground the heels of his hands into his gritty eyes and tried again. 'Right then, *señor*, I'm just going to fill these forms in with "unknown" and leave the custody officer to beat the details out of you.'

The man's dark eyes flickered over him. Did he detect a sign of agitation?

'You could just disappear down there – no name, no address, no record of ever having been here... No one would ever know.'

The thief clasped his hands together. Hamou saw his knuckles whiten.

'Anyway,' he pressed on, making as if to pack his things away, 'I'm off duty now, so I'll pass you on to Bilal. They call him Bilal the Butcher, you know. Can't imagine why.' He got to his feet and made for the door.

'All right.' The man swore in Spanish. *Madre de dios* was the least of it.

Hamou, still facing the door, grinned.

'My name is Raul Alonso.' He gave his address – out near the Roches Noires, a poor industrial area.

Hamou turned around and sat back down again. They filled out the forms and he took the thief's confession – yes, he had taken the old woman's money, but it was because his elderly mother needed medication that he couldn't afford.

'What exactly is wrong with her?' Hamou asked, his pen poised over the form, waiting.

Raul glared at him, then gave an exaggerated sigh. 'How the fuck would I know? She died three years ago. Look, I took the money because I wanted the money. I work all hours God sends but they don't pay me enough, the bastard French, and what the hell was that old woman doing with all that cash anyway?'

Hamou stared at him. 'What, you think all old Moroccan women should be poor?'

Raul shrugged. 'Look, don't blame me for it. You've been colonised: it's the way of the world. Your people know how to be poor in this shitty country. My people don't.'

Hamou thought about this later as he finally made his way to his uncle's apartment, having managed by dint of much persuasion to pass the thief into Martin's custody with the agreement that since he had confessed, he was not to be badly treated, though after his parting shot, it was sorely tempting to have him sent downstairs.

His people did indeed know how to be poor. They excelled in it: they had to. They eked out every coin they earned; they bolstered their meagre meals with cheap pulses and grains to make them last longer and to bulk them out so they filled the stomach; they threw nothing away, ate every scrap down to the gristle and the feet – nose to tail, brains to bollocks – and that was when they could afford meat at all. They repaired and reused everything: nothing was ever thrown away. They patched their clothes, added new collars and cuffs to old shirts, redyed robes gone shabby with age, resoled shoes time and time again. They shared with their neighbours and pooled their resources. They looked after other families' children and old folk to enable each other to work and earn. This was what it meant to have community; it was also what it meant to be oppressed in your own country. When tangible things were so sparse, you had at least to leave people their pride and their dreams, their religion, and their sultan.

The streets were beginning to fill up again, families strolling in the sunshine, children running around in new finery. Hamou had not himself had time to return home for a change of clothes, and in cognisance that the sight of an officer of the Sûreté entering his uncle's building was unlikely to go down well these days, he had taken off his cap and jacket. He had missed lunch, but he knew Aunt Jamila would produce enough food to feed the entire apartment block, so there were bound to be plenty of leftovers, and his mouth filled with saliva at the thought. Would there be *bstilla*? he wondered. It was his favourite, the rich pigeon-meat, delicate spices, golden onion, crisp layers of thin pastry, the topping of powdered sugar and cinnamon: a delicious balance of sweet and savoury that Jamila was so expert at producing.

Even before he reached his uncle's flat, he could hear the noise emanating from within. Were there more voices than usual? Hamou paused, listening. He could make out the bass note of his uncle's laugh and the light chatter of women, and he grinned. Full house, then. He knocked – unheard – then opened the door and let himself in, announcing himself loudly as he did so.

There was a break in the noise, then Aunt Jamila and his cousin Ali's wife, Khadija, rushed out in a cloud of perfume and a clatter of bangles and grabbed him, and a gaggle of children suddenly flowed around his legs. He had to hop to divest himself of his shoes as they all pulled him towards the salon.

'Come quickly, come on! Moha's fiancée's family is here. I think you know them...'

Moha's fiancée? This was the first Hamou had heard of such a thing. Moha had always professed himself far too busy to settle down, get married and have children as his brothers had. He had a business empire to run. He was a young man going places.

Hamou looked eagerly into the salon and, despite the intense warmth of the apartment, superheated by hours of cooking and packed, happy humans, felt his whole body turn to ice.

There, facing him, was Samira Chadli and her husband, Rachid, his downstairs neighbours. Next to them was Moha in a robe so white that it looked as if it might have been assembled by sewing together pristine snowflakes gathered from the tops of the mountains. With growing dread, Hamou's gaze slid to the banquette opposite, and there was Zina, perfect in turquoise, sitting between his cousin Tahar's wife, Naima, and another young woman he had not seen before.

He felt his throat constrict. How could this have occurred, and without him knowing a thing about it? Zina Chadli, engaged to his cousin Moha. Zina, with whom, he now painfully admitted to himself, he had fallen in love. And she was staring at him frankly, defiantly, as if challenging him to say anything about their recent night-time encounter. Her eyes burned brilliantly into his and he swallowed desperately and tried – and failed – to smile. His face was a mask, each muscle unresponsive.

His aunt's voice burbled on – '...your neighbours and their daughter Zina, whom of course you know...' – and Hamou

thought, *Yes, Zina, to whom I brought Moha when he got shot.*
Had that been the starting point for this unwelcome alliance?
he wondered. Had it been his own fault, this cruel twist of fate?
Had he brought them together, and in the process heightened the
danger to his uncle's family? Or did they know about her Black
Crescent affiliations and activities? Were they all involved? Was
he the only one here who wasn't?

Lack of food, a double shift and this sudden shock overcame
him. He muttered something about having an extremely
important task to complete that had somehow slipped his mind,
turned, and fled, retrieving his shoes as he went.

Outside on the street, he walked as if in a daze, barely seeing
the people he grazed against or even once properly bumped into,
without apology, stumbling on like some shameful drunk.

In the gardens of the Lyautey Park he subsided onto a bench
and put his head in his hands, appalled at his own behaviour.
What business was it of his if his cousin Moha married Zina
Chadli? Could he not at least have tried to camouflage his hurt
and shock at the news, to have pushed down his own feelings
for the sake of his family, and Zina's, and for the happy couple
themselves? He should have done so, he knew: put a brave face
on and congratulated them all and eaten and drunk and laughed
as part of the whole joyous group. Maybe by the end of the day
he would have felt better about it and managed to rein in his
own unrequited feelings. But now he had acted like a lunatic –
blundering in, then blundering out, mumbling gibberish. He had
embarrassed everyone, including himself.

And now he had no refuge. His home was the Chadlis' home.
He thought of their shoes lined up outside their door; their low
chatter a quiet, intermittent wave of sound through the floor of
his own apartment; the washing lines full of their laundry on the
terrace where he smoked. Where he had found the remnants of
the melon...

What was he going to do? Even when it had seemed that only
Zina was involved in terrorist activities, he had decided to turn

a blind eye, despite all his training and his personal concerns. But now, to say anything about the gun might bring his entire Casa family down. How could he continue in the police, given this dilemma? All his years of study, of striving to forge a career, to do good, to uphold the law, gone to nothing – to ash, to shit, to discarded pieces of melon peel with flies buzzing over them.

He turned his hands palm up and gazed bitterly at the incised zouhry lines that ran horizontally across them. Child of the djinns, indeed. He was a creature between worlds, who didn't fit in anywhere at all.

15

A Letter from Tiziane

Azul! Greetings, my son, may Allah's blessings be upon you and I hope that you have passed a good Eid with the family.

So much news! The fkih, Sidi Daoud, has remarried, to my second cousin Fatima, who lost her husband so tragically two years ago when imprisoned by those godforsaken… I will not speak the word here, for I do not want to bring down trouble. Such a prestigious match. It is always good to bring wisdom and status into the family, and even though he is quite an old man now, I am sure he will give her sons. Meanwhile, the baker's wife has had twin boys – you could hear the ululations of joy across the valley. She and Larbi are very proud and have been showing them off all over town. I must say it made me remember when you were born, my dear, and what a bold, black gaze you had, the bright regard of the zouhry. Everyone agreed you were by far the most handsome baby to be born in the village that year. Although of course this was only whispered and accompanied by many signs and imprecations against the evil eye – I did not want to alert the djinns, for fear they would snatch you back.

How well I recall knitting the mitts that I placed over

your little hands to hide the lines on your palms, because you know how people talk. We could do with your powers back here in Tiziane now, my son, for it is truly the driest summer I can remember, and water-divining would be a great boon to us all. The commandant and other officials are well provided for as water has been piped right to their door from the pool where you and your friends used to swim and there are no limits on how much they can use. Do you remember when we wanted to stop you all going there because we feared you might drown, and persuaded the muezzin to call out on his loudspeaker that a monster had been spotted in the pool and that the children should avoid the area for fear of being eaten? But it did not deter you: you led a band of your friends there and sent Anir in to investigate because you said he was the best swimmer? And poor Anir was petrified but did it anyway? Of course, there was no monster and Anir's mother came and banged on my door to complain that you had endangered her son's life. In the end, we laughed at your cunning, my son: you have the cleverness of djinns.

I also heard that the commandant's wife has an extra-ordinary new contraption which will do all the laundry at the press of a button! Her maid says they call it a washing machine. You just pile all your dirty clothes into it with some Omo powder, press a button, and *alakazam!* an hour later it all comes out as clean as when it was new! I don't entirely believe her. Anyway, we must make do with the old ways for now – they were good enough for my mother and my grandmother.

The best news, though, my son, is that I have found you two prospective brides. Both families are of good reputation and the girls are the eldest of their siblings, so whichever we choose can conveniently move from their family home into ours, where I can keep an eye on her while you are working away from home and in turn she can help with our household chores, for my hands plague me more with each passing month, and before too long your sisters will be of an age when they will take husbands and move away, leaving your poor old mother alone.

Hurry home, Hamou, my son, so that you can choose your bride, and make me proud. Your loving mother.

16

A few days after Eid, Hamou arrived at work to find the commissariat in uproar. A prominent French businessman, a close friend of the Resident General, had been shot and killed the night before. No one had witnessed the deed, but he had, according to the gossip buzzing around the corridors, been shot squarely between the eyes. A single shot, by someone with a steady hand using a small calibre handgun. Which meant that either he had known his attacker well enough to let him get close, or they were a stranger he had not seen as a threat.

Squads of police had been sent out into the Moroccan neighbourhoods and shantytowns – to intimidate, to harass, to flush out suspects. Hamou counted himself lucky that he was on a later shift and had not been roped in. This morning when he'd come into the commissariat, Saleh had told him with considerable relish that he'd heard rumours that a number of suspects had been taken into custody and had been taken to the interrogation cells.

Hamou's thoughts raced. Could the murder weapon have been the gun Zina had carried into the bidonville? Would she be implicated in the assassination? Perhaps interrogated in the cells downstairs? But eventually he chided himself for his irrationality. Neither he nor Zina Chadli were the centre of the universe. Then again, he knew how hard guns were to come by and what enormous risks people took to acquire or smuggle them in. He had heard all manner of bizarre stories: women hiding pistols in their babies' swaddling clothes, or tied to their inner thighs beneath demure, capacious robes. Guns broken down and concealed in the frames of prams, bicycles, mopeds, hidden inside bags of couscous and rice. Or inside a melon. Often, the ammunition arrived separately. And then a target would be selected, and the deed carried out. And only a tiny number of people would know anything about it, for the organisation of the resistance would have broken apart and dispersed.

Over the past couple of years, this had been the difficulty facing the authorities. Even the Istiqlal – the official opposition – was not monolithic. Parts of it had splintered off and acted independently of the leadership who spoke and negotiated like practised politicians, pressing their demands politely, reasonably, with a smile and a handshake. Some of the splinter groups – like the Sword of God, the Secret Organisation for the Victory of Mohamed V, the Black Hand, and now the Black Crescent – had shed their affiliations with the Istiqlal, like snakes shedding their skins, becoming covert, clandestine, autonomous, broken into tiny cells of activists who had little or no connection to one another. Under questioning, deep in the commissariat dungeons, it had become increasingly clear that even if you caught a member of one of these cells it would probably take you nowhere except into a dark cul-de-sac and an early grave.

So, he wondered: was Zina Chadli a member of such a cell? Was his cousin Moha? Clearly, Zina had acted as a mule, but how much did she know about the person or group to whom she had passed the weapon? How far did her involvement reach? And now he found he had to consider his cousin too. The whole family import business, for example... His visit to the Carrières centrales had already made him question the nature of that business. He thought again about poor dead Brahim, murdered during a political protest, followed by Moha being shot as he walked with the mourners. What a wretched mess it all was.

'Hey, Badi!' The crisp tones of Emile Fouquet broke into his miserable cogitations and his head snapped up.

'Sir?' He stood to attention, but the older man slapped him on the back.

'Lost in thought?'

Hamou managed a weak smile. He hadn't slept for three nights, had hardly eaten anything either, and felt like shit. But Fouquet had always been pleasant to him – not often the case for French officers, who used the informal 'tu' form whenever they addressed Moroccans rather than the more respectful 'vous'. Just as Fouquet's manners were impeccable, so was his uniform pristine, with knife-edge creases ironed into the trouser legs, and his shoes were polished to such a sheen as to repel every speck of dust. Even though he smoked incessantly, there was no trace of nicotine on his fingers: he used a silver holder for his 'tabac jaune' cigarettes, smoking them with his little finger cocked. When he removed his cap, every hair remained brilliantined in place, no matter the humidity of the day, and the scent of his aftershave, woody and expensive, lingered pleasantly in the air even when he had left the room. When he had been at the training college, Fouquet had been a guest lecturer and had taken something of a shine to Hamou, who had scored highly in his tests. Now he was his commandant, and his preference had probably been why Hamou had been assigned to weapons training.

'There's something I'd like you to do for me.'

'Of course, sir.'

'I left an important file on my desk at home last night. Be a good lad and fetch it for me, would you? I'd go myself, but I'm in the middle of something. Tell Edouard you need to borrow a mobilette and don't take any nonsense from him.'

'Yes, sir!' Hamou brightened. It was a lovely day and the chance to get outside and whizz through the traffic on a police scooter was attractive.

Fouquet turned to go and Hamou said in some alarm, 'Your address, sir?'

The commandant twinkled at him. 'Of course, you've not been to the villa, have you? We must remedy that one evening.' He took a small leatherbound notebook and a handsome gold fountain pen out of his inner jacket pocket and jotted a few lines, then carefully tore the page out and wafted it to dry the ink. Handing it to Hamou, he said, 'Ask the housekeeper to fetch it for you. It's in a blue folder in my study.'

Hamou took hold of the piece of notepaper, but Fouquet did not immediately let go. 'And, Officer Badi, do not delve into the file. It's strictly confidential, a matter of the utmost national security. Bring it to me, and only me. I'm entrusting you with this delicate task because I know what a trustworthy chap you are.' His eyes bored into Hamou's soul, which fled from such scrutiny. Then he released the page, and smiled. 'Slowly but surely, you are working your way up the ladder here. Don't jeopardise your progress by any foolish missteps, will you, Officer Badi?'

Hamou scanned the inked words, then folded the paper, stowed it in his pocket and snapped a salute. Did he know where the Rue Maupassant was? He thought he had a good idea where it was. 'Of course not, sir. I'll be right back.'

He checked the address on the map of the city in reception. As he had guessed, the address the commandant had given him was in one of the most exclusive European enclaves, towards the coast and the huge outdoor swimming pool near the corniche. As he collected a mobilette from the grumpy Edouard, under strict instructions to return it undamaged within the hour, Hamou felt his spirits lift. The sun was shining, the birds were singing and the prospect of seeing how the other half lived, even for a few brief minutes, was an enticing distraction from his inner weather.

He launched the scooter out into the Boulevard Maréchal and headed north and west, noticing how drivers gave him unwonted space and respect because of his uniform and the police markings on the vehicle. For someone who usually travelled on foot or on crowded buses that crawled through the traffic, it was exhilarating to cruise along like this. On a scooter, he could slip between other vehicles, zoom past bulkier traffic. Hamou tried a few overtaking manoeuvres and, cheered by his success as he passed a donkey cart and then an old Mercedes belching diesel fumes into the city's air, pulled out to pass a bus. A truck coming the other way blared its horn and missed him by inches.

Hamou swore quietly. He wondered about saving up for a scooter of his own. He sent nearly all his money, after rent and living expenses, home to his mother in Tiziane, but there was never enough. Perhaps after his next promotion... The idea of being able to nip around the city like this rather than trudging along hot, dusty pavements was enticing. He'd get more time in bed in the mornings, an extra cigarette or coffee before he set off for work; it would be so much easier to get to the cinemas in the Habous, or up to the coast. Maybe, in the interim, he could invest in a bicycle. He could keep it downstairs in the shared vestibule. One of his younger cousins was good at fixing up old bikes. He could learn for himself. But a bicycle was not a mobilette...

Lost in his reverie, Hamou cut across the path of a petit taxi, unaware until the driver leaned out of the window and yelled at him. Hamou jolted the scooter back into his lane, chastened. Dark thoughts came crowding back. Zina was going to be married to Moha. And he would have to go to the wedding, sing and clap and celebrate. He hoped it wouldn't take place for a long time. In truth, he hoped it might not take place at all. Now he understood why Zina had been so cool with him, so distanced and polite. How long had they been promised, and why had Moha never mentioned it?

These thoughts had been roiling through his mind ever since Eid. Whenever he thought about how he had made his ignominious exit from his uncle's apartment that afternoon he went hot and cold with shame. He wondered what they'd said about him when he was gone. *Don't mind Hamou, he's an odd one, like his father.* He thought Rachid Chadli might speak up for him, saying that his heart was in the right place, that he worked very hard, was under a lot of pressure. And his wife,

Samira, had a bit of a soft spot for him, he was sure: all the meals placed outside his door, all the welcoming words. In fact, up till last week he'd been convinced that Samira Chadli had designs on him as a son-in-law. What a fool he was. Perhaps he should have seized the moment and spoken to them about Zina himself, without waiting for a traditional intermediary? But he had always had his mother's voice in his head, her warnings about 'Arab' women. Well, it was too late now.

Again and again, he had circled back to his encounter with Zina at the bidonville, when he had held her, briefly, in his arms, trying to separate the incident from its circumstances, to add a romantic gloss to it, to make fantasy out of reality, but always it was spoiled by the clearer memory of her fierce struggle and the threat of the cyanide capsule and all that stood for. And once more he thought about the assassination and hoped the suspects who had been taken in had nothing to do with Zina.

Then he remembered again his urge to kiss her, his thoughts like moths to a lantern, and when he dragged his mind away it insisted on replacing the image with Moha kissing her instead and he almost ran into the back of a van that had stopped at the junction with the Boulevard d'Anfa. The idea of his younger cousin kissing Zina gave him a distinct physical pain in his chest. He wouldn't bet against it. Zina was aloof and demure with him, but Moha was an accomplished flirt, free with the sort of extravagant compliments women seemed to love. He had an easiness and confidence to him that Hamou could not emulate. He had become – he had to admit – too serious, too dour. Whatever happy-go-lucky joyfulness he'd had during his adolescence in Tiziane had long since evaporated. Perhaps it was just growing up, learning that the adult world was harsher than he'd imagined, full of responsibilities, moral dilemmas, pain and difficulty. Living alone, too, had turned him inward. He had few friends or allies here – just a one-handed beggar and the cousins he had now alienated. Working the hours he worked did not allow much time for socialising, and coming into daily contact with criminals and the poor and desperate had probably changed his demeanour, though it didn't appear to have had the same effect on his colleagues Yaya and Alphonse, Saleh and Driss, who were all around the same age as him, and also from poor Moroccan homes, who laughed and joked and took nothing seriously, least of all themselves. Truth be told, he felt uprooted, out of place in this huge, modern, European city, in which Moroccans were increasingly being shuffled off to the scruffy outskirts. The shining white buildings, wide boulevards, neat parks and smart villas were not for the likes of him. He was just part of the machinery that made the city function.

A big junction loomed ahead, and he was forced to pay greater attention. He was beyond the known extent of his world now, encroaching into the smart new residential area where only the richest Europeans could afford to live. He got turned around in the tangle of little roads north of the Boulevard de Bordeaux, crossing and recrossing the Rue de l'hôpital, but eventually stumbled upon the Rue Maupassant.

Hamou passed the address twice without seeing the number, for the plaque was obscured by tendrils of hibiscus tumbling over the high fence that concealed the house. Who needed numbers when everyone who needed to know who lived here knew, and privacy was paramount? He could hear voices over the fence, though. Female voices. He propped the scooter on its stand and opened the gate. Superintendent Fouquet's villa was the sort of place Hamou had seen only in the movies, or in a dream. Framed by palms and an orchard of citrus trees, it was a long slab of white concrete with steps leading to a huge double door in the centre, its form brutal, all straight lines and clean angles, its upper floor cantilevered out over the first. In a city of modern white European architecture, it was the most extreme example Hamou had seen, and he felt as if he had somehow stepped into a future which was neither his own nor Morocco's. It alarmed him, made him feel like a stranger in his own land.

This sensation was hardly allayed by the source of the female voices: to the right side of the villa lay a gleaming white area of marble in which sat a long, turquoise swimming pool, and beside that, two young women laughed and chattered. One of them saw him heading towards the villa and pushed herself to her feet. Walking fast, her wet feet slapping the hot stone, she made to intercept him, followed by her companion. Hamou could not help but stare, before dragging his gaze away and down. She was wearing hardly anything at all: just three triangles of damp cloth.

'Hello. Who are you and what do you want?' She stood before him with her hands on her hips. Her toenails were painted scarlet and her legs were thin and almost as brown as his own.

He tried not to look up. 'I'm an officer from the Sûreté, sent by Superintendent Fouquet for a file he left behind.'

'What's your name?'

Ton nom, not *votre nom*, even though she was barely more than a child. Hamou tried not to feel riled by this. He told her his name. She laughed. 'Ha-*mooooo!*' She turned to the other – not woman, as he had previously thought, but a girl, barely in her teens. 'He's called Ha-moooo.'

They both giggled. Neither of them offered their own names. The first girl took him boldly by the hand. Her own was clammy, from the pool, he thought, since the rest of her was wet, and with her other hand flung back her hair, which was waist-length and tangled. 'Well, Hamooo Badi, I think you should come and have a swim with us, don't you agree, Chloë?'

The other girl – a smaller version of the first, maybe twelve or thirteen – grabbed his other hand and together they began to tow him towards the pool area. Hamou started to panic. He had no training in how to deal with the precocious daughters of commanding officers when on an urgent errand; and when a small, pug-nosed dog came galloping out of the rosebushes to worry at his uniform trousers, he found that he had lost every single word of his painfully acquired French vocabulary and started crying out '*Sir bhalek, sir bhalek*' – get off, get off! in *darija,* to the vast amusement of the girls, who egged the animal on with shrieks of laughter.

He was beginning to think that between these three demons he was going to end up submerged and humiliated in the swimming pool when a shout pierced the noisy air, and the girls both instantly let go of Hamou, and the older one grabbed up the snarling, twisty little dog. The woman stepped towards him, shooing the girls away. 'And put some clothes on!'

Hamou took off his cap and ran a hand through his hair. He was trembling. He tried to hide that. 'Bonjour, madame!'

She looked Hamou up and down. 'How can I help you, officer?'

He explained the reason for his visit and watched her expression settle into some sort of professional understanding. She appeared to him to be a good deal older than the two girls she had sent packing; too old, he thought uncharitably, to be their mother, too severe and plain, surely, to be the superintendent's wife. He found it difficult to gauge the age of French women, though. Their clever use of cosmetics, their film-star smiles and fashionable clothing were in themselves a sort of uniform that disguised and confused.

'Follow me.'

She led him back onto the safety of the path, then up the steps to the immense door. This, she opened with a light touch, and when it closed equally lightly behind them, he realised that it must be fitted with some sort of hydraulic device.

'Wait here.'

She clicked away up the corridor, leaving him to take in the interior of the villa. Where it was baking hot outside, within the confines of the hallway it felt almost cold. As his eyes adjusted to the change in light levels, he noted that the floor was paved with black marble; everywhere the walls were unadorned white, unrelieved by any form of decoration – no paintings, photographs, stucco carvings; no niches, no wall lights, no vases of flowers or candle-lanterns. A wide staircase swept up to a galleried upper level. Through the balusters he could see that the first storey was also stark, although by some degrees brighter than the downstairs. It looked like an unoccupied, just-built house, rather than one inhabited by rich people, and it made no sense to him at all. If he were rich, he would fill his living space with colour and light; with fine cactus-silk hangings and rugs of Berber wool. He would commission the best *ma'alems* to tile the floors in geometric zellij and decorate the walls with stucco friezes and the ceilings with *muqarna* honeycombs; to carve the doors with interlaced stars and web designs. If you were rich, you would try to make yourself a palace, wouldn't you, rather than this sterile box?

He was beginning to feel a bit better about being poor when the stern woman returned with a blue folder in her hand, and then he felt even happier. He was about to accomplish his task, and would be back well within the hour, as instructed.

'It was the only folder on the master's desk,' she said, and something about her words and intonation struck him. She was Moroccan. Lighter-skinned than he was, but now that he studied the planes of her face and those dark eyes it was obvious, and he wondered why he had not seen it before. Moroccan, and a servant, but with the manner of a chatelaine. He took the folder and bowed his head, touched a hand to his heart. 'Shokran, lalla.'

For the first time, she smiled. 'Take good care of yourself, young man. We live in strange times.'

Stowing the folder inside his jacket, Hamou let himself out of the house and fairly ran down the path towards the gate.

'Salut, Hamooo!'

The girls appeared out of the citrus trees, grinning. At least they had some clothes on now, he thought, and there was no sign of the little devil-dog.

'Won't you come and swim with us, Hamoo? Please?'

'You're so handsome,' the younger girl cooed, gazing up at him beneath her long lashes in some horrible pretence of flirtation.

Hamou could feel himself getting flustered again. 'I'm sorry, I can't,' he said curtly. 'I have to get back to the commissariat.'

'You could spare us five minutes, surely?'

'I really can't, sorry.'

The older one pouted. 'I'll tell Papa you were rude to us.'

'Papa – Superintendent Fouquet – is waiting for me.'

She gave an exaggerated shrug. 'You're no fun at all, Hamou Badi.'

'Sorry.' He lunged for the handle of the gate and shot outside, desperate to escape. There was a sudden flurry of movement, then the clicking of claws on the pavement, and the dog ran past him and climbed onto the footplate of the police scooter, cocking its leg. Copious streams of piss suddenly cascaded over the clean metal.

'Nooo!'

Edouard would have a fit. The pissing went on and on. How was it possible for such a small creature to contain so much urine? He looked back at the girls pleadingly, but they just stood and watched, arms folded, sharing the exact same smile, as if they had somehow programmed the little beast.

Hamou moved forward as if to capture the dog, but it peeled its ragged black lips back to reveal sharp white teeth and snarled at him. When at last it finished its desecration of police property, it trotted back to be fussed by the giggling girls, who finally turned and left Hamou alone to stare woefully at the scooter. He took a handful of leaves from the roadside and did his best to clean the footstand. Then, gingerly, he got aboard and tried to start the machine, pulling down the start-lever and kicking the pedal.

Nothing. Not even a sputter.

Hamou stared at it in disbelief. This could not be happening. He took a deep breath and tried again. To no avail.

Something inside him shrivelled. Had the dog's urine had some malign effect? Had the machine run out of petrol? Was it simply broken? He cursed his ignorance of all things mechanical. Getting off, he examined the fuel tank, pushing the scooter from side to side. He thought he could hear fuel slopping inside, but he couldn't see anything. He broke off a twig of jacaranda, stripped it of its leaves, and thrust it down inside the fuel tank to gauge the level of petrol inside. The stick slipped from his fingers when he tried to remove it. So now he had a broken-down, piss-stained police-issue scooter with a jacaranda twig in its tank. Absurdly, he felt like crying. But that wouldn't get him anywhere. He pulled the lever, pushed the mobilette and jumped on, hoping that the illusion of motion would magically encourage the machine to remember how to do it for itself.

It didn't.

Hamou looked at his watch. Forty-five minutes had elapsed since he had joyfully left the commissariat, bound on his mission. There was no way in the world he would be back 'within the hour' as instructed. He would, he decided, abandon the scooter and take a petit taxi, no matter the cost. After all, no one was going to steal the thing from outside the superintendent's residence in this smart neighbourhood, even if it wasn't broken down.

He scanned the traffic on the Boulevard de Bordeaux for several minutes without once seeing a taxi, but then spotted a bus stop further down the street. A Moroccan couple with a pram and many heavy shopping bags stood waiting there, and now they were joined by a flock of noisy French schoolchildren. Hamou took his place behind the rowdy teenagers and willed a bus to appear. As if in answer to his prayer a municipal bus hove into view, drawing up at the stop with a hiss of brakes. At once, the French youngsters surged forward, overwhelming the Moroccan man and his wife. One of their bags fell over, spilling oranges, and the man ran to scoop them up before they were squashed in the traffic.

Hamou felt a sudden fury rise. 'Hey!' he cried. 'Let these people on first. Can't you see they've got a baby?'

'Just what we need,' said the boy at the back of the crowd now mounting the bus steps. 'More stinking Arabs.' And they all laughed.

Hamou felt his whole skin go cold. It was not 'just' the racism, or the rudeness, but also the total lack of respect for his uniform. He surged towards the boy, grabbing him by the collar. 'Get off!' he commanded. 'These people were here before you. Have you got no manners?'

The boy twisted away from him, shrieking, 'Get off me, you monkey!'

The husband pulled at Hamou's sleeve. 'We don't want any trouble, officer.'

Hamou glared at the driver. 'Aren't you going to do anything about this?'

The man turned his head, and Hamou saw that he was European. 'If you want a bus of your own,' he said contemptuously, 'why don't you ask your fucking sultan to buy you one?' And he drove off, leaving Hamou and the couple on the pavement.

Hamou turned to apologise to the man and his wife, but they avoided his eye, gathered their bags and started to push the pram down the road. Hamou stared after them, feeling his fury suddenly subside.

He looked down at his feet and saw a blue object had been left behind. Then he realised that it was the superintendent's folder. It must have fallen out of his jacket during the tussle with the French boy. It lay in the gutter now, dusted with grime. He grabbed it up in horror. Had it spilled any of its contents? He stared around, terrified that he might see pieces of white paper flapping beneath the wheels of the passing traffic, but no, retrieving it, he saw that the folder had been secured with an elastic band. His first piece of good luck. Alhamdulillah.

Looking up, he saw a petit taxi coming his way and waved it down.

Ten minutes later, he was back at the commissariat, only a little late. He dodged Edouard: he would explain the problem with the scooter later.

*

The superintendent was not in his office. Hamou laid the folder down on his desk, then hesitated. The angel on his shoulder warned him against opening the folder, reminding him of Fouquet's dire proscription. The bad angel whispered Zina's name. *If she's mentioned you could warn her, give her a chance to get out of the city.* The good angel won. Hamou turned on his heel. At the door, though, he turned back again. Hadn't Superintendent Fouquet said to put the folder 'in my hands'? If he left it lying around, even in the superintendent's own office, someone – anyone – might walk off with it. He crossed the room and picked it up again.

He met Sergeant Martin coming along the corridor and enquired where he might find the superintendent. The custody officer looked mildly surprised to be asked such a question but waved Hamou towards the staircase. 'Down there – Investigations.'

Something within Hamou quailed, but he gathered himself and set off down the steps to the lower floors, passing the custody cells and administration offices and heading further down than he had previously been called upon to venture. He passed the recruitment office and the room in which he had signed the firearms pledge, along dimly lit corridors lined by closed doors.

At one point he hit a dead end and had to double back and take a set of stairs he had missed. It was cold down here and felt unfrequented. Some bulbs in the light fittings were not working. At the foot of the next flight of stairs he missed his step in the semi-dark and almost knocked himself out on the facing wall as he turned a corner. The folder dropped from his hand as he reached out to save himself, and papers cascaded across the floor.

Hamou, leg- and wrist-bones jolted, swore furiously, got down on his hands and knees and scrabbled the pages together. He peered down the final flight of steps but could spy no escapees. For a while, he sat cross-legged, shuffling the pages back into some sort of order, trying hard not to read the typewritten words as he did so, his gaze skating across the densely packed information.

The word 'terrorist' appeared several times. Then Al-Hilal – the Black Crescent. His pulse began to thud in his ears. Shit. He looked up into the stairwell to make sure no one was coming down and scanned the next page. A lot of unfamiliar names. No Zina. No Chadli. No Derb Ghrallef.

His heart began to settle to a more normal rhythm. But on the next page a name leapt out at him. It was the street on which his uncle's business was situated. Moha and Brahim, the import business, including – under his cousin's aegis, drugs, and who knew what other illicit goods... Like guns...

Moha... and Zina. He had seen Zina in the market not far from Moha's apartment, taking the melon from the watermelon seller. And now the two of them were to be married...

He began to turn the pages over fast, searching for their names. Nothing on this page, or the next, nothing—

Footsteps echoed suddenly on the floor below, getting louder. In terror, he shuffled the papers together as neatly as he could, his hands feeling lumpen, and got them back into the folder. Of the elastic band that had held it shut, there was no trace. Oh God, Fouquet would know that he'd opened it. What could he say about that? That it hadn't been on the folder when he had been given it? He could hardly implicate the housekeeper... He tried and failed to invent a plausible scenario, his mind a great rushing blankness.

The officer who passed him a moment later regarded him curiously, but not too curiously.

Pull yourself together, Hamou told himself fiercely. He took a deep breath and walked smartly on down the corridor. Here, the air was chill yet fetid and there was a smell of drains, meaty but acrid. He shivered. From somewhere in the depths of the commissariat he heard a low moan, like a lowing cow.

There was an officer sitting at a desk as he moved towards the noise and Hamou saluted him and asked the whereabouts of the superintendent. The man got up from behind the desk and stared at Hamou, then at the blue folder. 'Oh yes, he's been waiting for that.' He held out a hand for it.

How tempting to just hand it over and flee. The man was French, a senior officer, and was waiting for the folder. But his orders had been clear, and he knew what he had to do. 'Superintendent Fouquet said to give the folder only to him,' Hamou said apologetically.

'Of course.' The officer gave him a strange little half smile. 'He's just down there. I'll unlock the gate for you. Shout when you need to be let out again.'

Hamou followed the man along the corridor to a sturdy steel gate and watched him unlock it with a key chained to his belt. Then the man stepped back, allowing Hamou to push the gate open and step beyond. Behind him, the door clanged as the officer locked it once more.

There were cells to either side of him now. Hollow-eyed men stared out at him. They all looked the same: heads shaved, dark cotton pants and shirts. *Doesn't show the blood*, said a voice in his head. Some nursed their hands in their laps. Hamou tried not to take in any details. He had some idea of what went on down here, but as soon as his mind ventured too close to the subject it shied away, an unwilling horse faced by a dangerous obstacle. He didn't look at their feet, either, but somehow details permeated his senses anyway: swollen, bruised flesh, contortions, crusted blood. Brown patches dirtied the concrete floor. Smears streaked the corridor, as if someone had been dragged.

Don't look. Don't look. His guts twisted. He could *not* be sick here.

A man stepped out into the corridor ahead of him, lit up a cigarette and inhaled deeply. The aroma drifted lazily to Hamou's nostrils. Tabac jaune. He fixed his gaze on the figure and saw how the silver cigarette holder caught the low light. He quickened his pace.

'Superintendent?'

The man turned. There was a dreamy expression on his face: calm, serene, almost blissful. Hamou knew the effect of a good cigarette, but he didn't think it was simply that.

'Sir.' He snapped a salute with one hand and held out the folder with the other.

Fouquet's gaze focused and steadied. 'Oh, Badi. Thank you.' He smiled. 'Come.' He gestured for Hamou to enter the little room before him.

Hamou's feet felt like lead. He did not want to go into that place. Something primal, intuitive, in him rebelled. 'I... I should get back to my d-duties,' he stuttered. 'I left the mobilette. It... it broke down... I should...'

A little crease appeared between the superintendent's eyebrows. He held up a hand. 'I have some papers I need you to take to Allizard,' he said, naming the man they called Tête Grise – head of the hit squads that went out into the neighbourhoods to pull in suspects.

Reluctantly, Hamou passed the superintendent, through a miasma of tabac jaune and sandalwood, into the small space beyond. His shoulders, which had been tense and rigid, dropped. It was only an office. There was nothing to see here.

Fouquet followed him in and picked up a few sheets of handwritten pages from a chair. 'Take these to Stéphane and tell him to get them typed up. Wait while he does, then take them straight to Allizard. Got that?'

Hamou nodded, took the papers and turned to leave. Superintendent Fouquet was gazing at the wall, his features smoothed once more. And then a guttural cry ripped through the air, so close that Hamou felt it as a physical sensation deep in his gut. The scream was followed by a gurgle, a moan, then silence.

Hamou wanted to run, but his exit was blocked by Fouquet. Of their own accord, his eyes followed the trajectory of the officer's gaze – at the wall, no, through it: a small glassless window... onto Hell.

In the room beyond, two men stood over the restrained body

of a third. Incongruously, they held tools – pliers, a hammer – like bad plumbers, the sort who beat badly fitting pipes into shape. The third man— no, he could not look at the third man.

Hamou wrenched his gaze away, stared at the floor instead. But that was no better. A glistening pool of something dark and viscous, wrinkling at the edges… Objects scattered, white against the grey of the concrete, jagged, weirdly shaped.

They were teeth. Teeth with roots.

Oh God… Hamou froze. He wanted to look away, but his body refused him. *Look*, it said. *No, look. There is no avoiding this.*

Unwillingly, his gaze travelled back to the unconscious figure. Even in the split-second in which he had initially glimpsed the face, he had known it was familiar, from the bushy beard to the jutting nose: Ahmed Choukri. Moha's friend, the radical one who had sat with them in Nabil's café; the one whose brother had been taken in by the police; the one who had assaulted him in the hammam before Ramadan.

One of the tool-bearers came to the window. His eyes skated over Hamou with what – complicity? contempt? – and settled on Superintendent Fouquet. 'Sorry, boss, we may have overdone it.'

Fouquet shrugged, insouciant. 'Can't be helped. Dispose of the body, Abid, and get the cell cleaned up. We got what we needed from him.'

The Moroccan turned back to his companion and said something in darija that Hamou could just make out: 'Take the fucker down to the incinerator. I'll get the cleaning gear.'

In a daze, Hamou left the antechamber and walked back to the gate, called hoarsely for it to be unlocked and made his way back up to the world of humans.

It was only after he got three flights up that he found a bathroom and was able to vomit compulsively until his chest muscles ached and his throat felt raw.

Ahmed Choukri. Tortured to death, his body about to be burned to ashes along with the rubbish. As if he had never existed. Had not walked and laughed and drunk coffee and raged about the protectorate in cafés with friends. And what about his family? Would they come asking his whereabouts? Would they be turned away with denials and deception, with blank stares? Or would they too be taken in for questioning?

Hamou's mind veered away. He picked up the forms he had been given. The shaking of his hands caused the papers to tremble, the words – even in Fouquet's small, precise handwriting – hard to decipher. At last, he made out a list of names and addresses. He read them avidly, then breathed out. No Moha. No Zina Chadli. No mention of anyone he knew. It was a relief. But still he felt sickened, horrified, wrung out.

It was a terrorist cell, he told himself. A small group of anarchists who had chosen the way of violence. They were at war with the French administration, and in war there were casualties...

But not like this. Not under torture in a basement cell, where information, teeth and nails and God knows what else were extracted. He leaned against the wall, trying to regulate his breathing, trying to think. He had known, deep down, that this was what went on here, hidden in the bowels of the chic modern building with the pots of jasmine at the entrance, amid the smart uniforms and the smothering layers of bureaucracy, all the rules and regulations and pretence at carrying on civilised governance, by the book, according to the training manual, and in the correct fashion. It was all a façade, a smokescreen. A smart suit on a rotting corpse.

And he – Hamou Badi – was paid to be a part of this pretence.

He wanted to get out into the air, to rip his uniform off, to walk away. Out of the commissariat, out of the quartier français; out of the city, into the countryside, the bled. All the way to the mountains of his home, where the air was sharp and clean and did not smell of blood and shit; or of tabac jaune and sandalwood.

But he did not. Like an automaton, he took the pages he had

been given to Stéphane, and stood there, sweating and nauseous, feeling the clatter of the typewriter keys in the bones of his face. Then he took the typed pages to Allizard, went to explain the circumstances of the missing scooter to Edouard, and finished his shift.

17

Hamou walked quickly to the Lyautey Park and lit up a cigarette to calm himself. But the smell of the tobacco reminded him of Superintendent Fouquet smoking nonchalantly outside the room in which Ahmed Choukri was being tortured to death. He remembered what the nationalist had said that day in the café: *You should stop smoking altogether. It's a political act.*

He dropped the cigarette, ground it underfoot and walked on, feeling sick. He knew what he had to do, and he didn't want to do it.

He strode towards the Rue Curie exit, looking back over his shoulder in case anyone was following him. He saw an elderly man stoop to retrieve his discarded cigarette. His robe, though clean, was ragged at the hem and cuffs. Something clutched in Hamou's chest. He turned and walked back towards him.

The man, looking up, saw the uniform, and quailed. 'I'm sorry, officer. You dropped it...' He held the barely smoked butt out to Hamou with shaking fingers.

Hamou placed a hand on the man's shoulder and felt him flinch beneath the contact. He also felt the man's bones, frail, close to the surface, not a scrap of spare flesh on him. 'Don't apologise, please. I dropped it on purpose.' He reached into his pocket, took out the packet of Anfas and the box of matches and held them out for the man to take. 'Here.'

The man looked at Hamou with a mixture of astonishment and suspicion.

'I don't smoke any more. You take them.'

The man squirrelled the Anfas and matches away in his robe in the blink of an eye, then took Hamou's hand and pressed his lips against it. 'God bless you, sidi. May he rain baraka down upon you.'

Hamou didn't feel there was much luck to be had in this city right now, but he wished the old man peace, and headed for the hinterland north of the Place de la Victoire.

His uncle's import business was situated on Rue Auvert. Normally, he would not dream of entering it in uniform, for tongues would wag, but right now he had no choice. Inside, he found Omar Belhaj and his cousin Hicham, packing oranges and lemons into crates. The air smelled clean and zesty and for a few seconds Hamou stood there, breathing it in. The two men looked up expectantly, then Omar stepped forward and gave him a bear hug, squashing Hamou against his ample belly. 'How are you, brother? What brings you here – are you on duty?'

Hamou gave him a tight smile. 'No, on my way home. I was looking for Moha.'

'He's out back,' Hicham said. 'I'll fetch him—'

'No, you carry on.' Hamou knew his way around the premises: he'd worked here alongside his uncle and cousins when he'd first come to Casablanca. Out the back there was a yard where they kept the non-perishable stock – vehicle tyres, gas cylinders, canned food, sacks and bales and barrels of whatever bargains they'd made. In the furthest corner, Hamou knew, was where Moha stored the illicit crates of wine and beer he sold 'sous le manche'.

His cousin was sitting at an improvised desk in a pool of sunlight, alternately feeding himself and an attentive black cat pieces of sardine out of a can. Moha looked up as Hamou came in, his expression of shock swiftly disguised. Getting to his feet, he wiped his fingers on his trousers, and at once the cat leapt lightly onto the desk, knocked the sardine can to the ground and ate the contents with the side of its mouth, growling quietly all the time.

'Madani, you little thief,' Moha said affectionately. He looked Hamou up and down. 'You look terrible.'

No time for pleasantries. 'I need to talk to you.'

'I'd say you do, after how you left us all last time!'

Hamou did not want to talk about that. 'Is this place private?'

'What can you have to say to me that Hicham and Omar shouldn't hear?'

Hamou just stared at him.

Moha shrugged and picked up his jacket. 'Come on, then.'

He let them out of the back door to the alley into bright afternoon sunlight, turning the corner and cutting between grubby, industrial streets till they came out in a small square where benches had been set around the walls. In the middle sat a fountain, and although its basin was dry and dusty, someone had set oilcans planted with geraniums around it, the bright flowers releasing wafts of spiced citrus scent into the heavy air.

They took a seat on the furthest bench and Moha offered his cousin a cigarette. Hamou shook his head. 'Given up.'

'What?' Moha barked out a laugh. 'Things must be bad.'

'Moha, your business is on a list.'

His cousin frowned. 'What do you mean, "a list"?'

'In the commissariat files about terrorist suspects. I saw it by accident. And...' Hamou swallowed. 'Look, you can't tell anyone where you got the information from – swear to me?'

Moha had gone grey in the face. He nodded. 'Of course. Tell me.'

'Ahmed Choukri. He's dead.'

'No!' Moha put his head in his hands. '*Merde*.' Then his head jerked up. 'How do you know?'

'I can't tell you. I just... can't.'

'They took him last night,' Moha said softly. 'Old Greyhead's men.'

Hamou nodded.

'And he's really dead?'

'Yes, I'm sorry, Moha. I know he was a friend.'

His cousin's expression had gone tight and pained. 'The fucking bastards.' He searched Hamou's face. 'There was nothing you could do to help him?'

Hamou, appalled at himself, burst into tears, turning away from his cousin's scrutiny, away from the sight of onlookers. In a cranny in the brickwork behind him, a large black fly was struggling in a spider's sticky web, its efforts becoming ever more ineffectual. He rubbed the sleeve of his jacket across his face, not caring if he covered it in snot. He found he did not care about much right now. Except that he did not want to see Zina, or Moha, or any of his family – in one of the commissariat's death cells.

'Sorry. I know there wasn't anything you could do. I shouldn't have said that,' Moha said miserably. There was a long pause before he said, 'And the business?'

Hamou mastered himself. 'I'm not sure if it named the business or whether it was just Rue Auvert I saw. But, Moha, you and Zina should get out of the city while you can. Just get to Tiziane, or somewhere a long way from here.'

His cousin regarded him curiously. 'Zina? Zina Chadli? Why? What's she got to do with anything?'

Hamou decided not to mention the gun, but instead said, 'Well, if you are implicated in any way, then she may be, by association, and—'

Moha cut him off. 'So that's why you ran off like that! I did wonder. We all wondered. Thought you'd gone a bit mad, to be honest.' Despite everything, he grinned. 'You think I'm marrying Zina Chadli, don't you?'

Hamou gritted his teeth. 'Your mother said so.'

'I'm sure she didn't.'

'She did. And they were there, her parents...' A strange doubt had begun to creep into his mind; a strange hope, too...

Moha snorted. 'You're a really crap policeman, Hamou. It's not Zina I'm engaged to, it's her cousin Leila.'

Behind Hamou's head the dying fly buzzed desperately. 'I don't understand.'

'Leila Chadli, Zina's cousin,' Moha said slowly, as if explaining himself to a child. 'She's come in from Tangier to stay with the Chadlis. Rachid and Samira brokered the betrothal on her parents' behalf.' He gave a small shrug. 'She's nice enough, pretty, only nineteen. I can't say I'm that bothered about getting married, but her parents have invested in the business: we use their warehouses. And they have excellent connections in the international zone, and in Spain. Not very romantic, huh?' Moha gave a short laugh. 'But no, I do like her, and affection will grow...'

Hamou remembered, now, that there had been a quiet dark-haired girl sitting beside Zina on the divan in his uncle's salon. His gaze had skimmed over her, discounting her, settled like a magnet on her cousin. He felt as if some part of his psyche had separated itself from the dark horrors he had witnessed and gone floating up into the sunlight like a child's balloon. 'You're not marrying Zina Chadli?' he checked carefully.

'She's a bit old for me, don't you think?'

Hamou bridled. 'She's not old, not at all.'

A massive grin split Moha's face. 'I knew it. You're sweet on her yourself.'

Reddening, Hamou said quickly, 'Look, that's neither here nor there. I just came to tell you about Ahmed, and the files, to warn you: to keep you safe.'

Moha nodded. 'Thanks, cousin. I know you're taking a big risk in telling me. But you know, you don't need to worry about me.' His expression became sombre. 'Shit, I'll have to go and tell Ahmed's parents. They've already lost one son.' He got heavily to his feet, as if he had aged ten years.

Hamou stood up, too. Moha held him by the tops of his arms, then hauled him into an embrace. 'The world's going to hell, Hamou. Try not to go down with it.'

Despite his cousin's dire warning, Hamou made his way home with a smile on his face for the first time in weeks. He passed the little yard where the old bicycle mender worked. Out on the pavement, the man was tinkering with an old rust-bucket resting upside-down on its handlebars. As Hamou approached, he straightened up. 'What can I do for you, officer?'

That was a change Hamou had noticed over these past months: fewer people called him by his name, even if they saw him every day, deferring to his uniform, perhaps distancing themselves from him by addressing his uniform. 'I wondered, Si Brahim, if you might have a bicycle I could buy?'

The old man beamed. 'How about this old beauty? She's elderly, but well-made. She'll last a lifetime.'

'I was thinking of something a little more modern.' His gaze strayed beyond the old man, into the little covered yard where, between piles of junk and parts, a chrome-and-blue bicycle was displayed on a stand. 'How much for that one?'

Having set eyes on it, a rush of images played through his mind – of him skimming through the traffic on a summer morning, the sun glinting off the chrome. He could go as far as the coast, to the grand piscine. He thought of all the women wearing tiny swimsuits like the superintendent's daughters; he thought – God help him – of Zina Chadli wearing such a thing, and came over all hot and vague.

Si Brahim made a face. 'I'm sorry to say that one's spoken for, officer. I'm just about to give it a final once-over.'

Hamou felt a stab of disappointment. 'That's most unfortunate,' he said, and it came out sterner than he'd meant it to.

The old man quailed, as if expecting Hamou to whip out his baton and beat him, or at the very least demand to see his documents, to pull him in for some spurious offence. 'I... I could perhaps ask if the purchaser might change their mind and wait for another model...' he started, and Hamou experienced a hot flush of shame.

'No, no. Please, no,' he said, placatory. 'I'll come back again another day, if you could ask around and see if you can find me something similar.' Seeing the expression of relief on the old man's face, he walked away.

18

The dog days of summer had set in. The sun beat down like a hammer, morning sea frets melding with heat haze shrouded the city, cloaking it in a smothering greyness that got into the lungs, made it hard to think straight, hard to move, hard to do anything much. To make everything worse, the refuse collectors were on strike in protest against the regime. The stink on the streets stung the nostrils. Criminals took advantage of the situation to dump corpses in alleyways and conceal them beneath mounds of rubbish. The rot attracted battalions of bluebottles, their nerve-shredding drone inescapable.

Hamou felt himself bogged down, in a morass not only of the body, but also of the soul, hating his job, hating the French, hating the ever-growing hostility around him. If he entered a café during one of his short breaks, conversations stilled and people turned away, not meeting his eye, or stared challengingly. He took to buying food from roadside stalls and carried with him a bottle of Oulmes, which he refilled at public fountains. He was sick of the sight of both crooks and victims; sick of processing thieves and brawlers, be they *colons* or Moroccan, sick of seeing kif-smokers in the parks and alleyways staring into space, of the beggars wheeling themselves around on trolleys, crying out for alms, of the old women with outstretched hands pleading for a coin. He always gave, but each time it made him angry – not at the beggars themselves, but that they should be forced to exist like this.

And every day, more brutality. There were citywide raids on the slums, the administration bulldozing shacks to drive the poor and the radical out of the city, resulting in mass arrests and harassment. Hamou had been involved in taking into custody a group of young men charged with killing another Moroccan known to be a police informant. He did not personally know any of the detainees, but he 'knew' them – they were the same age as his cousins and their friends, were passionate and defiant, politically engaged in a way that made him uneasy. They regarded him insolently, reproachfully, the question clear in their eyes: 'Why are you doing this to us? You should be on our side, not working for the enemy.'

He had seen terrible things – not just the dead bodies exhumed from beneath rotting garbage in alleyways, or the broken men in the commissariat cells, but the behaviour of his colleagues. Behaviour that till recently he could never have conceived of, especially from his fellow Moroccans: Saleh Zaoui deliberately dislocating a thief's shoulder by forcing an armlock beyond reasonable constraint because the youth insulted him; one of the French officers hitting a suspect so hard that his eye socket was smashed. 'He fell over,' the officer reported laconically, 'while trying to escape justice.' The other policemen said nothing to contradict his account. Even Hamou found himself tongue-tied in the presence of such barbarity. He didn't have the energy to intervene, had become mired in complicity.

Violent deaths became a daily occurrence. Regime collaborators killed by nationalists. Nationalists executed by the authorities. Moroccan activists killed by settlers. Settlers murdered by terrorists. Often the narrative became confused, the lines of allegiance twisted. Had the young Moroccan whose throat had been slit in a shack in the Carrières centrales been killed by one of the French murder squads, or by what many would deem his own side? The rumour abounded that the independence party itself, the Istiqlal, were killing members of the more militant factions so as not to jeopardise their own political negotiations, which they sensed were progressing.

Resident General Lacoste was to be replaced by Gilbert Grandval, who was believed to have a more moderate agenda and who would work to ease hostilities. The French government in Paris, rattled by increasing violence and fearing loss of control, were said to be seeking a negotiated settlement with the nationalists and the *colons*, seeing a threat to their comfortable way of life, and made their concerns felt not only in words but in attacks on those appearing sympathetic to the nationalist cause.

When the headless corpse of Ismail the Cockroach turned up outside the commissariat in the dead of night with his mobilette dumped on top of him, daubed with red paint and the Black Crescent symbol of Al-Hilal, there was general consternation, not at his loss, since he had few friends, but at what his murder meant and who had carried it out, especially since his head had been found atop a pile of rubbish on the edge of one of the most exclusive French enclaves.

'Who knows?' Driss Talbi said. 'It could have been anyone. No one likes a cockroach, do they?'

'But surely the Black Crescent...' Hamou started.

Driss shrugged. 'Could be them. Could be a false flag. By the settlers, or someone else.'

It was true that no one had liked the man, who was a snitch and a chkam, but nobody deserved to die in such a horrible way. It made everyone paranoid. Many times, after finishing a late shift, Hamou found himself looking over his shoulder, walking in the road, away from the entrances to dark alleyways, scanning every stranger and every passing car for signs of threat. Unable to carry his gun, he opted for digging his grandfather's amulet out of the drawer and placing it in his breast pocket for luck where he had previously always carried his cigarettes, even though he felt a peasant fool for doing so.

Sleeping was difficult. Plagued by nightmares and fearing that the stifling heat of his room might be to blame for his overactive imagination, he had taken himself up to the roof terrace, with a thin mattress, a cotton blanket, a cushion and a bottle of water. He lay staring up into the starry sky, narrowing his eyes to make out the patterns of the constellations. This was so absorbing that he failed to register the sound of quiet footsteps until they were almost upon him and sat up with a start that was almost as bad as stumbling out of his dream state.

'Oh!' they both exclaimed at once.

Hamou, who had undressed down to a pair of wide cotton trousers, sat up, pulling the cover over his naked chest. Zina stood her ground. They stared at one another warily until at last Hamou said, 'Sorry. It's just too hot to sleep downstairs.'

'Move up,' she said peremptorily and sat down beside him. 'I think we've moved beyond the usual rules of polite society, don't you?'

Hamou gave her a rueful grin. 'I suppose so.'

'Aren't you going to offer me a cigarette?'

Surely it was only French women and prostitutes who smoked? 'Er... I gave up.'

Zina's mouth quirked, the light of the moon limning her fine features with the palest silver. 'Well done. What more might you do, Hamou Badi, if you put your mind to it?'

They sat in an oddly companionable silence for a while. Then Hamou said, 'Might you consider leaving Casablanca for a time? I worry that you're placing yourself in danger.'

Zina gave a small guffaw. 'Of course I'm in danger. We all are.'

'You more than most.'

She considered this, then said, 'Let's not talk about such things, Hamou. We see things from different angles.'

'Maybe. But it's getting nasty out there, and I wouldn't want to see you fall foul of the administration.'

She raised her eyebrows. 'But you *are* the administration, Hamou. Like it or not. I suppose I should thank you for not giving them my name.'

'I want no thanks. I'd rather you stop taking such risks.'

'Nothing worthwhile is ever gained without great risk.'

Was this true? Surely hard work and dedication rendered the best rewards? This was what he had always been raised to believe. It was the Amazigh way. Everywhere you went in the city – probably in any city – each shop or stall you came upon open earliest in the morning and latest at night would be owned and run by a Berber family putting in hard graft and long hours. 'I'm not sure I believe that,' he said at last.

'Perhaps you should try taking a risk sometime and find out.'

Hamou's whole skin started to tingle. Blood rushed into his every extremity. Could he? Dare he? His bad angel won out. He leaned over suddenly, caught Zina by the chin and, angling his head towards her, pulled her into a deep kiss. It was a kiss that went on forever, while little fireworks exploded in his mind and in his blood, and yet it was over in seconds. But she hadn't pulled away. He registered this astonishing fact with the small part of his conscious brain that was still functioning. Not only had she not pulled away, she had returned his kiss, her lips moving beneath his. He thought so anyway, or had he imagined it? Had he imagined also the touch of her cool hand on his cheek? An enormous smile came bubbling up from deep within him.

He felt dizzy with delight, overcome by sensation, in such a daze that when she got gracefully to her feet and laid a hand on the top of his head, saying, 'Think some more about risks and rewards, Hamou. Think hard,' he did not realise she had gone until it was too late to reply.

'I will try,' he said into the dark, empty air. 'I will try.'

Hamou slept on the roof terrace during those hot nights, but Zina did not reappear to repeat the kiss, or even talk with him, and with each passing day he became more and more sure that he had somehow hallucinated their encounter, hallucinated or simply dreamed it.

He had of course seen her, but only from afar, although once she had, as if sensing his eyes on her from the terrace, turned and raised a hand to wave to him, and that simple gesture had made his heart soar like larksong.

Work was even grimmer than ever: a journalist had been beaten half to death earlier and Hamou had to break the news to his pregnant wife that her husband had lost an eye and was in hospital, barely conscious. She wailed so loudly that he was convinced she was going to have her baby right there in front of him and he found himself chanting '*La bes, la bes, la bes...*' as if by sheer force of will, he could somehow stop this from happening. He had no training for this sort of situation: he felt utterly at a loss. Hamou had met the journalist twice at nationalist meetings, had read his columns and admired his writing. It was hard to believe that this talented young man, father to two young children, nearly three, should almost have died at the hands of a group of European youths calling him 'filth' and 'son of a whore', on the streets of his home city, in his own country.

Walking home later in the dark, Hamou felt so angry that instead of his usual paranoia, he almost welcomed the idea of an attack on him. He felt in need of violent relief. But he reached his building without incident, wrestled successfully with the sticky lock and let himself quietly into the vestibule. There, propped against the wall, was the bicycle from Si Brahim's, the gleaming chrome-and-blue beauty he had set his hopes on. How had it come to be here, in his own hallway, the bike of his dreams? Had some friendly djinn, some zouhry relative, taken pity on him and intervened, as it surely had done to bring about the kiss stolen from Zina Chadli? Had the other deal fallen through, and the bike-mender thought to win favour with an officer of the law by delivering it to his home?

Hamou walked over and laid a hand on the shining vehicle to

assure himself of its reality. The metal of its frame was cold and glossy and super-real: his fingers closed around it. And then he was seized by a mad desire.

Reopening the door, he pushed the bicycle outside, threw a leg over it and started pedalling like a maniac. He rode past the cigarette stand and the grocer's stall, which was still open, its lamps still burning, past an astonished Didi laying out his sleeping mat in his accustomed spot, past the end of the Derb Ghrallef and then the shantytown, and on into the darkness.

But now he found it impossible to see. He braked and put his feet down. Dismounting, he fiddled with the front headlamp to see what was causing it to refuse to light up. When he twisted the front off, the headlamp rattled as if something lay broken inside. He moved his fingers in the space where only the wires to the bulb should be and came upon some small, heavy metal objects. In the darkness, his fingers interrogated them, but he already knew what they were.

He pocketed one, screwed the headlamp back into place, turned the bicycle around and pedalled back home quietly and carefully, as if the heaviness of his thoughts weighed down the vehicle, terrified that he might be stopped by one of the patrolling squads in their black Citroëns. He ignored the beggar's greeting, did not look at the grocer or the cigarette-seller, leapt off the high saddle as if it were burning him, pushed open the front door of the apartment block and replaced the bicycle exactly as he had found it, knowing it was not meant for him after all. Then, with great care, he relocked the front door.

Upstairs in his room, he removed the object from his pocket and stared at it under the unsparing light of his single unshaded bulb.

It was a bullet. Ammunition for a small-calibre handgun.

Hamou closed his eyes, feeling utterly bleak.

After this, he found he had gone off the idea of buying a bike. And when he saw Zina Chadli riding the shining machine down the road, with her dark robe hiked up to reveal a pair of slim, shapely calves, the sight made his breath catch in his throat. From then on, his every waking thought between tasks was of fear for her safety. He felt as if he were walking around several centimetres shorter, with his guts tied in knots.

19

Hamou was coming off duty one afternoon when he heard there was a fire in the old Bousbir that had started at a bakery and spread to surrounding buildings. At once he thought of Babrahim, the grumpy baker whom Aicha had woken to supply him with chebakia, and his son Zak, who had driven him home at breakneck speed on the back of his scooter. There were of course many bakers in the Bousbir, but it reminded him that he should call on Aicha to see how she and Sofiane were doing; besides, he might be able to help.

It was still sweltering at five o'clock. Hamou removed his kepi and uniform jacket with some relief, slinging the jacket over his shoulder. A brisk walk would probably get him to the medina faster than a bus at this time, so he set off through the park, passing beneath the cool shade of the trees whenever he was able to, then choosing streets with café awnings as he made his way north and west across the city.

The smell of rotting garbage was particularly strong today and Hamou's throat stung at the stench. He stopped at an umbrellaed stall and bought a cold bottle of water, relishing the passage of the chilled liquid as he gazed at the smart French shops offering dreams of beauty and plenty to those with money; at the tall white buildings, their lines so clean and modern and foreign, looming up into the pitiless blue sky. He gazed at the Europeans imperiously summoning taxis that swerved across three lanes of traffic to serve them. They knew the world belonged to them, that all they had to do was snap their fingers, offer a small denomination note, and some frazzled African would do their bidding, because it was the only way of bringing food to the table at home. He watched a couple laughing as they bantered about who was to ride where. The driver, a small dark-skinned man in a traditional robe, waited patiently. They gave him no thought, as if he were merely another moving part of the vehicle.

Hamou's gaze strayed to the talismans dangling from the taxi's rear-view mirror and remembered with a jolt the amulet that had been his grandfather's. He rummaged desperately in his jacket, at last finding it in a pocket, and thanked his luck that he had not lost it. By the time he looked up again, the taxi had pulled away, and he saw that by the side of the kerb lay a pile of steaming donkey shit. That about summed things up. Riches and rot. You could take over someone else's country and build your cities over the ancient bones of fallen civilisations, raise up your gleaming white modernist structures among dust and pisé. You could replace donkeys with gleaming automobiles. You could impose your bureaucracy, your infrastructure, ideas and your staff, but in the end there would always remain the stubborn will of the people, and a stinking pile of turds.

Flags were strung along the boulevards, zigzagging across the shopping streets: red, white and blue for the French holiday. *Quatorze juillet.* Bastille Day. He'd learned about the French Revolution at college. It had been presented to him as a great thing – the rising of an oppressed populace against a corrupt aristocracy living off the labour of the poor, hailed as heroes of the revolution. And in North Africa if people tried to throw off the shackles of their oppressors, they were called terrorists. Where was all their precious *liberté, égalité, fraternité* here in Morocco?

Hamou sighed. Well, let them have their holiday. At least someone was cheerful.

As he jogged across the huge square in front of the old Bousbir he could see the smoke in the air, lazy black drifts polluting the blue sky. Inside the old medina, people were scurrying. He stopped some young men and asked them about the fire. 'Follow us!' they cried and ran off through the maze of alleyways at such a lick that Hamou could hardly keep up. He joined a long line of people passing buckets of water in a human chain to try to douse the flames. The streets were too narrow to allow for the passage of big French fire engines, even if they were despatched to this poor Moroccan area.

After a sweaty hour of work the fire was eventually brought under smouldering control and Hamou found himself surfeit to requirements. Neighbours had gathered to take in those whose homes had been damaged; people brought armfuls of clothes and bedding, ushered children and the elderly to safety. The Bousbir's community spirit was in full flow.

Hamou retrieved his jacket, which now, like the rest of him, was covered in fine ash and stank of smoke, and made his way to the public fountain to wash his hands and face and slake his sore throat. He went to buy a handful of Carambars at a stall to give to Sofiane.

The stallholder handed over the sticks of wrapped caramel, then dropped his gaze to the uniform jacket over Hamou's arm. 'Nasty business, eh, officer?'

'Yes, terrible. It's great good luck that no one perished in the fire.'

'The attack on your lot in the new medina, is what I meant.'

'What?'

'Have you not heard?' The stallholder had a gleam in his eye, the joy of breaking shocking news. He leaned forward conspiratorially. 'Someone lobbed a grenade at a police jeep. An hour or so ago. Five officers injured, is what I was told.'

Hamou had been planning a cinema trip out that way tomorrow to catch *Rififi*, a film about the planning of the perfect crime. It seemed just the right sort of entertainment for a policeman, and he'd been looking forward to it. His first thought was that he might have been caught up in this atrocity; then, feeling ashamed, he considered the men who had been targeted. He would surely know some of them.

With a heavier heart, he made his way through the little streets to the building where Aicha worked. A lot of men were hanging around outside in the dusty square. A holiday trip to the brothel: how lovely. Hamou felt suddenly disgusted. Shouldn't these men – that one in the pink shirt and smart chinos, that one in a linen suit, that one in what looked like naval uniform; the man in the glasses who looked as if he should be sitting behind a desk in a bank; the loud group of young European lads laughing and pushing one another, filling the air with their obscenities – all be at home with their families on a national holiday? Did they all come here to ruin poor Moroccan girls, to pay them to do things they didn't get elsewhere, before returning sweet-faced to their girlfriends and wives and mothers?

Feeling irritable, upset and prudish, Hamou shrugged into his uniform jacket, jammed his kepi on his head and walked smartly to the door, past the waiting punters.

The brothel keeper recognised him at once: he supposed this was one of the particular skills one developed in her role – like a maître d' – that ensured the regular return of customers, and no doubt it was useful to memorise all the policemen, judges, diplomats, politicians, the rich and influential who came through her doors.

'I came to see how Aicha is. And to bring some sweets for Sofiane.' He brandished the Carambars in their gaudy red-and-yellow packaging.

The brothel keeper held up a hand. 'I am most dreadfully sorry, officer,' she said, 'but Aicha is no longer with us. Perhaps I could offer you some other young beauty?'

Hamou was aghast. 'She's gone?'

'For weeks. Actually,' the woman's regard narrowed, 'after I last saw you here.'

Of course. With the money he had taken from the charlatan and given to her. Good girl. She had taken herself and the boy out of this place, he hoped to somewhere better. He asked the woman if she had any idea where Aicha might have gone to, but the brothel keeper was dismissive. 'There are whorehouses everywhere.'

But Hamou did not think Aicha had gone to another brothel. He left with a swinging walk past the waiting men, sucking on one of the sweet caramel sticks as he went. It was almost as nice as a cigarette. God, he missed cigarettes. Then he caught himself feeling happy and chided himself. Five of his fellow officers blown up in the new medina. A hand grenade was a blunt instrument indeed, horrifying.

He had just reached the outer wall of the old medina and was emerging into the evening sun in the Place de France when he felt a rumble that seemed to transmit itself through both the air and the ground at once to tremble in his bones, and when he turned his head back towards the city, he could make out a rising plume of black smoke.

For a moment, everything seemed to stop. Then suddenly everyone was staring in the same direction, at first dumbfounded, then shouting for others to look. Had there been an earthquake? Had a building collapsed?

He found himself running – not, like any sensible person, away from whatever disaster had struck, but towards it, across lanes of stupefied traffic, across the junction at the Boulevard de Paris, through the Place du Maréchal, past the Municipal Theatre and the statue of Lyautey up on his horse, then the official house and gardens of the Resident General, apocalyptic scenarios tumbling through his mind, gripped by the irrational terror that Zina Chadli might have been caught up in this danger. He worried about her all the time: the entire city spread itself before him as a vast canvas upon which all manner of terrifying events might be played out with Zina cast at centre stage.

In the heat, his breathing ragged, each breath painfully uprooted from his lungs, his limbs moved too slowly, and his destination remained just beyond the next street, the next row of shops. A few minutes later he emerged onto the huge circular intersection at Mers Sultan, where so many of the city's great arterial roads converged, to a scene of devastation. The air was thick with the smell of char, of hot metal, of chemicals, and with the blare of emergency sirens. He found himself breasting a wave of panic, people running blindly towards him, others lurching, clutching injuries, blood seeping through their clothes. He passed a pharmacy where people milled around outside and glimpsed between shoulders a woman with long red hair stretched out on its tiled floor, a man in a white coat down on his knees tending to her, bloodied bandages strewn around, and felt ashamed at his relief in identifying her as European, and therefore not Zina, though what business Zina Chadli might have in this most affluent of French quarters on Bastille Day, he could not imagine.

He ran on, details lodging with hallucinatory force in his mind: a man with his suit in shreds and a fork embedded in his cheek; a woman hauling at the unmoving body of her husband; a tyre rolling silently along the road. Strings of red-white-and-blue bunting puddled in slicks of blood and other fluids on the ground.

He passed a young man sitting in the gutter, clutching a leg that ended obscenely just below the knee; then a child lying motionless in the road like a doll tossed carelessly out of a pram, while a grey-haired woman whose red dress had tattered away to show her underwear held a younger woman in her embrace as two men in medical uniforms ran over with a stretcher.

Police cars came to a screeching halt, abandoned at odd angles across the busiest traffic hub in this part of the city. Uniformed men milled around. Hamou ran towards the first policeman he found, a young Frenchman he vaguely recognised, who wore the distinctive white crossbelt and cuffs of a traffic cop. The man's face was pale, his eyes stark. 'What happened? What can I do?' Hamou asked, and had to repeat the question more loudly, because the man shook his head and touched his ear. Deafened by the blast.

'Are you all right?' Hamou shouted, and the other officer staggered against him. 'I just need to sit down for a moment.'

The man collapsed with his head between his knees, breathing in great gulps. Hamou ran his hands over his back and arms, looked over the rest of him for signs of injury. Just shock, he thought, and no wonder.

'I'll be all right in a minute, you go on,' the man said, too loudly.

Across the road, two men were getting out of a Citroën. Hamou recognised the divisional commissioner and Emile Fouquet, his deputy. He patted the traffic cop on the shoulder, sped across the road and snapped a salute. The divisional commissioner cast an unfriendly glance at Hamou, then transferred his gaze to a detachment of Sûreté officers piling out of a van on the junction. Fouquet regarded Hamou with an unreadable expression. 'Officer Badi, what are you doing here?' he asked, as if mildly surprised to find a junior officer at a smart cocktail party.

'Sir, I was off duty, but I hear the explosion, and I run...' Even to his own ears, his French sounded mangled.

The divisional commissioner turned back to Hamou. 'One of them,' he said, with something approaching a snarl. 'You're all savages.' And he spat on the ground, then walked away.

Hamou stared at the gob of saliva at his feet. 'I just came to help,' he said quietly.

'Check the interior of the café...' Fouquet indicated an area twenty yards away which appeared to be the centre of activity. 'See if there are survivors.' He reached into the Citroën, then passed something to Hamou. It was a large, black, rubberised torch, so heavy that it felt more like a club than a tool.

'What happened, sir?'

'A terrorist attack,' Fouquet said shortly. 'On Bastille Day. Quite, quite barbaric.' And he walked away to join his superior officer.

On this side of the roundabout were smart cafés and bistros accustomed to hosting affluent European clientele. Hamou was familiar with them from patrolling the area: the Chateaubriand, the Café de la Concorde and... Shock stole the name of the third. An eyeless black hole had replaced its gilded plate glass and shining lanterns, and the pavement that was usually packed with tables and chairs under a striped awning was now a vista of carnage. He picked his way between sparking electrical cables, mangled metal that had once been automobiles and bicycles, chairs and tables, a set of traffic lights. And what was that? An abandoned boot? No, a smart leather brogue, complete with a section of leg, the bone standing stark and white out of the ravaged meat. Oh God...

He managed, with utmost effort, not to vomit.

Inside what was left of the Café Gonin – the name came suddenly back to him – the electrics were out. Heart pounding in fear of what he might find, Hamou swung the torch beam from side to side, calling out, 'Police! Is there anyone here?'

Overturned furniture, floor tiles slick with liquid. Skidding as he went, Hamou made his way to the back of the café, but there the damage was minimal: the blast had clearly occurred either at the front of the café or just outside. He worked his way methodically forward, calling out but hearing only an eerie quiet as if the building were holding its breath. One of the big ceiling lamps had come down and lay like a vast metallic octopus, fat opalescent body and pendant chains sprawled possessively across a table as if devouring prey. Hamou crunched across broken glass and crockery, looking, looking. At the front of the café jagged teeth of glass were all that remained of the immense plate-glass windows. He dreaded to think of the wounds that flying glass must have caused.

Then suddenly, a weird gleam. Eyes! He yelped, and the eyes came at him – a cat, which ran past him yowling, ears flat to its head, out into the street.

Hamou's heart battered his chest. He steadied himself against the counter and his hand slid in something wet. An unholy mix of beer and blood, blood and beer. Impossible to tell: his sense of smell had ceased, so long in overdrive, it had become dulled and useless.

And then other torch beams converged on him, shining in his eyes, followed by a muttered, *sorry*. Hamou pulled himself together. 'No one left in here,' he said.

'No one alive,' the other replied, and he realised it was Driss Talbi.

'What happened?' Hamou asked. 'Was it an accident?'

'A bomb.'

He'd hoped Fouquet had been mistaken, that there had been a gas explosion or something. 'Do they know who set it?' he managed at last.

'The café owner's wife saw two young lads, seventeen or so, on a *triporteur*.'

One of those motorised tricycles the locals used for delivering goods, with a big cargo box up front.

'They stopped it at the lights outside the café, and one of them opened up the box, lifted out a stack of bread, and then they ran and the whole thing exploded.'

The mundane details made it all the more believable. 'How many dead?'

Driss shrugged. 'Who knows? It's fucking chaos. Walking wounded everywhere. Ambulances ferrying people to the Colombani. Someone will have to get down to the hospital and take details. Not me. It's the end of my shift.'

A bomb, set by youngsters barely out of childhood. Hamou remembered himself at sixteen, playing barefoot football and learning to smoke, and felt like weeping. There came back to him a flash of the woman at the pharmacy, her red hair spread across the dirty tiles, the broken child, the man clutching his ruined leg. What a terrible, pointless, vicious act.

'And the boys with the triporteur, have they been arrested?'

'Blown to hell, I hope,' Driss said savagely. 'One of our own was killed too,' he added, and for a moment Hamou thought he meant *Moroccans* before Driss continued, 'and that's in addition to the poor guys who were injured by the fucking grenade earlier,' and realised he meant *police*.

So, it had come to that, then, the demarcation of loyalty. Working for the administration trumped national identity, parentage, community, even religion.

It wasn't hard to understand why, when you were confronted by horrors like this, but then he remembered Ahmed Choukri dying under torture, and Zina Chadli preferring to swallow a suicide capsule than submitting to arrest, and he didn't know what he thought any more.

'What a world,' he said quietly. 'What a nightmare.'

20

He did not sleep well. Awful images from the previous evening kept ambushing him in garish Technicolor. If he caught them before they took root, he countered them with thoughts of Tiziane: the almond blossom turning the valley bottoms white and pink in the spring; the coconut scent of the wild broom and the feel of its coarse, flexible stems as he bent them into a knot just as his mother had taught him, while making a wish or a prayer – for Uncle Omar's knees, for his mother's arthritic hands, for (once, selfishly) a pair of football boots for himself. The idea was that a stranger would come upon the broom bush and, finding one of these knots, would add their own prayers while undoing it, thus enabling their wish to be granted. That was the theory, anyway – he never had got those football boots. He recalled the excitement of the travelling cinema stretching a white sheet between palm trees to act as a screen; sitting cross-legged on a blanket on the ground to watch the cartoons. If he concentrated hard enough, he could drive the horrors away. Eventually, he fell into a short but dreamless sleep.

Something woke him. He sat up, pulled on his robe, then got to his feet, the concrete roof still cool beneath his soles. He had slept through the first prayer. Down below, he could hear people going about their business – handcarts clanking, the rumble of vehicles, the insistent tweet of sparrows.

'Away with you!' he chided them, flapping his hands. 'I have nothing to give you. You'll have to wait.'

They flew off a few paces, unafraid. Promising them bread in due course, Hamou rolled up his bedding, took it downstairs, collected a change of clothing, a towel, some money, his keys and ran quickly outside. It was early enough that the hammam was quiet. The lad scrubbed his back with a rough cloth so hard that he lost a layer of skin and came out feeling if not exactly a new man, then at least clean.

He bought a copy of the morning edition of *Voice of the People*. The policeman in him demanded that he acquaint himself with the known facts of what had occurred at Mers Sultan, much as he would prefer to know no more about it. He scanned the shelves of cigarettes behind the storekeeper's head and his hands itched for a packet of Anfas – honestly, he would smoke anything, Kasbahs, or even Favorites right now. But his good angel won out in the end, and he came away with only the newspaper.

At the grocer's he bought a bag of pistachio nuts, fruit, yoghurt, *La vache qui rit*, and from the baker's a round loaf still warm from the oven, the solid feel of it in its wrap of paper a comforting assurance that some degree of normality remained in this city. Back at home, he brewed coffee and took a tray bearing his breakfast up to the roof terrace and read the paper while the sparrows pecked around his feet, chirruping their contentment.

Terror at Mers Sultan! screamed the headline above an image of the bombed-out café and photographs of victims' faces. Six dead, more than thirty seriously injured. The names were listed. Europeans mainly, Spanish and French. The manager of the café, a traffic officer, a boy of ten. He remembered the broken body of the child and the two grieving women, and his throat felt tight. The injured included another traffic cop: was he the deafened man he had spoken to? It seemed bad luck that two traffic policemen had been caught up in the blast. Then he saw

168

the name of an under-brigadier of the Sûreté listed among the injured. Maybe the café had been targeted because police liked to use it.

French families, too: groups of people sharing the same surname, a child of eight, two Moroccan waiters. Many unnamed victims had fled the scene to be treated at pharmacies, or at home. The final numbers are yet to be confirmed.

One witness stated that he had been in his car, stopped at the traffic signal close to the Café Gonin when he had seen two youths with a triporteur. He thought it had broken down: there was smoke coming out of it. 'They got out and opened the cargo-box and something made me suspicious. I'm not sure why, but I put my foot on the gas and sped away, even though the light was still on red, and a couple of seconds later there was an almighty explosion and shrapnel came raining down all over the back of my car. I had a very lucky escape.'

A very lucky escape indeed, Hamou thought.

The second eyewitness was the wife of the café manager, who said much of what Driss had relayed to him the previous night. He wondered at her strength of character, to give such coherent testimony in the immediate wake of her husband's death.

Hamou searched the article for any mention of the fate of the bombers, but they were not mentioned among the six named dead, nor had they been arrested, at least by the time the paper had gone to press.

There would have been battalions of police out in the Carrières centrales and other slums last night, he thought, and if they had not found them, then certainly they would be out today, too. He did not look forward to going in to work. He was on the evening and night shift. Almost certainly he would be sent out with the rest of his colleagues to root out those responsible – not just the two youths, but those who had prepared the bomb, supplied the triporteur, sourced the ingredients for the explosives, made the timing device. A number of Black Crescent cells, each assigned a specific task, or a single operation from beginning to end? Whoever it was worked on a greater scale than Zina Chadli and her associates. One handgun concealed in a melon; a scatter of ammunition hidden in a headlamp. It was hardly the stuff of wholesale murder, he tried to tell himself. But a single bullet could take a life.

Suddenly, the coffee tasted unbearably bitter. He poured what was left into the drain and took the tray and paper back downstairs. A slice of bright lemon sunlight slanted through the single window in his apartment, illuminating dust that rose in columns of sparkling motes as he crossed to the sink. When had he last cleaned his room? He imagined his mother walking into his apartment and felt ashamed. All he had was this small, rented space, and he could not even keep that clean.

He looked down at the red, black and white tribal rug his mother had insisted he bring with him when he first came to the city: 'It will always remind you of home,' she had told him. 'When you walk across it with your bare feet, pause and remember the hard work of the hands of the women who made it. Women do the greatest portion of work in this world, my son, never forget that. Always respect them for it. They bear the children and raise the children and teach them all the important things; they care for the crops and the animals, they cook, they clean, and they make the lives of men easy. It's hard to be a woman in this world, when men forget this.'

Recalling his mother's words, he looked down at the patterns. 'See these shapes...' She had pointed to the diamond lozenges marching across the rug in horizontal lines. 'These are the women of our tribe, working together, joining their power to keep everyone safe, warding off the evil eye. And here...' she touched the edges where lines of crosses and arrows formed a border, 'these are the men of the tribe, working to protect us from a distance. That's you, my son. One of the Free People. You may be a long way away, but you will always be part of the weave of life here in Tiziane. This is where your story starts...' she indicated the selvedge at the top, then ran her hand the length of the carpet to the other end, 'and this is your life ongoing. We never close off this edge, for who knows where the threads may lead?'

He touched the frayed edge now. Who indeed knew? In Islam it was said that the future was written by God, but in the older beliefs there was still plenty of room for chance, for decisions, for sheer random luck. He rolled the rug carefully and was about to take it up to the terrace to beat the dust out of it when his gaze fell on his uniform jacket, cast carelessly over the chair back when he had returned so weary and heartsick last night. With dawning horror, he realised that there was a dark stain on the right sleeve. A tangible reminder of the Mers Sultan atrocity.

He put down the rug, took up the jacket and emptied the pockets. He weighed his grandfather's amulet in his hand. It was an ugly thing. You couldn't wear it with anything other than a djellaba. Even in this modern apartment it looked out of place. He put it on the table, then emptied out his pockets – coins, an aspirin or something, a screw of paper, a couple of mints, a business card. He turned this over, remembering the American who had pressed it into his hand outside the brothel. What was his name? He scrutinised the printed words. *Charles W. Shelby Jnr.* What did 'Jnr.' mean? He had no idea.

He took the jacket to the sink and examined the stain. The summer light was merciless: blood, dark and dried. Whose blood? he wondered as he ran cold water into the sink, soaked the sleeve and saw the whorls of red unthreading themselves from the fabric. Was it that of the café manager, or one of his customers? From one of the injured waiters? Moroccan or French?

Did it matter? Blood was blood.

He wrung out the sleeve, and then, with the rolled rug over one shoulder and the dripping jacket in his hand, climbed the stairs back up to the terrace. He hung the jacket on one of the communal washing lines, hoping it would dry before he had to go to work. Then he hung the rug over another line and beat it with the stick Samira Chadli kept by the terrace door for this purpose and gave it a few good, cathartic whacks, gratified but at the same time appalled to see all the dust billow out of it. At last, feeling somewhat cleansed of spirit and a bit weak in the arm, he took the rug and hung it over the wall at the front of the terrace to be disinfected by the sun.

Down below, life was going on much as usual: a boy carrying a bundle of newly baked baguettes; the Javel man honking his horn to summon all the housewives who needed to replenish their supplies of bleach. An old man tapping his way down the opposite pavement, leaning heavily on his stick. Women with baskets over their arm heading out early to the market. It could be anywhere at any time, Hamou thought, were it not for the incessant roar of the traffic on the Mazagan, or the blare of distant police sirens.

He was about to go about the rest of his chores when something snagged his attention. A figure on a bicycle riding unsteadily towards the building. His stomach clenched: he knew exactly who it was. Zina swung a leg off the shining machine he had so coveted, staggered and let the bike fall to the ground, throwing out a hand to steady herself against the wall. For a few seconds, she bowed her head as if exhausted, then she raised her head and the light fell upon her face…

Hamou ran. He ran across the terrace and down all four flights of stairs. He flung the front door open before she even had time to fumble her key into the faulty lock.

They stared at one another.

'My god,' said Hamou, barely able to catch his breath, let alone form words. 'Who did… this?'

Zina's left eye was swollen shut, a dark bruise forming. Blood from a cut on her browbone was smeared down her cheek. She looked at him balefully out of her one good eye, and even one eye was enough to make Hamou's knees tremble. 'Get the bike in,' she ordered, and all but collapsed.

Hamou did as he was told, though all he wanted to do was to abandon the wretched thing, sweep Zina into his arms and carry her to safety.

'Lock the door,' she said hoarsely, and he did that too.

In the penumbrous light of the hallway they regarded one another silently.

'Tell me who did this to you,' Hamou said, 'and I will kill them.'

Zina gave him a crooked smile. 'Men,' she said. 'All the same. Just help me upstairs.'

At the door of her family apartment, Zina paused, listening. 'Have you seen my father today?' she whispered.

It seemed an odd question. Hamou shook his head.

'He should be at work by now, but...' She took Hamou's arm. 'Take me to your room quickly, quietly.'

Hamou felt himself go hot all over. 'If you're sure...'

'Just shut up and do it.'

Must have some Amazigh in her lineage – she was as bossy as his mother. Hamou opened the door to his apartment. Without the rug on the floor, the place looked miserable, uncared for, full of dust. 'I was just starting to clean it,' he said, but she waved off his words.

'Get me a bowl of water, a cloth, some antiseptic, if you have it, vinegar if you haven't, and a mirror.'

Hamou assembled the items, adding a brand-new towel he had not till now been able to bring himself to use, and a first aid box. He set his shaving mirror before her as she sat at the table. Sat on his chair. He couldn't quite believe that she was here, in his apartment, that they were alone together.

'Can I?' he offered.

'No.'

'Are you sure?'

'I'm a nurse,' she snapped.

He watched as she expertly cleaned the wound, dabbed antiseptic on it, applied a sticking plaster. 'What happened?' he asked at last, as she held a cold compress to her swollen eye.

Zina sighed. 'A patient with attitude. A settler – a *colon*. Came in behaving like the big man, complaining about how he'd been made to wait, and him a town planner and he had a meeting at nine. Then he moaned about not seeing a "proper doctor", that I was, of all things, a *woman*, and then he stared at me and realised I was Moroccan and started mouthing off about monkeys and savages, and the bomb at Mers Sultan. One of the doctors came and asked him to be quiet, said if he didn't want his boil dealt with, he could simply leave, and he quietened down for a bit. But as soon as he was alone in the treatment room with me, he started up again. Wasn't there someone better qualified? He didn't want to get infected or disfigured. I wanted to tell him he was one of the ugliest men I'd ever come across, inside and out, and that the very fact he had a boil meant he already had an infection, but he just went on and on about dirty foreigners and this "shithole" of a country.'

'But *he's* the foreigner, in our country!' Hamou was outraged.

Zina lifted a shoulder. 'I didn't say anything: what's the point? But I did lance his boil rather more vigorously than I might otherwise have done and he howled like a demon and punched me in the eye.'

'He should be arrested for assault! I'll track him down myself!'

Zina laughed. 'People like him don't get arrested, Hamou. Surely you know that by now? Anyway, he'd just accuse me of doing my job badly and they'd probably sack me.'

'But you're a good nurse,' he said, remembering how calmly she had dealt with Moha's bullet wound.

'I am,' she agreed equably. She glanced down at her ruined uniform, spattered with red and yellow stains. 'Fetch me a clean *gandoura*, Hamou Badi, and I'll change out of this thing.'

Hamou went to his single wardrobe and took out his Friday-best robe – white, with yellow embroidery at the neck and cuffs. It would probably fit her, he thought: she was almost as tall as him, and strongly built.

'Turn your back.'

Hamou turned, and shut his eyes tightly too, because the idea of Zina Chadli disrobing in his room was almost too much to bear. Almost.

'You can turn around now.'

He sucked in his breath at the sight of her. 'You look like an angel,' he said.

'I think that's probably blasphemy.' She stopped at the sound of voices on the stairs.

'And bring back some chickpeas,' came the voice of Samira Chadli, followed by a man's mumbled response.

'Thank heaven we came to your room.' Zina slumped back against the wall.

'But surely you have to tell them.'

She shot him a sharp glance. Something about the lopsidedness of her spoiled, beautiful face made him want to kiss her. He mastered himself, with difficulty.

'I don't want Father worried about me. He can be overprotective, and he doesn't like me working at the hospital as it is. I don't want him going there and making a scene.'

'Won't he see your bike down in the hall and know you're home?'

Zina swore, using a shocking phrase. 'I didn't think…'

'I'll let some air out of one of the tyres,' Hamou offered. 'You can tell him you left it behind because it was quicker to walk than to mend it.' He went to the window and looked down the street to see Rachid Chadli disappearing around the corner. 'It's all right, he's gone.'

Zina breathed out. 'We can go down now.'

'But won't your mother be shocked?'

She laughed. 'You don't know much about my mother.'

Samira Chadli took one look at her daughter's injuries and swore vehemently, using worse language than her daughter, then ushered them both into the kitchen.

'The devil!' she said when Zina told her the story. Then she set about concocting a poultice out of all manner of herbs and powders. 'That will take the swelling down, then it's a matter of cosmetics.'

Zina grimaced.

'Go and sit in the salon, both of you. I'll make tea. Tea solves everything.'

Hamou sneaked a look at his watch. He still had some hours before work, though the idea of going into the commissariat made a cold lump settle in the pit of the stomach that not even hot tea could dissolve.

When Samira brought the tea into the salon it was clear that her fury was still boiling. 'Give me the name of the man who did this to you and I will make sure he pays!' she said fiercely to her daughter.

Hamou eyed her with interest. He had never seen this side to his neighbour before. 'I said the same, lalla, but your daughter told me arresting him would accomplish nothing.'

'Who said anything about arrest? No disrespect to you, my son, you've always been kind and courteous to us, but the police have become no more or less than an arm of the state.' In case he was not entirely clear of her view, she banged a spoon on the table to underline her words. 'A weapon of French oppression.'

Even as little as a few weeks ago, Hamou might have disputed this and defended the force in which he was employed. Now, he shook his head sadly. 'There are still some good men in the Sûreté, lalla, but I know what you are saying.'

'Don't bait him, Yam'mi. He's confused and compromised. He knows he's on the wrong side but he won't admit it.'

'We all have to earn a living, Zina,' he said quietly. 'My family back home in Tiziane depend on me.'

'Your mother and siblings?' Samira Chadli clarified.

'Yes,' said Hamou. 'My mother is half crippled by arthritis and my sisters are not yet old enough to marry. I am the sole breadwinner: I send nearly all my salary home for them. The French have educated me and trained me as a policeman. I thought when I joined up it would be to do some good in the world. And I don't know how to do anything else.'

Samira Chadli clucked her tongue. 'There comes a time, young man, when principles must come before even family.'

'Mother,' Zina said warningly, but Samira's eyes flashed, and she looked like an altogether different woman to the one who had simpered and wheedled him to join them for meals. Had that been a front? Hamou wondered. And, if so, a front for what?

'My daughter tells me that you could have turned her in but have chosen not to do so. Oh, don't look so surprised: there aren't any secrets between us.'

Hamou's back prickled. He could feel Zina's one good eye fixed upon him – warningly? He weighed his words, not knowing how much Samira knew about Zina's activities and affiliations. 'All I wish for is the safety of your daughter. We live in dangerous times, and I would not want to see any harm come to her.'

Zina cut in now. 'Don't mince your words, Hamou Badi. My mother knows everything.'

'Everything?'

'Everything.' Zina was emphatic.

Samira Chadli smiled. 'My dear boy, you're not much of a policeman, are you? Certainly no detective!' She and Zina exchanged a conspiratorial glance, and both of them laughed.

'I found the melon peel and deduced its significance,' he said defensively.

'Well, that was careless of us,' Samira Chadli agreed. 'Maybe we underestimated you there.'

'How long have you been working with the Black Crescent, lalla?' he asked, uttering the forbidden words softly.

Samira chuckled. 'Oh, that is a recent development, my son. Have you heard of the Derb El Kebir massacre?'

He had heard about it, of course – they called it also the Slaughter of Casablanca. The French authorities, provoked by a great upswelling of Moroccan nationalism that manifested itself in widespread protest, had reacted with a violent crackdown that saw hundreds killed and imprisoned. April 1947. He was at college, wrestling with his studies, with a new language, with the pressure and unfamiliarity of examinations. He had not been paying proper attention to the world beyond.

'My husband, Zina's father, was killed during that atrocity. The French sent in the Senegalese, and they were butchers. I lost two of my brothers. It was a terrible time.'

Hamou was shocked, and not just for such loss: he had always believed Rachid Chadli to be Zina's father.

Samira took in his bemused expression. 'Nearly every woman I knew who lived in the Derb El Kebir then lost a husband, a son, a brother, a father. We got as many of the resistance fighters out as we could, hid them in our homes, smuggled them out wearing our robes, our veils.'

'I was only fifteen,' Zina said, remembering. 'I had no idea women could join the fight. I remember seeing a photograph in the newspaper of a woman resistance fighter in Palestine, holding a machine gun, and after that it was all I could think about. I had no idea, for years, what my mother was involved in: she kept her associations and actions secret from us – from me, and from Rachid. He's a peaceable man, Hamou, rather like you. He doesn't approve of direct action.'

Hamou looked down at his hands. 'If you'd witnessed what I saw last night, you might be less sure that what you call "direct action" is any sort of solution.'

The man roaring in the gutter, clutching his ruined leg.

The broken child.

The woman with the red hair...

He started to shake.

The two women exchanged a look. Then Samira Chadli rose heavily to her feet and put an arm around Hamou's shoulders.

This motherly gesture proved almost too much for Hamou, whose throat swelled with unspoken sorrow. He swallowed and blinked desperately, determined not to break down in tears in front of these two fierce women. *Be a man, Hamou Badi*, he told himself furiously. *The Free Men do not weep.*

Into the silence, Zina said, 'Yesterday evening I treated a two-year-old shot by the police.'

Hamou's head came up. 'What? Where?'

'In the new medina. When the police jeep was attacked, they started shooting into the crowd. A ten-year-old girl died, the toddler caught a bullet in his leg. Another three people died, just ordinary shoppers.'

The jeep attack. He had forgotten all about it, did not even know who among his colleagues had died or been wounded, had no idea there had been such indiscriminate retaliation. He could, though, imagine the panic that came from having a grenade thrown at you, death exploding out of nowhere, threat perceived everywhere. Did that also explain the Slaughter of Casa? The French lashing out in terror at losing control. He could feel that same terror in the city now, both sides poised to mete out violence.

'The child's parents tried to make a police report,' Zina went on. 'But they were waved away. Just collateral damage, wrong place, wrong time. When Moroccans die or children are injured, they don't care. We are nothing to them.'

'Even so,' Hamou said quietly, 'I cannot condone the use of bombs and grenades.'

'Then what's your answer, Hamou Badi? When our people are brutalised and the colonisers treat us like slaves in our own land, and take everything, including our sultan and our dignity, what should we do? Smile and bob our heads and thank them for the clinics and schools and roads and say, "*merci, Papa*"?'

'Now then, Zina,' her mother chided. 'Can't you see he's still in shock? Don't browbeat him. He has to make up his own mind, you can't do it for him. In my experience men take longer to make decisions than women do when it comes to the hard things.' She shrugged. 'Women are used to having to be ruthless.'

Zina was about to reply to this when there came a loud hammering at the front door downstairs. They all looked at one another, startled and alarmed.

'Go peer through the shutters,' Zina hissed to her mother. 'See who it is.'

Samira went to the window. Zina set aside the compress and turned to face Hamou. Seeing her wounds afresh made him blench. 'I'm so sorry,' he said, though for what, exactly, he could not say.

'It's a cop,' Samira reported. Her fists were balled, as if she was ready to fight.

'Just one man?' Hamou asked.

'Yes.'

'French or Moroccan?'

'He didn't look up.'

'Is he armed?' asked Zina.

'I couldn't see.'

Hamou thought fast. 'Was he wearing a kepi?'

'No.'

The hammering came again, accompanied by a shout.

'Stay in here and bolt the door,' Hamou told the two women. 'I'll go down. If I shout, arm yourselves with whatever you can find.' His gaze locked upon Zina, who looked pale but determined.

He ran down the stairs, threw open the big iron door, its hinges grating in protest. For a few seconds he did not recognise the man outside, then he saw the mobilette propped on its stand. It was Yacoob, the replacement for Ismail the Cockroach. He felt his shoulders drop. 'What do you want?'

It came out more abrupt than he'd intended: the young man looked angry.

'Hamou Badi? You're to report for duty immediately.'

'But my shift doesn't start till five—'

'We're on high alert. All free time is cancelled. You're on duty from now till your commanding officer tells you to stand down.'

Hamou thought about his wet jacket hanging on the line upstairs and sighed. 'Give me five minutes and I'll come with you.' And he had to let the air out of Zina's tyre too.

Yacoob gave him a nasty grin. 'I'm not a taxi service. Make your own way to the commissariat, and do it fast.' And he walked to the scooter, mounted it and puttered off down the road.

21

The atmosphere at the commissariat was at once frenzied and tense. People ran here and there, shouting over one another, getting in each other's way. Hamou forged a path through the mêlée to report for duty, only to find the throng that had converged on the roster room impossible to penetrate. Officers assigned their duties pushed out past him, looking grim and pale around the eyes; others seemed invigorated, keen for a fight.

He caught the eye of Driss Talbi, who waved him over. Redoubling his efforts, Hamou shoved a passage towards him.

'You're with me!' Driss shouted. 'Derb Omar!'

The area centred on the Place de la Victoire. Hamou knew it well: it was the heart of the Moroccan business area.

'What's happening there?'

Driss tapped his ear. 'Tell you outside.'

Hamou was ticked off the roster and he and Driss escaped the press of bodies and went as instructed to be equipped.

'Counterdemonstration got out of hand. Started at Mers Sultan, reasonably peaceful, then they marched up the Lorraine and spread out into Derb Omar, causing trouble, beating people up, and it's got a lot worse since then.' He stretched his neck with an audible crack. 'I wish they'd give us our guns,' he said savagely. 'It sounds like a bear pit out there.'

Hamou was glad it had not yet come to guns and said so. Driss regarded him with disbelief. 'What's the point of being trained as a firearms officer if you don't get to shoot the bloody things?'

'It's not just a gun you're shooting, though, is it?' Hamou reasoned, sliding his baton into place at his hip. It was not, he thought, likely to be much use against a mob, but even so. 'It's another human being.' Then he thought about the Frenchman who had thumped Zina in the eye that morning and wondered what he would have done if he'd been an armed witness to that assault. Probably best not to think about that.

'These rioters, they're animals,' Driss went on. 'Mind you, so are the fuckers who set that bomb off yesterday. The world's gone mad.'

It was hard to disagree with that sentiment, Hamou thought, as they neared the Place de la Victoire. Smoke hung over the quarter in a dark pall, rendering the heat of the day even more oppressive. At the junction with the square they came to a halt, backed up by the battalion of police already engaged there. The commanding officer, a frazzled-looking man with a clipped moustache, took one look at them and cried, 'Ah, reinforcements, thank the Lord!' He sent Driss and Hamou's contingent forward immediately. 'Your turn at the front!' he shouted. 'Give my chaps some respite.'

The forty or so new arrivals made their way through the crowd. Driss and Hamou made sure they stayed close together. They had just come within a rank or two of the forward line when something struck Driss full in the face. He swore loudly. Hamou did not even have to look to know what it was: the stink was unmistakable. Faeces. His nose wrinkled in disgust. And as if there could be any doubt as to the provenance of the projectile, a man screamed, 'Dog shit! That's all you are! Dog shit in the land of dog shit!'

Driss drew his baton and went for him, howling in red fury, straight into the crowd.

More missiles followed, one hitting Hamou's freshly laundered jacket square on the chest: not shit, at least, but the sweet corruption of rotting fruit. Then a stone, and another.

'Sons of whores! Sons of whores in the land of whores!'

The men they were facing were all European – dressed in shirts and slacks, brandishing the poles of tricolour flags like weapons.

'We'll burn it all to the ground!' someone jeered.

'It's all it's good for. Breeding ground for terrorists and monkeys!'

'Clear the city and start again!'

'Murdering bastards!'

Another hail of projectiles, nothing large or heavy – yet – but designed to infuriate.

A French officer beside Hamou shouted, 'Shut up and go home, you idiots! You're just making everything worse.'

'What good are you?' retorted a settler. 'You should be on our side!'

'I'm here to keep order, you maniac!'

That earned him a well-aimed orange that took off his kepi. The crowd cheered. Then a piece of rubble followed, and another. An officer a few feet away from Hamou fell to his knees, shouting in agony, and was hauled out of the firing line by two colleagues. A chunk of concrete whistled past Hamou's cheek and hit the man behind him.

'Shit, this is getting serious!' Driss said grimly.

A settler launched a flagpole like a javelin. '*Vive la France!*'

'Fuck this.' Driss charged at the *colons*, hammering his baton down at random, carving out a channel into which other officers poured. All around batons rose and fell, but the fighting became more intense as Moroccans attacked the baying settlers, launching sorties out of the smaller streets around the square, hurling stones and insults.

'Get out of our country!'

'Go back to France, where you belong!'

'Cowards: go back to the land of cowards!'

Soon it was impossible to tell who you were hitting – *colon* or colonised, European or Moroccan. Hamou found himself squeezed between uniformed figures, carried along on a tide. At one point, he felt both feet leave the ground. The situation felt dangerously out of control, and he found himself wondering whether, if they had been armed, they might have been able to exert greater influence over the mob, by threat rather than force. But seeing the wild joy of his fellow officers as they battered heads and backs at random, he knew deterrent would not be the end of it if lethal arms were involved.

Step by step, minute by minute, they drove the mob back. Smoke stung the eyes. Sirens wailed, fire engines screamed down the Boulevard de Marseille and forced their way through the square.

Officers with megaphones ordered the mob to disperse. 'Go back to your homes! Get off the streets! If you remain, you'll be arrested for riot!'

Hamou's baton-arm, jarred by each strike, ached to the bone. He glanced down at the baton. Whose blood had stained it? Frenchman or Moroccan? Shopkeeper or office worker? Baker or chauffeur? He felt ashamed to have drawn blood, anyone's blood. The ache in his arm was dwarfed by the ache in his heart. He was not a violent man, had not joined the force to mete out beatings and blows. He might be keeping the peace, but that very phrase seemed absurd in the midst of such brutality.

At last, there was breathing space. He found Driss in front of him, bare-headed, his kepi gone, grinning like a madman through a mask of dried blood. 'God, I enjoyed that!' he declared. 'I needed it: all that poison's been building up for months. Whoo!'

Again, Hamou thought of the man whose carbuncle Zina had lanced, the man who had hit her in the eye. The whole city was like that poisoned wound, he thought, resentment and hatred boiling up beneath the surface, swelling and infecting, waiting to burst and spray its putrefaction everywhere.

'You all right?' Driss asked at last, coming down off his high.

Hamou nodded. 'Think so.' He appeared miraculously unscathed, as if he'd floated disembodied throughout the entire encounter. He rubbed his face, sniffed. 'What's on fire, do you know?'

Driss shrugged. 'Half of Casa by the look of it.'

Hamou looked around. They had fetched up partway along the Strasbourg, in the hinterland behind the Place de la Victoire. With a sudden cold thud in his stomach, he realised that the smoke was emanating from the Rue Auvert.

'Oh no!'

He took off running, his feet slapping the ground. He could see flames leaping from a building fifty metres away and he knew – just knew – it was the family business. His fears were confirmed by the sight of Omar Belhaj, his robe covered in soot, at the front of a line throwing bucketfuls of water hopelessly into the blaze.

Hamou grabbed his arm. 'Moha?' he croaked.

Omar's eyes were red and wet. Hamou searched them desperately, but the big man shook his head. 'I don't know. He was here, but—'

Hamou bolted up the road, turned the corner, and emerged into the alley behind the warehouse. From here he could see that the building was ablaze. Orange flames shot skywards, climbing over one another as if in a race to the clouds. He found the back gate and tried to open it. It was latched from the inside. He rattled it hard, yelling his cousin's name. Shinning up the wall, Hamou got his arms over the top and surveyed the scene. The patchwork of tarpaulins that covered the yard was still largely intact, but the corner bordering the back of the storehouse was starting to char and smoke.

'Moha!' he yelled again, but there was no reply. Hamou ran his feet up the wall and boosted himself over, landing heavily on the other side, the baton at his belt dealing his left ankle a painful blow. He looked around. No sign of his cousin, just the usual clutter of piles of stock, crates, boxes, tins, truck tyres.

But if those cans got hot they would explode like grenades, and as for the tyres... The place would become an inferno in no time. Everything seemed to slow down. Hamou found himself thinking coolly and clearly. With more forethought than he had ever dreamed he possessed, he unbolted the back gate so he had a means of escape if things got bad, then grabbed a length of sacking, soaked it in the water butt, and swung it around himself up over his head and shoulders and the bottom half of his face, leaving just his eyes uncovered. Then he kicked in the door to the storehouse and hurled himself inside.

A great billow of smoke and superheated air engulfed him. Hamou's eyes streamed. He couldn't see a thing.

'Moha! Moha!' He roared it like a battle cry, but the fire was louder.

He waved his arms in front of him and the flames swirled like dancing djinns. The fire was at its worst towards the front of the building: already the partition wall was gone. The smoke was thick and black and acrid: he coughed and choked. He wouldn't have much time before the fumes got him. 'Moha!' he cried again, and heard a faint mewl of sound. He stumbled toward the noise, staring down at the ground, looking for the fallen body of his cousin. His foot hit something low and solid and for a moment he thought he had stood on Moha, but no, it was a sack of rice, white grains spilling out into the darkness. Beyond it, a pair of eyes showed green-gold, shining out of an impossibly small space. Not human eyes, those: a membrane shuttered briefly, and the sound came again, throaty and pathetic.

He bent and dragged the cat out by the scruff. It hung limp in his grasp, rendered kittenlike and compliant by fear. He remembered Moha feeding it sardines. Madani, that was its name. He opened his jacket and stuffed the animal inside, expecting it to fight and claw, but it squirmed down deep inside and settled itself under his arm. He could feel it there, pulsing like a second heart, fast and scared.

'Moha!' he rasped once more, but there was no force to his cry and now little hope left to him. An explosion cracked somewhere to his right. The fire had engulfed some bottles and shattered the glass so that the liquid contents hissed across the floor, then something else went off like a bomb. Cooking oil: he could smell it. In fear for his life, Hamou turned and stumbled towards the backyard, tripping over a chair – no Moha – a crate of oranges – no Moha – sacks of flour.

Back outside, he sucked in a deep breath and coughed long and loudly. Once more he called out his cousin's name, with no expectation of response. There was nothing more he could do here. He had to hope his cousin had got out and Omar Belhaj simply had not seen him amid the chaos. But surely this could not be true. Moha would never leave his family business to burn – he'd be out front, organising the chain of water carriers, yelling orders, trying to save whatever stock he could.

He let himself out of the gate just as the tarpaulin came swirling down across the yard like a malign cloud of fire. If he'd been caught under that...

Then he thought about the gate being bolted from the inside, and knew dully that Moha had not got out that way. Discarding the sacking that had surely saved him from the worst effects of the smoke, Hamou stood head down, hands on his knees, chest heaving, feeling a terrible sorrow well up inside him.

His cousin. His little cousin. Whom he had loathed and despised, resented and envied; then come to cherish and admire. Gone. Dead? It was unthinkable. Moha was too full of life, too savvy, too streetwise, to burn to death in an arson attack by belligerent *colons*.

A movement beneath his jacket: the cat changing position. Hamou pulled it out and surveyed it miserably. The last time he had seen it, Moha had been sharing his lunch with the creature. He had loved this unkempt, scrawny little animal. He set it down gently on the path. 'Off you go, Madani. You're safe now.' The cat regarded him with its unblinking, lambent gaze. When he walked away, it followed him. 'No, go on. You're a stray. You can look after yourself.'

The cat clearly disagreed. It miaowed, accusing him of abandonment. Hamou shooed it away. Madani coughed and shook his head as if to displace an annoying insect. Then he ran at Hamou and butted his blunt black head against his leg, demanding his attention.

'Oh hell.' Sighing, Hamou retrieved the animal, settling it back inside his jacket. 'Just for a while,' he told it. 'To make sure you're all right.'

Back on the Rue Auvert, the fire engine had at last arrived and firefighters were running around with hoses and a pump linked to a water bowser. Saving Moroccan businesses was clearly not a priority. Omar Belhaj was sitting on the steps of a building on the other side of the road, his head in his hands. Hamou crossed the street and sat down next to him. 'I couldn't find him.'

Omar's head came up. 'What? Who?'

'Moha. I couldn't find him.'

Omar looked appalled. 'You went in?'

Hamou nodded.

'I'm so sorry.' Omar rubbed a hand across his face. 'Alhamdulillah you're safe. Moha, he went to the Roches Noires, around two o'clock. I – I'm sorry, Hamou, I completely forgot. I was in shock – the *colons*, they beat me up, Hicham too, and set the fire. I hardly knew what I was saying when I saw you.'

Hamou regarded him steadily, but his heart was beating at twice the normal speed. 'You mean, he wasn't in the storehouse?'

Omar looked broken. 'He left me in charge and look at the place.' He gestured towards the gutted building. 'There were a dozen of them, French lads looking for trouble. They asked for Moha by name.' He looked at Hamou. 'That must mean he's on a list, mustn't it? He was a target.'

Hamou nodded grimly, remembering the papers he'd scanned all those weeks ago. Was there any connection? Moha and his father were well known in the community and the business was successful. 'Who knows?' He squeezed Omar's shoulder. 'You couldn't have stopped them.'

'I tried.' Omar was almost in tears.

'I'm sure you did. Where's Hicham?'

'Someone took him to the clinic – he tried to get some of the stock out and burned his hands. He'll be all right.'

'What a wretched mess. I have to report back – I'm still on duty.' Hamou started to fish Madani out of his jacket, thinking to hand the cat over to Omar as the next best thing to Moha, but the animal dug its claws into the fabric and held on tight.

Omar put his hands up and shuffled his bottom along the step. 'Sorry. I can't stand cats. Especially this one. It's a djinn – you've only got to look at it.'

Black, ruffled and affronted, eyes lit as if from within, Madani did look like a small, angry demon. Defeated by its will, Hamou stowed the animal away again. 'I'll hang on to it till Moha... If you see him or Hicham, let them know I was looking for them, will you? I'll try to visit Uncle Salim as soon as I'm off duty.'

Back in the Place de la Victoire, he found his team rounding up suspects and bundling them into vans.

'What happened to you?' Driss Talbi asked curiously, noting the smears of char on his face and hands.

'My cousin's place – the family business – up in flames,' Hamou said shortly.

Driss looked sympathetic. 'Shit. Sorry to hear that. Everyone OK?'

Hamou nodded. 'My cousin's at the clinic with some minor burns. At least I hope they're minor. They beat up the warehouse manager but he's not too bad.'

Driss made a face.

'They're trying to bring the fire under control, but I don't think there's much to save.'

'Officer Badi.'

He turned to find the captain with the clipped moustache behind him, and snapped a salute. 'Sir.'

'Your family business? Did I hear that correctly?' The officer jerked his chin towards the tower of smoke, which appeared to have thickened with the arrival of the firefighters.

'Yes, sir.'

'Sorry to hear that.' He looked at his watch. 'Why don't you knock off now? I'll sign you out till tomorrow morning. Back on duty at eight sharp, right?' He looked to Driss. 'You too, Officer Talbi: you did well under difficult circumstances.'

Driss and Hamou exchanged a glance as the officer walked away.

'Praise from the high-ups. Cherish the moment, Hamou. It may never happen again.'

Hamou took a bus to the Maarif and wearily climbed the stairs to his uncle and aunt's apartment. The building felt preternaturally cool and quiet after the heat and noise of the day's events and his footsteps echoed mournfully off the walls of the stairwell. His head was full of the awfulness of the day – first Zina Chadli's assault, then the baying mob, the arson attack on his family's business, thinking his cousin was dead. He craved his aunt's embrace and some tea and normality. He wanted to sit down with his family and be reassured that all would be well. He needed to see that Hicham was not badly injured, that his uncle was not too downhearted at the destruction of the storehouse, and to know that Moha was safe. But when he rapped on the apartment door he was met by a resounding silence. He knocked, and called, again and again. At last, a neighbour came puffing up the stairs, heaving shopping bags. A big woman, she huffed with the effort, and even after she had set the bags down, took several moments to catch her breath.

'They're gone, son.'

'Gone?'

'Packed up and left a couple of hours back.'

Hamou felt panic seize him. 'But where? Where did they go?'

The woman patted his cheek. 'Sorry, my boy, I have no idea. Somewhere away from this godforsaken city. Goodness knows, I'd leave too if I had anywhere else to go.'

She shuffled off down the corridor.

Hamou bent his forehead against the cool wood of the door and felt like weeping. Inside his jacket, the cat changed position as if reminding him of its presence.

'All right then,' he said eventually, feeling like an idiot for speaking aloud to a cat. 'Let's go home.'

22

There was no word from Moha, or any of his Casa family the next day, or the one after that. Hamou resigned himself to living with a companion he had never planned for or wanted.

For his part, Madani made himself very comfortable and soon started to boss Hamou around unmercifully, requesting food as soon as he returned exhausted from duty, demanding caresses and attention. And yet this routine calmed Hamou: he could feel his heart rate slowing. The two of them slept together on the roof terrace, Hamou wrapped in a cotton blanket, Madani pressed so close against him that he could smell the fish on his breath.

As the sparrows came to life, rather more warily now, so did Madani, and he seemed determined that Hamou should share the dawn with him. First, he would purr loudly in Hamou's ear, then he would nudge Hamou's head with his own. If Hamou continued to lie there with his eyes closed, pretending to be asleep, Madani would resort to more direct methods: tapping his cheek firmly with a velvet paw, and once, horrifyingly, attempting to open one of Hamou's eyelids with a cunning claw. *I know you're in there, you can't hide from me.* Loud miaows would drown out even the muezzin's call to prayer, and Hamou would rouse himself groggily and feed himself and the cat once more. He had even brought up a bucket of sand for its toilet; as he flushed the cat's waste down his own facilities, he would shake his head sadly. Reduced to slaving for a feral cat...

He made plans for releasing the animal back into the streets. Maybe in the tin-can city, where there were pickings to be had for a stray cat. But then he remembered all the wild dogs wandering there after dark and worried that he would be sending Madani to his death. And there was, he had to admit, a certain degree of comfort to be had from sharing his space with a cat. Apart from the shit and sardines, Madani was very little trouble. He slept in whatever pool of shadow he could find during the daytime and no matter what hour Hamou returned from work he would find the little cat sitting on the mat at the top of the stairs, feet together and head up, waiting to trot in at his heels as soon as he opened the door.

'I see you have a friend.' Zina stood over him now, silhouetted by the sun, a basket of washing balanced on the jut of one hip.

She put the laundry down and at once Madani jumped into it.

'Oh no you don't!' She snatched him up and put him back down on the ground, where he wove sinuously around her ankles. 'Well, you're a little charmer, aren't you? Been taking lessons from your master?'

'I'm not sure that's quite how I'd describe our relationship.' Hamou held out his fist and the cat bumped its head against it, purring furiously.

'Looks as if he's got you trained,' Zina said with a grin.

'Do you mind him being up here?' This was, after all, where the washing was put out, where rugs were spread out in the sun. 'He seems very clean,' he finished lamely.

Zina lifted a shoulder. 'Cats do as they like and come and go as they please. They have more freedom than us Moroccans.' She lifted her face to the sun and Hamou saw that the swelling around her eye had gone down, leaving the bruise a sallow yellow.

'Are you feeling better?'

'I heal quickly,' she said. 'Good job, it's been busy.'

Hamou imagined all the victims of beatings and baton charges, brawls and arson who must have passed through the hospital where she worked. 'I've never known anything like it,' he said after a long pause. 'It feels like the end of the world out there.'

Zina gave a short laugh. 'Why are men so melodramatic?' Then, seeing the expression on Hamou's face, she reached out and laid the flat of her hand on his cheek. 'Poor Hamou. How much further can they push you? Where's the line you will not cross?'

He captured her hand and held it there, and the cat, jealous, clambered over Hamou and inserted itself between them like a spoiled child. The tense moment dissipated. Zina kissed him lightly, as if it were a trifling gesture, but it made Hamou tingle from head to foot. 'I'd better go,' he said forlornly, not wanting to break the connection, and Zina rose and retrieved the laundry basket.

'We all have work to do, Hamou Badi.' Her mouth quirked as she regarded the cat, now lazily washing its face with one paw. 'Well, maybe not all of us.'

Walking to the commissariat, Hamou felt a sense of dread weighing upon him. If he'd had whiskers like Madani's, they would have been twitching.

Near the junction with the Mazagan pieces of paper lay scattered across the road and in the gutter, as if someone had dropped them in a hurry and fled. Out of curiosity, Hamou bent and retrieved one, turning it over to read the Arabic script. At the top of the page ran the rubric 'Al-Hilal', and beneath that the symbol of the Black Crescent.

Under this, the exhortation:

Rise up, people of Morocco!
The French are weak and in disorder.
Now is the time to strike.

Rise up and join us.
Fight for the independence of our country.
Let us defeat our oppressors once and for all!
Y'Allah!

Feeling guilty merely for reading the words, Hamou glanced around to be sure he hadn't been observed and saw a black Citroën gliding off the boulevard towards him. He folded the flyer swiftly, stowing it in his jacket pocket, then walked on, a man on a mission, keeping his gait casual, his eyes straight ahead. Even so, as the Citroën cruised by, he could see the men inside and knew them to be special forces, and his heart began to beat faster.

He didn't know what he had expected on arriving for duty, but it wasn't to be allotted a day in the office, processing paperwork and taking statements. His relief was so great he felt like laughing but managed simply to nod and make his way to the interview rooms. His relief was short-lived. Just half an hour into his shift he heard wailing and just knew it was coming his way. A moment later, Driss Talbi's head appeared around the door. 'Sorry, brother,' he said. 'I need you to take this one's statement. She'll only speak Tachelhit and I'm missing two words in three. So, I thought, who here speaks the lingo? And, well, here I am. She's all yours – oh, and her sister, too, though she's a bit less, how shall I say? Hysterical? I've got her son – I'll be down the corridor taking his statement, all right?'

And before Hamou could object or even ask what the hullabaloo was about, two black-robed women bustled in. The first was the one shrieking. She was small and round, with a pale face framed by a headscarf and the pulled-up corner of her haik. The kohl that had been painted around her small, dark eyes was smeared grotesquely down her cheeks and the silver bangles on her arms clattered as she waved her hands to punctuate her cries.

'*Tassanou! Tassanou!*'

Her liver? Why was she shouting about her liver?

'La bes, la bes, lalla. Calm down.' And then he remembered. Had it really been so long that he had heard people, particularly old women, cry that very word in Tiziane? He could hear his own grandmother calling it now, weeping over the death of her son, his father, dead in a car accident in the mountains. At the time he had hardly been able to take in the enormity of the event. The loss of a father, and he was so young, and his mother and grandmother so wrecked by it, that it was this inconsequential detail he recalled most clearly.

In their culture the liver was the seat of all emotions, all life and health, more important even than the heart. '*Waccha, lalla,*' he tried again. 'It's all right, speak to me, tell me your troubles, gently now, sit down, slow down, talk to me.'

Perhaps it was the sound of her own dialect spoken back to her, but at last she subsided into a chair and buried her head in her hands, sobbing. Her sister put a hand on her shoulder, then looked at Hamou. 'Give her a moment, son. She's had a terrible shock.'

But the next thing he knew, the old lady was pushing up the sleeves of the blouse she wore beneath the robe to expose her arms to him. '*Chauf!* Look! Look what they did to me! Imagine what they're doing to her right now, my sweet, my little one, my angel! Aieee! My baby girl, my little Jenane!'

Bracelets of bruises. Someone had grabbed her with real force. Hamou was shocked. 'Please, tell me what happened.' And when she started to shriek again, he looked pleadingly to her companion, who gave her sister a shake. 'Calm down, Hafsa, and tell him. How can he help us otherwise?'

Bit by bit, the story poured out. That morning in the old medina her son had been attacked by a group of European men – or *tarwa lhalouf* – sons of pigs.

'No, sister, you can't call them that, not in here! She means *iromaen*, sir, just settlers, you know?'

Hamou assured her she could use whatever words she wanted to him, but he wrote down 'Europeans'. 'Go on.'

A group of European men who appeared drunk, or just mad, had set fire to her son's taxi, which was parked just outside the family home, in the early hours of the morning. Her son had run out to stop them and they had poured petrol on him and tried to set him alight too, so she and her daughter and granddaughter, Jenane, had rushed out and tried to stop them. She had been wrestled to the ground and kicked and punched...

'I cannot show you or any other man those other bruises on my body,' she said, and he assured her it would not be necessary. Her son had been beaten around the head with a piece of wood, and the men had made off with his wife – the old woman's daughter-in-law – and with Jenane, who was only fourteen.

'And your daughter-in-law, what's her name?'

The older woman shook her hands at him. 'She will be fine, she's used to the ways of men. It's my little Jenane I worry about.'

Nice. 'Names, I need names, and where this happened,' Hamou tried again.

The second woman gave the family's name and address.

The old lady stabbed a finger at the form Hamou was trying to fill in. 'While you're doing all this writing, who knows what's happening to my angel? Raped! Murdered! Write that down!'

Hamou filed a report of battery on the man and his old mother, of destruction of property regarding the taxi, and of abduction. He tried for specific descriptions of the attackers, but the old lady sighed heavily. 'They all look the same to me.'

Hamou made his excuses and went down the corridor to check in with Driss, who was sitting across the table from a man with a turban of bandages. The taxi driver, Hamou surmised. Driss slipped outside and the two men compared notes.

'Nasty business,' Driss said.

'I couldn't get much in the way of useful description from his mother.'

'He says the ringleader had different-coloured eyes,' Driss said.

'How do you mean, "different-coloured"?'

'One blue, one brown. That means the father was a djinn.'

Hamou had never told Driss about being regarded as a zouhry, and made a mental note never to do so. 'Anything else?'

'One of them spoke Spanish, but the rest were French, and no older than twenty.'

It took some time to usher the witnesses out, with promises that they would do their best to find the abducted woman and girl and return them to their family. 'The sooner you go, the sooner we can get started,' Hamou told them.

He went to see his commanding officer, but Captain Latour could not have looked less interested if he'd tried. He barely cast an eye over the witness statements before sliding them back across the desk to Hamou. 'We don't have time for this sort of thing now.'

Hamou stared at him. 'But two women—' he corrected himself, 'a woman and a girl of fourteen, have been abducted. Anything might happen to them.'

'Let's not prejudge events, Officer Badi.'

'They burned the husband's taxi and beat him senseless, tried to burn him too.' Hamou could feel rage rising in him at the man's indifference, and suddenly, viscerally, he understood the grandmother's emotional outburst in the face of what must have seemed to her implacable bureaucracy.

'My job is to look at the bigger picture,' Latour said with a small, tight smile. 'Events like this are no more than hearsay and we will deal with them in due course. For now, there are more pressing matters, and I am sure the two ladies will make their way home in their own time. Now then,' he stood up, 'I'm transferring you to Fouquet's team. You're firearms trained, aren't you?'

The feeling of dread that had been hovering settled coldly over Hamou. He nodded.

'Go downstairs and get kitted out.'

Dismissed, Hamou seethed. That poor old woman, placing

her trust in him. In the system. And the system didn't give a damn for her, for her daughter-in-law, her little Jenane.

Downstairs, he found Saleh Zaoui and Driss Talbi as well as Ahmed Haddadi, a young Moroccan he'd trained with, and a group of French officers, all being allocated rifles and magazines of ammunition. He took his own weapon and a magazine and signed for them. Slinging the rifle over his back, he followed the others upstairs and out to the yard, where they piled by the dozen into waiting transport.

'What the hell's going on?' Driss asked once they were settled in the back of one of the vans.

It was Saleh who answered. 'I heard a mob from the medina joined forces with another from the Derb Sultan and they're marching on the European quarter.'

'They're flying the national flag from all the mosques in the old Bousbir,' Ahmed said. It was the first thing Hamou had heard him say outside their training class. Now he spoke with an air of quiet authority. 'The people have risen. They want revenge against the *colons*.'

One of the Frenchmen stared at him. 'Might I remind you it was your lot who planted the Mers Sultan bomb? Don't talk to me about revenge!'

Your lot.

'They're animals,' Saleh said. 'They disgust me.'

'I heard they've deployed the Senegalese *tirailleurs* and the Foreign Legion,' one of the Frenchmen said, with eyes bright with anticipation. 'I don't know why they need us as well. Those guys are *extreme*.'

'They've brought Duval in and put him charge,' another officer said gleefully. 'He'll sort those bastards right out.'

Hamou and Ahmed exchanged a glance. Even Hamou knew who General Raymond Duval was. They called him the Butcher of Algeria. He'd overseen a passage of brutal crackdowns over the border. The Istiqlal had made much of one particularly horrible event, and it had been the subject of one of the talks Hamou had attended with Moha years before. As he recalled, there had been a large but peaceful demonstration in the town of Setif, in North Algeria, the protestors carrying placards demanding an end to French rule and equality for their own people. A boy of fourteen had waved a forbidden Algerian flag, and on the orders of Duval, the French troops had opened fire with machine guns, mowing down the boy and hundreds – maybe thousands – of protestors. The numbers varied, but the story remained essentially the same: peaceful demonstrators gunned down without mercy. One shocking atrocity among many. It had happened a decade ago, but here was Duval again, drafted into Casablanca. The prospect of any peaceful resolution seemed vanishingly remote. Suddenly, the weight of the rifle on Hamou's back was unbearable. He felt sick, his mind drifting to the wording on the Al-Hilal pamphlet. *Now is the time.*

Now was the time. It felt like war.

He did not have the luxury of turning this disturbing thought over in his mind, for they were ordered to load their weapons, the van's brakes screeched and the back doors were thrown open and they all piled out into the oppressive heat.

They were in the northern quarter of the Maarif, but given the chaos they had descended into, Hamou could not precisely locate himself. He gazed at the buildings, tall and white and smart. When he looked up, everything seemed normal. There were pigeons gathered on the ledges and windowsills, gulls drifting on invisible air currents, white contrails searing through the blue. Further down, he saw washing draped on clotheslines – a little bit of Morocco penetrating the European glamour – and for a brief, lovely moment he was reminded that Zina had kissed him, quite unprompted, on the roof terrace that morning, and a little bubble of gladness rose in his chest. Then he spotted a figure on the terrace and was about to avert his eyes, for it was rude to stare at women going about their private business, when he realised it was not a woman at all, but a man wearing a kepi and army fatigues, setting up a sniping position. And now he had seen one, he could see them everywhere, snipers on the roofs and balconies, looking down the sights of rifles, weapons pointed towards the boulevard.

Now, there was no way for Hamou to perceive any normality in the scene. Wherever he looked, there was some new imposition on ordinary city life. Shops boarded up to protect the shining plate-glass windows and expensive stock; apartment windows closed and shuttered where ordinarily they would be thrown open to the sun. There were military jeeps and armoured cars where usually there would be bicycles and buses, donkey carts and taxis. And beyond the security forces – the police, the goums, the legionaries, the tall black tirailleurs – he saw a tide of people advancing.

Men in robes, men in shirts and trousers; women in djellabas, women in western dress. They walked slowly and purposefully, carrying placards bearing the face of the deposed sultan, waving the Moroccan flag with its interlaced green five-pointed star on a scarlet background. Five for the five pillars of Islam: faith, prayer, charity, fasting, and pilgrimage; red for the blood of the ancestors, for unity and strength; for nationalism, pride and identity.

Hamou shivered, remembering the boy in Setif, abruptly recalling his name now – Saal Bouzid – that was it. *Saal Bouzid.* The name tumbled in his mind as he went where he was instructed. 'Over there, to the front, reinforce the goums!'

The goumiers were Moroccan troops serving under French command. There they were in their khaki uniforms, lined up at the head of the security forces with their rifles trained on the advancing crowd of protesters. A deterrent, Hamou told himself. Just a deterrent, a loud message: *this far and no further.* It was somehow obscene, though, to see uniformed Moroccans pointing guns at their own people. He reminded himself that they were hardened fighters, that they had seen bitter action in the war in Europe, had then been deployed by the French to fight their dirty war in Indochina, and had lost much of their humanity as a result.

But what was his excuse? Here he was – Hamou Badi – a young man from a remote village in the Anti-Atlas Mountains – wearing the uniform of the regime, one he had been proud to don when he had graduated from the college and taken his oath to obey his superiors in all that pertained to his service, to use the force entrusted to him for the maintenance of order and the enforcement of the law. He had thought he was doing a good thing, a worthy thing, by joining up. He had thought that to be a policeman would mean helping people. He had never thought he would be forced to drop an investigation into a woman and child abducted by thugs, or to be ordered to face off an advancing crowd of people peacefully demonstrating for the return of their sultan and their freedom.

'Raise your weapons!' Fouquet ordered his men. 'Fire over their heads!'

Glad to be given this simple order, which offered threat but no direct violence, Hamou raised his weapon and nestled the stock against his shoulder as he had been trained, feeling the polished wood cool against his cheek. But even so, his hands shook, and his rifle barrel shook too. He slid a sideways glance at his comrades and noticed that his were not the only hands to be trembling. Settling the butt of the gun more firmly into his shoulder, he pressed the trigger and felt it kick back against him as he shot into the blue air.

The ragged thunderclap all around dazed him, made his eardrums hurt. A hundred pigeons exploded off their ledges with a clatter of wings, shining, shining against the sunlight.

'Again!'

The bolt ratcheted the round into place, and he fired again. The crowd halted, and Hamou's heart leapt with sudden optimism. Those warning shots had worked, then. Good. Perhaps violence could be averted after all.

The protestors were close enough that he could clearly see their faces. His eyes fixed on a man who looked just like his uncle Omar, only twenty or so years younger. He was angry, shouting, waving a picture of the sultan, shouting 'Youssef! Youssef!' A woman beside him in a robe and hijab was shouting too. Young men all around them, waving flags, punching the air with angry fists.

'Fire again!'

Again, they fired over the crowd. The volley was less staccato this time, as if they were becoming parts of a smoothly working machine.

A moment of deep silence followed. But that silence was broken by a solitary shot and, turning, Hamou saw Superintendent Fouquet with his pistol pointed directly at the crowd, his face dark with blood. And then he saw the man who looked like a young Uncle Omar crumple slowly to the ground, a dark wound staining the pale brown of his robe.

Had Fouquet just deliberately shot him? Hamou's heart galloped. This wasn't deterrent or maintaining order. It was murder, pure and simple.

For the second time that day he heard a woman wail in grief and watched as the woman in the hijab went to her knees beside her dying husband.

That was when the stone-throwing started – at first just a half-dozen, then a hail of them, and not just stones, but bottles, potatoes, bricks, oilcans. A car was pushed over, employed as a barricade: protestors flowed in behind it, using it as a shield. Hamou saw a young man, arm raised ready to throw his missile, fly suddenly backwards with a red hole through his face, and looked up to see the sniper who had shot him sighting his rifle for the next shot. A bottle came whizzing past Hamou's head, and he heard someone behind him cry out as it struck home. Another rain of projectiles and the goum in front of Hamou fell to his knees, leaving Hamou exposed, on the front line, staring right into the chaos. Fouquet, to his left, drew a bead on another protester and calmly shot him through the chest.

Hamou howled, an inchoate cry.

Fouquet flourished his pistol towards his own men. 'Shoot them! On General Duval's order: show no mercy!'

All around him, his fellow officers with varying degrees of willingness shouldered their weapons. He saw Saleh shoot into the crowd then calmly sight and shoot again; he saw Driss's eyes wide with shock, then squeezed closed as he pulled the trigger; Jamal with tears running down his face. More missiles came flying at them. Hamou lifted his rifle, then angled it higher and deliberately fired over the heads of the crowd into the empty air. He felt Fouquet's cold eyes upon him.

'Shoot *at* them, you fool! Or by God, Badi, I'll shoot you myself!'

Hamou raised his weapon again. He thought about Ahmed Choukri in the torture chamber of the commissariat, the blood and teeth on the floor, and the desire to turn the gun on Fouquet was suddenly red and urgent. His trigger finger itched to do it. But he could not. He had never intentionally harmed another living being in his life and he could not do it now. He could feel the superintendent's gaze on him, feel even at this distance the fury boiling off him. But he did not care. He would not kill at the order of this murderous man. He would not shoot his own people; he could not even shoot this monster.

A moment of intense clarity came over him. If he could no longer follow orders, what was the point of being a policeman any more?

Hamou dropped the rifle. Just threw it down. He took off his kepi and threw that down too. He was about to cast off his jacket when an immense blow hammered him in the chest, as if someone had taken a huge swing with a mallet to the top of his ribcage.

And Hamou fell.

23

'Is he dead?'
Fingers on his neck.
'Not quite.'
'He'll wish he was.'
'God save him.'
'God save us all.'

Hamou's eyelids opened a slit. The light was too bright: he closed them again. His chest felt as if a bus had driven over him. Where was he? It sounded like hell. Shouts, cries, moans, howls, prayers, curses, weeping. Had he died? The voice had said not. But how could you trust the voice of someone you could not see?

He forced his eyelids open, found himself staring up into a merciless light. A face loomed over him. He tried to shrink away from its scrutiny, but the only hiding place was within his own head. He jammed his eyes shut again.

'Hey! Come on.' Someone gave him a shake – not gentle, but not rough, either.

'What's your name?' Another voice.

'Is he unconscious again? We should try to keep him awake.'

A poke in the side. 'Wake up!'

Hamou felt angry. Couldn't they just leave him alone? He wanted to sleep, even if it meant not waking up again. He took a breath, and it was like being knifed.

'Ahhhh!'

'He spoke! Alhamdulillah!'

Hands held him upright and he felt as if his ribs might crack apart. But then he was sitting, and the pain was somehow abated. He half opened his eyes. This time the light was less stark. He looked down. Were those his hands? He was handcuffed. Why was he handcuffed? He tried to make his brain function, but it refused him. Better to sleep than to know. Knowing felt like an irretrievable step – once taken there was no way back.

The shrieking again. He'd heard that somewhere before. And the smell…

Hamou's eyes came fully open. His memory knew where he was before the rest of him did.

And there was the corroborating evidence: the bars, the stained floor, and now more of the smells broke through the walls he had thrown up to prevent the knowledge: blood, piss, faeces; tabac jaune.

He retched.

'Bucket!'

Someone thrust a foul-smelling pail under his face, and if he hadn't actually needed to vomit before, now he had no choice.

Sweating and trembling, his chest burning, Hamou sat there with tears leaking out of the corners of his eyes. He was in the cells deep within the commissariat. The antechamber to hell. He groaned.

'It's OK, man. You'll feel like shit for a while, but it's better to get it out.'

The disgusting bucket was taken away, one thing to be grateful for. Gingerly, Hamou touched his ribs, winced. Had he been run over? But then he would have been in hospital, being treated by nurses, like Zina, not… here.

Shooting: he remembered shooting. The image of the man who looked like Uncle Omar. Emile Fouquet, his pistol aimed… at him.

Panicking now, he looked down, expecting to see a flood of

red across his chest, but there was just white shirt, grubby, but not bloodstained. It smelled, weirdly, scorched, sulphurous. His fingers fumbled ineffectively at the buttons.

'Hey! Calm yourself, brother. Are you hurt? Let me.'

The fabric parted and fingers touched his ribs. Hamou sucked in his breath and tried not to shout out his pain.

'Well, would you look at that?'

'What?'

'Look. Isn't that incredible?'

'Bismillah. It's almost a perfect square!'

None of this made sense. Hamou waved his hands at the spectators to make some space for himself. Tucking his chin in tight, he looked down. Just to the left of his breastbone was a black bruise, as square as could be, the corners just slightly flared. He frowned, bemused. And then he thought about his grandfather's amulet, kept carelessly in his breast pocket. It must have taken the force of Fouquet's bullet. That was insane, impossible.

'Hey, look!' one of the voices said. 'Look at his hand.'

'What?'

'The line, there on his palm.'

Someone took hold of his hands and held the palms out flat so that they could all see. Hamou found he didn't have the strength to pull it away.

'Zouhry,' someone said reverently.

'What's that?'

'Don't you know anything?'

'Of course he doesn't know anything, he was born in this shithole of a city.'

'He's the embodiment of luck, the luck of the djinns. You can tell a zouhry by the straight lines across their hands, by a light in their eyes, and some have little horns on their heads. They can detect treasure and divine water. All the things of the world are easy and open to a zouhry.'

'Apart from this cell!' someone said, and they all laughed.

'It's just a legend.'

'No wonder he's still alive – the djinns keep an eye on him!'

'Was it a piece of djinn treasure that saved him?'

'I reckon so. Hey, zouhry, what's your name? Tell us your story.'

Hamou hesitated. How could he tell these people anything? They were criminals: he was police. Did that distinction still hold true after what had happened? He thought that being in this place meant it did not. But that did not necessarily put them on the same side.

He began to fear everything now – the cell, the light, the noises down the corridor, the people causing the noises down the corridor, the men in the cell here beside him. He should have died, he thought. Just not woken up: it would have been simpler. All his grandfather's stupid amulet had done was to preserve him for worse, far worse, to come.

He looked around. The others were not handcuffed. Why was he the only one to be restrained? He tried to pull the cuffs from his wrists. Someone tried to stop him.

'Calm yourself, brother. They'll remove them, I expect, when they come back.'

Hamou did not want 'them' to come back, to identify and crow over him. And he certainly did not look forward to whatever came after that.

'What's your name?' he asked the man who had probed his wound, turning the question around on him.

'Tareq Slaoui.'

With a name like that, he was from just up the coast, from the old city of Salé.

'And what do you do, Tareq Slaoui?'

'Fish-packer, up at the port.'

'And you?' Hamou asked a man with a lazy eye.

'Mahmoud. I work in a factory near the Roches Noires.'

'What are you in here for, Tareq?'

'Protesting, that's all. Just marching to make my voice heard.

They arrested me for being proud of my country. Didn't even throw a stone, let alone a punch.'

'Me too,' said Mahmoud. 'I didn't throw any stones.' He paused for a moment. 'Threw some donkey turds, though.' He grinned, showing gapped teeth.

'How about you?' Hamou turned his attention to a man with a close-cropped black beard, sitting quietly on a bench at the back of the cell.

'I don't know anything about you,' the man said, regarding Hamou narrowly. 'How do I know you're not some cockroach? Dropped in amongst us to pick up the shit?' He stood up and towered over Hamou, looking down.

'What, you think they knocked him unconscious and threw him in?' Tareq scoffed. Having given details about himself, he was invested in not being proved a fool.

'They're clever, the French, I'll say that much for them.'

'He's not French, though, is he? He's one of us.'

'Is he, though? He's not saying much about himself, are you, zouhry? What's *your* name and where are you from?'

Hamou looked him in the eye. 'My name is Hamou Badi and I come from Tiziane.'

'He does have a Soussi accent,' Tareq said.

They had to concede this.

'What are you doing such a long way from home?' the nameless man asked.

'Working, to keep my family at home fed and clothed.'

They nodded to this. A lot of them were doing the same.

'What's your job, then? What is it you do, all this way from the mountains?'

It would be easy to lie smoothly, to tell them he was a carpenter, or a baker, or a bicycle-mender, but he did not want to hide behind falsehoods any longer. 'I'm a policeman,' he said softly.

'You see?' The bearded man was triumphant. 'I knew it. A spy, a chkam, sent in amongst us to get information. Well, you've failed! We aren't talking.' He turned to the rest of them, assuming a leadership role. 'Keep your mouths buttoned, lads, right?' He looked back at Hamou. 'As for you, you should be ashamed of yourself.'

'I am.' Hamou paused. 'At least, I was.'

There it was, he was alone again, stranded in that no-man's land between the rock of the French regime and the hard place inhabited by his own people. But he was also a stone in the grinding quern, grit in the cogs of the machine. He lifted his chin.

'After my father died, I came to Casa to work and get an education. I went to college, I did well. When they offered me a choice between the civil service and the police service, I thought I could do more good by joining the police, to even things up a bit, offer a different perspective, some understanding and support to my own.'

The bearded man started to object, but someone quieted him.

'When I was a boy,' Hamou went on, 'I found a body. A body, stuffed into a oued, a Moroccan woman bundled into the side of a dry riverbed like a bit of old rubbish. And no one seemed that bothered about it. No one in the administration, anyway. They said she was a prostitute, with no family or anything. As if that meant she didn't matter. Even at the age of eleven, I knew that was wrong. Our local mokhaznis were useless, and the French didn't care – they just buried her in the village cemetery, and because there wasn't any family to tend to the grave, to pile stones and thorns on it to keep the wild animals away, the jackals dug her up and desecrated the corpse. And that really upset me, it seemed such a terrible thing. So when I had the chance, I became a policeman so that I could do better for my people.'

He took a deep breath – they were all listening, and he remembered the other thing they said about zouhrys: that they also had the gift of storytelling.

'But when it came down to it, all I could do was small things. The weight of the establishment was against me, the system, the bureaucracy. Every day I saw something that broke my spirit a little more. And then my mother sent me my grandfather's amulet, a reminder of my heritage, of who I was. And you know what? I nearly put it in a drawer. Ugly old thing, I wouldn't wear it, but then I thought about the care my old mother had taken to have it repaired and filled with protections by the fkih, and then sent all the way from Tiziane to Casa on the bus, and I put it in my uniform pocket.' He watched understanding dawning on the faces of his cellmates and paused to let it sink in. 'I was policing the demonstration in the Maarif with the rest of my unit when we were ordered to fire on the crowd. I watched my commanding officer shoot down a man in cold blood, an unarmed protestor, and I knew I couldn't do it. I threw down my rifle and my kepi and he turned that pistol on me.'

Hamou touched his fingers to the bruise on his chest and a small flame ignited beneath it, deeper and darker than the pain that the bullet had inflicted on him. Yes, he had refused to follow orders to fire on unarmed people. That was not a shameful thing. He had done something good. He felt the heat of this thought flow through him like molten silver, as if he had absorbed the amulet and his body had subjected it to a form of alchemy. Shame and fear transmuted to a sort of – if not pride, then a searing, liquid sense of honour and solidarity.

'Yes, it saved my life, that amulet. That bit of old Tuareg silver from out of the desert. There must be a reason for that, mustn't there?'

'It is written,' someone said reverentially. 'Allah's word is fate.'

'I still don't trust him,' the nameless man said.

'Does it matter? We're all going to die. Only difference is whether it's easy or hard,' said Tareq.

As if to punctuate this pronouncement, a terrible cry echoed down the corridor and then ended abruptly. An eerie silence followed, then a door clanged, and footsteps sounded on the concrete, coming their way. Hamou felt the hairs rise all down his spine.

A uniformed man appeared outside the cell. He peered through the bars, and his gaze settled on Hamou. 'I see you're awake, Officer Badi. Superintendent Fouquet will be delighted.'

Hamou could only half-recognise the man whose face was shadowed beneath the brim of his kepi. It was the malicious amusement of his tone that made him recall the custody officer who'd been on duty the day he'd brought the file of documents down here for the superintendent, the one who'd unlocked the gate for him with a smile, knowing exactly what he would see beyond.

'I have a message for Fouquet,' Hamou said.

'Oh, do tell. I'll be happy to pass it along.'

Hamou said something, but so quietly that the man could not catch the words and had to step a little closer.

'This,' Hamou said, and shot a gobbet of sputum through the bars, where it landed on the officer's fastidiously pressed uniform trousers.

The men in the cell laughed uproariously. 'Good on you, Hamou Badi!'

'This will be added to your account, you son of a whore!' the officer swore. 'I'll make damn sure of it.'

'That showed him,' Mahmoud said, as the custody officer stamped off down the corridor.

Hamou shook his head. It had been a petty gesture, the small defiance of a petulant toddler.

Payment was not to be exacted immediately, though, it appeared. A tray of food turned up some hours later: stale round loaves and a pot of soup in which grey vegetables and pale twists of unidentifiable gristle floated, and the prisoners fell upon it, dipping hunks of bread into the pot to scoop up the sustenance, no matter how horrible it was. It was only when the soup was half gone that someone remembered Hamou.

'Hey, give the zouhry some help – he's still handcuffed!'

JANE JOHNSON

And so his fellow detainees fed Hamou, picking the more palatable morsels out of the pool of greasy soup for him, until the pot was empty.

It was almost noon on the next day when they came for him.

24

Two uniformed men took Hamou down the corridor and into a small, brightly lit room. As soon as he entered it, he knew it was the place where he had seen Ahmed Choukri. Of course it was. That was just the sort of thing they would do. He knew how intimidation tactics worked. He'd been taught about them, he'd seen them used by his colleagues, albeit in smaller, less horrifying ways.

He did not recognise the men in whose custody he found himself, and perhaps that was deliberate, too. Down here, he was not Hamou Badi, officer of the Sûreté, but just another prisoner, without status; alone and insignificant.

They removed his handcuffs, and he flexed his fingers and rubbed at his chafed wrists, but that relief was fleeting, for a moment later his shirt and trousers were forcibly stripped from him, and he was bound, forearms and ankles, to a chair whose feet had been riveted into the concrete floor.

It was hot in the cell, but Hamou shivered, exposed and vulnerable, his dignity taken with his clothes. He bowed his head, looked down at his thighs, which were a paler brown than his arms and sparsely haired, the muscles rigid with the urge to fight or run. His legs wanted to help him but they, like the rest of him, were helpless to do anything at all.

The smell stung his nostrils. Disinfectant, the cheap sort, without any perfume to disguise its nature, and beneath that all the essentials of a man: urine, shit, blood, and a sharp, meaty smell he could not quite identify, until he realised it was his own sweat, made rank by fear, as if every vile particle within him had risen to the surface to poison the air.

'Comfortable?' one officer asked, sarcastically, in darija.

Moroccan, like himself. Not French: ah no, the French did not like to get their hands dirty. Hamou raised his head. '*Hashouma!* Have you no shame, treating your own people like beasts in an abattoir?'

The man replied with a casual, open-handed slap that knocked Hamou's head sideways. His eyes stung with tears. He did not remember the last time anyone had struck him so. Even the confrontation in the hammam – when he had been similarly unclothed – had not been much more than a tussle. He recalled, though, the reason for the attack: Ahmed Choukri's anger at the brutal treatment of his brother, here, in these very cells where later he was to lose his own life, and Hamou's defiance seeped away, as if he were a holed-bucket.

'It is not me who should be ashamed, son of a pig!' the officer snarled.

He took off his kepi and his jacket and rolled up his sleeves, and Hamou realised with sudden, horrible understanding that he was one of the goons who had extracted Ahmed Choukri's teeth and nails and left them strewn across the bloodied floor. Abruptly, his jaw and hands shot through with sympathetic aches, anticipating the treatment to come. It was all he could do not to beg for mercy before they had even touched him. What a useless terrorist he would make: he would be ready to blurt out every scrap of knowledge he had at the first intimation of torture. Then he thought about Zina, and what he knew about her and her mother and their work for the Black Crescent, and his sweat pooled and stank.

'We'll make a start, shall we, Jalil?'

'Shouldn't we wait for Fouquet?' the second man said doubtfully.

'The superintendent appreciates those who take the initiative, men who show a bit of enterprise.' He gave Hamou a nasty grin. 'Hook up the electric box,' he told the second man, without taking his eyes off the prisoner. 'We'll soften him up a bit for Fouquet.'

The other man, knees bent under the weight, hefted a big wooden box to the table and opened it. It was full of switches and dials and snaking thick black rubber cables ending in jaw-like clips.

Hamou dragged at his bonds. He knew it was useless, but he couldn't help the reflex. 'What the hell do you think I can tell you that you don't already know?'

The first man leaned in closer. 'How about telling us who got you into the Sûreté in the first place? How did they infiltrate you into the ranks? Who do you report to?'

Hamou stared at him. 'Captain Latour.'

Another slap, the other cheek, whipping his head to the right. 'Don't be facetious with me, nationalist pig!'

'I— What?'

'I'll take over from here, Abid,' a voice said smoothly.

The man stepped aside, and there was Emile Fouquet behind him, applying a flame to the tip of a cigarette in an elegant silver holder. With an utterance of satisfaction, he breathed a wisp of cool smoke out into the air and smiled fondly at Hamou. 'Officer Badi. I can't tell you how it pains my heart to see you here, in this place, in the hands of these...' he swept his hand to indicate Abid and Jalil, 'gentlemen. This is not where you belong. A talented young officer, promoted through his own good efforts. An officer for whom I had high hopes. I'm sure there must be some misunderstanding that has landed you in this unfortunate predicament.' He leaned in and Hamou caught a whiff of the sandalwood aftershave the man habitually wore. It made him gag. Emile Fouquet raised an eyebrow. 'Are you unwell?'

Hamou shook his head, though the bruise on his chest,

marking where the man had shot him, burned as if in response to the presence of his would-be murderer.

'You had a remarkable escape,' Fouquet went on, as if the shooting had nothing to do with him. 'Really, quite miraculous. I think the good Lord must have saved you so that you could tell us what you know.'

'What I know about what?'

'I fear that you have nationalist sympathies, Officer Badi.'

Hamou stared at him. 'You tried to kill me.'

The superintendent's expression hardened. 'Don't take that tone with me, young man. Your... well-being lies in my hands. I could take all your troubles away, promote you beyond any concerns about divided loyalties. Moroccans with a good heart and mind do well in our organisation. We make sure they are well rewarded for their service to us. A young officer with your potential might well one day afford an apartment in the Maarif, maybe even a villa out on the coast. So, if you were to divest yourself of the troubling information I feel sure you are tormented by, we would, shall I say, be grateful. On the other hand...' He took a long drag on the cigarette so that its end glowed vermilion and tiny luminous flecks spun off into the air. Hamou's eyes tracked them obsessively. 'If you choose not to cooperate, well, that would be unfortunate. Which is it to be, Officer Badi?'

'I have nothing to tell you.'

'Do you know the creature I most dislike in this world?' the superintendent said at last, so conversationally that Hamou had to strain to hear the words. 'Snakes. I really have quite the antipathy to the things. Not a fear, mind you.' He wagged a finger at Hamou. 'No, never a fear, but a visceral dislike. A loathing of the way they slither, their slippery sideways movement. The serpent, on its belly, in the dirt, intent on doing harm. Cursed above every beast of the field, made to eat dust all the days of its life.'

He sent a wisp of smoke wreathing and coiling through the

air to gather around Hamou's head, filling his nostrils with the hateful aroma.

'Is that you, Hamou Badi? Have you been sneaking through the grass, looking for damage to do? Spreading poison in the shadows. Snakes do not have the courage of the assassin or the bomber, or even the stone-throwing protestor. No, they work by insinuation. By creeping around, pretending to be one thing when they're something else entirely. Maybe even wearing the uniform we have bestowed on them, with blackness in their hearts. All the advantages we have given them, all the education, the training, the elevation above the common peasants they were born to be – cast away, thrown back in our faces. We try to raise such folk up and make them into something more than the common clay they came from, and they repay us with betrayal and disloyalty. Does that description fit?'

Hamou firmed his jaw. 'You ordered me to fire upon unarmed people.'

'You think guns are the only weapons in this world?' Fouquet waved this nonsense away with his free hand. 'I trusted you, Officer Badi. I trusted you so far as to send you to my own home, where you made my daughters uncomfortable with your lascivious staring and lewd suggestions—'

'I... I... didn't!' Even in his position of perilous vulnerability, Hamou was outraged. 'If they said I did, they're lying.'

The next thing he was aware of was a hiss and a sudden stench of burning, an acrid-sweet scorch. Then the pain came, like a red shout. He tried to raise his hands to his face to protect himself, and of course was unable to. Fouquet looked at the end of his cigarette with dismay as if it had disappointed him. Then he removed it from the silver holder and dropped it to the floor, ground it out underfoot.

'A waste.' He shook his head sadly. 'You see what you made me do? I do not like to see things go to waste – a fine French-made cigarette or a man who could have made something of himself.' He shrugged. 'It seems to be the trajectory of the modern world. We create great things, beautiful things: a shining white city where before there was nothing but the ordure of animals, a civilisation where before there were uneducated tribesmen. We brought order to a disorganised country which was rife with corruption and violence, where people died of disease like flies. And what gratitude do we receive? What thanks do you give us for the clean new schools and hospitals, for the networks of roads and railway lines? For the sanitation, the gleaming boulevards, the chance of an elegant, civilised life of the European rather than the bestial existence of an African?' He dug in his pocket and brought out a piece of paper, unfolded it, then threw it into Hamou's face. 'This! This monstrous provocation!'

The page slid down Hamou's chest and came to rest on his bare thighs. Even though it was upside down, even though his eyes were watering from the pain of the burn on his cheekbone, he saw the symbol of the Black Crescent and recognised it to be the political flyer he had picked up out of the gutter in the Derb Ghrallef the previous morning.

'It's nothing,' he said dully. 'Just a thing I picked up off the road.'

Fouquet's blue eyes were shards of broken glass, and contempt curled his lip. 'There is also this.'

On the palm of his hand, held close enough for Hamou to see it clearly, sat a small white tablet. For a moment he frowned, perplexed. An aspirin? Why was the superintendent showing him a headache pill? Then he remembered, and his guts turned to ice. It was Zina Chadli's suicide pill, the one she had been given by the resistance, by someone in Al-Hilal, to be taken if she were ever captured by the authorities, rather than give up her contacts to the police, as Mohammed Zerqtouni, the carpenter who had blown up the Central Market, had done. The cyanide tablet he had wrestled away from her in the bidonville, picked up off the ground and pocketed to keep it away from her. He stared at it now and wished that he could crane his neck just a little further, far enough to be able to flick out a tongue as long as a snake's and scoop it into his mouth, swallow it down and welcome the brief agony and then the permanent oblivion it would bring.

Fouquet's fingers closed over the tablet. 'So, you see, we have you. What we do not have is your network. You will give me names. The man who recruited you. The one who gave you the propaganda and the man who gave you the cyanide. If they are all three the same, you will give me other names: the rest of your organisation. The ones who make the plans, those who source the weapons and the bomb-making equipment, those who carry out the acts. If you give me the names, now, without delay, without putting me to the trouble of having to… encourage you, I will make sure you are dealt with leniently. That is, that you are not executed. Do you understand me, Hamou Badi?'

Hamou's tongue felt as if it was coated with sawdust. His mouth moved, but no sound emerged. He closed his eyes, prayed for guidance, for courage.

Zouhry.

The memory of the other prisoners uttering the word in awe returned to taunt him. But he was no zouhry. There was nothing lucky about him. He wondered just how much pain he could withstand before he blurted out any names. Could he be strong enough to protect Zina, or would he cave in immediately, whimpering like a kicked dog?

I will find out something about myself now. It was not a comforting thought.

He opened his eyes and fixed them on Fouquet. 'I am not a nationalist and I have never worked for any organisation other than the Sûreté. I'm not a member of any dissident group, I've had nothing to do with attacks on the regime. Whatever you do to me will not get any information out of me, because I do not have any information to give you.'

Emile Fouquet gave an exaggerated sigh. 'How very disappointing. I had thought you more intelligent.' He beckoned to his colleagues. 'Abid, be careful where you place the electrodes, try to keep the visible marks to a minimum. Family, you know.

Although, I gather your family has fled the city. That's curious timing, isn't it, Officer Badi?' His gaze flicked over the burn he had inflicted. 'Perhaps a couple of carefully placed blows to the face, the sort he might acquire resisting arrest? You understand?'

Abid nodded.

Footsteps approached, and then the custody officer appeared. He saluted the superintendent. 'Sir—'

Fouquet stopped him with a hand. 'Of course, I promised Officer Penaud some recompense for his trousers being soiled by this creature. I'm sure you'll think of something, Abid.'

'Yes, sir. My pleasure.'

'Sir.' Penaud looked pinched and pained.

'You have a suggestion?'

'Ah... no, sir, not that. Message from the divisional commissioner.'

Fouquet looked displeased. 'Well, you'd better deliver it, then.'

'Not here, sir. Not in front—' He tilted his chin towards Hamou.

'As if that mattered.'

'It is... ah... relevant. Sir.'

Fouquet looked back to the torturers. 'Keep an eye on the prisoner. I'll be back.'

He was back, twenty minutes later. Hamou could detect the anger in his walk: his footsteps were loud and fast, his heel strikes echoing off the walls of the corridor.

'The prisoner is to be transferred. Penaud has the paperwork. You are to discharge him into Penaud's custody, and his alone, hear me?'

The goons nodded.

'Dress him and put those things back on him.' Fouquet pointed to the discarded handcuffs. 'Leg irons, too. I'm taking no chances. You have leg irons, and a key?'

Abid nodded. 'Yes, sir. One minute.' He scuttled past Fouquet off down the corridor.

'Don't get your hopes up, Badi.' The superintendent glared at

Hamou, rage boiling off him. 'You'll get what's coming to you. This is just a delay, not a reprieve. It'll give you more time to consider your situation. Maybe come to the right decision and tell us what we need to know, then I might be prevailed upon to plead your case with the commissioner, see if we can come to a mutually beneficial arrangement.'

Hamou narrowed his eyes. This man had shot him in the chest and burned his face with a cigarette. 'There's nothing you can offer me, Superintendent Fouquet. Not a single damn thing.'

25

The Ghbila. They didn't call it the 'Little Jungle' for nothing. Once the police car had passed beneath the great carved arch over which the words 'Prison Civile' were inscribed and Penaud handed him over to a pair of uniformed guards, Hamou found himself surrounded by a swelter of noise and bodies.

Handcuffed, and with his ankles linked by chained leg-irons, he clanked beside his captors down corridors lined with cells whose prisoners reached through the bars, catcalled, whistled, shouted. The stench was unbearable.

'Where are we taking him?' one guard shouted across Hamou to his colleague.

'The warden wants to assess him. He'll decide where he's to be incarcerated.'

'The warden himself, eh? He doesn't look important enough to be taking up the great man's time.'

They laughed. It was as if, Hamou thought, he wasn't there, as if they were accompanying an animal, rather than an individual human being with ears and feelings.

They emerged from the first prison block into a high-walled yard floored with scuffed sand. Barbed wire topped the walls: only a gecko could skitter up them to freedom. Through another arch and into an administrative block, quiet corridors of closed doors, astonishingly white and pristine after the little hell they had left behind. At the end of this was a large wooden door, ornately decorated like the entrance to a palace. A uniformed man stood to either side, rifle butts resting on the ground. When they saw the guards approaching with their charge they came suddenly to life, as if someone had switched them on.

'Papers?'

One of Hamou's captors handed over a sheaf of documents. The guard took the file and passed through the door. His colleague looked straight ahead, making no acknowledgement of the presence of the other three men. A housefly buzzed around, then landed on the man's cheek. He swatted it away and it fell to his feet, where with a vicious stamp he ground it into the dirt. Within seconds, a pair of ants converged upon the fallen fly and began to push at its body, making little headway given the disparity of their sizes. They were soon joined by one more, then another, then out of nowhere a small column of them, and at last they made progress, marching towards their hidden colony with the corpse borne aloft. Hamou watched, fascinated. Such efficiency, such teamwork: it was impressive.

The first guard returned. He thrust three sheets of paper at one of Hamou's guards and saluted. 'You can leave him with us now.' The papers had been signed and covered in many coloured rubber stamp marks.

This was what he was now, Hamou thought. A piece of administration, a number in a logbook, a statistic in a file. He followed the guard beyond the wooden door. They crossed a small paradise garden laid out in traditional quarters, a fountain in the centre, rills leading outward. Jasmine and roses, hibiscus and bougainvillea. Citrus trees provided shade around the edges, benches set between them. It was so beautiful, so unexpected, that Hamou felt his eyes sting.

On the other side of the courtyard, the guard rapped on a door carved with geometric stars, and a voice replied, '*Entrez!*'

Hamou found himself standing in a handsome room set with European furniture and expensive rugs. Books lined the walls.

Behind a large wooden desk covered with piles of paper, inkpads and a carousel of rubber stamps, a man sat, holding a telephone to one ear. '*Oui*,' he said. '*Bien sûr. Absolument.* I quite agree. *A bientôt*, Colonel.'

Colonel? The back of Hamou's neck prickled. But it probably had nothing to do with him. He and the guard waited as the warden ended the call. The man stood and regarded Hamou with an unreadable expression. 'Remove his restraints, then wait outside,' he told the guard. 'You may sit in the garden.'

The warden watched impassively as the man unlocked Hamou's cuffs and shackles and took them away, and when the door closed, crossed to a window as if checking on the guard's whereabouts. Then he returned to his desk and sat down, ran his eyes over the paperwork, and after what seemed many minutes, looked up at Hamou. 'Sit down, please.' He indicated an armchair upholstered in pale yellow velvet.

Hamou lowered himself gingerly onto the edge of the seat, afraid to mark the fabric.

'I am told that you are a member of the Sûreté, Monsieur Badi.'

Hamou confirmed this.

'Can you tell me why you were arrested?'

Hamou frowned. 'I'm not aware that I was arrested. I was… knocked unconscious, and when I came to, I was in a cell in the commissariat central.'

'Tell me what you were doing immediately before falling unconscious.' The man linked his fingers and stared at Hamou. He had brown eyes, an egg-like face, and a neatly trimmed moustache. His skin was smooth and unwrinkled, and his hair was slicked back. Hamou could not tell his age: he could have been anything between forty and sixty. He found it hard to know with Europeans – life did not mark them as distinctly as it did his own people.

'I was policing the protest in the Maarif, sir.'

'And?'

If he told the man the whole story, would he be quietly done away with as an embarrassment to the regime? Shot for disobeying orders? Hamou hesitated.

'What happened to your face?'

The man was peering intently at the burn on his face. What to say? That a protester's stone had struck him? But the wound was still raw and unscabbed. He looked down at his hands.

'Tell me the entire truth, Officer Badi. I need to know exactly what I'm dealing with.'

Hamou looked up unhappily. 'My commanding officer shot me for not firing on the crowd,' he said quietly. 'That's how I lost consciousness – it must have knocked me off my feet and I hit my head.'

'You don't know?'

'I don't have any recollection beyond the sensation of the shot slamming into me.'

The warden looked sceptical. 'Where is the wound?'

If I tell him, he'll think I'm mad. Hamou took a deep breath and touched his fingers to the place on his chest where the bullet had struck home. 'It hit... an object in my breast pocket and must have deflected.'

The warden nodded slowly, said nothing. He didn't even look surprised, so he must already know. Surely Fouquet had not admitted to shooting him? Now, the man steepled his fingers. 'I can understand you may have suffered some shock and concussion from the episode, Officer Badi.'

Hamou waited.

The warden leant forward. 'I believe you may have been struck by a stray bullet. It was – was it not – a riot? At least,' he looked down at the papers, 'this is what the divisional commissioner tells me.' He lifted his eyes and regarded Hamou dispassionately.

'It's... possible,' Hamou said, feeling his way.

'And the fresh wound on your face?'

Hamou felt the cigarette burn flare with renewed heat. He said nothing, knowing very well it would not go well for him if he were to accuse a superintendent of the Sûreté of the torture of one of its own officers. He waited to see where this was going.

The warden's mouth moved in the faintest intimation of a smile. 'All right then. I gather, Officer Badi, that you have been an exemplary member of our police force. That you graduated from the training college with good marks and have carried out your duties diligently and meticulously. All your reports are excellent, and you were recently promoted to bearing arms, yes?'

Hamou nodded.

The man picked up an exquisite fountain pen, removed its cap, made a mark on one of the sheets of paper, replaced the cap, turned the barrel of the pen in his fingers over and over. Hamou followed the movements, half mesmerised by the flash of gold each time it caught the sunlight.

'So why,' the warden said at last, 'would you be in possession of terrorist literature and the sort of suicide pill favoured by extremist elements?' He fixed Hamou with a piercing gaze, all bonhomie gone.

'I… ah… picked the leaflet up off the road. Someone had let them fall, as if they'd fled in a hurry. I was curious to see what it was, so I picked one up and read it and then stuffed it in my pocket.'

The warden nodded slowly. 'Plausible, I suppose. And the pill?'

'I… found it.'

'Where did you find it?'

'On the ground. In the bidonville in the Derb Ghrallef.' It was a partial truth. He already felt he had said too much.

'Just lying on the ground? Where any child might have found it and swallowed it?'

'Yes.'

'Don't you think that's a little unlikely?'

'Someone must've dropped it.'

'People do seem to drop a lot of things in your proximity, Officer Badi.'

Hamou could feel himself reddening. A long silence ensued.

At last the warden broke it. 'Tell me, and tell me frankly – because if you do, things will go a great deal better for you – are you a member of the independence party, and have you played any part in the nationalist uprising?'

Hamou felt so skewered by the man's unblinking gaze that he felt guilty even though he was not guilty. 'I am not, and I have not.' This much, at least, was true.

The man sat back. 'I wish I were able to take your word for it.' He looked pained. 'You must understand that I will be unable to help you unless you are completely truthful with me. Now, what does the name Charles Shelby mean to you?'

Hamou wanted to please this quiet brown-eyed man, but he had never heard the name before. 'I'm sorry, I don't know.'

'You don't know what it means to you, or you don't know the man?'

He came upon so many people in his work. The name sounded European. Hamou scoured his memory for recent cases, victims of violence, of theft, and came up empty. 'I'm sorry, I can't think of anyone.'

The warden sat back in his chair and closed his eyes. In repose, his face looked older than it had when he had been interrogating Hamou, the skin corrugating into tiny wrinkles and folds, frown lines and laughter lines. He did not look like a bad man, Hamou thought, or a cruel one. He wondered how he had come to be the warden of this prison, which was surely not a position a man of substance would choose for himself. His gaze wandered to the books, some leather bound and gilded, others more official-looking, less decorative. On a low bookcase to one side a more varied selection of spines. Names jumped out at Hamou: Simenon, Christie, Malet, Guillaume, le Hallier…

'Are you a reader of detective novels, Officer Badi?'

Those cool, sharp eyes on him again.

'I've read a few.' It had been one of the ways he'd improved his French, at college and just after, before the exigencies of police work had pressed in upon him.

The warden selected a volume from the low bookcase, opened the cover, flicked through a few pages, and smiled. Then he closed it again and slid it across the desk to Hamou. 'I'm afraid you're likely to be with us for some time, Officer Badi, while we get to the bottom of this affair, and I fear the prison, as a result of current troubles, is rather overcrowded and uncomfortable. Perhaps you might like to have something to take your mind off the situation.'

Hamou did not know what to feel. 'Situation?' he echoed. 'I haven't done anything wrong. Except refuse to shoot innocent people.'

'Nobody is innocent, Officer Badi. Not these days.'

He was issued with two blankets: one thin, the other of rough wool. 'One for the summer, the other for winter,' the guard informed Hamou, who stared at him. Was that it, then? 'Some time' stretched into months, maybe years. He felt sick.

The cell he was taken to was crammed: bodies lounged on the floor, on benches against the walls. Too many in too small a space. The inmates groaned when the guards opened the door and shoved Hamou in. He stumbled and fell, landing on top of two men, who grumbled and swore. One picked up the object Hamou had dropped when he put out his hands to save himself, and laughed. 'Well, at least we can wipe our arses now!'

His neighbour took it from him and cast an eye over the cover. '*La Peau du Loup!* Who are you, bringing a novel in here, some sort of professor? Or perhaps it is you who are the wolf in sheep's clothing, huh?'

Hamou tried to make himself small, drawing his knees up to his chest.

They had all been swept up during the recent protests, it seemed, though none had yet been charged for any offence. 'They say they're holding us here for the "good of the state",' a young man called Nacer said. 'Till it can be proved we're no danger to the regime. My uncle's a *khalifa*: I'm sure he'll get me out soon.'

There was some jeering: clearly, Nacer had been saying this for a while and still no help from his uncle, who worked for a judge, had arrived.

Larbi, the man who had picked up the novel and laughed about it, was a gardener; Issa – the man who had retrieved the book – was in the civil service; Mustafa worked for a grocer; Amine was a street-sweeper; Yakoub a fisherman; Samir a plumber; Kabir a postman; Khalil a pharmacist and Darid a businessman. Hamou thought he recognised the eleventh man from somewhere and for a moment feared he might once have arrested him. Then it came to him. 'Are you... you look like... Salah Medkouri?'

The young man grinned shyly. He had widely spaced eyes and a mop of springy brown curls.

'You are! I saw you score for Raja against Wydad last year!'

'Last year! You're not much of a fan if that's the last game you saw me play in.'

Hamou looked away. 'I was policing the match.'

'Policeman?'

He told them his story. They were incredulous. 'He shot you? Just like that?' Samir stared at him. 'Your commanding officer? Why isn't he in here?'

Yakoub the fisherman snorted. 'Because he's French, you idiot.'

'Are you sure you didn't turn your gun on him first?' Darid wanted to know.

'I threw my gun away.'

'That's a shame,' said Larbi darkly.

Days came and went without change, without news. Time fell into patterns: lights up, lights out. A shower every three days (the place stank); a twenty-minute walk in the scuffed sand of the exercise yard, where they saw other prisoners like themselves, yet not like themselves, some shackled and cuffed, thinner, harder and meaner-looking than Hamou's cellmates. Some limped, dragging swollen feet; others wore clothing bearing dark stains. Some whose eyes burned with anger; others who gazed down like beaten donkeys.

Hamou began to think this might become his future, that he might become one of the empty-eyed ones, shuffling around the perimeter like a walking corpse, and he shuddered. During the days he did his best to keep his mind blank, to let his thoughts skip across the surface of things like a stone skimmed over a dark pond. He talked and laughed with his cellmates, and even read the detective novel to them by chapters, but it was set in Paris during the war, and none of them could picture the setting or connect with a tale of French spies and Nazi oppressors.

'Why was their resistance considered heroic, while ours is called terrorism?' Amine asked, and no one had a good answer for that.

At night, though, the terrors engulfed Hamou as he lay on the concrete floor with his head in one man's armpit and his legs draped over another, fitting into one another like pieces in a puzzle. He wondered if the authorities had found out about Zina and her mother. Had they been captured and interned, even tortured and abused? He thought about his Casa family, about Moha and Hicham, his uncle Salim and his aunt Jamila, his cousins Ali and Tahar and their wives and children. Where had they gone? Were they safe somewhere? He hoped so. He wondered about his mother and sisters, who would have received no word from him, and no money either. Would they have questioned the bus driver who came each week to Tiziane from Casablanca, asking if he had seen Hamou? He wondered if anyone would come looking for him, how long it would take before anyone realised that he was missing. And if they did, would they be able to track him down? The warden had said he was 'in the system', but the system presented an implacably blank façade to the outside world, concealing the vast, intricate, inward-facing machine. It would take courage to make enquiries, determination to persevere despite all the blocks and barriers that would be thrown in front of them, bad enough in a time of peace and surely worse in these times of chaos and unrest, as the mechanisms of state began to fall apart.

One night, as he fell in and out of fitful sleep, Hamou thought about the scruffy black cat he had rescued from the fire, how trusting it was, how it had followed him around, butting him with its oily little head, how it had settled down to sleep with him on the roof terrace; how Zina had teased him about it. Had it patiently waited for him to come home, night after night? Had the poor thing starved to death? He found himself crying silently into the crook of his arm.

'It's Eid al Adha tomorrow,' Nacer announced one morning.

'Perhaps we'll get better food than the usual shit,' Mustafa said hopefully.

'You're kidding, right? The French don't care about Eid,' Larbi observed. 'It's just another day to them.'

'They know about Eid, all right,' Issa said. 'Don't forget that was the day they took our sultan away.'

How could they forget?

A man came to the cell later that day, calling Hamou's name.

Hamou felt sweat prickle under his shirt. 'That's me.'

'Visitor. Come with me.'

Zina Chadli sat at a table in a small room with a man stationed outside. Hamou, cuffed and shackled, was ushered in. When he saw her sitting there in her terracotta robe and neat hijab, his knees buckled, and he stumbled inelegantly to the chair opposite her. The guard who had fetched him took a seat beside Zina.

There would be no privacy, but even so, Hamou devoured her with his eyes, taking in her long, straight nose and hawk's-wing brows, the slightly mocking curve of her lips. He could hardly believe she had tracked him down, had had the nerve to come right into the heart of this terrible place.

They made their polite exchange of greetings; Hamou enquired after the health of her parents, then, hesitatingly, '... and Madani?'

Zina frowned. 'Oh, you mean the cat?'

Beside her, the guard smirked. Absurd to waste a second of the allotted ten minutes with talk of a cat!

'Madani is being treated like a little prince.' Zina's brown eyes twinkled, and if Hamou had not loved her before, now he felt as if his heart might burst. 'I have brought you couscous and chebakia, to celebrate Eid.' She turned to the guard, giving him a devastating smile. 'For you too, sidi. Eid Mubarak.' She passed the man a wrapped package. 'I am sure you would rather be celebrating with your family on such a day than here in the prison.'

He took it from her and immediately opened it and started to eat one of the pastries, closing his eyes in a sort of ecstasy. Knowing she was not seen, Zina touched her fingers to her heart and gazed at Hamou.

Even though he was detained in the Ghbila, in a filthy cell with eleven other men, without charge, without hope, Hamou thought he might never have been so happy.

'I found you a good lawyer: he'll come to see you next week. He'll get you out, I'm sure of it,' Zina said fiercely.

The guard laughed, spraying crumbs. He had heard it all before, but no one ever got out of the Little Jungle. 'Time's up,' he said. For the gift of the pastries, he felt he had already extended a little leeway.

Zina got to her feet and leaned across the table to kiss Hamou.

'Hey!' said the guard. 'That's only allowed if you're married.'

'We are,' Zina lied magnificently, and drew Hamou to her.

*

The food, which had been checked for smuggled items, had lost its heat, but it was still delicious. Hamou shared it between his cellmates, his heart too full to begrudge them his gift. They feasted upon flat loaves, spiced lamb, couscous and vegetables in a sauce that, even cold, seared the tongue and had them all licking their fingers as they savoured every morsel.

'Your wife?' Amine asked.

'Not yet,' said Hamou. Almost, he could believe there might be a future in which he could be with Zina, married, away from here.

'Better hurry,' Samir the plumber chuckled. 'Any woman who can cook like this must have suitors queuing up for her.'

Issa and Salah both received visitors that day – the older man his wife; the young footballer his mother – and both brought Eid treats which were also shared around. That night was the first many of them managed to sleep without hunger gnawing at their bellies.

The next day it was back to the usual routine, and the next, but the following day Darid left them, apparently released. 'Someone paid a decent bribe,' Larbi said bitterly, but the very fact of his liberation filled them with varying degrees of hope – perhaps it was possible to get out of this place after all.

Then Issa fell ill with a fever and a sharp pain in his side that got steadily worse till he was rolling on the floor, groaning like a wounded ram. He was sweaty but felt both hot and cold; when he pissed, there was blood in it. For hours the guards ignored their cries for aid, but when at last Issa fell unconscious, they came and hauled him away.

'Is he going to die?' asked Salah fearfully.

Khalil touched him gently on the shoulder. 'Inshallah if he gets proper treatment, he'll be fine.'

Issa did not return that week. There was more room to stretch out for sleep, but they worried about him. Neither was there any sign of the lawyer Zina had promised. Hamou was glad he had not mentioned this possibility to his cellmates now; the disappointment was a private thing that he hugged to himself until hope was smothered.

But then, two miracles at once! Issa was brought back to them in clean clothing, no longer sweating and grey in the face. A kidney stone, he told them, followed by an infection. He rattled the bottle of pills he'd been given. Khalil looked it over. 'Penicillin, good,' he declared, handing it back.

And within half an hour of this, a guard came for Hamou.

This time Hamou found himself sitting in an office. A man stood sentinel outside, the guard inside sat in a corner, pretending not to listen. The lawyer was young and French, elegantly dressed, with keen grey eyes, and the lean frame and tanned skin of a man who played a good deal of outdoor sport. He wondered how Zina knew the man and felt a sharp pang of jealousy, a thought he cut off as unworthy, and shook the lawyer's hand with as much dignity as he could muster.

'It's an interesting situation,' Monsieur Leclerc – 'call me Jean-Claude' – said, as they sat down.

Hamou gave him a wry smile.

Leclerc leaned across the table. 'Why didn't you tell everyone right away that you're a friend of Charles Shelby?'

That name again. Hamou regarded him curiously.

'It took a fair bit of digging to find out about him and then some time to make contact, since he's been out of the country, but I gather he owes you a favour.'

A little spark went off in Hamou's brain. Feeling suddenly energised, he sat bolt upright, snatching at a thread of memory. The day of the demonstration when he had found Sofiane and shown him the sultan's face on the moon, the day that had ended with him paid in bundles of cash for blessing the charlatan's crystals with his zouhry hands. That day, yes! He recalled the tall man who spoke execrable French, Aicha's customer at the brothel, who had shaken his hand and given him the business card he had kept in his pocket ever since, with the instruction to call him if he ever fancied a good meal, or anything. Could it be?

'An American gentleman?'

'Indeed. And a very important one, too. The diplomatic attaché responsible for liaison between us and US Strategic Air Command in the matter of establishing their airbases. Friend of the US president. It seems you have friends in high places, Hamou Badi.'

Hamou's thoughts whirled. What was the favour that he could ask for? What did it all mean? He formed a careful question. 'And you think he can help me?'

Leclerc grinned. 'He's got them all running around like headless chickens. That man's on 'The List'. The big list, the one that starts with Eisenhower, Auriol and de Gaulle. I hope they've treated you well, or you could end a few careers!'

Hamou goggled at him. How tempting it would be, he thought, to have Fouquet disciplined, demoted, even dismissed. His hand went subconsciously to the burn on his face, no more than a crusted mark now. 'I... I just want to be released,' he said after a while.

'And then what?'

Hamou hadn't thought that far ahead. He could hardly step back into his job, policing protestors, expected to shoot upon them. He looked at Leclerc, overcome by conflicting emotions. 'I don't know.'

'I gather discussions have been going on behind the scenes,' the lawyer went on. 'The Sûreté, the military, the diplomatic service. You have the ability to embarrass a number of people. Professionally, I mean. You could wreak a considerable amount of havoc if you had a mind to do so.' He paused. 'Where do you come from, Mr Badi?'

'Tiziane. Down in the south-west. In the Souss, the Anti-Atlas.'

'Have you ever considered a different career?'

Hamou felt a stab of panic. 'No, not really. It's all I've ever done. It's my profession, I took exams, I have six, seven years' experience... I need to make money, for my family. My father's dead, I have no brothers, that's why I had to come to Casa...' The words came tumbling out.

Jean-Claude Leclerc held up a calming hand. 'Leave it with me.' He looked down at his expensive watch and got to his feet. Patting his pocket, he withdrew something and pushed it across the table. 'I think this belongs to you.' He beamed at Hamou. 'I have a meeting with the warden now. He seems to be a civilised man.'

Hamou's heart, which had been racing, seemed to skip a beat, to stop. Only this morning he had thought he might die in this place, neatly shuffled away, forgotten. Then he had been given this unexpected offer of – what? Salvation? And now, he was to be abandoned again? He could not bear the loss of hope, it seemed too cruel. 'Please, don't leave me here,' he said, and was mortified by how craven he sounded. He thought of his cellmates – of the young footballer, the sarcastic gardener, Issa with his painful kidney, Mustafa the grocer, Amine and Kabir, the fisherman and the plumber, Khalil the pharmacist. It felt like a sort of treachery, to abandon them in the Ghbila: a selfish act, and yet he knew he would take the chance, and it shamed him.

Leclerc smiled – a brief, professional smile – and left.

Hamou stared after him, then down at the object on the table, a twist of blackened metal, almost unrecognisable. His grandfather's amulet, or what was left of it. He picked it up wonderingly, smelling the acrid burn of chemicals, his fingers running over the tortured edges. He held it against his heart, remembering. Baraka. His mother had had it filled with luck. Perhaps he should trust to fate.

26

Hamou was flying through clear, uninterrupted air, the pale, distant blue of sky far above the land. He experienced nothing but a sense of movement, though it was as if his surroundings moved rather than himself. It appeared, in his dream of flying, that all he had to do was exist, to allow the universe to take him into its flow, to carry him where it would. Arms stretched out, eyes open into blessed blankness, he sailed on...

...until suddenly there was hubbub. Shrieking, howling, an inhuman noise that grated inside his skull. Abruptly, he was back in the torture cells beneath the commissariat, listening to other people's agony, waiting for his own to begin. And then, somehow, the sound of an affronted chicken intruded itself into the human cries...

He jolted awake... and there was an affronted chicken, running lopsidedly down the aisle, clucking insanely, pursued by a small, black, yowling creature. Coming sharply back into himself, he leapt to his feet. 'Hey, Madani!'

The cat took not the least scrap of notice.

Bumping first one hip then the other against successive seats, Hamou caught up with Madani just as it cornered the chicken. He grabbed him up and the cat writhed in his hands, one big furry muscle bent on murder. Another of the bus passengers retrieved the escaped chicken, which was then passed back to its owner, a small woman in a traditional black haik, whose earrings jangled as she shouted imprecations at Hamou and his demon cat.

Hamou stuffed Madani back into his basket, then apologised to the old lady, and in the end she blessed him not only in the name of Allah but also of Lalla Tirza, the female marabout whose white stone shrine sat beside the road that wound up into the mountains.

It appeared that he was back in the land of marvellous Berber women. The thought felt so surreal that he felt compelled to tug back the window curtain. He looked out onto tawny, rock-strewn hillsides and knew at once exactly where he was: on the grindingly slow ascent up the Afoud. He gazed at the familiar landscape rising steeply to either side of the narrow road, dotted here and there with bursts of dark green argan trees – trees that grew only in this region of Morocco – and felt his pulse slow. It was real. The detail was too exact, too consistent, for this to be part of his dream. On the argan trees, the fruits would be ripening, nearly ready for harvest, amid their wreaths of waxy leaves and cradles of thorns, and suddenly he could smell the aromatic oil extracted from the roasted kernels rubbed through the last steaming of his mother's couscous. He experienced a sharp pang of anxiety. His mother did not know he was coming home. He had not even had a night in his own bed. The police car that had removed him from the prison had waited for him outside while he packed his few belongings. When he had knocked on the door of the Chadlis' apartment, hoping to steal a few words with Zina, as well as retrieving the cat, the door had been opened by Samira, who had lamented over his imminent departure. For every moment that passed while she adapted the basket in which Madani had been sleeping in Zina's room so that he could be safely transported, Hamou had hoped that Zina would suddenly appear, but no such luck. Now it occurred to him that he might never see her again and his heart clenched. Who knew what would happen to her in these dangerously uncertain times?

Up the twisting mountain road the bus laboured, passing tiny villages that clung to the hillsides, their walls and roofs of the same dusty red ochre as the surrounding rocks. Skinny cows plodded around a field of mostly bare earth; a white dog lazed in the lee of a wall, tongue lolling: Hamou could sense the heat even at this early hour. They traversed rocky gorges in which prickly pears studded the sides and pink-flowered oleanders rose from the canyon beds. As they descended towards the plain, the driver made unscheduled stops to take on passengers from the outlying villages laden with baskets, boxes and bags and Hamou realised today must be the day of the souk in Tiziane. He had lost track of the days.

Before long he had to squeeze himself against the window to make room for three young women in embroidered white robes who flashed dark, kohled eyes at him and giggled behind their hands. Feeling both discomfited and disengaged, Hamou sat looking straight ahead, listening to their chatter. Clearly, they thought him a foreigner. And he felt like a foreigner. The Hamou who had left Tiziane would have laughed and flirted with them, but the Hamou who was returning was a man, and a damaged one at that.

As they passed the great rock formation that marked the descent into the valley, he turned his face to the window and reflected on the chasm between life in the city, with its violent brutalities, and life in the rural heartland to which he was returning and wondered how he was going to reconcile his passage between the two.

With a screech of brakes, the bus came to a halt in the centre of Tiziane. Hamou waited for other people to get off, then loaded up his bags and suitcase, tightened the cover on the cat basket, and stepped down into the dazzling heat and light of his village. He stood there while tides of humanity washed around him, taking in the smells: dust and spices, cooking oil and baking bread, diesel and donkey shit. He was home. But somehow it no longer felt like home. Or rather, he felt he did not belong here.

Perhaps he did not belong anywhere…

'Hamou Badi?'

Three men stood waiting for him, two in dark, official-looking djellabas, one in military khaki. Panic flooded his mind. Had they come for him? Was he to become another of the thousands of disappeared, incarcerated in a rural jail far away from the political hotbed of Casablanca, where he could be quietly forgotten? Had the promise the French authorities made to Charles Shelby been nothing more than a lie? He knew he would never be able to withstand more time in prison: the destruction of hope would annihilate what little was left of his spirit. He looked desperately around. Should he run? Could he run? But he felt rooted to the ground.

'Come with us, please,' one of the men said, in Berber, not French.

Hamou realised the man was a civilian, probably a *moqqadem*. And the uniformed figure was not a policeman but a mokhazni, one of the caid's men. None of them was armed. His senses still prickled with suspicion, but he no longer felt inchoate panic. Gathering himself, he asked, 'Can't I go to see my mother first, to let her know I'm here?'

'That can be arranged later. We have our orders.'

The other moqqadem introduced himself as Brahim, and his companion as Hassan. The mokhazni put a hand to his heart, bowed and named himself as Houcine. None of this was behaviour that marked them as hostile, but Hamou decided to reserve judgement. A boy was summoned to lug his bags, and they made their way along familiar streets that had grown unfamiliar. Throngs of people flooded past and around them, heading for the souk, and Hamou clasped Madani's basket close, feeling the cat shifting its weight. If he escaped here, he'd never see him again. Not losing the cat suddenly took on huge significance.

They crossed the river at a bridge that hadn't existed the last time he'd been home, wide enough to accommodate two lanes of traffic and currently jammed with trucks, cars, donkeys, carts and scooters. Groups of men stood talking and smoking. Their eyes travelled over the small cavalcade without great interest or recognition, but even so, Hamou felt scrutinised and self-conscious. Soon they were in the greater calm of the main street over which the mosque's minaret towered, clay-pink and white. Seeing it, Hamou felt more centred: it was his waymarker, his guidepost. They passed the old market square and the hammam and the tunnelled alley leading up to the big house where he and the other children had queued in trepidation to collect the daily milk from Taba Tôt. How long ago his childhood seemed, long ago and far away.

The main road led on through a built-up area that had spread since Hamou was last in Tiziane so that in all truth the village could no longer be considered such and was now a small town. The new buildings comprised shops and offices, garages and finally stables, and led past the oasis where bunches of orange dates hung high in the palm branches to a high-walled compound behind which lay the judicial centre.

'Nearly there!' Brahim declared.

It struck Hamou abruptly that the village jail was on the other side of this compound. He'd spent a night there when he and his gang had been caught raiding grapes from a rich man's garden, trampling down the vines like cattle. Was this their destination? He experienced an innate sense of guilt and fear. His defiance these days was greatly diminished from what it had been when he was twelve. 'Why are we coming this way?' he asked nervously.

'Haven't you been told anything?' Hassan asked.

'Nothing.'

The moqqadems exchanged a glance. 'Will you tell him, or shall I?'

'Tell me what?'

Brahim grinned. 'You're the new *hakam*.'

It was not a word Hamou was familiar with. His face must

have shown his puzzlement, because Hassan went on, 'The caid will explain when you see him this afternoon. Once you've had a chance to settle in.'

'Settle in?' Hamou echoed. They were almost at the place where the old cells had been, but they appeared to have been replaced by a series of new constructions, low-lying and white-painted. The new jail?

Brahim pointed to one of the whitewashed buildings. 'That one's for you.'

Hamou went hot, then cold. What sort of trick was this?

The mokhazni snapped a salute. 'Permission to be dismissed, sir?'

Hamou realised Houcine was talking to him. 'Ah... yes?'

The mokhazni marched smartly back towards the judicial compound. Hamou gazed after him, wondering why he had needed a guard.

Hassan handed him some keys. 'Go ahead! It used to be the adjutant's quarters, but he's moved out, so now it's yours.' He indicated a door at the end. 'We'll be back for you in an hour. Taïb can run errands if there's anything you need, can't you, son?' The bag-carrier nodded eagerly, anticipating a tip. 'See you later.'

Hamou watched the moqqadems leave, understanding nothing.

'Go on,' Taïb encouraged. 'Open the door.'

As if in a dream, Hamou set the cat basket down, unlocked the door and stepped inside. Sunlight pooled on honey-coloured floor tiles and cast spangles on the walls where it refracted from the hanging lanterns. He flicked a switch on the wall and those lanterns glowed gold and green.

'Wah!' exclaimed the boy, letting fall the bags. 'You've got electricity!' He gazed at the sumptuous surroundings and Hamou felt his own wonder sharpened by the boy's astonishment. His searching gaze took in a smart modern kitchenette, a copper kettle on a stove, plates and glasses behind the glinting windows of a cabinet. A seating area comprising settee and armchair in the European fashion, a low table, a fireplace, good local rugs, a shelved alcove. At the back of the room were two further doors. How could all this be for him? He stood staring, feeling dizzy and amazed, but also uneasy and distrustful.

A yowl interrupted his reverie: Madani had had enough of being confined. Snapped back to practicalities, Hamou retrieved the basket and brought the cat inside.

'What you got in there, mister?' The boy was right behind him.

'If you close the front door, I'll show you.'

The lad looked suspicious but did as he was told. Making sure there was no escape route, Hamou opened the basket, and Madani shot out and raced around the room as if someone had released a pent-up spring.

Taïb shrieked, 'It's a djinn!'

Hamou held up his hands. 'It's just a cat. He's been cooped up for hours.'

The boy backed away. 'Zouhry,' he yelped, and made the sign against the evil eye. 'Zouhry!' He scrabbled at the door handle, all thought of payment forgotten.

'Wait!' Hamou cried, but Taïb was gone. He ran to shut the door in the instant before Madani reached it, then slumped against it, shaking with adrenalin. Things had happened too fast. Within just over twenty-four hours he had gone from sharing a stinking cell with a crowd of other prisoners to a last goodbye to his apartment and neighbour, seventeen hours on a bus and now here he was, in a handsome little house for a hakam. Whatever that was.

He sat down heavily on the cool, tiled floor, fighting tears and a fearsome headache, trying to make sense of it all, and returned to himself only when Madani stalked up to him and gave a questioning miaow. He scooped the cat up and buried his face in its cool, musty fur, and Madani put up with this for a short time, then extricated himself and walked around their new quarters with his tail hoisted like a flag, an explorer claiming a new territory.

Hamou pushed himself to his feet and followed the cat across the living area to examine what lay beyond the other two doors and found a bathroom furnished with an enamel bathtub, an overhead shower, and what appeared to be two European-style toilets, one lower than the other. The second door gave onto a large, elegant bedroom full of light and the scent of roses. In all his life, Hamou had never had a dedicated room in which to sleep. He had slept, as most people did, on the couch in his living area, wrapped in a blanket. But here was a huge, brass-framed bed made up with sheets and pillows and quilts. He staggered to it and sat down. The mattress welcomed him so soothingly that suddenly all he wanted to do was to climb into the bed and sleep for hours.

Madani, however, had other ideas. He launched himself up beside Hamou and gave him a hard stare. Hamou knew that look. 'Oh. I'll see what I can find for you. Just hold on.'

He could see vegetation beyond the windows, and a wall. And actually, that window was a door. He crossed the room and looked out onto a small, walled courtyard garden. Bougainvillea tumbled over the walls and roses grew in the flowerbeds. Hamou unlatched the door and stepped out, closing it quickly behind him. A pot and some earth had been his first thought, but now that he was out here, he thought better of it. He reopened the door and held it ajar. Madani stalked very deliberately to the end of the bed, made a neat jump over the brass footrail and glided to Hamou's feet, sniffing the air, then snaked swiftly through the gap and paced the perimeter of the courtyard, interrogating each stone, pot and plant for information. At last, satisfied that he had got the measure of the space, Madani walked to the far flowerbed and, half-hidden by the shrubs, made use of the facilities. There followed a good deal of scrabbling, then he came trotting back to the house, demanding food.

Hamou located his supplies in one of the bags the boy had dropped and emptied a tin of sardines he had brought seven hundred kilometres from Casablanca onto a rather too-nice saucer and watched as Madani snorted his way through the fish, leaving not even a scale or flake behind. The cat seemed to have a great deal more confidence in these new surroundings than he did, Hamou thought. Maybe he should take a lesson from that.

He made himself unpack and put his few belongings away, but still it felt as if he were trespassing. Washing and changing into a clean robe made him feel a bit better, but he still jumped nervously when someone knocked on the door.

'Ready?' Brahim and Hassan had returned, and the mokhazni was waiting at the end of the path. Hamou followed them to the judicial compound, a walk of maybe two minutes. They delivered him to a waiting room, and the mokhazni joined a colleague outside.

Hassan consulted the clock and knocked on the office door. A voice invited him to enter, and he did so. Then he came out again. 'The caid will see you now. We'll wait for you outside.'

Behind the desk sat an older man in a dark woollen robe, with an immaculate white turban on his head, his bone structure clearly marking him out as from the local area. He came out from behind his desk to greet Hamou, who was surprised when he was suddenly enfolded in a bear hug. 'Welcome, young man – I knew your father well!' He indicated a chair and Hamou sat down.

Ten minutes later he was out again, his head spinning. He stood on the threshold, staring out at the far mountain range, the Djebel Kest, a burning rose-red in the afternoon light, at the deep blue sky, and tried to steady himself. Hakam Badi. A new position for Tiziane, one created especially for him. He would, apparently, do a job that linked the caid's office with the French administration. It felt like a gift, but also like a trick. Was this the regime's way of keeping an eye on him? One false step and he might find himself behind bars again.

The mokhaznis and moqqadems were all smoking. Hassan saw him and ground out his cigarette, looking sheepish. 'Shall we take you to your office now?'

Hamou shook his head. 'I'm not starting till tomorrow. I'll go for a walk.'

They made as if to accompany him.

'On my own.'

It took a few more minutes to escape them. They had their orders but, as Hamou explained, he was not yet officially in his post, so they could stand down. He would go to see his mother and sisters. In his pocket he had a bundle of francs: an advance on his new salary, the caid – Hajj Abdullah – had explained. Their eyes had met. Hamou had felt as if he were taking a bribe. Was this hush-money to smooth over Fouquet's attempt to murder him? To stop him talking about the torture that so routinely was carried out in the cells of the commissariat? The thought was corrosive. He pushed it away and walked purposefully towards the town.

As he neared the mosque, he began to notice a number of well-turned-out people hurrying in the same direction. He stopped a passer-by and asked the occasion.

'Funeral,' the young man said succinctly. 'Some old woman.'

Hamou's heart stuttered. He was suddenly irrationally convinced that something had happened to his mother because he had not immediately gone to see her. He wanted to ask more, but the man had moved on. He walked faster, fuelled by alarm. More mourners, some of them wailing. Somebody well-established here, then, someone well known. Hamou caught up with a man of middle years. 'Excuse me, who's died?' Terror made him abrupt.

The man shot him a suspicious glance. 'If you have to ask, you're clearly not from around here.'

Fighting his panic, Hamou headed for the old family house, across the river, past the souk. The front door was closed. He knocked hard. No one came. He called out, stepping back to shade his eyes in case someone was on the roof terrace, hanging out washing.

'Yam'mi? It's Hamou.'

Still no answer.

Some old woman...

He ran back the way he had come. Back across the bridge, in the centre of Tiziane, he caught up with the procession. Up ahead, a white-swathed body was held high. Was it the right size to be his mother? It looked larger, but maybe that was the shroud. A gaggle of women followed, veils pulled close to their chins, wailing and ululating. He scanned what he could see of their faces. Oh! There was Iza, his childhood friend, now a woman, willowy in her flowing robe, her huge dark eyes emphasised by kohl.

'Iza!'

She looked around, startled, and clearly didn't recognise him. He didn't blame her – it was hard to believe he had any connection to the gangly, exuberant youngster she'd known. But then her eyes widened, and she gasped. 'Hamou! We thought you were dead. Your mother...' She paused as people turned to look at them, and Hamou's pulse juddered.

'My mother?'

'Your mother, have you seen her?'

'I... I just got home.'

'This way.' Iza pulled him by the sleeve, forging a passage through the mourners, and suddenly there was Mimouna, a proper young woman now, and his little sister Sofia. They looked solemn, but not grief-stricken.

'There—' Iza said, and a woman turned around and stared Hamou right in the face.

'Yam'mi!'

A shriek, more piercing than the mourners' cries. 'Hamou!'

He folded his mother in his arms, widening the embrace to include his sisters. His relief was so great he thought he might faint. He held them as if to reassure himself of their corporeal reality, so tightly that Sofia broke free, complaining he was crushing her.

'But who is dead?' he asked at last, and they told him it was Taba Tôt, and he became very still, remembering how she had terrified him back then, with her meaty arms, her unpredictable temper, her protruding, bloodshot eyes and talk of djinns and magic. Back then, she had seemed like some sort of monster. But he had known true monsters now, and true fear. Now, she would have held no terrors for him. Indeed, an overwhelming sadness came over him that his return to his home should coincide with the loss of one of Tiziane's great characters, one who embodied the old ways of superstition and magic, and it was as if something else had been taken away from him, another skin peeled away from his frail defences.

Hamou remembered her telling him, 'You have the luck. You have baraka. It makes you strong.' He did not feel strong, but he knew he must garner whatever resilience was left to him in order to honour her.

Falling into step with them, he joined the mourners. They walked along the bank of the river, past the great house where he had collected the milk every day. They crossed at the old ford and went on towards the cemetery under the rock formation the French called the Tower and known, by the rather earthier locals, as the Prick and Balls.

His mother and sisters stayed with the other women by the low wall of the cemetery to chant and wail; Hamou went in with the men to pray and to lay to rest the mighty old slavewoman in a hole dug into the rocky ground. Boys had cut thorn branches to keep the jackals and wild dogs at bay. These were interlaced over the grave and two shards of rough granite were placed upright at the corpse's head and foot. Hamou, who had seen the grandiose mausoleums and statues rich people bought for themselves in Casablanca, was profoundly moved by the simplicity of the ritual and the grave. Every soul was equal in death. He bowed his head, breathing in the air of his homeland, feeling the rocky ground beneath his feet.

And then, just as he started to feel some equilibrium return to him, he remembered the poor woman who had been interred here when he was a boy, the one whose body he had found hidden in the riverbank, and remembered how no thorns or stones had protected her grave, and how her body had been ravaged by wild animals.

What a shame upon the village, he thought. What a shame upon them all.

27

The last time he had been at a family gathering, he had run away. Hamou took deep breaths in the alley outside his old home, fortifying himself before going in. There had been no refusing his mother: Lalla Saïda was an indomitable woman, and an indomitable Berber woman at that, and when she determined there was going to be a homecoming party, there would be a homecoming party, even if it was at fearsomely short notice, and he hadn't been given any choice in the matter.

Hamou approached the door half an hour later than the prescribed hour, then swung sharply away. He wasn't ready to go in yet, to smile and charm and give himself over to small talk and celebration. Quickening his stride, he took a turn around the side of the house to where the animals were kept, to gather his composure. The sheep and goats would be wandering freely around the village, as was the custom in these parts, to forage whatever they could find, before returning to their pen before sunset to be kept safe from the wild dogs. But the chickens – six brown-feathered matrons with long legs and fine pink-red crowns and wattles – were scratching around in the dirt and he watched them for a time and allowed his thoughts to settle. None of them took much notice of him but after a while the rooster, noticing his presence, came running across the patch of ground with his neck feathers frilled out like an angry lizard's and his tail and wings spread threateningly, to stand between the newcomer and his harem. A furious low-pitched warble shook his throat.

Hamou grinned, remembering his mother's letter. 'Hello, Agulez. It seems you're doing an excellent job of guarding the coop.' A shame that Izum was gone: the old rooster had been quite a character, and he was glad he hadn't had to eat him. He took a couple of steps back to indicate that he posed no threat, but still the Wolf stood there, neck and wings outstretched in challenge, regarding him with battle-ready eyes. Stepping back once more, he collided with something. Someone. A high-pitched complaint and then an angry curse as a tin can went flying, spilling seed everywhere.

Hamou turned, and there was Sofia. 'Where did you learn to swear like a soldier, okhti?'

His little sister coloured, then bent to retrieve the seeds and corn that had spilled in their collision. Hamou squatted to help her. 'How is it in there?' he asked after a while.

Sofia gave an exaggerated sigh. 'Oh, it's all so tedious. I don't blame you for taking your time out here, there's a ton of them all chattering away, and Yam'mi fussing: it's why I volunteered to feed the chickens. Mother is insufferable: everything you move she moves back, everything you do she criticises. She made me change three times and put this old thing on.' She bunched the black fabric of her traditional robe and shook it in disgust. 'Just look at the embroidery on it.'

Hamou didn't know what he was supposed to say. He looked at the wide embroidered edging. 'It's very… handsome,' he said at last. 'Very striking.'

'It's ancient, is what it is,' she returned sharply. 'Nanna made it. Imagine! I'm wearing a dead woman's clothes that my mother wore before me.' She sounded disgusted.

'Just think of all the history that haik has seen,' Hamou said gently. 'Think how it represents the strong women of our people, of our family – Nanna, then Yam'mi, now you.'

Sofia pursed her lips. 'It smells old,' she complained. 'It stinks of camphor and dead moths and old wee.'

Hamou leaned closer, then laughed. 'It really does!'

His sister swiped at him, and he rocked back on his heels, then lost his balance and sprawled backwards in the dust.

'Now look what you've done!' He got to his feet, brushing off his djellaba.

They were both giggling now and he remembered their mock-fights when he was her age and she was six. There was a little over ten years between them, but she had always been the sister to whom he was closest. Mimouna, though older than Sofia, was more serious, more fierce, indeed sometimes as overbearing as his mother. Hamou felt a sudden rush of love for his little sister, for his family, for Tiziane. Perhaps coming home would make things right after all.

'Who's in there?' he asked as Sofia scattered the seeds and the hens all picked up their skirts and clucked joyfully.

'Oh, you know.' She shot him a look. 'Uncle Omar and Aunt Zahra, Lina and Farah, Amir and Hasan and their wives and kids, Cousins Hamsa and Nabil and Saïd and Rachida.'

Hamou groaned. How could he face all these smiling, happy people, having seen the things he had seen, experienced all he had lived through? They could not possibly understand, and he had no wish to enlighten them.

Sofia inserted her free hand in his. 'Everyone's so happy you're home, and Yam'mi and Aunt Zahra have cooked and cooked. Come on, it'll be fine.'

Hamou followed her in like a lamb to the slaughter.

It *was* fine, as long as the conversation stayed light and touched on local gossip and news, prices in the market, recent births and marriages, a couple of scandals involving local chiefs taking French money. 'You'll be seeing plenty of that in your new position, I'm sure,' Uncle Omar had chuckled. The old man looked a good deal more frail than Hamou had been expecting, and stayed sitting throughout the festivities, with his stick propped against the wall beside him. He saw how Aunt Zahra's gaze slid to her husband during quiet moments, and noticed the worry lines in her face; noticed also how hale Omar's sister – Hamou's mother – appeared by contrast, even though there were no more than a few years between them.

The children ran in and out of the room, stealing pastries without reprimand, and Hamou smiled inwardly. Had he done the same at their age he'd have earned a smacked bottom, from his mother, never his father. Probably because his father had almost never been around for gatherings like this. The cousins were all getting on with their lives, farming, selling, toiling, though Hamsa complained about having lost the rights to a plot of land in a dispute. The fellow who had taken it had contacts among the French administration, he said darkly, shooting Hamou a look, and with a sinking heart Hamou intuited that he was going to end up embroiled in such matters. Then he chided himself: after all he had gone through in Casa, handling irritations like this would be as nothing.

The word 'Casablanca' passed no one's lips, for over an hour, but it hung in the air, unspoken, and Hamou had the distinct impression that the guests had been instructed to leave political discussions at the door, unless he raised the subject himself. He could sense their curiosity, though: it prickled in the air. How had young Hamou – who had been just a lowly policeman in the Sûreté – landed this new job that everyone was talking about? He knew his mother would have been boasting about it all over town, and he knew he should talk a little about it to curb their curiosity and make them feel included in what they would see as his good fortune, but he just couldn't find the words.

In truth, he still didn't understand the situation himself, and feared to consider it too closely, because doing so brought back bad memories, fears and heartache. When Lina had asked after their cousin Moha, Hamou had gone cold all over. With all eyes on him, he had managed to stutter out the short truth, that he had no idea where the Casa family were now, but that they had packed up and left the city for somewhere safer, and he hoped they would be in contact in due course. Then, knowing he was on the verge of tears, he pushed himself to his feet and, using the excuse of clearing some plates away, fled the room.

He deposited the plates in the kitchen, then went into the small family sitting room away from the gathering for some quiet, taking deep breaths and trying to calm the shudders that ran through him. His fingers ran over the scar on his cheek. Thankfully, no one had remarked upon it. It had probably left more of a psychic mark than a physical one by now, but he could feel the little ridged depression where no stubble grew. *Be a man, Hamou Badi*, he told himself, tapping the scar compulsively. *The Free Men do not weep.* And then he remembered the last time he had told himself this, and his heart yearned for Zina Chadli. Without her, he would not be here. It was she who had found the French lawyer, had worked so resolutely to get him out of jail; had even looked after his cat. Would there be repercussions for her, even for the family? He could not imagine that the administration would have taken their defeat over his case – as he was sure they must see it – with equanimity. He must write to her, although maybe for propriety he should write to Rachid... but then he would not be able to say what he wanted. But even writing to the family could endanger whoever delivered the letter for him, and it would tie the Chadlis closer to his escape from the clutches of his tormentors. It might make them a target for Fouquet's vindictiveness...

Frustration made him groan. He hammered his fists on his forehead. Surely there must be a solution? But if there was, it wasn't going to occur to him now. He rolled his shoulders, tried to calm himself enough to go back into the fray before he was missed.

Too late.

'What are you doing hiding away in here?' Lalla Saïda bustled in. 'Come along, back into the salon with you. Your guests will be wondering where you are!'

'*My* guests?'

'Of course, your guests. Why else has everyone gathered but to see you and welcome you back home?' She fussed at his djellaba, straightening the shoulders. 'You should have worn your grandfather's amulet,' she chided. 'It would have looked very well with this robe.'

Hamou started to tremble, feeling the impact on his ribcage again, his nostrils stinging from the sulphurous kbrit. The amulet had saved his life, but he couldn't form the words to tell his mother what had happened. How to explain to her that his commanding officer had shot him, tortured him, killed and tortured other Moroccans as if they were less than animals? That this was what was going on in Casa now, that it was outright war, and a dirty war at that, that he did not know if it was coming here too, or what he would do if it did. He didn't know anything.

His mother caught him as he collapsed against her. Lalla Saïda was strong: she took her son's weight, manoeuvred him to the divan set against the wall, sat down beside him. 'Hamou, what is it?'

For a long time, he was silent. 'I... can't, Yam'mi. Can't talk about it. Just can't.' He couldn't meet her eyes.

For a time, she just held him. Then she pulled away and patted his hand. 'I want to show you something.' Huffing to her feet, she crossed the room, opened a drawer in the cabinet and came back with something that she placed in his lap.

Hamou looked down at a deckle-edged black-and-white photograph, a little out of focus, or maybe hazed by sun and time, of a slim, handsome man leaning up against a truck, wearing European clothes, a cigarette in his hand. It took him several seconds to recognise the figure as his father, but his father looking as he had never seen him, so young, maybe in his twenties. He looked happy and confident, a man with a bit of swagger and not a care in the world.

'You look just like him.'

Hamou looked harder and was suddenly shocked by the resemblance.

'I loved him more than anything in the world. When he... died, I thought I would die, but I couldn't do that. I had you and your sisters to raise, and my own life to live. The world is a cruel place and there are wicked people in it. But, habibi, there is also so much good to be done, so much wonder to be found. And I know you have that good in you, that wonder. I could tell as soon as I saw you that you had lost your sense of baraka: I thought at first it was the shock of Taba Tôt's passing – such a sad thing to come home to – but it's more than that, isn't it?'

Hamou nodded dumbly, looking down at the photo in his hands, at the beautiful, shining young man who had given him life. 'I'm trying, Yam'mi, I really am.'

'I know you are, and I know you'll get your baraka back. But maybe you need some help with that. I'll think about that, my son. Whatever you need.'

'What I need is a little quiet time, Yam'mi. To find my place in the world again.'

Lalla Saïda nodded slowly, and took the photo back from him, gazed down, then ran her thumb over it lovingly. 'I will tell them you were called away. On hakam duty.' She looked up, gave him a crooked smile. 'I am proud of you, my boy. I will always be proud of you, Hamou Badi.'

28

No one seemed to understand precisely what the job of the hakam entailed, and Hamou soon found this to be both a blessing and a curse. It afforded him a freedom he had never enjoyed in his adult life, but at the same time it seemed everyone considered him their personal problem-solver.

As Hajj Abdullah had explained it to him, his new role sat between the judiciary of the French administration – with its inexorable mechanisms, written laws and scads of bureaucracy – and the traditional tribal courts of his people. He was there as a filter between the two, sorting out conundrums that were not straightforwardly addressed by either of the existing structures.

The hakam was the person locals came to when there was a suspicion they had been cheated or short-changed at the market – the thumb on the scales, the watering-down of honey, the addition of alloy to silver. He registered long-standing boundary disputes and talked to nomadic herders about the traditional rules of grazing and watering rights; women came to him to complain about the behaviour of relatives and errant husbands, about money problems and inheritance difficulties that had been left unresolved by the tribal courts. He was a sort of pressure valve, allowing the local community to let off steam, taking the heat out of long simmering disputes. Hamou began to suspect, though, that he was also seen by the French as their eyes on the local population during these times of political tension. They read his reports, he knew, so he was careful to keep his wording neutral and names to a minimum.

He settled back into life in Tiziane with determined focus on the here and now. Being back in the bled, the rural lands beyond the reach of central government, was shockingly different to life in Casablanca. Here, the hands of the French lay less obviously heavily upon the people. There was no Sûreté and no significant military presence here: everything went through the local commandant and his deputy the adjutant; a handful of soldiers kept the peace – the rest had been posted to Marrakech and Casa, where there was the greatest need of them. There wasn't even a jail, as such, in Tiziane any more – lawbreakers were taken away to the region's administrative centre of Tiznit on the coast. And so Hamou went to the hammam, to the barber, to the mosque; he walked around the market, ate with his family, enjoyed tending his little garden, sat reading with the cat curled up beside him, took herbs to help keep the nightmares at bay, had a pair of new yellow babouches made to fit him…

And learned to ride.

The mule had come as something of a surprise. Hamou had been hoping, indeed expecting, that his new role would come with a form of transport – maybe nothing so grand as a car, but at least a mobilette, so he had been dismayed when Hassan appeared at his office just as he was sending on her way a woman who heard he was a zouhry and sought a blessing for her baby son.

'To protect him from the djinns, you know. They will listen to you.'

He had assured her they would not, but had, out of kindness, laid a hand on the child's head and muttered a prayer over it, and this seemed to please the woman well enough.

Hassan, leaning on the doorframe, grinned after her. 'Hope your magic works on animals, my brother.'

Hamou knitted his brows. 'Why?'

'Come with me and you will see.'

Hamou followed him out of the judicial compound – where he spent several hours a day at a desk, in his own office, with a lad, Saïd, who would run errands for him, and his very own secretary, a quiet young man called Aziz, sitting outside – and down the road towards the town to the stables.

Hassan greeted the boy inside – they appeared to be cousins – and ushered Hamou in. 'This is Raphäel. He belongs to the commandant,' he said, stopping at a stall where a handsome black horse gazed out at them, liquid-eyed, inquisitive. 'He's pure bred, from the Suleiman stud near Marrakech.'

'He's beautiful.' This much Hamou could appreciate: the animal had a noble bearing and a handsome profile, but by heavens, he was huge!

The commandant must be a keen *chevalier*, for he owned three other fine animals. The other two horses stabled there belonged to his adjutant, Officer Boulanger.

By now, Hamou was feeling increasingly nervous. He wasn't going to be expected to ride a horse, was he? he asked Hassan anxiously.

The moqqadem laughed. 'A horse? Of course not!' But before Hamou could relax, he added, 'This is your mount.'

They had come to a halt by a stall over which another creature looked out. It eyed the visitors in an unfriendly manner and snorted.

'Mine?' Hamou regarded the beast in dismay.

'He's called Makouda,' Hassan said, laughing.

A *makouda* was a round, often viciously spicy, potato dumpling. Hamou considered this nomination and felt concerned.

Hassan had the boy open the stall and coax the animal out. The mule was smaller than the fine Arab horses owned by the French, but it still seemed a monster to Hamou, especially when it rolled back its lips and showed him its enormous yellow teeth – in greeting, or in warning? He patted Makouda's nose hesitantly, and the beast threw its head up and stamped, missing Hamou's foot by an inch.

'Shit!' Hamou couldn't help but leap backwards. 'I'm supposed to ride this thing?'

'How else are you going to get up to Tagtout and Amalou?' Hassan asked guilelessly, referring to two of the more remote mountain villages that came under the purview of Tiziane.

Later that evening, Hamou had returned to the stables alone. The boy was still there. 'Can you ride?' Hamou asked him.

The boy grinned. 'Of course.'

'Can you teach me?' He pulled a small denomination note out of his pocket and the boy's grin widened.

'Waccha, sidi.'

Every night for the rest of that week, Hamou had returned to his little villa with his backside and thighs aching to the bone. He rode like a sack of rice, but he rode. Makouda had a taste for carrots: he was mad for them. Hamou bribed the mule for its cooperation, which was given grudgingly, though what would happen when the carrots ran out?

It occurred to him that he was a lucky man indeed if managing a mule had become the greatest of his concerns, and gave a rueful smile.

Everybody wanted to see the new hakam. Hamou was invited to gathering after gathering. He had no idea he had so many cousins, could not keep track of their names or the internecine connections and rivalries (even feuds) between them. And every single one of them seemed to have a niggling little problem they thought he could help with. Hamou, pleading inexperience and the need to get to grips with his new position, managed to hold them at bay, but he began to feel like a twig caught between rocks in a torrent of floodwater.

Then there were the local tribal chiefs. Each of the settlements around Tiziane were affiliated to a *takbilt*, and each tribe had a chieftain or *amghrar* and its own sheaf of petty officials, and they all wanted a piece of Hamou. He was invited to dinners and feasts in one village after another in the valley and amongst the mountains, which meant endless treks on the surly Makouda, and an ever-closer relationship with the carrot-seller in the Tiziane market. On each of these ventures Hamou was forced to take with him an armed guard, to fill in a form in advance for the hours of service of his mokhazni and for the rifle and ammunition the man had to carry.

At these gatherings the only people Hamou seemed to meet were men puffed up with their own importance, all landholders and power brokers looking to gain advantage in their petty squabbles with one another, or to use him as a foothold within the French administration. After the traditional greetings, drumming and dances, he would be subjected to an endless succession of embraces and reminders of their dealings with his father and uncles, their daughters' marriages with this or that cousin in his family, and of course suggestions of single girls who might make him a fine wife, and by the end Hamou would leave feeling drained and frustrated.

At the fourth gathering, in the village of Amalou, which as its name suggested lay in the shadow of the mountain range, he finally ran out of patience. 'It's very pleasant to meet your clan,' he lied to the chieftain, 'but the people I really need to get to know are your teachers, your doctor, the imam, your blacksmith, your farmers, your water diviners.'

The amghrar looked appalled. 'But those are just poor people, folk with neither influence nor power.'

Hamou had been thinking about this on the winding path up through the foothills during which journey he had passed a lot of poor peasants scratching sparse crops out of dry soil, scrawny sheep and goats scrambling up streambeds where no water flowed, women trying to wash laundry in a pool scummed with algae, children who should have been in school gathering argan nuts. Surely, he should try to do some good in the world with this little bit of power he had been given, to make the lives of such people better rather than continuing to reinforce the system of corruption and preference that was contributing to such poverty? He spoke earnestly. 'As I see it, my role as hakam is to improve the lives of ordinary people, to be the oil between the cogs of the villages and the authorities.'

The amghrar regarded him sceptically, then laughed. 'Oil costs money. Nothing comes for free. Now about that building permit we were discussing earlier…'

Later that week, Hamou returned from work to find an envelope propped against his front door. When he picked it up, he found the paper was soft and creamy, and his name was written in flowing black ink in a formal French hand. Opening the envelope, he found an invitation within:

> *Commandant and Mme Martinot*
> *Request the pleasure of the presence of*
> *M. Mohammed ben M'barek*
> *To attend a drinks reception*
> *This Thursday evening at their home*

Hamou stared at it. The French commandant and his wife had been away from Tiziane to avoid the worst of the punishing heat, gone to their villa on the coast at Essaouira. He had been inaugurated into his new job by the adjutant, Jérôme Boulanger, a cheerful young Frenchman with very blue eyes and a disarming manner. He had been dreading their return. Martinot would surely know his history, would have contact with the administrative chiefs in Casa, possibly even with Fouquet and his superior. Till now, Hamou had gone about his new job as if playing a role, but now reality was crowding in. He sighed. There was no chance of refusing the invitation, he would have to attend, but it would feel like walking into the enemy camp.

He would need armour.

*

At six thirty on Thursday evening, Hamou put on the suit his sister Mimouna had arranged to have made for him. She had a fierce eye for cut and detail and had overseen the poor tailor mercilessly. The man looking back at him from the mirror on the interior of the wardrobe door appeared soigné, ridiculously elegant.

Madani, however, regarded him through slitted eyes, not taken in one whit by this cosmetic transformation. He loudly demanded more sardines.

Hamou shook his head. 'Oh no you don't, little saboteur. I know your game.'

The commandant's villa was situated on a rise overlooking the town. A guard stood at the gate and saluted the hakam as he approached, then demanded his papers. 'Can't be too careful these days,' he apologised as he handed the identity card back. 'Especially not after the attempt on the governor in Tiznit yesterday. Rumour is the gunman was a member of the Black Crescent. They shot him dead before he did any harm, but you know, terrorists everywhere.' He tapped his semi-automatic fondly.

Hamou's spine prickled. *Even here*, he thought. *They have a long reach indeed.* He tucked the card back into his jacket pocket and walked up the path to the villa. On the threshold he took a deep breath, braced himself, and entered, to be met by a hubbub of noise and a miasma of expensive tobacco that triggered horrific memories, and for a sharp moment felt the distinct urge to flee. He forced himself into a room full of men in suits and smoking jackets and women in cocktail dresses, jewels and high-heeled shoes, and felt his head spin.

'Ah, Hamou, good to see you!' The caid, Hajj Abdullah, held

him at arm's length and looked him up and down. 'Good effort, young man.' Like Hamou, he was dressed in European style but, as if refusing fully to conform to French standards, had added an extravagant turban pinned with a silver amulet. 'Before I introduce you, remember you are a proud member of this clan: I stuck my neck out to vouch for you when this hakam plan was suggested by Casablanca, so don't let me down. And whatever you do, try not to stare at the ladies – it's hard, I know – but they have different ways, the French, and we must be gentlemen. Got that?' He narrowed his eyes at Hamou in much the same way Madani had. *Sardines later, then...*

Hamou nodded and the caid guided him to where an austere-looking man was deep in conversation with a group of other men. Something about the set of his face reminded him of Fouquet, but perhaps that was just his paranoia. He turned his attention to the woman beside the commandant, whose blonde hair was arranged in gleaming rolls that tumbled to bare white shoulders and a luscious sweep of bosom. Hamou fixed his stare at a point on the wall behind the guests to ensure his eyes did not fall on forbidden territory but as soon as the woman caught sight of him, she leaned across and caught the caid by the arm. 'Dear Hajj Abdullah, who is this extremely handsome young newcomer?'

'Ah, Madame Martinot, this is the estimable young man who was recently returned to us from service in Casablanca to be our hakam. He is Mohammed ben M'barek ben Ali, though he prefers to be known simply as Hamou Badi.'

The woman beside the commandant's wife now turned around and blew a puff of menthol-perfumed smoke into the air between them, then took a step forward, breaching the smoke ring, grinned slyly at Hamou, and said quietly in the local dialect, 'Hello, darling Hamou. It's lovely to see you. But here you don't know me: *comprends?*'

Hamou's gaze widened. The woman standing between him and the commandant and his wife wore a dress of violet satin, cinched at the waist by a wide, jewel-encrusted Moroccan belt, but everything else about her looked French, from the styling of her shining auburn hair to her deep red lipstick and elegant cigarette holder. Despite her sophistication, he would know her anywhere. Those eyes, green-gold ringing brown irises, the colour of the river stones where he had fished as a child, down past the orchards, where dragonflies had darted and crested larks soared…

Aicha Ghazaal dropped him a slow wink, then turned back to the commandant's wife. 'You know what *"badi"* means in Arabic, don't you, Isabel? "Marvellous", that's what it means.' Her accent was perfect: what a chameleon she was. 'Hamou the Marvellous. Perhaps he can perform miracles!'

Madame Martinot shouted with laughter. 'Oh, Leone, how delightful, I must tell Jules.' She plucked at her husband's sleeve. 'Come and meet the new mediator, Monsieur Badi – his name means marvellous, and didn't you say this place needed a miracle-worker?'

As the commandant greeted and questioned him, Hamou sensed Aicha regarding him with irrepressible complicity. His head spun. It might be the champagne, which he had never had before, but he didn't think it was just that. For the rest of that strange evening, he found his eyes straying across the crowded room to where Aicha stood, apparently perfectly at ease in this company, laughing with the women, flirting with the men. One man in particular seemed much taken with her: an ugly bull of a fellow with a thick neck and the roughened red face and veined nose of a seasoned drinker. When Aicha moved through the crowd to join another knot of revellers, his eyes followed her. Hamou could hardly blame him: she was entrancing. He wondered where she had learned such ease and poise, let alone such perfect French. But of course, he knew: she had learned it in the brothel in Casablanca, catering to her most privileged clients. But it was a long way from Casa to here, and not just in geographical terms. He recalled now how they had called her

Aicha Soussi in the old medina, and that she had the accent of the area when she was not curating her image. He wondered what had brought her 'home'.

He watched the bull-necked man – introduced to him as a local landowner called Baptiste Meline – walk up to Aicha now and touch her familiarly on the hip. How did she not shrink away from the old lecher? Instead, she turned her gleaming smile on him, accepted a cigarette and allowed him to light it for her and they stood for a short time in the group, talking and laughing. Then Meline drew her aside and, lowering his head, said something to her alone. Aicha smiled up at him, but the smile did not reach her eyes. Hamou saw something undefinable in it; something hard. She shook her head, kissed his veiny cheek quickly, and returned to the Martinots' group. Shortly after this, Hamou saw Meline leave the party with another woman, very young, and the pair did not return.

How Hamou wished he too could escape, but Hajj Abdullah kept guiding him around the room to meet one person after another whose names he knew he'd never retain. After a while, the adjutant came to steer him away.

'Tedious things, these parties. How are you finding your new quarters?'

Hamou remembered that Boulanger had lived there before him. 'It's very pleasant. I hope your new quarters are comfortable.'

'The old place was a bit small,' the adjutant said airily. 'You must come up and have a drink with me in my new house. It's jolly nice, actually.' He hesitated, then added, 'Were you leaving? I saw you look longingly towards the exit.'

Hamou laughed. 'I wish I could.'

'Well, you can: you're your own man here. It's a neat position you occupy, between the two administrations – makes it a lot harder for anyone to tell you what to do.'

'Maybe it means everyone can tell me what to do.' Hamou grimaced.

'I dare say it'll feel like that sometimes, but I don't think you need to worry too much. Everything's moving in the right direction,' the adjutant said with a conspiratorial wink. 'But I've been asked to bring you to the commandant before you leave.'

'Must I?'

Jérome Boulanger's blue eyes sparkled. 'Believe it or not, I hate these occasions too: but you have to do your bit. Come on.'

Martinot greeted him as if they were old friends and asked him, 'So, Hamou, do you hunt?'

This was such an unexpected question that Hamou was struck dumb for several embarrassing seconds, before replying that he had been out on one or two expeditions (though he did not add that these had been with his uncle, shooting rabbits with an old blunderbuss, or that he had thrown up).

'Capital!' the commandant exclaimed. 'You'll come out with us next time we go after boar.' And then he'd turned his back on his new hakam and started talking politics with his neighbour.

Hamou caught the words 'Black Crescent', and he walked away.

29

Early one morning at the end of the summer, Hamou
was listening to the radio with half an ear while trying
unsuccessfully to coax Madani into eating the chicken scraps
the butcher had given him the previous day, which the cat
had decided were greatly inferior to tinned fish, when a news
bulletin came on about an incident in the north of the country,
at a settlement called Oued Zem. There had been an uprising
among the Berber tribes in the region, and many Europeans
had been brutally murdered. The details that followed made
Hamou's skin crawl. By the time he heard the newsreader
mention the involvement of dissident nationalists, and that it
was believed the atrocity had been timed to mark the second
anniversary of the sultan's exile, he felt sick. Immediately, he
thought about Zina. He hadn't heard of any atrocity taking
place in Casa, but who knew what made the news reports, and
what didn't?

He got ready for work, let Madani out to patrol his new
territory, and walked the little way to the judicial compound.
Above the Djebel Kest, where the ravines and overhangs were
marked by sharp maroon shadows, the sky was a pristine blue,
untouched by cloud or contrail. And yet, his heart did not lift
as it usually did when he headed for his office to do some good
in the world, and when he arrived it was to find Aziz, Saïd and

Houcine deep in conversation out in the courtyard. They stopped talking when he appeared.

Aziz said, 'Did you hear the news from the north?'

Hamou nodded.

'A terrible thing,' Saïd said, but his eyes were bright.

'Terrible,' Hamou agreed, but he meant it. The details from the news report had been appalling. Women and children murdered, including a boy who had his throat slit on the operating table in the local hospital.

'Fifty dead, they say,' Aziz added.

'I heard it was the Black Hand,' Houcine said.

'I'm not entirely sure the Black Hand are still operational.' Hamou said it without thinking. Now they were fascinated. Because he had recently come from Casa, they thought Hamou knew everything there was to know about the complexities of the political resistance. There were stories that he had been involved, that exile to Tiziane had been a way of removing him from the cauldron in the north. He amended quietly, 'Though what do I know? There are so many splinter groups. It's impossible to keep track of them all.'

'They're saying this may be the last straw for the French,' Aziz said hopefully.

Hamou was not going to be drawn in. 'Nothing is ever that simple,' he said. He was surprised by their avidity. Did the nationalist cause enjoy support even here in this rural community so far from the political centres?

'Well, blessings on the head of the true sultan,' Houcine declared. 'May he be returned to us soon.' There was a chorus of 'inshallah'.

The hakam's waiting room was full. Hamou operated a strict first-come first-served system and had instructed Aziz and Saïd that on no account were they to accept bribes for preferential treatment, even in non-monetary form. As it was, he found himself beset by compromise at every turn, but especially at home: his mother's kitchen was full to overflowing with jars of oil, pots of honey, bags of grain and piles of fruit, and when he had asked her where it had all come from, she had been uncharacteristically evasive.

'Our family has many friends, dear son.'

Hamou had eventually cornered his little sister Sofia, whose tongue was more easily loosened than Mimouna's. Eagerly, she had explained that the delicious provisions had been gifts from hopeful suitors.

'Ah,' Hamou had said, relieved. 'Well, I hope Mimouna has some say in the choice of her future husband.'

Sofia had giggled. 'Of course not for Mimouna. For you!'

'For me?' Hamou had been aghast.

'Yam'mi's been interviewing candidates ever since you came home. She said you're at the peak of your marriageable value and it's the perfect time to capitalise on that.'

Hamou knew well enough the customs of his people, and how they vied for every iota of advantage for their families and strengthened clan bonds by forging alliances by business, trade, and most of all by marriage. Such delicate investigations were traditionally carried out by the women of the family, who were the most sensitive to the shades of benefit to be acquired, to the infinitesimal degrees of social differential, to assessments of character, age, appearance and stock; to the quantity and nature of dowry to be assigned. How many times had Hamou's mother pressed him on the question of marriage? How many times had he – he thought successfully – managed to evade it? She had clearly decided to take matters into her own hands. Was this what she had meant when she had spoken about him needing some help with getting his baraka back? Did she think marrying him off against his will would achieve that?

In fact, it seemed Lalla Saïda had more than one strategy up her sleeve when it came to dealing with Hamou's baraka; on his next visit home, he had been ushered by his mother into the room off the vestibule, and there found the fkih, Sidi Daoud, waiting for him, with a number of objects laid out on a low circular table – a little clay brazier, a pot of incense crystals, a glass of milk, a long spoon, some eggs, and a quill and ink. Such accoutrements belonged surely in the realm of Al Attar and other charlatans, but Hamou knew the fkih to be a wise man and a scholar, and of course now he was part of the family, so rather than running a mile, as had been his first instinct, Hamou had greeted him cordially and sat down with him.

Behind them, the door had closed stealthily.

After the traditional greetings had been exchanged, the old man regarded Hamou closely. Then he closed his eyes and held a hand before Hamou's face, moving it as if trying to touch every part of it but was prevented from doing so by a force field. Hamou had watched the seamed palm pass before his eyes, travel eastwards, then south to his chin and neck, then finally back up to the crown of his head on the other side.

Sidi Daoud's eyes flew open and his pupils seemed so wide and dark, it was as if they had sucked in the night. Without a word, he had fanned the coals in the brazier, added a few nuggets of incense and then taken Hamou's hands in his. 'You have seen much suffering, my son.'

Hamou had wanted to wrest his hands away and bolt. But he forced himself to stay. 'Yes,' he said after a long silence, 'I have.'

'No one but I will hear your words, you have my solemn promise on that. Not even your mother. Tell me, Mohammed ben M'barek ben Ali, all the things that have given you pain while you were away from us. Do not stint. Do not hold back. I am here to help you.'

And so, slowly, haltingly, Hamou had talked about his time in Casa. About the general brutality and injustice. About the specific events he had witnessed, and those in which he had been at the centre. When he came to the retelling of Fouquet's attempt on his life, the fkih's grip had tightened.

'Your grandfather Ali's amulet? It took the force of the

bullet?' He seemed somehow energised: for he had been the one to whom Lalla Saïda had taken the amulet to fill with kbrit and alum and other magics.

'It saved my life,' Hamou had said quietly. He thought about the blackened, tortured twist of metal that had been returned to him by the lawyer at the Ghbila, and felt again the creeping, uncanny acceptance that there might indeed be some unearthly power at work in the world.

When Hamou had talked it all out, Sidi Daoud wafted the fragrant incense towards him so that he was enveloped by it. 'For purification,' he said simply. Then he took up the largest and whitest of the eggs, opened the little bottle of ink, dipped the quill in it and for several long minutes wrote upon the shell in tiny letters.

ⴽⵔⵀ; ⵛⵥⵜⴰⵏⵅⴰⵣⵍⵀⴰⵔⵟ
ⵔⵚⴰⵚⴰⵏⵛⵏⵖⵄⵎⵜⵜⴰⵙⵛⵓⴱⵜ

Sidi Daoud handed the egg to Hamou, who stared at it in wonderment, turning it over and over to examine the glyphs he had made. It was, he knew, his own language – Tamazight – written in its own ancient alphabet, the Tifinagh. But no one knew how to write the Berber language now: it was almost entirely lost. He recognised ⵣ though, as the symbol of the Free Men. He gazed from the markings on the egg to the fkih in wonder.

'We are a proud people with a long heritage, Hamou,' Sidi Daoud said quietly. 'You are Amazigh; you are Chleuh. No one can take your pride and your strength away from you.' He traced the words he had marked. 'Hatred. Pain. War. Bullets. Murder. Curse. Now, break the egg into this glass, and throw the shell into the coals.'

Hamou did as he was told and watched as the flames licked up in the brazier and charred the pieces. The fkih swirled the egg into the milk and added honey and a sprinkle of some powder which smelled like cloves and nutmeg, then handed the glass to Hamou.

'The bad is gone but there is always some good to be had from every experience. Drink down the good and let it nourish you, my boy.'

And he had. It had tasted better than he had expected, and when he had walked home he had felt somehow lighter and more optimistic. He was Amazigh, one of the Free Men. He was in a position to do good in the world, and that was what he would do.

This morning his first case was a woman who had agreed a price for a carpet in the market, had gone home to fetch the money but, on her return, the carpet-seller had told her he had received a better offer and that if she still wished to purchase it, she would have to top that price.

'Did you clearly agree the sum?' Hamou asked gently.

'He touched his heart and swore on God's name.'

'I will come with you at lunchtime to see this tradesman,' Hamou promised her.

The woman was most satisfied with this. 'They told me you'd take his part because he's your cousin!' she crowed, and Hamou's heart sank. Still, there was the principle of honest dealing to be upheld and family would have to come second.

There followed a widower who complained that his neighbour was stealing his figs. 'She's brazen about it!' he declared, incensed. 'She hangs them up to dry on her washing line along with her underwear, right in front of my house!'

Hamou sent his clerk to ascertain that the woman had no fig trees on her land, then agreed to meet the man later in the day to have a word with the neighbour.

The next two problems – both involving tangled inheritance claims – he referred up to the tribal courts, with the promise that if the matters remained unresolved, he would take up their cases and make further enquiries on their behalf. These were followed by a couple of easily dismissed petitioners looking to enrol him on their sides in vexatious claims: he sent them on their way, accusing them of *tamqant*, finger-pointing.

Next came a young woman, who stared at Aziz until he took the hint and left, closing the door carefully behind him. Hamou waited, pen poised to take his own notes. The plaintiff was striking, with boldly arched brows, heavy kohl and silver filigree earrings.

'How may I help you?' he said at last.

'I think I may require a divorce.'

'That doesn't really fall under my remit,' Hamou said carefully. 'It's a matter for the customary court.'

'I've come to you first, before I take it to court. I need some advice.'

'Of course.'

'It's my husband, you see.'

'Well, yes. Go on.'

'He doesn't make enough effort.'

Hamou waited, a polite question on his face, feeling a twinge of sympathy for the man. Was he expected to help with housework, children and livestock, as well as whatever he did to bring money in?

'In bed.'

'In bed?'

'He's supposed to do his best to give me pleasure, isn't he? That's what my mother told me, that according to the Prophet my conjugal rights are equal to his. He is bound to satisfy me, just as I am bound to take him to my bed and give him pleasure.'

Hamou swallowed. 'And he doesn't?'

'No. He just gets on me without preamble and sets about his business.'

'Oh dear. That doesn't sound very satisfactory.'

'It isn't.' She looked very fierce.

'Have you tried to talk to him about this?'

The woman gave him an odd look. 'No.'

'Don't you think that would be a good place to start?'

'Why should I have to instruct him in his duty?'

'Perhaps he is… ignorant of this duty?'

'Tell me, Hakam, what should I tell him to do?'

Hamou, flustered, said quickly, 'I may not be the best person to ask. I am not yet married.'

The woman smiled and Hamou felt the blood rising in his cheeks. 'Well, I am sure that were you married, you would make an effort to please your wife.'

'Ah, yes, without doubt.' He looked away from her probing gaze and wrote a few words in the notebook in front of him. The words were 'bread, olives, cheese, bottle of water'. He wrote them as a shield for his confusion, trying to think about lunch rather than sex. Calmed, he looked up again. 'Tell me, Lalla…?'

'Ouaziz. Fatima Ouaziz.'

'Tell me, Lalla Fatima, why did you marry him?'

Her eyebrows shot up. 'He seemed a good prospect.'

'What does he do?'

'He's a mokhazni.'

Oh no. Hamou had a nasty feeling he knew what was coming next. 'A mokhazni, in Tiziane?'

She gave him a look bordering on the contemptuous. 'Of course, in Tiziane. His name is Houcine.'

Hamou's heart sank. 'I see.'

'Yes.' She smiled. 'Now you do see. So, I thought, because he works with you, perhaps you could have a word with him about this. Man to man. Because if he doesn't make more effort to do his duty by me, I shall have to consider divorce.' She got to her feet, nodded to him, and left.

Hamou sat there, feeling shaken. Then he took a deep breath, crossed the office and opened the door. Outside was a single old man, the old woman who had seen him about the carpet, and Aziz. Hamou let a long breath out in relief. 'Come in,' he said to the old man and his scribe.

The old man seemed reluctant. 'Could I perhaps talk to you... alone?'

Hamou and Aziz exchanged glances. 'Yes, of course,' Hamou said. 'Why don't you run along and get yourself some lunch?' he suggested to Aziz. To the elderly woman, he said, 'I will be with you shortly, Lalla Hasna.'

The old man shuffled into the office and lowered himself creakingly into the chair opposite the desk. Hamou closed the door and took his seat. He laced his fingers together and leaned forward. 'What can I do for you, sir?'

'I bought something in the souk last week, and it didn't work.'

'Go on. I'll need some details. Tell me what it was you bought, and from whom, and I'll do what I can for you.'

'I did everything I was told. I waited three days, until the first crescent of the moon showed itself, and sat beneath a fruit tree.'

Hamou frowned.

'And then I waited and...' The old man looked shifty.

'And?'

'Nothing.'

'I'm afraid I don't quite understand. What was this thing you bought?'

The man mumbled something unintelligible.

'I'm sorry, could you repeat that?'

'A stimulant.'

'Oh. A drug, you mean?'

'I suppose you could call it that. Though the seller said it was completely natural, an extremely rare plant picked in the desert under a full moon, and all I had to do was to grind it up, mix it with a little honey made by bees that have fed on thyme and some water blessed at Lalla Tiaza's shrine, then take it while sitting beneath a fertile fruit tree by the light of the new moon. So that's what I did.' He leaned forward. 'Do you think the water or the honey may have been at fault?'

'I doubt it very much,' Hamou replied. 'Tell me, was the gentleman you bought it from thin, dark and around forty or so, dressed in a Saharan robe decorated with gold frogging and a dark blue turban?'

'Yes, that's the one!'

'I am afraid, sidi, that you've been duped. That man is a charlatan, a fraud. He poses as a Tuareg sorcerer, but the plant he sold you has no magical properties. He's been warned off from the souk here more than once. He sells his aphrodisiac for an extortionate sum, gives complicated instructions and tells people not to take the potion till he's well on his way to fleece his next set of customers. I'm very sorry. If he comes back, I will do what I can to help you get your money back from him.'

The old man looked miserable as he limped out of the office and Hamou's heart went out to him. He must be at least eighty. Did the sexual urge never loosen its hold?

After quickly filling out some forms, he walked into the town with Lalla Hasna to see the carpet-seller, who leapt up and embraced Hamou enthusiastically.

'Cousin! How good it is to see you. Let me brew you some tea.'

Hamou indicated the old lady. 'I'm here on behalf of Lalla Hasna.' He couldn't remember the man's name, so he resorted to a neutral greeting. 'My brother, this lady claims she struck a deal for a carpet but that when she returned to pay for it, you upped the price.'

The carpet-seller spread his soft hands. 'I had a better offer, and you know how it is, cousin. I have a wife who expects to be well looked after, and three children under the age of five. How they run through clothes! They grow and grow, the little ruffians, it's so expensive. You remember how we wrecked our djellabas playing football as boys? You tore a hole in your new one and wouldn't go home till after dark in case your mother saw it!'

Hamou narrowed his eyes at him. Ah, now he remembered: it was Qasem, always on the edge of the group, not very bold or good with his feet, always a bit of a coward. He did not much like the man invoking childhood events in this manner – it felt like a form of emotional blackmail – and he spoke abruptly. 'Now then, Qasem, a deal is a deal.'

Qasem looked affronted. 'Not until the money changes hands.'

'I can't believe that you aren't a man of your word,' Hamou said, modifying his tone. 'As I recall, you were always truthful and much looked up to for it by the rest of us.'

Qasem appeared taken aback by the statement, also somewhat mollified. 'That's nice to hear. But you know, cousin, times are tough, and a hard-working man needs to make every centime he can.'

Hamou nodded. 'Of course. And this lady also needs to count every coin.'

'I am not poor!' the old woman screeched. 'And he's a liar and a cheat, beg your pardon since he is related to you, but I speak only what I know.'

Hamou rounded on her. 'Please leave this to me. I am the hakam.'

She subsided, though her beady black gaze shuttled between the two of them as if they might, by dint of hand signals or some secret family language, be hashing out an agreement that would see her hard done by.

'Now, lalla, tell me: do you see the carpet in question here in the shop?'

The old woman pointed to a traditional rug woven in red, black and white. Hamou had seen hundreds of similar rugs, and indeed there were others like it in this very shop. He turned to Qasem. 'If you received a better offer, why is the carpet still here?'

The carpet-seller lifted a shoulder and gave a half-hearted shrug. 'I daresay they'll be back for it shortly.' Hamou held his gaze until Qasem looked away. 'Or maybe not.'

Hamou firmed his lips. 'Do you have the money?' he asked the old woman.

She muttered, and rummaged about in the depths of her bosom under her robe. Hamou and Qasem both looked away, discomfited, until she handed a roll of notes to Hamou. 'You count it,' she said.

It seemed a lot, but Hamou supposed it was a fair price for the good workmanship. 'Qasem, you struck a deal with Lalla Hasna, and you must honour it: I am sure you wish to maintain the good reputation of the town. The lady has a good many relatives scattered through the country: we would not want word of sharp practice to get around.'

With ill grace, Qasem took the money and rolled the carpet up. There was no more talk of tea or family.

Hamou carried the carpet for the old woman to her house, and was surprised, given the cost of the carpet, to find it to be no more than a mudbrick one-room addition to the side of a larger residence. A large feral tabby cat sat outside, and as soon as Lalla Hasna appeared, it trotted to meet her, bumping its head against her legs and purring loudly. She bent and stroked it, and as soon as she opened the door, it went inside.

The old lady invited him in. Despite the warmth of the day, inside it felt cold and dank, like being in a cave high up on a mountain. Hamou had not seen such poverty in all his life, even in the bidonvilles of Casablanca. On a floor of beaten earth there was nothing but a reed mat, a cushion, and a blanket, where the cat had made itself comfortable, a lamp recycled from an oilcan, a small clay brazier and some pots and pans. On the wall, a gilt-framed portrait of the exiled sultan added a little tawdry glamour. When he started to unroll the carpet for her, she stopped him. 'No, no, it's not for me. It's for my daughter. Her husband died and she's getting remarried. It's my wedding gift to them.'

Feeling humbled and unbelievably lucky in his own lot as he strolled around the sunny market later, Hamou bought a baguette and some olives for his lunch and wondered what else he might do to help Lalla Hasna. He remembered her adamant 'I'm not poor!' It wouldn't be straightforward.

He returned to his office. The man who had reported the theft of his figs was waiting for him outside, holding the reins of his donkey, and with a sigh, Hamou remembered that he had promised to accompany him to his home, a village beyond Tiziane, this afternoon. Tucking the bread under his arm and stuffing the bag of olives into his pocket, he signalled for the man to follow him and went to fetch Makouda.

30

Makouda was friskier than usual. He evaded the stableboy's attempt to capture him and kept throwing his head up. Once out of the yard, the beast danced around in circles to prevent Hamou from taking the saddle, and showed considerable interest in the other man's donkey.

The widower, Azzedine ('call me Azzy'), seemed amused by all this, and when Hamou took a step back from the animal, he realised why. 'Oh. Oh, my goodness.'

The mule's penis was vast and extended, as long as a man's forearm, ending in a fist that bobbed like a cobra's head beneath its belly.

'Makouda, Makouda, behave! Please, stop.'

Now the mule was trying to mount the donkey, rearing up and snorting furiously. The jenny, bemused, since she was not in season, bore this attempted assault for a patient minute, then rounded on Makouda, teeth bared. And just like that, the mule quieted. Hamou and the widower exchanged glances. 'I'm so sorry,' Hamou said.

Azzedine grinned, the smile lighting up his dour face, and Hamou saw for the first time that the man was barely middle-aged. 'You can't blame him, it's just nature.' He paused. 'Are you married, sidi?'

'No,' Hamou said shortly, and did not elaborate.

They took the hill out of Tiziane towards the high plateau.

At first, Hamou had tried to lead the way, but Makouda kept turning to make eyes at the jenny, so in the end he let Azzy ride ahead, giving the mule the enticement of the donkey's neat hindquarters, and he trotted along, as docile as a lamb.

Azzedine told Hamou his history. For years he had worked away in Tiznit for a jewellery maker in the silver quarter there, to provide for his elderly parents and younger siblings, before returning in his thirties to settle down to work the family's land. 'You should have seen it! An orchard full of apricots, peaches and pomegranates. The fig tree, of course, right beside our own well. We grew tomatoes, peppers and chillies, and so many herbs. By the time I got it all in order we were eating like sultans! And I got married – to the prettiest girl you can imagine.' He fell silent.

Hamou waited, sensing tragedy.

'Our first boy was stillborn; the second, a girl, lived for two weeks. Jehane – my wife – lost two other babies before term. The third grew big inside her – a boy, all the women said. They put her to bed before the birthing date and everyone brought her delicacies. Figs were her favourite – fresh and juicy, or dried and threaded into a ring. She craved them all through her pregnancy...'

Again, a silence stretched between them, broken only by the sound of the animals' hooves in the sandy dust of the lane and the call of hoopoes in the trees.

'The boy wouldn't come out right and she tried so hard she died of exhaustion.' He wiped his face. 'Then drought took the farm, too. I gave up the animals after Jehane died: she was the one who took care of them, and I couldn't stand the sound of their bleating when she'd gone. I sold off parcels of land – my parents had died, my sisters were married, it was just me, and I didn't need much. Just the orchard and the well, and a few chickens. And my fig tree.' He turned and looked into Hamou's face. 'Is it too much to ask that what little I have left isn't robbed from under my nose?'

'Of course not.' Hamou couldn't think of much to say.

They crested a rise beyond a huddle of pisé buildings and Azzedine got off the donkey, unlatched a gate, and led them along a smaller lane, past ancient stone cisterns and into a tidy smallholding. Here, he released the donkey into a field to graze what little it could find and suggested that Hamou tether Makouda to a post near the house. The mule, separated from his love interest, set up a fierce braying like a tortured door hinge, and had to be placated with a carrot, much to the widower's amusement. Then Azzy picked up a pair of copper pitchers and led Hamou past the house to the well and fig tree.

The field they crossed was so dry that little dust devils rose from it in the afternoon wind off the plain. It was hard to believe it had once been lush and productive: now the only green to be seen came from the odd weed and the area around the well. The fig tree, though, was a beauty, its fingered leaves large and handsome, and what was left of the fruits in its branches were ripely dark. Azzedine reached up and picked one. He handed it to Hamou. 'They're the sweetest you'll find,' he said softly. 'Jehane always said so.'

Hamou took a bite. The skin resisted his teeth for a moment, then gave way in an intense, sugary release. He closed his eyes. 'Exquisite.'

Azzedine beamed proudly. Then he pointed beyond the stone wall around the well to the neighbouring house, and there, Hamou saw stretched between two trees, the washing line draped with...

...goodness! Such a range of undergarments he had not seen since he'd been stationed on the Rue de Strasbourg. He felt the blood rising in his cheeks as he took in the lace-trimmed panties and brassieres, a corset with a mass of frills at bosom and hips. Between these items, threads of drying figs, like flattened circles of cork, swayed provocatively in the breeze.

After a moment, Hamou grinned. 'Let me go and talk to your neighbour, to see what she has to say for herself.' He suggested that it might be better if he went alone to speak with the woman and asked for her name and circumstances. Azzedine told him her name and that she lived alone, after her mother's death earlier in the year. Hamou left him drawing up water with which to fill his pitchers.

He climbed easily over the low stone wall that separated the properties and went to the neighbouring house. The woman came out, her arms crossed over her chest.

'Are you Rafika, the daughter of Adel Bahou?' he asked, and she nodded, her mouth quirked just a little, as if they shared a secret, which Hamou supposed they did.

'Here about the figs, are you?' She gave a throaty laugh, showing the gap between her front teeth. An air of female confidence swelled the air between them.

'Yes. I'm the hakam, down in Tiziane. Azzedine asked me to talk to you.'

Her eyes slitted, and Hamou was reminded of Aicha regarding him with amused complicity at the commandant's soirée, the delicious, unspoken truth sparking in the air between them. 'Have you been taking his figs?' he asked bluntly.

She cocked her head and her grin widened. 'Well, there's taking and *taking*. I haven't been *eating* them, if that's what you mean. Just picking and drying them. For him. They'd go to rot otherwise. Azzedine doesn't look after them, or himself.'

'I see.' And he did see. 'Might I bring your neighbour here so we can talk?'

'Please do,' she purred. She pulled up a stool, hitched up her robe and sat down on it, legs stretched out in front of her, crossed at the ankle. She had very neat ankles, Hamou noticed, small-boned and slender. She made quite a picture sitting there, with her haik pulled up and bright geraniums in the pots around her. 'It's a shame that such a fine man should live all alone, letting the world go to waste around him.'

For a moment, Hamou wasn't sure whether she meant him or the widower, but her gaze had already transferred itself towards the spot where Azzy stood, balancing his pitchers on the wall.

'Fetching water,' she clucked. 'It's not a man's business.'

Hamou went to fetch Azzedine. He put a hand on the man's shoulder. 'I don't think she's stealing your figs,' he said quietly.

Azzy bridled. 'She is! Look – just look at them all hanging there!'

'Calm down. She said she hasn't eaten a single one – she's saving them for you.' Hamou paused. 'I don't think that's all she's saving for you.' He gave Azzy a telling look and watched as understanding dawned.

'Oh.'

'Yes, oh. How long have you been on your own, Azzedine?'

'Nearly five years.'

'That's a long time.'

'It is.' Azzedine was thoughtful. His gaze roved over the artfully arranged washing line, and that transformative grin broke out of him once more.

Hamou clapped him on the shoulder. 'Perhaps I should leave you to talk to your neighbour alone?'

Azzy ran a hand over his turban, neatening it. He smoothed his djellaba. 'Perhaps that would be for the best,' he agreed.

Hamou walked back to retrieve Makouda, a silly smile plastered to his face. He could not remember the last time he had felt such satisfaction. He was still congratulating himself as he let the mule out onto the main track once more and headed back through the little village.

'Hey!'

The voice snapped him out of his reverie.

'You're the hakam, aren't you?'

'Hamou Badi, yes.'

The man approached. He looked to his left, then his right, as if concerned at being overheard. 'You're not police, are you?'

Hamou shook his head. 'No.'

'If I ask you something, it's in confidence?' The man fell into step with Hamou. He was fifty or so, heavy-set, with a limp, and wore a grubby shirt over wide Berber trousers.

'I share any information that comes to me in the course of my work with other authorities only when asked to by those who seek my aid.'

'Swear to God?'

'As Allah is my witness.'

'The thing is my friend... paid for a service, and it has not been carried out. To his satisfaction.'

'Go on?' Hamou encouraged.

'I probably shouldn't be seen speaking to you.' The man ran a tongue over dry lips as he looked around again. 'Would you meet me up at the *agadir*?' He motioned with his head to the old stone grain store perched on the hill overlooking the village.

'Are you sure that's necessary?' The climb looked steep.

But the man had already taken off in a fast, lopsided walk in the opposite direction so that he would come at the agadir from the other side.

'Come on, Makouda. Now we'll see just how surefooted a mule can be.'

He urged the animal up the scree and boulders and headed for the tor. These old agadirs had been built in ages past when tribes warred with one another and there was always the threat of famine. It was where the community stored its grain and dried goods and sometimes even its valuables, under lock and key. French rule had at least lessened the likelihood of both war and famine in the region, and the agadirs were used less than they had been. Was he being lured up there for nefarious purposes? To be robbed? Even killed? But he hadn't had that sense from the nervous man. He ate his lunch – better to die on a full stomach – swallowing the bread and olives, throwing the pits to the ground. Precious little chance of them taking root here, though, in this stony soil.

Makouda complained at the steep gradient but put his head down and plodded onward. From the top of the tor, Hamou could see the geography of the whole area, from the Djebel Kest in the north to the sprawl of Tiziane in the valley, with its radiating spokes of new roads, the school the French had built on one side, the oasis on the other; he saw the villages dotted here and there, and if he turned, he could see the road to Tiznit winding across the plateau and into the far-off hills of the Afoud range. Looking out over the whole area for which he worked as hakam, he felt like the king of the djinns.

Then he heard someone breathing heavily and the crunch of stones underfoot. The memory of the morning's radio report came back to him. Were there people here working for the nationalist cause who would see him as a traitor for taking a salary from the administration? He also took a stipend from the caid's office – yet again, he stood between worlds – this time between the Amazigh and the French, but he doubted that nuance would be appreciated. Hamou cursed his foolishness for not bringing Houcine with him. He had just thought he was going to deal with a petty dispute about figs!

The man appeared now, a bit grey in the face from the effort of the climb. He didn't look much like a crack assassin. Hamou scanned him for signs of a weapon, but he carried no gun that he could see. A knife, then? You could hide a knife anywhere. Hamou wished he had not dismounted from the mule: they could have taken off down the track at speed. He positioned himself on the other side of the animal. 'Sorry, old boy. But better you than me.' Though if anything bad did happen to the mule, he knew he'd be upset.

The man stopped, and bent double, wheezing.

'What's your business?' Hamou called. 'What did you want to talk about that couldn't be done down there?' He indicated the village below, which seemed a speck from up here. Would anyone hear him if he shouted for help? It seemed unlikely.

The man straightened up, one hand on the ancient stonework of the grain store. 'In here,' he said, nodding to a small door.

There was no way Hamou was going inside. 'I need to keep hold of my mule,' he said pleasantly. 'He's a nervous one.'

The man shrugged. 'Ah well, there's no one to hear us in this godforsaken place.' He wet his lips. 'The thing is...' He came closer, and Hamou watched his hands. 'The thing is, this... friend of mine paid for a man to do a thing, and the thing wasn't done.'

A failed transaction. That was all. Hamou's shoulders dropped. All the years in Casa, all the death and brutality had left their mark. 'What was the "thing" that wasn't done?'

'Swear again you won't go to the police.'

Hamou put his free hand to his heart. 'I swear.'

'You're from the area, aren't you?'

Hamou nodded.

'So, you understand honour.'

'I would hope so.'

'Good. Because some people seem to have lost all concept of it. The French came along and muddied the waters. Time was the tribes sorted these things out for themselves. It was clear. A man dishonoured another and he paid for it. "A life for a life, eye for eye, nose for nose, ear for ear, tooth for tooth, and wounds equal for equal" – that's the *qisas*. Isn't it?'

Hamou had a bad feeling about this. 'Yes,' he said hesitantly.

'So, if a man dishonours another man's daughter, he should have recourse to retribution, or at least like for like payment?'

What, was he suggesting the other man's daughter be dishonoured to match? That was barbaric. 'We have other laws now,' Hamou said bluntly.

'My friend's daughter was promised to another, but this rich man came along and plucked her like a flower. So now she has lost her worth as both wife and daughter, for the other party pulled out of the marriage agreement, further dishonouring her, and the family. Now she sits at home, crying that no one will have her. And no one will!'

'Poor girl. Her betrothed won't forgive her?'

'Why would he? She is spoiled goods! My whole family is dishonoured. Why would they ally their family with ours now?'

'I thought it was your friend's?'

The man sighed. 'I am so angry it has made me stupid. Yes, it's my daughter. And I went after the bastard who did this to her, and he just laughed when I explained how her bride price was now lost to us and he owed us a debt of honour. Called me a savage and threatened to set his dogs on me.'

'Dogs?' Hamou frowned.

'He's a *kafir*.'

'I see.'

'So, then I talked to one of the elders on the council and he said there was nothing that could be done because the man was not of the tribes. This happened before you were appointed as hakam, or I'd have come to you.'

Hamou felt a small, profound relief that this awful thing had occurred before his time. 'You spoke of a service unfulfilled?' he asked at last.

'I went to see the public assassin,' the man said defiantly. 'I put my case to him, and he agreed that the man had been given the chance to make good on his crime and had failed to take the opportunity, and so his death was fully warranted under the old laws.'

'But good heavens, man.' Hamou was aghast. 'Those old laws don't operate any longer, not here. This is a modern society, with modern laws—'

'I see they were right about you,' the man said bitterly. 'You work for the French.'

Oh, here it came. 'I worked for the French in Casablanca, but now I work for the community of Tiziane,' Hamou said reasonably. 'I report to Caid Hajj Abdullah.'

'And to the commandant.'

'And to the commandant.' Hamou agreed. 'However, my job is to help resolve matters that fall between the two.'

'That's why I'm here.'

'I can't bring the man who dishonoured your daughter to justice,' Hamou said.

'I know *that*!' the man exploded. 'I want you to go and see the public assassin and get my money back from him. He was supposed to get rid of that bastard – but I saw the man walking the streets of Tiziane this very week! I am robbed and abused on all sides!'

So it was just a dispute over a transaction in the end, a nasty one, certainly, but a solvable problem all the same. 'All right, then,' Hamou said. 'I'll see what I can do for you.'

'And you swear you won't go to the cops?'

'On my life.'

At the family house that night, Hamou picked at his food. He had, perhaps, never fully realised before that his mother was a terrible cook, having been spoiled in Casa. The memory of Zina Chadli's couscous sauce thrilled through him, setting a tingle to his senses that had nothing to do with the heaped dish on the table in front of him. But the prospect of the conversation to follow also dulled his appetite. As his sisters cleared away the dishes, Hamou got to his feet, offering to help so as to procrastinate, but his mother shooed the girls away and called him back. 'We have much to talk about.'

Hamou gave in to his fate and sat back down.

'How are you feeling, my son, after the time you spent with Sidi Daoud?'

He considered this, having not given his encounter with the fkih too much thought, brushing the old man's antics off as the usual superstitious flim-flam. Besides, he had been so busy, learning and applying his new role. But he had, he realised, been sleeping better. He felt more energised, lighter in spirit; more engaged with the world. He had experienced fewer nightmares, fewer jolting memories. The news out of Oued Zem had shocked him, but it had not sunk him in depression or drowned him in the horror of his time in Casa. He wondered now whether the talking had helped settle some things in his mind. But if he told his mother he felt better, would she see it as the perfect time to press a bride upon him? Likewise, if he said nothing had changed, would that mean she would use his weakness as the reason he should marry as soon as possible, so that he had a wife to take care of him? It appeared he was damned either way.

'It was good to talk to Sidi Daoud,' he said carefully. 'And in time I'm sure I shall begin to feel better.'

She narrowed her eyes at him, and Hamou felt sure she saw straight through his evasiveness. 'Good, good. Well, let us proceed to the matter of your marriage.'

So, there was to be no escape. He started at once to explain he didn't want to get married, not right now, and that to maintain any semblance of integrity in order to do his job well and be accepted by the local community he must be seen to be impartial and fair-minded. His mother sat through his long peroration serenely, her hands folded in her lap, but when he reached this last point, she flapped them at him dismissively.

'My son, everyone knows the good standing of our family. Marrying well will merely strengthen your reputation and ties to the community. You have been away a long time: it would be good for people hereabouts to see you take one of their own to wife.' When Hamou started to protest, she held up a hand. 'I have made a shortlist!' she announced triumphantly. 'It has been winnowed down by every skill in my possession. The chaff has been cast to the four winds, leaving only the best grain, and even those I have sifted through to find the most wholesome kernels amongst them.'

She touched the thumb of her raised hand. 'Firstly, there is the Benasser family. They are first cousins to Hajj Abdullah – you could not ask for better connections to cement you in place as hakam. Their eldest daughter, Zohra, is nineteen. They brought me some cheese she had made – she rises at dawn to take care of the milking, and then get on with the household chores – and it was very fine. It would be excellent to welcome such a good little worker into our family—'

'She is too young!' Hamou cut her off. 'Where will I find common ground with a girl so much younger than me?' He knew before he had even finished speaking that he was making a capital error in engaging her on the merits and demerits of her preferred candidates. To enter into debate weakened his position.

Lalla Saïda grinned like a cat that had caught its mouse and could now toy with it until the death. 'Under the blankets, my boy. That's where you'll find your common ground. She has a lovely figure – I have seen her in the market – good hips and large breasts. She will bear you many children!'

Hamou's shock must have showed, for his mother chuckled loudly.

'Then there is Warda, daughter of Cherif Okba, the chief of Azaghrar village.' When Hamou made a face, remembering one of the pompous amghrars with whom he'd had dealings, she went straight on, 'And we have Amina Fikri, the scholar's daughter. Not as pretty as the first two, and rather short-sighted. I heard from the optician she needs glasses, but—'

'Mother! Have you been all over town with your investigations?'

'But of course! I am not going to make a poor bargain for my only son, am I? I ruled out two other girls from good families on the advice of Si Tami, the dentist, on account of their teeth, and another because a doctor at the clinic told me her heart was not strong.'

Hamou struggled for words. At last, he said, 'You sound like a farmer at a cattle market checking out the milch cows!'

Lalla Saïda pursed her mouth. 'That's a crude way of putting it, but not entirely inaccurate.'

Hamou pushed himself to his feet. 'I'm sorry, Yam'mi, to have put you to so much effort, but I'm just not having it! If – and I do mean if – I take a wife, she'll be a woman I choose. A woman, not a girl. And certainly not some willing little worker brought in to take care of your wretched chickens and goats and clean your house and clothes.'

His mother narrowed her eyes at him. 'I do hope you don't already have a candidate in mind?'

He stared at her. Did his mother know about his tenderness

for Zina Chadli? Did she have spies even as far as Casa? Then it dawned on him. Of course she did. His mad behaviour at his cousin Moha's engagement party might well have made it back to her via the chatty gossip of family members, before the Casa family had fled the city. He groaned inwardly. What a fool he was. No doubt she'd started fervently interviewing the families of all the eligible young women in the region on the very day she'd heard that bit of tittle-tattle.

He firmed his jaw. 'No more of this now, Yam'mi. And please make no promises nor accept any more... gifts' – he had been about to say 'bribes' but managed to hold it in – 'until I've had more time to consider my future. All my thoughts are consumed by my new job. I have no energy to spare on such things as marriage.'

Lalla Saïda looked calculating. 'Well, if I am not to have a nice young woman to help me around the house, I will need something to make up for it.'

'Of course,' Hamou said, relieved. 'I can give you a little more money each week and you can hire a local woman to come in and help with your chores—'

'I want no strangers in my house!' she declared furiously. 'What I want... is... a washing machine!'

Hamou regarded her incredulously. 'But you have no electricity.'

His mother gave him a gimlet stare. 'Now that you're so influential, I'm sure you can sort that out!'

Hamou walked home with his head spinning, feeling almost nostalgic for his life in Casa. On the way home, he stopped at the tabac cart, bought three cigarettes and smoked all three of them, one after another, in a fury of self-loathing. He paused as he neared his house in order to finish the last one and was grinding the butt into the dust when a figure moved out of the darkness, a man in a hooded robe.

'We are watching you, Hamou Badi,' the figure said in a deep voice.

Hamou's throat closed up. He could not speak.

'The end of the oppressors is coming and there will be consequences for those who collaborate too closely with the enemy. Make sure you know which side you're on... hakam.' The last word was uttered with an intonation suggesting contempt.

And then the man was gone into the night. Hamou stared after him, heart thudding. He could have been killed – stabbed, shot – where he stood, and no one would have seen, or been able to save him. He let himself in, locked and bolted the door, and placed a chair beneath the handle.

The next morning when he rose after a wretched, sleepless night, he opened the door to find an odd-looking item on the step outside. Bending to examine it, he realised it was a comprehensively charred croissant, and knew at once what it signified. He had heard of such objects being left outside collaborators' houses in Casablanca. It was a warning; a message. From the Black Crescent.

They were watching him. They were everywhere.

31

Slimane Chafari lived in an isolated house high in the valley above Tagtout. It took Hamou and his mokhazni over an hour to find the place, partly because it was so remote, partly because when they asked directions, people turned away and pretended not to have heard or understood the question. It was a couple of days after his warning from the Black Crescent and though nothing more had happened, he was still feeling unsettled.

'Is he really an assassin?' Hamou asked.

Houcine made a face. He looked so ludicrous astride his donkey, with his toes nearly trailing the ground, that Hamou felt too sorry for him to address the matter of his failure to satisfy his wife. The problem weighed upon him. How was he going to raise such a difficult subject without giving offence? Every time he approached the idea of doing so, his mind shied away from it like a spooked horse. 'It's what everyone says he used to be. But he's very old now. It seems unlikely.'

'And yet, people still pay him to... kill their enemies?'

Houcine laughed. 'People love to make up stories.' His expression darkened. 'Especially people in Tagtout.'

Hamou looked around. It seemed a pretty, prosperous village, the eponymous oleanders lining its steep watercourse, pink blossoms pushing their apricot scent into the warm air. The houses were old but well cared for, and there were cats everywhere. 'Do they have a reputation for falsehood here?'

'They're a strange lot, very insular, all related, one way or another. And they have a lot of sorcerers and marabouts. I mean, look, they've got no mosque.'

'They probably go to the one in Tafla,' Hamou said reasonably, referring to the village they'd passed on the way up.

Houcine made an unconvinced noise in the back of his throat. 'People go missing around here, never to be seen again. You won't get anyone from Tagtout coming to seek your help. They deal with everything themselves, the ancient way. You don't cross a Tagtouti.'

Hamou remembered what the nervous man had said, *A life for a life, eye for eye, nose for nose, ear for ear, tooth for tooth, and wounds equal for equal*, and shuddered.

'Remind me why we're here?' the mokhazni asked again.

'I can't say anything other than that I'm making enquiries. On official business.' He put his heels to Makouda's barrel to encourage him up a steeper stretch. When they crested the ridge, he saw a single home built in an enclosure, with large windows that looked out across the landscape. Berber homes usually had small windows set into thick walls; it made them easier to defend, and to keep warm in harsh mountain winters. This suggested an owner with little fear of the outside world.

No livestock were in sight, and apart from an area where herbs and other cultivated plants were growing, the garden seemed to have been allowed to run wild: bindweed, mallow, prickly pear and jujubier bushes flourished, though someone, or something, appeared to have worn tracks through the vegetation.

Houcine looked dubious. 'It doesn't look much like an assassin's house.'

Hamou grinned. 'What, exactly, does an assassin's house look like?' He was struck by a memory of Emile Fouquet's immaculate villa and gardens and pushed the thought aside. 'You wait here,' he instructed the mokhazni. 'I'll knock and see if anyone's in.'

He slid down from Makouda and tethered him to a nearby tree. The mule set about stuffing its face with the wild mountain plants. Hamou fervently hoped none were poisonous. Who was to say the public assassin wasn't growing murder weapons in plain sight?

As if reading his mind, Houcine said dourly, 'Don't drink anything he offers you.'

Hamou picked his way through the vegetation to the front door and rapped hard upon it. Nothing but silence, except that he had the oddest sensation that he was being observed. After what felt like a very long time, he heard sounds within the building. A voice called down to him, 'Identify yourself!'

He looked up into the mouth of a long-barrelled gun pointing down at him from an opening in the upper storey. 'I'm Hamou Badi – Mohammed ben M'barek – the hakam from Tiziane.'

The weapon remained steady. 'What's a hakam doing here?' A pause. 'In fact, what the hell is a hakam?'

Hamou explained his role patiently and said that he had come on behalf of a disgruntled client. The man with the gun gave a low chuckle. 'You'd better come in.'

A couple of minutes later, Hamou found himself sitting in a comfortable salon with brocade divans on three sides, and a silver-topped table on a tribal rug of exceptional quality. A portrait of the exiled sultan took pride of place on the wall, beneath which a gold-embossed copy of the Quran lay on a green silk cushion. On the opposite wall hung a pair of ornamental daggers. The gun, a bouchfar, like the one Uncle Omar had used on those long-ago hunting expeditions but with a longer, more decorated barrel, was propped by the door.

Slimane Chafari reappeared bearing a tray of refreshments.

'Nice place,' Hamou said.

The skin around Chafari's eyes crinkled. 'You like the Taznakht rug?' He prodded the beautiful carpet, in blue and red, orange and gold raised patterns of diamonds and triangles, with a socked foot. 'You know why good examples cost so much?'

'To be honest, I know nothing about carpets.' All Hamou knew was that he had seen nothing so fine in Qasem's shop.

'They're made by the women of the Ait Ouaouzguite. Each one is unique and carries the personal story of its weaver. Part woven, part knotted, part embroidered. It takes a great deal of time, skill and craft to create such a work. And this...' he ran his hand over a spangled cream rug draped over the end of the divan, 'is a *handira*, an Amazigh wedding cloak, from Imchil.'

'They're beautiful,' Hamou said sincerely. 'You have family in the High Atlas?'

Chafari smiled but did not answer. Instead, he devoted his attention to pouring tea from a great height into two small, decorated glasses without, Hamou noted, spilling a drop. And yet the man was old, seventy, or more. He had the fine-boned features typical of the region, a nose like a blade, eyes as sharp as those of a bird of prey. He moved like an elderly person, placing his feet with exaggerated care. But he had a very steady hand. The fragrance of mint filled the air. Hamou remembered what Houcine had said: when the man pushed a glass towards him, he took it, but hesitated to drink until his host drank. Again, Chafari smiled to himself. Hamou felt observed and assessed. He didn't much like it.

'Perhaps I should get to the reason I'm here,' Hamou started, but Slimane Chafari held up a hand. 'Please. Tea should never be tainted by business. Let us enjoy what Allah, peace be upon him, has provided in peace and with gratitude first.'

The tea was not as sweet as he had grown used to, and it had more complex flavours. At last, curiosity got the better of him. 'Tell me, Si Chafari, what's in your tea?'

The hawk eyes gleamed. 'You see, if we had been talking business the nuances would have passed you by. Of course, three types of mint – classic Moroccan mint, water mint, strawberry mint – that last one I raised myself, a rare variety bred true from my grandmother's plants; a handful of Chinese gunpowder green tea, a pinch of thyme, green nettle, a few fennel seeds, sugar of course, and... a little magic.'

'Magic?'

The assassin's grin broadened. 'A true artist never gives away all his secrets.'

Hamou had the distinct impression they were not just talking about tea any more. He held the man's gaze. 'Even so, I must ask you about a claim a member of the public has made to me about a broken contract.'

'Oh yes?' The old man placed his tea glass down on the tray and set his features in an expression of polite interest.

'He told me he had engaged your services to carry out a task for him, that a significant sum of money was paid for the – ah – execution of that task,' Hamou chose the word carefully, 'but that the service was never completed to his satisfaction.'

The public assassin leaned back against the wall cushions and interlaced his fingers in his lap. 'And what might this service have been?'

'You are known hereabouts as the public assassin,' Hamou said.

Chafari looked pleased but said nothing.

'And apparently the task was to kill a man who had dishonoured his daughter.'

The assassin laughed out loud. 'Goodness! If a man were paid to carry out killings for such a reason, he would be rich indeed, and the country half populated!'

Hamou pressed his lips together and waited.

'Look at me,' Chafari said at last, when he had finished laughing. 'An old man, half-crippled by arthritis, an assassin? I should take it as a compliment. But the truth is...' he leaned forward to fix his predatory stare on the hakam, 'I take all sorts of medicinal herbs just to get up and down my own stairs these days.'

'I remember,' Hamou said quietly, 'that when I was growing up in Tiziane, people called you the public assassin back then. Child that I was, I thought it sounded daring and exciting, to be a gun for hire. We used to play games of being the killer and the victim. My friend Aziz always wanted to be the assassin: we used to fight over it.'

'How sweet,' Chafari said. After a minute, he added, 'I knew your father, I believe. M'barek ben Ali. A trader, yes? Travelled south a lot.'

Hamou felt his skin prickle. 'Yes.'

'He did well for himself, didn't he?' The assassin flicked his thumb under his chin, the gesture for 'too much'. 'Salt, spices, linen, dyes...' He paused. 'Guns.'

Hamou stared at him. 'Guns?'

'Ah, we old folk have our secrets still. I dare say you thought he was a most upright fellow, but if you dig deep enough you may be surprised by what you turn up.'

Hamou, rattled, pulled the threads of his task back together. 'My father is long dead. Don't confuse past and present. I have a job to do, so let's return to the case at hand. Did you take money for a contract killing from a gentleman from Imouane to kill a man?'

The assassin, put out by Hamou's refusal to rise to his bait, sat back on the couch. 'Why don't you run along, lad? I have nothing more to say on the matter. Time was, the tribes handled their own business, and issued the right to take action according to the slight.' He nodded to where the bouchfar leaned against the doorframe. 'I bought that from your father, you know. Bit of an antique now, but I'm fond of it. It costs thirty thousand francs for a gun licence nowadays. That's a lot of money! Perhaps you should check with the French administration as to who holds a gun licence... though of course, all that red tape won't help if someone's managed to get their hands on a gun by some other, less official, method.' And, levering himself up from the couch with what seemed to Hamou rather theatrical effort, he got to his feet and ushered the hakam out.

'And do give my regards to your mother,' was Chafari's parting shot. 'She was a pretty one, ripe as a peach.' He kissed his fingers.

Hamou stomped back to where Houcine waited with their mounts. Seeing his boss's face, Houcine said nothing, just untethered Makouda and handed the reins over. Hamou managed to mount the animal without the usual rigmarole, as if Makouda had intuited that any playful behaviour might be punished harshly, and they headed back down the track towards Tagtout.

'It's a puzzle to me,' Hamou said after a while, 'how a man that old and, as he claims, disabled by arthritis, manages by himself all the way up here on this mountain. I mean, it's a fair trek just down to the village for bread, and I saw no sign of any mule or donkey. Perhaps he has his family to deliver groceries and look after him.'

Houcine barked out a laugh. 'He's got a Chevy parked round the back.'

Hamou wheeled around to stare at him. 'A Chevrolet?' Then he remembered the tracks in the vegetation. 'What an idiot I am. Perhaps we should go back...' He thought for a moment. 'He does appear more well off than you'd expect for a solitary old man with no obvious income. But you'd think if he were a public assassin still – if he ever was at all – he'd surely have a better weapon than an ancient bouchfar.'

Houcine grinned. 'Those things'll barely hit a house!'

Hamou bridled, remembering Uncle Omar's skill with his blunderbuss. 'As with all these things, it rather depends on the care and skill of the shooter.' A thought occurred to him. 'If you think about it, a bouchfar is rather like a woman. It can be temperamental, unpredictable. You need to take care of it, to treat it with love. You can't just ram the powder in and hope for the best or it'll blow up in your face. You've got to take your time with it. Clean and polish and caress it, get to know its little ways, be observant of its characteristics. You need to oil it and coax it and bring it gently to bear. Then it will suit you well and fire true and strong and never let you down. It'll be the only gun you ever really need.'

Houcine gave him a long, reproachful look. 'Fatima came to see you, didn't she?'

*

Some days later, Hamou was woken by someone rapping at his front door before dawn and, having shifted a disgruntled Madani, got out of bed to open it and found Jérome Boulanger, the adjutant, outside with a tin of sardines for Madani and an invitation from the commandant to attend upon him at once for a hunting expedition.

Hamou started to object. He had no interest in hunting, no wish to attend such an event. And how would it appear to onlookers, to spies working for the Black Crescent, for example, if he were to be seen out hunting with the French? Of course, he did not voice such concerns, but said only that he was extremely busy at work.

Jérome waved an arm. 'Aziz will handle everything today.'

'He's only nineteen!'

'Hamou, you can hardly say no to the commandant.' Jérome's blue eyes were altogether too bright for such an unearthly hour, but his tone was firm as he added, 'I'll wait for you to get ready.'

Hamou emptied the sardines into the cat's bowl and watched as Madani applied the side of his face to scissoring the fish apart. Then he pulled on a pair of wide cotton trousers and a knee-length djellaba, belted to stop it flapping. He rubbed his chin. No time for a shave. He wound a long blue turban around his head: the year was wearing on and it was a chilly morning.

When he emerged, Jérome looked him up and down, and grinned. Hamou made a face at the adjutant's back as he followed him. What were you supposed to wear on a boar hunt?

Apparently, what you were supposed to wear on a boar hunt was the costume of an English country gentleman. Commandant Martinot stood outside the stables with a shotgun broken over his arm, wearing a curious pair of woollen pantaloons tucked into long socks, a checked jacket, yellow silk kerchief, and a jaunty cap with a feather sticking up out of it. His companion wore a gilet bulging with pockets and garlanded with bandoliers of ammunition like some sort of mountain bandit. On his head he wore a wide-brimmed hat decorated with dangling talismans. Hamou overheard one of the local lads handling the saluki hunting dogs say snidely to another, 'He looks like a bazaar water carrier!' and had to cough to mask his amusement. It was an accurate description: a *guerrab* wore garish clothing and a huge hat decorated with tinkling bells and tassels.

When the man turned around, Hamou recognised his huge moustache, shock of iron-grey hair and bull neck: he was the man from the cocktail party who had left early after talking to Aicha. Baptiste Meline. A local landowner, Hajj Abdullah had said. One of those *colons* who had profited greatly from the chance to take up all the best farmland and use the native population to turn it to huge profit. At the party, formalwear had constrained his bulk, but there was no disguising the size of the man today: he looked like a warthog. So Hamou was shocked when Meline took one look at him and called out to Martinot, 'I see your young hakam has gone fully native!'

The commandant eyed Hamou with something approaching pity, then shook his head. 'What on earth are you wearing?'

Hamou looked down at his djellaba. 'It was my father's,' he said quietly. It was good quality camel wool.

'Do you at least have a gun?'

'No, sir.'

The commandant sighed, then called for Jérome to bring a rifle. 'Used one of these?'

Hamou looked the weapon over. It was more modern than the one he had trained with, but he nodded. 'Yes, sir.'

The dogs were circling and yipping with excitement. More men arrived – local beaters bearing rods and drums, a man in a leather butcher's apron stained with old blood; the amghrar of Aflawassif mounted on a bay pony tricked out in tasselled headpiece and breastplate, as if he were about to ride in a *fantasie*;

two of his men, bearing silver-ornamented guns. The tension rose. Hamou felt a bit sick, at having to ride the mule, at the prospect of violence and death, at his inexperience in such company. He patted Makouda's neck, hoping that the beast would not decide to parade his prodigious equipment today of all days.

Soon, they were riding up through the oasis towards the plateau. Women out early in the fields gathering forage stopped and stared, and when they called and ululated, the amghrar's men flourished their rifles like heroes riding to war. They passed through the village of Imouane, with its clifftop agadir and its ancient stone houses built into the rocks, and Hamou wondered in which one lived the man who had paid money to the public assassin.

The granite formations became increasingly idiosyncratic as they climbed, standing proud on the horizon like figures – a hawk here, an old man with a long nose there. The more you looked, the more you saw. Hamou and his friends had made up tales about them as children: that one was a giant turned to stone by a local witch; that a lion pretending to be a rock in order to lure unwary travellers (how they had squealed when they ran beneath it); further on was a hare and its leveret; a tortoise; and the tall hill of tumbled stones was in fact a pyramid in which an ancient king was entombed, ready to be summoned to the aid of the local tribes in their time of need.

Except that the French had come, and the ancient king had not risen.

There was a haze over the plateau as the coolness of the dawn met the warmth of the rising sun, and argan trees and thorn bushes showed as dark shadows against the tawny ground. Small birds flittered away from their approach, swooping and calling, and Hamou experienced a jolt of nostalgia for early mornings out here on the plateau during his boyhood, chasing rock-squirrels and eating Barbary figs. As the beaters dispersed to run up into the rocky outcrops to search for boar tracks and scat, he found himself riding near the back of the hunting party, mainly because Makouda, feeling surly, was tackling the steepening ground unenthusiastically and there was only so much chivvying he could do. But it proved to be an excellent position from which to survey and listen. He heard the amghrar greasing around the commandant and the landowner, Meline, reminding them of his need for funds, and suggesting they should grace the annual festival in his village with their presence, for the food would be exceptional, and the girls would perform an *ahwach*. Hamou found himself wondering whether the Black Crescent had spies in Aflawassif, and whether blackened croissants might be left on the amghrar's doorstep.

Martinot politely declined, saying that Madame Martinot's stomach was delicate, and she could not take the bumpy roads into the hills; but Baptiste Meline avidly wanted to hear more about the girls: were they virgins? Did they have good breasts? But even the venal tribal chief drew the line at this, and returned to ride with his men. Martinot and Meline pulled away to one side on their handsome stallions and after a while fell into a different tenor of conversation, clearly unaware that the young hakam was still within earshot.

'Word from France is they may pull out, give the fuckers their sultan back,' Meline grumbled. 'Load of cowards, not a backbone between them.'

Hamou did not catch everything the commandant said in reply, but enough to gather that he agreed the situation was becoming untenable. More killings, general unrest in Casablanca, and in other cities across Morocco, the Istiqlal sensing victory.

'Those bastards,' Meline growled. 'Fundamentalists and terrorists, the lot of them! We should have destroyed them all when we had the chance. Rounded them up like they did after the attack at Oued Zem and strafed the bastards till the valleys ran red with their blood. That's the way to deal with these people; there's no reasoning with them, force is all they understand, men, women and children, all.'

Hamou's skin went cold.

'Will you go back?'

'Me?' Meline laughed. 'I'm finished in France. There's nothing there for a man like me. I've made my fortune here, have the sort of life I always dreamed of as a young man. The girls here are luscious – you don't know what you've been missing. Not that Isabel isn't a beauty, but fucking a native girl, you can't beat it: they put up a good struggle. And as long as there are corrupt fools like,' he named a couple of the local chieftains, 'to keep the tribes in order, I'll have no trouble. They always like my coin. Besides, these fellows, they can't govern anything. It'll become a lawless wasteland, as it was before we came. When our lot pull out, we'll leave them with a bureaucracy they aren't educated enough to use and an infrastructure that will fall to bits around their ears. All the more opportunity for men of ambition, eh, Jules? You should stay. We could make this area our own little kingdom.'

Hamou could tell from the set of Martinot's shoulders that he found the discussion distasteful. He caught the tail of his response: '...villa in Essaouira, enough for me.'

Anything else they might have said was lost as the beaters up ahead in the rocks started shouting and drumming, and the dogs were let off the leash to drive the game towards them. The commandant, switching abruptly into full military mode, started to order the shooters into position, a semicircle, regularly spaced, waving Hamou up to join them, but suddenly there was dust in the air and the amghrar and his horsemen were charging wildly ahead, waving their weapons and whooping like demons.

The commandant swore. Then he and Meline galloped after them.

Hamou watched them go, since he was unable to persuade Makouda into anything more than a brief canter, which almost dislodged him from the saddle. He couldn't make out what was happening up ahead, but it looked like pandemonium. A shot rang out, but whether it was at animals that had been flushed out, or whether it was the amghrar or one of his idiot outriders firing into the air, he didn't know.

Then two of the saluki hounds came flowing towards him, ears flat, tails down. One was streaked with blood. Hamou tried to halt them, but the dogs took not a scrap of notice and bolted past. He urged the mule with his knees but when it dug its heels in had to smack its hindquarters, then hold on tight, his rifle jouncing on his back. He tried to make sense of the scene. Beaters were running in different directions. Horses milled, kicking up dust. Dogs barked and whined. In the midst of it all, something was squealing and thrashing. The sound of its agony grated on Hamou's brain, making him grit his teeth against it.

When he got closer, he saw that it was a man on the ground, not a wild boar, and that he had a leg wound. One of the beaters was winding his turban material tight around the wound, but the white cotton flowered red with every turn. 'Was he gored?' Hamou asked the man nearest him, one of the *bahra*.

The beater shook his head. 'I don't think so, but it all happened so fast. We flushed some boar out of a cave and shouted the find, and then the amghrar and his men came charging towards us, followed by the rest, and there was shooting, and he fell off his horse. I thought he'd just lost his seat, but it seems he was shot.'

'By a stray bullet? From one of the hunting party?'

The man shrugged. 'Who knows? It was chaos.'

The man was still shrieking, but more slowly and at a lower pitch, like a clockwork toy running down. The commandant stood over him.

'Can you ride, Boulanger?'

Oh no, it was Jérome. Hamou felt a sudden rush of empathy. The officer had always been decent to him, never condescending or unpleasant.

The adjutant was pale with blood loss, but even so, he said, 'Yes, sir.'

'Get him up on his horse, and tie him on,' Martinot ordered the beaters, and they shovelled Jérome into his saddle, where he swayed, teeth gripping his lip against the pain as they strapped him in place. Then the commandant ordered the amghrar to escort the wounded man back to Tiziane and get him to the hospital there.

The chieftain looked thunderstruck. 'Who are you to order me around?'

Martinot stared at him coldly. 'I'm the man whose hunt you and your undisciplined idiots have wrecked. I'm the commanding officer of the man who's been shot, no doubt by one of those idiots. So, unless you want me to send an army of tax inspectors to your village to go through your finances, you'll do as I tell you. I hold the authority in this region, you uneducated savage, and you'll do as you're told.'

The amghrar went red in the face and swore in the local dialect. 'Not for much longer, kafir,' he growled. Then he waved for his men to follow him, and they galloped off, leaving the wounded adjutant sitting on his horse amid clouds of their dust.

'I'll go with Officer Boulanger,' Hamou offered, desperate to get away.

The commandant wheeled around. 'If I wanted you to go with him, I'd have told you so. You can damn well stay here till I've bagged my boar.'

Hamou watched the injured man urge his horse into a walk and slump across the animal's neck. It was three miles back to Tiziane. He hoped he'd make it.

There were no more boar to be found that morning. No doubt the noise and commotion had warned them all off. By lunchtime, the returned beaters and hounds had flushed out a mountain hare, which set the salukis coursing joyously, a jackal and some feral dogs, and the commandant and Meline had shot half a dozen partridges. They halted beneath the shade of a huge argan tree beside an ancient well sunk in a natural depression in the rocks. The water level was still quite high, despite the long period of drought the region had suffered. Small brown birds flew in and out of the trees and came down to drink; frogs croaked and splashed into the water when the dogs investigated too closely.

The sun beat down, hotter than might be expected for the time of year, and Hamou began to feel quite drowsy after eating bread and mutton-sausage, cooked meats, olives, cheese, grapes and patisserie. At a little distance away, the beaters sat around a small fire they had made to brew up tea, eating their lunch of *mahrach* – little brown loaves – tinned sardines and dates, smoking Favorites, or something even cheaper. Hamou's nose twitched. How he would love to join them. Though, even more, he would prefer not to be here at all. He wondered how the adjutant was, whether he had got to the hospital, and felt miserable to be trapped here, unable to help him.

Suddenly Meline leapt to his feet, unexpectedly nimble for such a bulky man. 'There!' He pointed to the horizon.

Hamou stared where the man indicated. High up on the distant ridge, a movement. He couldn't make out what it was, but Meline was already reaching for his gun. The commandant shaded his eyes. 'What is that, a wild ass?'

'You need spectacles, my friend!' Meline took off running, crouched and low, from one argan tree to the next, zigzagging across the sandy plain, threading a path between cacti and spiny euphorbia. Then he raised his rifle, sighted, and a single shot split the afternoon's serenity. Whatever was up on the rocks crumpled.

Martinot caught up with his friend. '*Mon dieu*, you got him! What a shot!' He turned to the hound-master and beaters. 'Come on!' He ran for his horse and brought Meline's too, and the two Frenchmen galloped towards the ridge.

Hamou pushed himself to his feet and retrieved Makouda, tethered in the shade of a tree. The mule rolled an eye at him and danced away: it took Hamou a good five minutes to get him under control. The rest of the hunting party were well ahead now, even the runners. He urged Makouda into a trot, then to a reluctant canter, and held on tight. By the time he reached the top of the ridge and slid off his mount it was all over. Meline was kneeling over his kill, mantling like a crow, as if to keep others away. Hamou almost did not want to see what it was the Frenchman had brought down, but he could hardly slip away now.

The gazelle lay on its side, its pale fawn flanks moving in quick shallow breaths, one delicate foreleg pawing at the air as if it might somehow gain enough purchase on it for sudden escape. A dark hole marred its soft white belly fur; blood leaked startlingly red from it to pool on the sandy ground. Hamou gazed at the lovely creature in dismay, taking in its huge dark, terrified eyes, outlined in black, then white, its twitching ears, wide black muzzle and elegantly curved horns. He had never seen one of these desert animals up close: they were wary and alert, always on the edge of flight, rarely seen during the daytime or in the open. To be this far north, hundreds of miles from its usual habitat, it must have been seeking water. It had run and bounded all the way from the edges of the Sahara, across rock, desert and dunes, over mountain ranges and through rocky chasms, to reach the Tiziane plateau, there to be gut-shot by a fat man in search of a bloody thrill.

Hamou felt his gorge rise. To kill a gazelle was unlucky: it was a spirit of the wild. He watched in horror as Meline demanded the butchering knives from the man in the leather apron and started to hack at the creature's neck, laughing and joking about where he would mount his trophy, and at last Hamou could stand it no more.

He led the mule away down the rocky defile and back towards the well, where the sounds of the frogs and birdsong soothed his mind. He thought about waiting there for the rest of the party to return, then decided he would not be missed, and turned the mule for home.

32

The hospital in Tiziane was in truth no more than a clinic: a low, modern concrete building operated by three French medical staff and some locals who tended to wounds, cleaned, and ran errands. It had been one of the first constructions the administration had raised when they arrived in the region twenty years before. Hamou had been inside many times during his childhood, for vaccinations and health tests, after various accidents, to be X-rayed and bandaged. Memories of needles and pain still held a frisson of anxiety for him as he passed beneath its arch and entered the wide hall in which voices echoed like those of lost djinns.

He asked the first person he saw – a man with a broom – about the wounded French officer and was relieved to be directed to a room off the main corridor. Somehow, Jérome had managed to get himself to the hospital.

The adjutant lay pale and motionless on a metal cot with his eyes closed, his bandaged leg elevated on two pillows.

'Jérome?' Hamou said softly.

The wounded man did not stir. Hamou looked around the cell-like room and found that the officer's uniform jacket had been hung carefully over the single chair. Beneath the chair lay the reddened rags of his trousers, which had been cut off in pieces. Hamou picked them up gingerly. The hole on the front of the thigh where the projectile had entered was clearly delineated. He turned the fabric around and found a larger, more ragged exit hole on the other side. A curious smell came off the material, not just the meaty, metallic tang of blood, but something pungent, almost spicy. He raised the piece of cloth to his nose.

'Do you often hang around hospitals sniffing other people's clothes?'

Hamou leapt guiltily and dropped the gory rag. 'Sorry, sorry! I came to see how you were.'

Jérome gave him a wan smile. 'As you see. The bullet went right through. Trouble is, it took a fair chunk of muscle with it. They say I'll heal, but it'll take a while. You'll see me hobbling around the village on a stick like some old codger.' He looked thoughtful, then brightened. 'Perhaps they'll invalid me out on a decent pension.'

'I can't blame you for wanting to leave.'

'I don't really want to leave... well, I didn't. I like it here.'

Hamou was surprised. 'What is it you like?'

'Oh, you know. The climate is good, the people are, I was going to say "kind", but... Well, they are kind, for the most part. Generous, hospitable – even the poorest of them would give you their last drop of tea or piece of bread. Back home... it's... different.'

'Go on,' Hamou encouraged. The adjutant was a different kind of Frenchman to those he had regularly encountered in Casa.

Jérome hesitated. 'It sounds rather selfish, I suppose. But back in Angers, I'm just the third Boulanger son: no money, no prospects. Here, I'm, well, someone.' His shoulders moved in an awkward shrug. 'I'd have to scratch my way up the pole, start again from almost nothing. All these rumours about us pulling out... I don't know what I'll do.'

'You could stay.'

Jérome laughed. 'What's the point of a lone French officer with a gammy leg?'

'You'll heal, my friend. You will, inshallah.' Hamou left a pause, then asked, 'But how did it happen? Did you see?'

Jérome made a face. 'No idea. There was chaos after the beaters called the boar and those idiots from Aflawassif galloped in and started shooting.'

'Do you think you caught a stray bullet, or could it have been deliberate?'

The adjutant looked shocked. 'Deliberate?'

'Have you upset anyone here?'

Jérome laughed. 'Well, of course I have. It's in the nature of the job. I've put people behind bars, sent them to prison in Tiznit...'

'Nothing more... personal than that?' He was thinking about what the man from Imouane had said about his daughter. But he was also thinking about the man who had stepped out of the shadows that night to warn him off collaborating with the French, and the attack on the governor.

'No, of course not! Are you missing being a policeman, Hamou?'

Hamou laughed. 'Not really.'

Silence fell between them, then Jérome asked, 'Did they really carry on with the hunt after they sent me off on my own, tied to my horse?'

'I couldn't believe it,' Hamou said quietly. 'I offered to go with you and Martinot ordered me to stay. I should have followed my instincts and ignored him. I hate hunting anyway.'

'Did you really offer to do that? For me? An enemy?'

'You aren't an enemy.'

'After all the French have done here, you can say that?'

Hamou shook his head. 'You may be French, but you are not France. It wasn't your plan to take over Morocco, to steal its sultan, oppress its people, was it? To me, you're Jérome, who is kind to cats.'

Jérome grinned. 'No, but I'm part of the regime that enabled all that.'

'Remember, I too wore a French uniform in Casa. I know

what it is to feel complicit. All you can do is try to do good in the world, in whatever way you can.'

The adjutant regarded him askance. 'That's a very old-fashioned view, Hamou.'

'Perhaps I'm an old-fashioned man.'

Jérome reached out a hand and Hamou took it. 'I like old-fashioned. Thanks for coming, my friend.'

Hamou was on his way back to his office when a man stopped him in the street. 'You're the one they called the zouhry, aren't you?'

'I prefer to be known as the hakam,' Hamou said gently, hoping to deflect him.

'Yes, yes.' The man, round as a barrel in his striped robe, was impatient. 'But it's not a hakam I need.'

'I may not be able to help you then,' Hamou said, trying politely to extricate himself.

'Please. Will you give me your hand?'

Frowning, Hamou extended his right hand. The man took hold of it and turned it palm up, then gave out a great sigh. 'You are! I thought they were mocking me when they told me to look for you. I urgently need a zouhry, you see. My well's run dry and I must sink a new one.'

Hamou had to refrain from laughing. 'I'm very much afraid I don't dig wells.'

'I know that! But the local *maf-aman* is sick, so I need a zouhry.'

Hamou took back his hand and stuck it in the side pocket of his robe, out of sight. A maf-aman was a water diviner, prized for near-magical skills. 'I don't think I can help you with that. I've never done any divining.'

'Can't you see I'm desperate?' the little man cried. There were three days of stubble on his chin and a mad light in his eyes.

'Well, yes, but—'

'I have a car,' the man said quickly, as if this sealed the deal. 'I'm not poor, I can pay you! It'll take no time at all and then I'll drive you back again.'

'Tell me your name and where you live,' Hamou said at last, 'and I'll come tomorrow.' He would take Houcine with him: he felt rattled by what had happened to Jérome.

'I'm Hajj Yazid from the farm beneath the Eagle's Head, everyone knows me.' As if to prove this, he raised a hand to a pair of men walking on the other side of the street, and they waved back. 'Please come now. The well-digger has already arrived all the way from Tata.' He named a town far to the south. 'He's the best well-digger between here and the Sahara and it's taken months to get him. If I postpone, it will take weeks more before he can come back and by then all my animals will have died, and probably me as well. I've been hauling water for them twice a day from the river down here in the valley, and I'm not a young man. Please: I'm begging you.' Tears stood in his eyes.

Hamou remembered what he had said to Jérome. How could he not go with this poor, desperate man? He said at last, 'Hajj Yazid, I'll come, but I can't promise you a good outcome. The lines on my hand are just a quirk of nature. I've got no special powers. It's all just superstition and nonsense.'

Hajj Yazid beamed. 'You will find water for me, I know it. It's not just in the hand, the mark of the zouhry, but in the eyes too: and you have a zouhry's eyes!'

And with that he towed Hamou along the road to a tragic-looking Renault that had been crudely converted into a pickup truck by dint of having the back half of its roof cut off and the seats removed. This area was laden with so many heavy jerrycans that the vehicle sank on its haunches like an exhausted animal.

They chugged up what seemed an endless hill till the Eagle's Head loomed before them, a tall outcrop of wind-sculpted granite ending in a rounded block with a great, hooked beak that looked poised to strike passing travellers. Dust devils swirled in the air as the wind off the plateau teased into play the surface of the unpaved road and sent it flying against the car's windscreen. Only one of the Renault's wipers worked, and only then with a piece of string that Hamou was instructed to pull at intervals: Yazid kept sticking his head out of the side window to see where he was going. It was not a relaxing drive.

At the farm, Hamou felt obliged to lug the water containers off the truck to fill the troughs. He watched as animals converged on them at the sight and sound of water – scrawny sheep and thin, dark goats, two cows with their ribs showing, a yellow dog, chickens and geese. The farm looked as run-down as the animals, its fields parched and dusty. A single donkey tethered to a far-off post brayed disconsolately.

Yazid took Hamou to the failed well and they both stared down into its opaque depths. 'Could the well-digger not deepen this existing well?' Hamou asked.

'The walls won't hold, he says. Something complicated about the formation of the rock strata here.'

'I really don't know what I can do for you,' Hamou said again, feeling like a fraud even though he had been honest with the man.

'Well, we shall see. Let me go fetch Bilal Boanou, the well-man.'

Hamou shook his head to himself. He sat down with his back to the sun-warmed stonework and surveyed the view, imagining what it must be like under better conditions. Meadows of wheat and wildflowers, probably; pasture and plenty. Lush and beautiful, and with the hazy blue of the Afoud range on the horizon, a lovely outlook marred only by the stark outline of a tall electricity pylon and the thick black wire that reached from it all the way to the farm. Closer, ochre stacks of granite towered up on the far side of the dusty track. Hamou narrowed his eyes, recognising some of the formations, and realised he was looking out over the back of the outcrops where they had been hunting that morning. Standing up, he shaded his eyes. Yes! There was the giant, albeit from an unfamiliar angle, and there, the hare. The track they had driven along must run almost parallel, but a kilometre or so apart from the one they had taken this morning on horse- and mule-back. He'd thought they were in the middle of nowhere, but the hunting ground appeared to be a good deal more accessible than he'd thought. He was struck by a question. Had someone known about the hunt and gone out to shoot one of the regime's officers? Perhaps they'd meant to assassinate Martinot, and hit Jérome in error.

The sound of voices broke through his thoughts, and he turned to see Hajj Yazid approaching with a short man wrapped in a desert robe. This must be the well-digger. Hamou stood up to greet him. Bilal was small and weathered, with corded muscles in his neck and forearms. He looked both ancient and youthful at once, and although his face was wreathed in wrinkles, he moved as easily as a boy. His shining dark eyes searched Hamou's face, then he asked to see his hands. 'A true zouhry,' he breathed, tracing the horizontal lines. 'Well, this is something indeed. On both hands, as perfect as can be.' He placed his own hands flat against Hamou's, and Hamou felt a strange, hot tingle in his palms, as if a current of electricity had passed between them. The well-digger laughed and turned to the farmer. 'Well done for finding such a one!'

'I've never divined for water,' Hamou said quickly. 'I'd rather you didn't get your hopes up.'

Bilal cocked his head. 'You need to trust your instincts, son. I can read the ground; I have a feel for the geology. Between us we can do this, I am sure. Let's get to work.'

For half an hour, the three of them walked around the perimeters of Hajj Yazid's land, discussing the merits and demerits of every possible well placement, and Hamou felt nothing, and by the end nothing but despair: he had no special powers, as he had always known. But then Hajj Yazid clapped a hand to his forehead and ran off back to the house, returning a couple of minutes later with a pair of metal rods. 'It looked easy when I saw Si Aman do it, so I had the smith make me a pair. They don't work for me but I bet they will for a zouhry!'

The farmer handed them to Hamou who turned the objects over in his hands. They were thirty or so centimetres long, made from copper, slender and light, with a right angle at one end to make a handle, which fitted into his palm and felt comfortable to hold. He held them out and they balanced finely, swinging slightly from side to side. 'What are they?'

'Divining rods!' Hajj Yazid said triumphantly. 'You hold them out in front of you and they tell you where the water is.'

Hamou was far from convinced, but 'Now we shall prevail!' the well-digger declared.

He walked Hamou over to the failed well, brought up the bucket and peered into it. 'Ah, good.' Tilting the bucket so that the tiny amount of water left in the bottom gathered to one side, he instructed, 'Wet your hands and the rods with this so you will both recognise what you seek. The water in each place has its own signature, its own silent song. You must listen for it, with the rods.'

The last time Hamou had felt so ridiculous was when the charlatan in the Bousbir had made him bless the crystals for his customers, but he did as he was told.

They followed an incline from the existing well, and he felt the rods pulse once or twice, then the sensation died away. Some steps further on, he experienced the urge to move sharply right towards where a huge old argan tree spread its gnarly limbs. For a few moments he stood close to the tree, but the rods were quiet. Beyond the tree, the land dipped again, and here the rods jumped and crossed, and Hamou felt his hands come alive with a sort of internal fire. He stared at the well-digger, who smiled back enigmatically then knelt and began to sniff the ground.

Hamou and Hajj Yazid exchanged a glance.

'Argans know,' Bilal said, straightening up. 'But this is a big old tree. Four hundred years or more this tree has stood here, sucking water out of the ground. You were right to pass it by.' He beckoned to Hamou. 'Come here. Extend the rods and walk around me. Let's make this as precise as we can to save on the dynamite.'

On the what? Hamou felt suddenly alarmed.

With the well-digger shuffling on his knees, and Hamou holding the rods as if they might bite him, they made an odd tableau, but after another couple of minutes, Hamou uttered a yelp as the rods kicked up suddenly and one spun right out of his grasp and hit Bilal squarely on the head.

'Ow! That's what comes of having double divining strength!' The well-digger rubbed his forehead, then retrieved the rod and stuck the long end vertically into the ground. 'We dig here!' Then he ran back towards the house to fetch his kit.

Two charges were enough to hit the water table. Once the dust had settled, the three of them stared down into the ragged hole to see clear liquid bubbling, and Bilal explained that tomorrow a group of men would be assembled to help him dig the well and build its walls.

Hajj Yazid embraced Hamou with tears on his cheeks. 'You're a miracle worker. I shall always be in your debt. Name your price! Anything, anything I have is yours.'

Hamou smiled. 'I'm just so happy to have been able to help. It's been the most extraordinary experience.' He felt elated.

'I know you won't take money, but a goat? A sheep? As a feast for your family? I know your mother, you know: a fine woman. I'm sure she'd love some *mechaoui*...'

'Honestly, no, keep your animals. You've worked so hard to keep them alive.'

The farmer frowned. 'You dishonour me if you won't take something.' He considered Hamou's kilted-up old robe, and added, 'My wife's a fine seamstress. Perhaps she could make you something more befitting your status.'

Again, Hamou shook his head. 'Truly, it's been my pleasure.' A thought occurred to him. 'Tell me, Hajj Yazid, how did you get electricity all the way out here? I've had people in the middle of Tiziane complaining to me they can't get connected.'

The farmer said excitedly, 'My son's the engineer in charge of laying the cables!'

'Well now,' Hamou said thoughtfully. 'Perhaps we can work something out.'

Hajj Yazid invited Hamou and Bilal for tea and almond biscuits and to meet the rest of the family, but Hamou shook his head. 'I don't mean to be rude, but there's something I must do before the light fails.'

While Yazid took Bilal back to the house, Hamou took off running across the dusty track, up the rocky bank, then over the open ground toward the outcrops. Fifteen minutes of this at a fair lick left him panting and sweaty, looking up at the granite towers on the plateau from the less familiar northern side. He jogged along, trying to pinpoint his position. It was more difficult when you were right up under the cliffs like this, but after a short time he recognised the upright rocks that at certain angles appeared like a hare's ears. He thought back to the day of the hunt, visualising the scene when the beaters had shouted out the prey and the amghrar and his men had galloped towards the outcrop. The hare had been to the left, maybe fifty metres. If he could just get to the other side before the light failed... Turning, he looked back to Hajj Yazid's smallholding. It stood out clearly enough now, as the red light slid across the plain, but when the sun went down it would be a different matter. He ran on, searching for access to the other side of the formation, and at last came to a place where a hole through the rocks gave him a view of the plateau beyond.

Hamou scrambled through, feeling the granite cool and rough with crystals against his palms. Again, he sensed that curious sense of energy flowing through him, just a whisper of it in comparison to the jolt he had experienced through the divining rods. Some awkward manoeuvres saw him emerge on the other side of the outcrop, and now it was much easier to see where he was. It was brighter on this side, where the sun still hit strongly, though at a reddish slant. A few hundred metres away he could see the big argan tree and the natural well where they had stopped to eat, and further on, now in shadow, the ridge where Meline had shot the gazelle. He ran out into open space and turned back to pick out the hare and other granite towers and now could easily make out the scuffed sand and flattened euphorbias that the hunt had trampled, where Jérome had been shot. Concentrating, he quartered the ground in much the same way he had walked with Bilal with the divining rods, searching, searching.

And then at last he saw what he was looking for. He went down on his knees, till his nose was no more than a couple of centimetres away. There was no mistaking it for anything else. He sniffed and received a wisp of aroma, but whether it was from the object, or the ground, he could not tell. Closing his fingers around it, he picked it up. It weighed heavy in his hand, a curious, rather gruesome shape. He tucked it carefully into the pocket in his djellaba and started to make his way back towards the cave through which he had climbed.

The boar came out of nowhere. Not a huge one, not as large as some he'd seen, though always at a distance, but large enough to do serious damage. It shot out of wherever it had been denning among the rocks and stared at him, panting, its big wedge of a head appearing as ancient as a dinosaur's, its small eyes catching the rays of the dying sun so that it looked as if its skull was full of fire. Two wickedly sharp tusks curved up on either side of its muzzle. He had seen what a wild boar's tusks could do to a man. He started to sweat, could feel each drop burst out of his skin and trickle down his spine. His heart raced; his palms, stretched out before him as if as a plea, felt hot. *Don't run*, he told himself. As if he could anyway: the soles of his feet had taken root.

He gazed back at the creature that had the power to take his life and felt that in some profound way they were connected. As if a hot wire ran arcing between them, eye to eye, face to face, mind to mind; as if element spoke to element, thought to thought.

Then the boar dropped its head, and it kicked up its heels and ran off along the base of the outcrop, away from Hamou, and vanished into the deepening gloom.

Hamou was very quiet on the ride back down to Tiziane with Hajj Yazid, not even commenting when the headlights on the old Renault failed. All he could think about was the fire in the boar's eyes, the kick of the divining rods that now lay in his lap – a gift from the grateful farmer – the water bubbling up from Bilal's blast site, the shuddering flanks of the dying gazelle, the blood-specked object in his pocket. These images whirled around his head in a kind of weird alchemy, leaving him dizzy with sensation and a sort of delayed shock. He exited the car in a daze and upon arriving home fell into a sleep so deep that he was deaf even to Madani's increasingly loud complaints about his missed supper.

33

Hamou had been hoping to return to see the work done on Hajj Yazid's well, but his duties pressed in and he found himself stuck in his office, writing reports. He had already discovered that missing dates drew rebuke: someone, somewhere, had the job of checking the receipt and contents of regional reports and were assiduous in this task. So, he outlined his cases and outcomes, marking them as resolved, dismissed, or passed to the tribal courts or upwards to the commandant's office, and all the while he remembered Baptiste Meline's scornful remarks about indigenous people being too uneducated to handle French bureaucracy or anything else, understanding only force and violence. This drove him harder: he would show them how efficient and capable an educated young Berber could be. More – he would show them that even the smallest problems experienced by the local population were worthy of attention and effort.

While checking regulations for local building work, he found the work roster for Hajj Yazid's son, and during his lunch break went to find him on site, laying electricity cables to an extension of the Tiziane school. Tahir bin Yazid was a softly spoken man of maybe thirty-five with a neat beard and the same dark, liquid eyes as his father. He embraced Hamou fiercely upon introduction. 'Finding water on our land will save not just my parents and their livelihood and animals, but also my whole family: many households depend on Baab's farm.' He dipped his head. 'Truly,

I thought he was going to lose not only his mind when the well failed, but also his health – maybe even his life! The men in our family are not long-lived, and when Baab was lugging those canisters of water around, and would not wait for me or my brothers, I feared the worst.'

'Honestly, I think the well-digger had the true knowledge and skill.'

Tahir shook his head. 'Bilal swore he couldn't have done it without you to show him the exact spot to sink the well. He said you found a perfect synclinal aquifer between the rock strata and that he would never have been able to locate such a thing on his own.' He laughed. 'I'm an engineer! I've never believed in magic, until now. So, tell me how I can help you.'

Hamou did.

That evening he had an invitation to join Jérome for a meal, so having showered and changed and fed Madani, Hamou strolled the short distance to the adjutant's house on the edge of the village, and was surprised to see a gleaming Mercedes outside. He hesitated before entering – perhaps he had misunderstood the date or time and Jérome had another visitor. But the adjutant came hobbling out as soon as Hamou came into the garden.

'I have the use of the commandant's car!' he crowed.

'That's kind.' Hamou was surprised. Given how he had treated Jérome after the shooting, he could not see Jules Martinot as a particularly caring man.

'Well, it's army issue, so it doesn't really belong to him, and they still have Isabel's Alpine. But they're off back to France shortly.'

'Another holiday?' Hamou asked, but Jérome shook his head.

'No, for good. He's taking up some government posting. Getting out while the going is good, before the flood of French returning from this place take all the best jobs.'

'So, the rumours are true? The French really are pulling out?

What will happen next?' Hamou asked. It seemed too good to be true, a fantasy becoming suddenly manifest.

Jérome shrugged. 'There will be some sort of handover of power. Some of us will stay on to facilitate that.' He grinned. 'Soon you'll be able to tell people you're a friend of the new commandant of the Tiziane region!'

Hamou stared. 'Really? But this is wonderful news.'

'Our secret for now. Come on in, let's toast my coming promotion.'

Inside, a table had been set for two, with glasses, a bottle of wine, and a jug of fresh orange juice, in deference to Hamou. Jérome reached for the jug, but the hakam grinned, feeling light-headed from the news, which was too huge to take in. 'I can't toast all this with orange juice.' He took a small glass of wine instead, but finding it horribly bitter, set it aside.

They sat talking till Jérome's young manservant brought in a fine meaty stew, and Hamou realised that he was famished. After a while he asked, 'How's your leg?' He had been hoping Jérome would raise the topic himself, since it was not politely done in his own culture to make such a direct enquiry.

Jérome's face fell. 'Oh, you know. It hurts like stink, especially first thing in the morning and late at night, or if I sit for any length of time, but exercising it is a fearful bore. I get so impatient with how slow I am. But I suppose it's improving a bit. I've been getting some physical therapy, but the doctors are leaving next week for Marrakech. There's been a fair bit of trouble there. I doubt they'll come back.'

'Will they be replaced?'

Jérome lifted a shoulder. 'That could be one of the things that falls between jurisdictions. I will ask, but perhaps you could make enquiries too.'

'Me?'

'It'll be important to train up local doctors and nurses, people who will stay for the long term. People who speak the language and understand the local customs.'

Hamou nodded slowly. 'Yes, that's important,' he said thoughtfully.

They had just reached the cheese course when there was an urgent knock at the door. Jérome looked up, alarmed. 'It must be important to interrupt dinner!' He got slowly to his feet, groaning with the effort, and retrieved his stick. There were voices in the hall. 'Stay here,' he told Hamou. 'It's probably best you're not seen. Fraternising with the natives isn't encouraged, though that will change in due course!' He limped out into the hall, closing the door behind him.

Hamou sat there, feeling somewhat resentful, but he was pragmatic enough to understand that the slight wasn't personal. He strained his ears, but the voices moved away down the corridor. He had been drinking orange juice for the past hour, but now picked up his glass of wine and drained the remnants in a single swallow. Standing at the window, he watched the light fade over the distant mountains and wished fiercely for a cigarette.

A few minutes later, two figures walked out of the house, through the garden and disappeared through the archway, and Jérome came limping back into the room. 'It's Baptiste Meline,' he said, a bit breathless. 'He's disappeared.'

'Disappeared?' Hamou echoed.

'Hasn't come home for three nights. They waited till this evening in case he'd been caught up in some... bit of business that overran, but there's been no sign of him. They say he's a man of regular habits, gets furious if his plans are derailed.'

Hamou had formed a considerable antipathy to Meline from his two short encounters with the man in which he had shown himself to be both boorish and predatory. 'And you're supposed to do what, exactly?'

'Investigate, I suppose. Try to find him.'

'Isn't this a matter for the commandant? After all, they seem to be friends.'

Jérome laughed. 'Baptiste doesn't have friends.'

'Does he have enemies?'

'Too many to count. Apparently, the commandant has washed his hands of the matter. Said there's little point in starting something he can't finish. So, it looks as if I'm stuck with it.' The adjutant sighed. 'God, I loathe the man. If someone's done away with him, good riddance is all I can say.'

Hamou raised his eyebrows.

'Oh, I know, I should put my personal feelings aside, but honestly, he's – and I don't use such words lightly – an evil man. I don't know if you've ever encountered true evil...'

'Oh, I have,' Hamou said quietly. 'Believe me, I have.'

'Will you help me with this, Hamou? I don't speak Berber; I'll need someone to interview the staff and any other witnesses.'

'You've got the moqqadems, they're all local. And the mokhazni report to you.'

Jérome made a face. 'Come on, would you trust any of them to investigate a missing teapot?' He held out a hand to Hamou. 'Work with me, Hamou: it's the way forward, don't you think? How can you say no?'

Hamou smiled, then took his hand. Maybe it was time to try to patch together a working alliance, joining the best of what the French administration had brought with local knowledge and sympathy, and maybe just a bit of his own policing nous, too.

'I can't.'

The next morning, Hamou wrote a letter to his old address in Casablanca. It was maybe the fourth of these letters he had written, addressed to himself, in the hope that Samira or Zina would pick one up and realise it was meant for them. But he had never had a reply. This time he decided to make the effort to meet the bus from Casa as it came in and waited until the driver Mehdi had finished helping the passengers off with their luggage.

They greeted one another and Mehdi looked around at the

bustle of Tiziane on souk day. 'I think maybe one day I'd like to retire here,' he said wistfully. 'Things in Casa are bad. It's no place to raise children.'

'We're not getting much news through,' Hamou said. 'Not after Oued Zem.'

Mehdi stared at the ground. 'I lost two cousins in that bloodbath.' He looked up again. 'There have been reprisals, a lot of resentment on both sides.' He lowered his voice as he added, 'Even when the handover of power comes, and they're saying it will come soon, that won't be an end to it. There will be grudges settled, mark my words.'

Hamou nodded. There would be no magic wand waved over Morocco even if the French pulled out. He handed Mehdi the letter he had written. 'It's a good deal to ask, but would you wait for a reply this time, even if it's just a verbal one?'

Mehdi's mouth turned down. 'No one answers at that address,' he said softly.

Hamou's heart lurched. 'No one?'

'I've knocked and called out, but in the end, I've just had to slip the letters under the door.'

Hamou imagined his letters piled up, gathering dust in the hallway where Zina had kept her bicycle, and wanted to weep. His dismay must have been clear, for the bus driver placed a consoling hand on his shoulder.

'Is there no one else who might know where they are?'

Hamou had long ago explained the need not to implicate the Chadli family. He had thought of and dismissed the idea of writing to Zina via the clinic where she worked, and all official channels were closed to him: no one in the Sûreté would want to be seen to be in contact with Hamou Badi. It was bad enough that he had placed the bus driver in danger.

And then he had an idea. 'Wait here!'

Hamou dashed up the road to the stalls near the mosque and there purchased some soap, rosewater, and a traditional local tunic, and bundled them up with some string helpfully offered by the stallholder. On the way back, he added a packet of Favorites and tucked them inside the bundle, which he thrust into Mehdi's hands. 'There's a beggar with a withered arm who spends most of his time on the street corner near the apartment block. His name is Didi. If he's still there, would you give him this package, and the letter, and ask him if he has any news of the family?'

Mehdi grinned. 'I've seen him. You're a most determined man, Hamou Badi. I hope she's worth it.'

'Ask Didi about her cooking.'

The bus driver laughed, and Hamou came away with a lighter heart. Surely, if his baraka were returning to him, this latest attempt would bear fruit?

When he got to his office, he found the commandant's Mercedes pulled up outside.

'Sorry, I need you to come with me right now to Meline's place. I'm afraid a missing Frenchman trumps living villagers!' Jérome got out awkwardly, leaning on his stick. 'God, this thing makes my leg ache: the pedals are abominably stiff. I say, can you drive, Hamou?'

'I've never driven a car in my life!'

'Excellent time to learn, old chap.' Jérome grinned. 'Come on, if you're going to learn to drive, you may as well start with the best!'

Against his better judgement, Hamou found himself in the driver's seat and as he struggled with the controls the car bunny-hopped inelegantly down the track. But by the time they'd reached the centre of Tiziane, he'd pretty much got the hang of the pedals, which was just as well, since it was market day and the road was thronged with people, donkeys, bicycles, scooters, cars and trucks following no discernible rules of the road. Jérome had to bark 'Brake!' only once, and then helped him restart the motor when it stalled, but then they were out onto the road down into the valley and the big machine rolled along so smoothly that even the potholes barely gave it pause. Hamou could sense the power of the engine, purring quietly away under the long, sleek bonnet, and remembered how he had aspired to owning nothing more than a mobilette, or even a bicycle, when he was in Casablanca. Well, he was a long way away from ever being able to afford a car, but even to drive one gave him an amazing sense of freedom.

'Take the next right,' the adjutant instructed as they passed beneath the sun-bright cliffs of the Djebel Kest, 'and follow the road to the end. It was constructed for Meline – all the land from here to the mountain belongs to him.'

Hamou performed the turn with only a little fish-tailing, despite the loose gravel, and had to curb his self-congratulation in case he attracted the evil eye. On either side, the fields were lush and green, in marked contrast to the farms they had passed. There were orchards of citrus trees, pomegranates and plums, a hectare of almond and olive trees, then several of harvested crops. At last, the house came into view, a modern two-storey affair that looked as if it could have been transplanted here from Casablanca's corniche, complete with ornamental flowerbeds and swimming pool.

Hamou thought about Hajj Yazid and the other farmers struggling to keep their crops and animals alive through the drought, and the dry fields they had passed before they turned onto Meline's land. In his culture they said 'aman iman' – water is life. How had the man managed to channel so much of this precious resource that he was able to maintain a swimming pool? He felt anger rise in him.

'I wasn't expecting this,' he said quietly.

Jérome mistook his tone for awe. 'The man's as rich as Croesus!' He laughed, and then had to explain who Croesus was. 'Sorry, I don't suppose you have much use for the Classics here.'

'Not really,' said Hamou, trying not to feel patronised.

'It's all just stories really. Very old stories,' the adjutant added apologetically. Then he laughed. 'Oh, I just remembered that

Croesus's son was accidentally killed on a boar hunt! See, we all tell the same stories, don't we?'

Hamou told him about a local tribe who mistook another clan's donkey for a boar and accidentally killed it. 'It happened hundreds of years ago, yet they still fight over it, and the tribe whose donkey was killed still mockingly bray at the others.'

Jérome stared at him. 'Long memories!'

'Oh, yes. Nothing is ever forgotten or forgiven here.'

'I see I shall have to watch my step,' the adjutant said quietly. 'Oh – pull in over there by the Avant.' He pointed to where a sleek black vehicle was parked. 'Just try not to hit the pots or run over the flowerbeds and bring it to a gentle halt... Ow! I said gentle.'

Hamou looked over at the big Citroën. 'Perhaps he's back.' He felt unaccountably disappointed.

'I'll go and find out.' Jérome levered himself out of the passenger seat and hobbled towards the house. He'd barely walked a dozen steps before a woman came running out, looking distressed. Hamou watched as the two talked, then Jérome turned and beckoned to him.

'He's still not returned. Jacqueline hasn't seen him since he left the house three days ago.'

As they followed the woman inside, Hamou touched Jérome's arm and mouthed 'Wife?' at him. Jérome shook his head. 'Housekeeper.'

The house was shabbier inside than Hamou had expected. Not untidy or dirty, but unloved and in need of maintenance. Hamou stared at the mounted gazelle's head in the hall. It looked grotesque and dolorous. Was it the one he had seen shot? He made to follow the adjutant and housekeeper into the salon, but the woman turned and shooed him away. 'Not you, go out the back, where the servants are! Tell the cook you're the driver and she'll give you coffee.'

Hamou was about to explain that he was the hakam when Jérome gave him a minute shake of the head, so he nodded meekly and followed the corridor to the back of the house. Hearing voices, he opened a door into the kitchen, and conversation instantly ceased. Four people in there: two men and two women, all local in appearance. Hamou addressed them in Tachelhit, explaining who he was – not the police, just the driver for the adjutant, who was trying to find Meline, and he was born in Tiziane, too – and saw shoulders drop and expressions relax. The younger woman ushered him to a stool and started to pour coffee from a pot on the gas stove. When she began to ladle sugar in, Hamou stopped her, saying he was too young to lose all his teeth, and they laughed. General conversation enabled him to classify them as the maid, the cook, the gardener and Meline's manservant, an older man in spectacles.

'So where do you think he is?' he asked after a while.

'Monsieur Meline doesn't share his plans with us, we're just the staff,' the cook said, tucking a strand of her hair under her headscarf. She had a severe face and hooded eyes.

'But you must have some ideas of your own?' he pressed.

She gave him a look that would quell a camel. 'You're very nosy, for a driver.'

'Just trying to help find Monsieur Meline, in case something has happened to him.'

'Would serve him right,' the younger man said sourly.

'Brahim! Don't forget who pays your wages!' the cook snapped. Then she turned to the maid. 'And, Fawa, you have work to do. Go on, don't hang around making eyes at the visitor, go!'

The girl coloured and fled. Hamou wondered how he would escape the cook's sharp eyes so he could ask the maid more questions: he was sure she had been about to say something. He turned his attention to the manservant. 'Do you have any idea where Monsieur Meline might be?'

'I keep his diary,' the older man said hesitantly.

'Is there anything in there that might give a clue where he went?'

The cook physically interposed herself between Hamou and the bespectacled man. 'If you're just a driver, why are you behaving like a policeman, asking everyone questions? Go on, out of my kitchen. I have groceries to buy and luncheon to prepare for when the master returns.'

Hamou put up his hands, placatory. 'Sorry, I don't mean to intrude. But can you at least tell me who reported your master as missing?'

'That would have been Jacqueline.' The cook rolled her large, expressive eyes. 'That woman worships the ground he walks on.' She laughed. 'But as far as he's concerned, she might as well be invisible.'

'I drove her into Tiziane so she could make the report,' the gardener said.

'In the Citroën outside?'

'Yes.' He dipped his head.

'Nice car,' Hamou observed, and the man grinned.

'I don't usually get a chance to drive that one: it's a bit big to go up some of the mountain tracks round here—'

'Brahim!'

The gardener cringed. 'Sorry, but...'

'The master has another vehicle?' Hamou asked quickly.

There was an awkward silence, then Brahim said, 'He has a 2CV. It's not as smart, but it has a higher suspension for the ruts and potholes.'

'And he took it out when he left? I didn't notice a 2CV parked outside.'

Brahim and the cook exchanged a complex look, and at last the young man said, 'He did.'

Hamou turned to the bespectacled man. 'Do you know where he was going?'

The manservant shook his head. 'There was nothing in his diary...' He hesitated. 'But he's supposed to be visiting the amghrar of Aflawassif this afternoon.'

'An official meeting?'

The manservant shrugged. 'That's all it says: Cherif Zakour, Aflawassif, written in the afternoon section.'

'No specific time?'

'Just afternoon. Monsieur Meline never makes appointments for the morning or evening if he can help it.'

'And why would that be?'

'Abdelhafid, enough of the tittle-tattle!' the cook said warningly. She turned to the gardener. 'I must go to the souk now or there will be nothing left but rubbish. Get the car started, I'll be out in a minute.' She turned to Hamou. 'Off you go! Abdelhafid has work to do and so do the rest of us. You can wait for your officer outside.'

Hamou, shooed out like a stray cat, and with Jérome nowhere in sight, walked around the house, his footsteps crunching on the gravel. It was situated in a fine position, with the Djebel Kest rising to the north of the property, its shadowed gullies peppered with little villages and the white minarets of two or three mosques. To the west the ridges receded in definition till they were little more than a hazy dream of mountains dissipating into the distance. He turned his face up to the sun and sighed, wishing he could share this moment with Zina Chadli.

A small stone landed near his feet, and Hamou jumped, shaken out of his reverie. He looked around, but there was no one in sight, though dust was rising on the lane where the big Citroën was making its way up to the main road. Another pebble, closer. He looked up. On the roof terrace of the house, silhouetted against white sheets billowing on the line, a figure – a girl: the maid, Fawa. Their eyes met and she raised a hand shyly in greeting. Hamou walked towards the house, wondering how he could get back inside without being seen. A few moments later a small door opened at ground level and the girl beckoned to him. 'Inside, quick, before you're seen!'

Hamou found himself standing in semi-darkness very close to the young woman, could hear her breathing, a little rapid; could smell the detergent soap she had been using. It felt compromising, a bit transgressive.

'We don't have much time before Abdelhafid notices I'm gone.' Fawa was panting from her run down the steps.

'Did you want to tell me something?' Hamou asked softly.

She made a movement of her head. 'You mustn't tell anyone, promise me.'

'I promise if I do have to pass on whatever you tell me, I will keep the source of the information secret.'

She seemed to make up her mind. 'He raped my sister.'

He recoiled. 'Baptiste Meline?'

'Yes. He raped her and got her pregnant, but she was lucky: she went away to relatives and the baby died.'

What a terrible definition of 'lucky'. 'That's very sad. Where's your sister now?'

'She stayed in Azoura.' Fawa named a village to the north, then hesitated.

'Go on?' Hamou encouraged gently.

'He... touches me sometimes.' She bowed her head, and Hamou could feel the heat of her shame warming the air between them. 'I don't invite him in any way.'

'It's not your fault, Fawa.' He remembered the Frenchman's distasteful remarks to the commandant, and added fervently, 'He's a horrible, horrible man.'

'He is!' She looked up at him and the meagre light slicked off her eyes. 'I hope he's dead. There, I've said it. I hope he's dead and one of the women he has hurt or dishonoured has killed him. Go to any village and you'll find one. Sometimes he brings them here for the night, or several nights. You hear things, not nice things. If you find him alive, *you* should kill him!' The venom in her voice, even at a whisper, was shocking.

'I can't do that,' Hamou said. 'But I do promise that if he lives, you will see him stand before a court.'

'I won't have to testify, will I?' From defiant she had shrunken back to terrified.

'It probably won't come to that,' he said gently, 'though I may need to talk to your sister.'

'You can't! She's married now, her husband must never know!'

So many secrets in the world, so much evil. 'We'll ford that river when we have to. Where do you think he's gone?'

'He went to see a woman.'

'How do you know that?'

'He made me iron his underwear and lay out a new shirt.' Such disgust in her voice.

'And he doesn't usually do that?'

'Him?' Fawa was derisive. 'He's a pig.'

'Do you know where he was meeting the woman?'

She shook her head. 'One of the mountain villages. He took the little car.'

The 2CV. 'He's probably still with her, then.'

'He wouldn't stay one night in one of the village houses, let alone two or three: someone would kill him. Anyway, he always comes home. Says he can't sleep anywhere but in his own bed. I've been here three years and he's never broken the pattern, not once.'

Footsteps outside on the gravel: they both froze. Then Hamou heard Jérome's voice, calling him.

'Take care, little sister,' he whispered to Fawa. 'And if Meline does come back, get yourself another job.'

'That's not so easy,' she said. 'My aunt and cousin work here too.'

Hamou had failed to recognise any family resemblance, but then, he hadn't been looking. 'The cook and the gardener?'

She nodded.

Outside, the footsteps receded, and Jérome called for him again from further away.

'Look, if he comes back, come and see me at my office in Tiziane. Ask for the hakam, Hamou Badi, all right? I'll help you find work, I promise.'

He opened the door a crack, then slipped out and heard it

close quietly behind him. By the time he reached the front of the house, Jérome was leaning up against the car, smoking. He regarded the hakam sardonically. 'A little tryst with the pretty maid?'

Hamou stopped dead. 'What? No!'

Jérome grinned. 'Just teasing. Saw her going upstairs with a load of laundry: lovely little thing.' He threw the stub of the cigarette down and ground it out with his heel. 'So? What did you find out?'

'I'll tell you on the way.'

'On the way where?'

'To see Cherif Zakour, in Aflawassif.'

'Oh God, not that clown.' Jérome rolled his eyes. 'His men tried to kill me. Why there?'

'Meline has an appointment with him this afternoon. Let's see if he turns up.'

As he drove, Hamou told Jérome all he had discovered while he was banished to the kitchen, and that at least three of the servants were connected by family ties. 'The cook in particular did not want the others talking to me, kept snapping at them if they looked as if they might disclose something sensitive.' He was still considering how much of what Fawa had told him to pass on to the adjutant.

'Interesting. The housekeeper was oddly tight-lipped, too. And she'd been crying, though she'd tried to disguise it with make-up.'

It was hard to believe anyone would miss Meline enough to weep. Then he remembered what the cook had said: *That woman worships the ground he walks on.*

'If you ask me,' Jérome went on, confirming this, 'I think she's in love with him. She was getting hysterical, is convinced he's dead.'

'In love with Meline?' Hamou yelped, and the car swerved suddenly towards the ditch. He oversteered and the back end slid away. Jérome took hold of the wheel, and between them they managed to get the Merc under control. Hamou's heart beat hard: it would get a lot worse than this soon – there was a steep climb up to Aflawassif, all hairpins and precipitous drops. 'How could anyone love that… that…' he remembered the word Fawa had uttered with such loathing, 'that pig?'

'He does have a look of the warthog about him,' Jérome mused. 'Are warthogs pigs? Must look it up when we get back. Yes, the poor woman broke down several times. That's why it took so long, though goodness knows what you were doing.'

Hamou said nothing.

'She's been with him for twenty years or more,' Jérome went on.

'Twenty years? Here, in the valley?'

'Certainly in the region. He was one of the first French settlers around here. I suppose that's how he's got himself such a prime spot.'

'Well, she should be able to see him for what he is,' Hamou said, guiding the car carefully around a tight bend. The gears crunched loudly, and Jérome winced.

'How about pulling in up ahead and I'll drive us up to the village?' he suggested.

Hamou was glad to relinquish the driving: concentrating so hard had made his shoulders rigid with tension. 'So, what else did she say?' he asked, walking around the vehicle, and easing himself into the passenger seat. 'Does she know where he might be?'

'He didn't tell her anything, but that wasn't unusual. She says he often disappears during the day but that he's always back for dinner, and never, ever sleeps anywhere but in his own bed, so for him to go missing for three days is out of character.'

'It was implied by one of the staff that he didn't always return alone.'

'Women, you mean?' Jérome shot him a look.

'That's what I understood.'

The adjutant drummed his fingers on the leather of the steering wheel. 'Maybe that's why Jacqueline is so worried.'

'Jealous husband?'

'Or brothers, or fathers, or cousins, or clan chiefs. Gosh, this is going to be awkward. Your people are a bit sticky about this sort of thing, aren't they?'

'It's a matter of honour,' Hamou said stiffly.

'Quite, quite. I've been here long enough to understand that. Mind you, there are other reasons people might dislike Meline enough to… abduct him, beat him, or whatever. Rich men don't always come by their wealth honestly.'

'So, we can add criminals, gangsters and business partners to fathers, brothers, husbands, cousins and clan chiefs!' Hamou paused, then added with a laugh, 'Oh, yes, and he's French!'

Jérome did not laugh. 'And now is the perfect time to do away with someone, in the interregnum between protectorate control and whatever comes next,' he mused. 'There could, as you suggest, be a political element: an assassination, say. Or a criminal currying favour with those on the up, bumping off a mutual enemy to score points. Or maybe someone just wants his land…'

Hamou hadn't thought of any of this. 'Of course, he may not be dead at all. Maybe the car broke down or he had an accident.'

'We'd have heard,' Jérome said. 'You know what Tiziane's like, especially on market day with people coming in from all over. Someone's always seen something. There's nowhere so remote that it isn't in sight of a shepherd or nomad.'

'True. So whatever has happened to him was out of sight, en cachette.' Hamou thought about this some more. 'Better ask about the car. Not too many 2CVs around here.'

But there was no sign of the vehicle on the road up to Aflawassif, or in the village itself. Jérome asked directions to the amghrar's residence, took one look at the track, and parked the Mercedes in the square near the mosque, leaving two boys playing football with a handful of small coins to keep an eye on it. Hamou was reminded painfully of his cousin Moha doing the same near the Carrière centrales in Casablanca and felt a deep pang of loss. No one knew where his Casa family had gone, not even relatives in Tiziane, not even suppliers to the business whom he'd tracked down and called on on some other pretext. What if he never saw any of them again?

The amghrar's residence was an old Berber house built from irregular blocks mortared with pisé and with traditional zigzagging designs around the door and windows to ward off the evil eye. Upright stones had been set at the edges of its flat roof, pointing heavenwards to mark the deaths it had seen within its walls: a stark reminder that life was transitory.

It was the amghrar himself – Cherif Zakour – who opened the door. He ushered them into the salon a little testily and without a word about Jerome's wound or limp, so if the adjutant had been expecting an apology, he was to be disappointed.

'No, I haven't seen Meline,' Zakour said when they explained why they had come.

'But he's due to arrive this afternoon?' Hamou asked.

The amghrar pursed his lips. 'My business is my own.'

Jérome gave him a cold stare. 'This is an official enquiry: you are bound to answer our questions.'

Zakour's lip curled. 'You'll be gone soon, I hear.'

'Not me. I'm staying on, so I'd suggest you cooperate.' Jérome held the man's gaze. 'If you think there will be a free-for-all, I'm afraid you are greatly mistaken.'

The amghrar turned to Hamou. 'What's the matter with you, working with the fucking French?' he asked in a guttural rattle of Tachelhit. 'Have you no loyalty to your own? Why are you interested in that fat *chelb*, anyway?'

'Your name's in his diary, for this afternoon. What's your meeting about?'

'Oh, this and that. It's not a fixed thing.'

'What, the timing, or the subject?'

'Just a possible bit of business, a passing suggestion.'

'You'd do business with a – what was the phrase, a "fat chelb"? And why would he come all the way to Aflawassif? Couldn't you have met in Tiziane, or his house? Does Meline come up here a lot? To the village? I've not heard anything good about this man, especially when it comes to women.'

'And girls.' A young woman leaned on the door jamb, regarding them. Her eyes swept over the adjutant. 'Got a watchdog with you, have you?'

'Away with you, Illi.' The amghrar regarded his daughter fondly. 'Men's business.'

Illi rolled her eyes so hard Hamou thought they would disappear into her skull. 'Who is the handsome foreigner?' she asked Hamou, not moving from her position. She had a river of black hair and fine, straight brows, and despite her precocious bearing, could not be more than fifteen or sixteen.

'He's the adjutant of Tiziane,' Hamou said, and had to bite his tongue before he told her Jérome was soon to be the commandant. 'An important man.'

'Why's he looking for that pig Meline?'

'Rude. We are making enquiries.'

She shrugged. 'Into Meline? You should leave him to the jackals.'

'Illi!'

'Already leaving.' She lifted a shoulder in a gesture of insouciance, gathered her robe up to reveal peep-toed shoes that showed off toenails polished a deep blood-red, and flounced off.

Zakour's eyes were misty. 'Little beauty, isn't she? Reminds me of her mother.' He breathed in, remembering, then returned his attention to the adjutant. 'Always has to be the centre of attention. The bride at every wedding, the corpse at every funeral.' He said this as if it was a good thing.

'Could someone please translate?' Jérome said in clipped tones, and Hamou gave him a brief résumé.

The adjutant looked thoughtful. He looked at the chieftain. 'So, sir, you never answered my original question. Why has Meline got an appointment with you written in his diary for this afternoon?'

'Why exactly do you keep asking about my private business?'

'The gentleman has been reported missing,' Jérome said.

The amghrar sat back with his hands in his lap. 'Oh dear. Well, I doubt it's anything serious. I'm sure he'll turn up.'

'Perhaps we could wait for him, to see if he comes to his meeting with you?'

Cherif Zakour rolled his eyes as theatrically as his daughter. 'As you wish.'

They drank tea, brought in by a silent headscarfed woman far too meek to be the wife, and still there was no sign of the Frenchman. Jérome passed the time talking with excessive politeness with the clan chief about village finances, the construction of a new road, water rights, then they sat in an awkward silence. At last, the amghrar checked his watch. 'Look, he's clearly not coming, and I have work to do.'

The adjutant edged his way off the couch and, using his stick, managed to stand. The amghrar glanced at his leg, then looked away. He said nothing, but when they reached the door, Hamou said to Jérome, 'I'll see you back at the car – give me ten minutes.'

'The day of the hunt,' Hamou said quietly, when the adjutant had disappeared from view, 'was it you or one of your men who fired the shot that struck him?'

The amghrar looked thunderstruck. 'Are you out of your mind?'

Hamou dug in his pocket and pulled out the ball of lead shot he had retrieved from the site of the shooting. It was round on one side, flattened and splayed on the other from impact, but it was clearly handmade, for an older style of weapon, and flecked with dried blood. 'Only you and your men carried guns that would use shot like this.'

Zakour burst out laughing. 'Stay here.'

Hamou heard him calling at the back of the house but couldn't make out the words. After a few minutes, the amghrar returned, bearing a long-barrelled, muzzle-loading gun. He thrust it at Hamou. For all its antiquity, it was a beautiful thing, its stock covered in silver engraved with Berber tribal markings.

'It's not been fired in the best part of fifty years. I don't know if it even works any more!'

Was this the weapon the man had brought to the hunt? Hamou examined it; sniffed it. Nothing. He stared down its barrel. Cobwebs! There were actual cobwebs in it. He handed it back. 'And what about your men?'

As if summoned, the door opened to admit the two riders who had accompanied the amghrar on the hunt. Each bore a rifle similar to the chieftain's, though less ornate. 'This fellow thinks we shot the French officer!' Cherif Zakour declared.

They chuckled. 'That'd be a fine trick!' The first man tossed Hamou his weapon. It was very light – too light – and Hamou realised it was not a real gun at all, but an ornamental replica. 'Oh.' He handed it back.

The second looked like a real gun, but it only fired blanks, the man explained, and showed Hamou the cartridges he used for it, little more than fireworks that generated a muzzle flash and an explosive sound. Hamou frowned. 'Why would you take these to a hunt?' He remembered the spectacle they had made of themselves, prancing around on their caparisoned horses, tricked out like exhibition riders at a fantasie.

The amghrar shrugged. 'When we hunt, we hunt: but never boar. They are *haram*. That was just a picnic with guns,' he said contemptuously. 'So, we thought we'd attend in style, add a bit of local colour. We weren't expecting to be insulted by those kafir.' He made a rude gesture.

'But you still do business with Meline?' Hamou asked.

The amghrar's gaze was cold. 'It's clearly going to take you more time to understand how the world works here, boy.'

'I'm sorry to have wasted your time,' Hamou said formally.

'I suppose you think you're sitting pretty when the French pull out, but don't get too many big ideas, eh?'

The amghrar narrowed his eyes, but Hamou regarded him levelly. 'I'm here only to help the adjutant and to do my job.'

'We never needed a hakam before, I don't see why we need one now. We do things our own way around here.'

'I'm sure you do.'

Hamou let himself out into the dusty street.

When he got back to the car, Jérome was not in sight, though the young footballers were still kicking their ball around. Had they been here all this time, or had they gone home for lunch and returned? Hamou leaned against the Mercedes and watched them appreciatively till the ball came rolling towards him. He trapped it neatly and kicked it back into play, earning a whoop. After a while, the players drifted off one by one until only the two lads to whom Jérome had given coins remained. They came over, no doubt hoping for further recompense.

'Who are you, mister?' the first one asked. He had mismatched eyes, one green, one brown.

'I'm Hamou Badi, the local hakam. I work for the community, helping people with their problems.'

'What sort of problems?' asked the smaller, darker boy.

Hamou outlined the simpler aspects of his job and they looked bored. Before he lost them altogether, he asked, 'Do you ever see the man known as Baptiste Meline here in the village?'

'The one who looks like a *boutagant*?' He used the local word for wild boar.

Hamou grinned. 'Yes, him.'

The first boy laughed. 'He comes to visit Ider's mother!'

'He does not! Shut your mouth!' And the smaller boy flew at the other, fists swinging.

'He does, too! She's a *tadgalt*!'

'Hey!' Hamou separated them. 'Don't use that word. It's cruel and nasty,' he admonished the larger boy, who looked unabashed, but sulky. Then he made a rude gesture at Hamou and ran off.

'Are you all right?' Hamou asked Ider gently. The boy's eye was starting to swell.

Ider nodded, but his gaze was hot. 'He's lying about my mother.'

'I'm sure he is,' Hamou said quietly.

'But that man comes here for girls. Sometimes he gives them money, sometimes just bruises. Lots of people want to kill him: I've heard them say so.'

'Have you seen that man recently?' Ider shook his head and his lip wobbled. Hamou watched as he mastered himself fiercely. 'Do you have a favourite football team?' he asked quickly.

Ider's eyes lit up. 'Raja, of course!'

'I met Salah Medkouri. In fact, we spent a fair bit of time together!' Hamou omitted to add that it had been in a Casablanca jail.

The boy was transported. 'Wait till I tell the others that I met a friend of Salah Medkouri!' He raced off, equanimity restored.

Hamou watched him go, feeling nostalgic – for his own boyhood; for a simpler life; even, strangely, for his time in Casa. So, Meline was not just a womaniser, but a brute too. Fawa's story about her sister echoed by the words of a child. He had known in his gut that she spoke the truth. He scanned the road up from the valley floor for Meline's vehicle, but there were just people on foot, and on donkeys, returning from the souk in Tiziane with their purchases. He turned back to look for any sign of Jérome and saw him come walking, stick swinging, in the company of two women in black robes decorated with bright embroidery. The adjutant looked positively sprightly.

Hamou straightened up. 'There you are!'

'I was waylaid by these charming ladies. They took me up to their sacred spring and doused my leg in its healing water. Then they massaged it till I howled like a dog – I'm surprised you didn't hear me! But look how much better I'm walking. They're miracle workers, better than the doctors. Would you tell them so, Hamou? My Berber's not up to it.'

Hamou translated and the women hid their mouths and giggled. The younger asked if Jérome was married. 'Not yet,' the hakam said, 'but I don't think he's looking right now.'

'Tell him when he is he should come back and ask for Naima.'

The older woman tutted, then scrutinised Hamou. 'You're the zouhry, aren't you?'

'I'm the hakam,' Hamou said patiently.

'I heard you divined water for Hajj Yazid.'

'That was more the well-digger, Bilal Boanou.'

She was having none of it. 'I will send my brother-in-law to you. He was round here complaining that his neighbours have stolen the water assigned to his crops and he's too feeble to do anything about it. Perhaps you can find him a new water source.'

Hamou sighed. 'Perhaps. But I'm very busy, he may have to wait.'

He and the adjutant got back into the car and waited till the sun disappeared over the ridge. 'He's not coming, is he?' Jérome said at last.

'Doesn't look like it.'

A long silence fell between them. Then Jérome gave a little laugh. 'You're becoming something of a local celebrity.'

'I'm afraid I'm about to become something of a local fraud,' Hamou said quietly. After another long silence he added, 'Illi, the amghrar's daughter, said "leave him to the jackals". It's a common turn of phrase, but...'

'But?'

'The more extreme nationalist elements call themselves jackals sometimes. Actually, it's a common term for those who kill vermin.'

Jérome raised an eyebrow. 'Interesting.'

'It's probably nothing.' But Hamou's mind was turning again.

34

Baptiste Meline was still missing over a week later. Mokhazni from across the region had been sent out to every village to make enquiries, but no one had seen the man or his vehicle. Hamou went back to his duties as hakam and put in long hours to clear the backlog that had built up.

The news coming in from the wider world was encouraging: a deal had been hammered out between the French and the Istiqlal and it was said that the sultan would soon be on his way back from Madagascar to resume his rightful throne once more. Hamou wondered what would happen to the puppet sultan Mohammed Ben Arafa then. Indeed, he wondered what would happen to anyone who had collaborated with the administration. It seemed likely there would be a long period of upheaval as power was handed back to Moroccan authorities, during which a great deal of patience and goodwill would be required. He remembered what Mehdi, the bus driver, had said about reprisals. He remembered the man stepping out of the shadows by his home with his dire warning. He remembered the symbolic blackened croissant on the step, and hoped he had managed to stay on the right side of whatever arbitrary line had been drawn. There were certainly scores to be settled, and it appeared some were not waiting for the interregnum. A French army jeep was blown off one of the mountain roads by an explosive device: the three occupants survived but were injured. People whispered the words 'Black Crescent' with a mixture of awe and alarm, but Hamou had heard other versions of the incident: it was the work of nomads; it was a reprisal for the death of a local man jailed in the uprising in Marrakech; and even that the soldiers had made the story up as cover because they had got roaring drunk and lost control of the jeep, which had been comprehensively wrecked.

The mood was nervy and febrile. Jérome had his hands full, and Hamou hardly saw him. Some of the French settlers had been forced off the terrain they farmed near Ait Baha. The rumour had gone out that *all* the French were leaving and there had been a scramble to lay claim to ancestral land. Long-buried inheritance quarrels were resurrected; tribal feuds reignited over boundary disputes. Hamou spent hours in various councils of elders, taking notes, trying to calm tensions, watching in admiration as Caid Hajj Abdullah trod difficult lines and negotiated temporary settlements. He kept his nose to the grindstone and got on with the small things he could do to improve people's lives, driving himself harder every day.

Which was why, returning home late one night, he was stunned to find he had more company than usual. Revealed by the sudden snap of the light switch, Madani lay stretched out on the couch, nursing what appeared to be five kittens: two tabby, one tortoiseshell, one fully red, and the last patched black and white. Man and cat stared at one another, one uncomprehending, the other reproachful. Hamou let drop his coat and went to his knees for a better view. He regarded his cat with astonishment. 'Madani, what have you been up to?'

Well, it was clear what Madani had been up to, but how had he never deduced that Madani was not the tomcat he had always taken him to be? Had he never thought to examine the animal's nether regions? He had not.

So, now he was responsible for a household of seven – as well as his mother and sisters and their livestock. For a moment, this realisation weighed upon him, then he was struck by a sense of wonder, as he watched the tiny bundles with their eyes tight closed and their little mouths hungrily sucking. Madani knew how to be a mother, and her kittens knew how to feed. How powerful nature was, driven by unstoppable instincts and urges. He reached out and stroked Madani's head and the cat narrowed her lambent gold eyes at him in a communication of trust, then yawned hugely.

'I thought you were getting fat,' Hamou said. 'I put it down to indolence and a good life. Little did I know what you were getting up to while my back was turned!'

What on earth was he going to do with five kittens? Tiziane already had a large feral cat population, and now he had added to it. He shook his head: yet another problem for the hakam to solve.

The next day dawned fair. Another day of no rain, another day of unhappy people coming to seek his help. He had moved the divining rods Hajj Yazid had given him into a cupboard and had patiently explained to all comers that he was a hakam, not a water diviner. And thank heaven the maf-aman was now largely recovered and able to help find water sources, though with decreasing success, since the water table kept falling.

Even so, the queue for his attentions was a long one: plaintiff after plaintiff, dispute after dispute. By afternoon he was exhausted, and hungry. He left Aziz in charge as he walked quickly into the town to buy provisions. When he told Rachid the butcher about Madani, the man laughed, then gathered a bagful of scraps. 'She'll need to keep her strength up to feed that lot!'

Word passed from the butcher to the fruiterer, from the fruiterer to the spiceman, from the spiceman to the herbman, from him to the baker, and on. Hamou went to the square of artisans and purchased a cheap blanket and a large, flat basket, then drank a coffee standing outside the café. By the time he reached the grocer, word about his 'tomcat' giving birth was all over Tiziane. The man behind the counter tallied up his shopping, then popped a tin of beef into his bag: 'A treat for the new mother!'

Hamou was touched by such kindness. There was no tradition for pet-owning here – people's lives were hard, and animals had to earn their keep – so when he got home to find on his doorstep a jar of cream, a clay dish and some handfuls of combed sheep's wool for bedding, his eyes filled with tears.

He made the feline family comfortable out in the courtyard garden, carrying each kitten to the blanketed, wool-covered basket with the care he would give to porcelain, leaving the back door ajar so that Madani would not feel banished, and made his way back to his office, fuelled with even greater fire to give back whatever he could to his community.

It was gone four by the time the almond farmer came to him. He said they called him Azam Tagulla, because barley porridge was all he ate. Hamou had come to recognise real suffering when he saw it. Azam was reticent, but Hamou drew his words out with gentle encouragement.

'My... my sister-in-law said I must come to see you, but I've been... I don't like to make a fuss. I don't want to... bother you. And I don't want anyone... to get in trouble.' Hamou realised this was the relative of the older woman who had taken Jérome to the sacred spring in Aflawassif.

'My trees are dying,' Azam Tagulla went on miserably. 'Almonds are well known for resisting drought, and they've survived so far against all the odds, but now they're dying. My neighbours still have water – we share the *targua*, the irrigation system from the spring above the village which is regulated by the water officer – but it seems only to be me who has been affected. I went to see the *asrayfi* to make a complaint, but he said he'd been turning on my water as usual, so if there was a problem, it was my problem. I've been carrying buckets of water for my trees up and down day after day, but now the women have chased me away from the well for fear I will use the last of their water, and I can't do any more. So, I am begging you to come and help me.'

Hamou felt awful for what he said next, but he knew he had to say it. 'I can follow up your complaint with the asrayfi, but if you want to find a new water source, you need the help of the maf-aman, not me.'

Azam Tagulla leaned across the desk. 'I don't need you to find a new water source for me. I need you to find *my* water!'

'Have you checked the irrigation system to make sure it isn't faulty?' Hamou asked reasonably.

'Everyone but me is getting water.'

'Are you on good terms with your neighbours? Might someone be holding a grudge against you?' Hamou had come upon one instance where a group of farmers had conspired against one of their number and cut off his water supply to drive him off his land because he was so disliked. He did not want to suggest this might be the case with Azam Tagulla, but you never knew. People fell into feuds that continued for decades over the smallest of things. He sighed. 'I'll come with you, and you can show me the irrigation system, and if your neighbours are around, I will have a word with them. And then if that doesn't get us anywhere, I will talk to your asrayfi and amghrar, and will try to get to the bottom of this.'

Makouda tried to bite him as Hamou saddled him up. 'Yes, yes, I know,' he told the mule. 'I thought my day was over, too, but I'm afraid there's no help for it.'

There was no mokhazni available to accompany them, all were engaged on official business for the adjutant, but Hamou reckoned that a quick visit to Tafla did not warrant the presence of an armed escort. The village was easy to access, and generally peaceful. It was quite pleasant to trot along the valley road in the warmth of the afternoon, looking up at the rufous slopes of the Djebel Kest, watching large birds riding the thermal air currents in search of prey, wing feathers spread like fingers. Eagles, maybe, or Barbary falcons: he was no expert, and it was hard to judge size at this distance. Beside him, sitting side-saddle on his donkey, Azam Tagulla stared off into the distance, his torrent of words dried up as fully as his water.

Even before they reached the man's property, Hamou could tell, looking up from the road, which strip of land was his. The parcels to either side, though dry, still maintained a degree of verdancy, while Azam's lay dull and brown, his almond trees visibly withered. He took in the situation of the smallholdings: serried rows of cultivated terraces, the narrow track up to Tagtout far above, zigzagging up the mountain. As if they had seen him coming, no other farmer was out on his land: the whole place was deserted.

They passed through the village, and that too was preternaturally quiet. Azam pointed out his home – a tiny house with a single door downstairs, and a single window above, in a row of similarly small abodes. 'As you can see,' he said, 'I'm not a rich man. My trees are all I have.' He sounded broken.

'Show me the boundaries of your land and your irrigation system and I'll take a look, in case there's something you might have missed.'

Azam nodded glumly. 'That's good of you, Hakam. I'm not a young man and my eyes and legs are not what they were. That's why we planted almond and olive trees, planning for the future: I can't plough or hoe or scythe any more.'

They walked through the village, its collection of old houses all in the same ochre-red as the surrounding earth and towering cliffs, the little mosque standing out like a single white chicken in a flock of brown hens. On the outskirts, where habitation gave way to agriculture, Hamou tethered his mule alongside the man's bony donkey. Makouda stared about at the dearth of pasture, and his doleful cries followed him up the track. Above and below them, the land had been dug in undulating terraces to maximise the use of the steeply sloping ground. It looked stony and unproductive to Hamou, but when he got his eye in, he could make out drainage channels leading down the slopes, tilled land, and crops. Azam Tagulla's patch was noticeably dry. His trees, which should be in full leaf, were in a miserable state, the leaves curled, the fruits shrivelled.

The farmer, as if seeing the devastation afresh, sank to his knees in the dust. Hamou placed a hand on his shoulder. 'Just point me to where the water source is.'

Azam pointed feebly up the slope. 'Follow the channels up to the ravine – that's where the spring emerges. I can't climb up there any longer.'

Hamou left him there and made his way uphill. The extent of Azam's land was relatively clear: three wide terraces, separated by drystone walls, the first planted with olives, the other two with almond trees spaced at regular intervals. Seeing the exposed roots of the poor trees where the thin, dry topsoil had worn away made him sad: he wanted to bend and cover them, as if they were indecent.

At the top edge of the first terrace, he followed a path around the end of the retaining wall and climbed onto the second terrace. A concrete channel ran down the edge of the field: it was dry as bone. Hamou looked around and saw no one else in the fields. He stepped over the barrier of thorns and entered the adjoining terrace, where the neighbouring cultivator clearly had a penchant for turnips, row after row of them with flourishes of leaf and their blushing crowns just showing through the soil. Despite the generally dry conditions, the turnips appeared healthy and reasonably well watered.

Back on Azam's land, he climbed up to the third terrace, which was narrower than the previous two and more broken up by cactus and thorn. Getting to the water channel was more of an effort here, but still when he did locate it, he found it dry to the touch. It required some effort to make his way behind the retaining wall, which incorporated huge fallen boulders from the cliff that loomed above him. From here, he could see a network of channels leading up into the deeply shaded ravine beyond and ultimately, he deduced, to the water source. They were widely spaced here, but must converge above. Therefore, whatever problem had stopped Azam's irrigation must lie between here and the spring.

Hamou tried to make a direct assault on the slope above, but the spiky undergrowth rebuffed him, and after a while he gave up and walked towards the village. A couple of hundred metres along he came upon a track leading up towards the ravine. With a sigh, he looked upwards. A pair of birds circled, wings spread, silhouetted against the darkening sky. There was maybe half an hour of good light left, and he didn't much want to be up in the ravine after the sun had set, for that was when the wild boars became active.

Glancing back down the terraced slopes, he could just make out Azam Tagulla sitting on the wall at the bottom, staring up hopefully. He couldn't let this poor man down.

The higher track must be the path the water officer took each day when turning on and off the water allocations to the different channels: it was clear and easy to negotiate. He could hear the spring long before he reached the source and eventually arrived at a long cistern into which clear water tumbled joyfully. He looked in: it was maybe a third full and he could see from the dark stain on its sides that the water level was usually much higher. From the cistern ran a system of pipes and blocks. This was what the asrayfi was in charge of: ensuring that every cultivator had access to their fair share of water: two hours a day, no more, no less. Hamou went from channel to channel, touching each in turn. Every single one was damp, so it appeared that the water officer had not lied.

So, the problem lay between here and the third terrace. He tried to follow the channels down, checking them at intervals for traces of water. It was hard going: no one ever entered this dense undergrowth. He availed himself of a fallen branch and started whacking a path down towards the terraces.

The light was fading now, the sky acquiring a violet tint streaked with gory red. He laid about himself more fiercely, frustrated that a simple task had become so unpleasant, but driven by the commitment he had made to the poor farmer, and by his own obstinacy.

A little way ahead, he noticed a depression in the tangle of vegetation and made for that. He had determined now that the middle of the three channels he had been following fed Azam's land, so he followed it down towards the depression. Wet, still wet: his hand confirmed with a touch on the concrete. And a little lighter here, too, as he emerged from beneath the mountain's overhang. He could see Azam's top terrace now, so he had narrowed the problem down to a stretch of perhaps twenty metres.

And this was where he hit a thicket of thorns. Swearing, Hamou lashed the bushes, and wished he'd worn stouter clothing and footwear. With great effort, he broke a path through to clearer territory. There was the channel, brimming with water. There must be an obstruction damming it up. With effort and further bushwhacking, he came to the problem: a wild boar appeared to have collapsed across Azam Tagulla's irrigation channel, blocking the flow. And now he remembered the circling birds that he had seen from the valley road, and again when he had checked the sky for light. What a dolt he was! Of course, they were carrion birds, vultures probably. He had forgotten everything Uncle Omar had taught him.

If he could move the boar, he could restore Azam's water to his crop at once. What a triumph that would be! Hamou scrambled the few metres remaining between himself and the dead creature, trying not to take any notice of the smell, or the angry clouds of flies he disturbed. He wedged the end of his branch under the middle of the beast and heaved. It didn't shift. He leaned all his weight on the branch and put in a huge effort.

One, two... The branch snapped with a mighty crack and the sharp end came at him so fast that he thought it was going to impale him. Instead, it clipped his ear painfully so that he yelled out, and went tumbling.

Hamou landed in a tangled heap on top of the body, and the dead boar released a great huff of air so that he was enveloped in a foul miasma, making him gag and cough. He scrambled clear in disgust. Shuddering, he brushed himself down compulsively, and his hands came away wet and sticky. Despite his revulsion, he could not help but look back. The boar had shifted just a little, enough that he could make out paler underparts, which were bloated and swollen. A great spiral of blowflies rose, buzzing angrily, disrupting his view, and dispersed into the noisome air.

And now his night vision kicked in, and Hamou made out a face, and a pair of pale, clouded eyes, eyes that dully trapped and reflected the last light of the day.

He turned away and retched.

The creature was not a boar at all. It was Baptiste Meline.

35

Meline's body was wrapped in a tarpaulin and taken down to that part of the abattoir dedicated to processing pork for French military provisions, which seemed to Hamou remarkably apposite.

The Frenchman's corpse was in a wretched state after many days lying in the backed-up irrigation water and it was hard to immediately determine the cause of death. The adjutant had sent to Marrakech for a medical examiner, who had just arrived. Jérome and Hamou were to attend his inspection. Hamou was not looking forward to it: his discovery of the corpse had him waking in the middle of the night, covered in sweat, engulfed in the old Casa nightmares again.

Hamou had expected the gleaming Mercedes to roll up outside, for the abattoir was a stiff walk beyond the village, but instead Jérome came sauntering down the road with his stick balanced on his shoulder, accompanied by a bespectacled young man with premature baldness, introduced as Georges Pinot. They shook hands and Hamou fell in beside the Frenchmen as they headed down through the town, ever watchful in case there were eyes on him marking his company.

'You're walking better,' he said to Jérome when they passed out of the village

'Almost completely healed.' The adjutant grinned.

'They say the waters of the Blue Spring have miraculous properties.'

The medical examiner raised an eyebrow.

Jérome laughed, then became solemn. 'I reckon I'm lucky not to be lying where Meline is now.'

Meline was lying on a table, thawing.

'Why's he that colour?' Hamou asked in a loud whisper, as if the dead man might hear. Parts of Baptiste Meline were the purple-black of an aubergine; other patches the colour of a ripe plum, and there were little rips and tears in his skin.

'Tell me how you found him,' Pinot asked him.

'He was in the fields outside the village of Tafla, under the mountain.'

'I meant his position,' the medical examiner said patiently.

Hamou felt a fool. 'He was face down, across an irrigation channel.'

Pinot nodded. 'That would make sense. After the body's circulation ceases, the blood pools where gravity dictates, creating this lividity.' He indicated the puce areas which, along with the bloating, rendered Meline even more monstrous than he had been in life. Then he prodded the corpse's abdomen, which was darker yet in colour, and greenish, and Hamou remembered the foul rush of air when he had fallen on the Frenchman's remains, and felt nauseous. 'Some of this distension will be caused by the gases of putrefaction, but I would hazard he was not a small man in life.' A little smile: a man in his element.

As the body succumbed to the environment outside the refrigeration unit, it softened and parts flopped. Pinot manipulated the limbs one by one, turned the head, made little noises, examined closely the rips in the skin. Then he went back to palpating the chest and belly, and Hamou tried not to look at the dead man's private parts, remembering with revulsion all the harm they had done.

'Turn him over,' the medical examiner asked the two abattoir workers, and with a lot of puffing they did so, and suddenly Jérome strode to the door and disappeared outside. Hamou covered his mouth and nose with his scarf.

'Ah, interesting.' Now Pinot had a gloved finger inside a hole on the man's back. It rooted around for a minute there, then re-emerged. He looked disappointed. 'Thought he'd been shot, but apparently not.' He went to the sink, ran his hands under the tap.

The adjutant came back in, looking clammy. He looked to the medical examiner. 'Cause of death?'

Pinot pursed his lips. 'I can't say definitively, the body's in a pretty poor state. Nine, ten days outside? And it looks as if he's taken a big fall.'

'A fall that would kill him?'

'I can't really say. There are a number of broken bones – neck, ribs, sternum, leg, pelvis, and some tears and puncture wounds that may well have occurred at the same time. Quite a deep hole in his back, but no correspondent hole on his front, so it doesn't look as if he was shot. Could be a blade, or it could have occurred during the fall. He took quite a bashing.' He looked to the hakam. 'You said there was a mountain?'

Hamou nodded. 'Yes, right above where I found him.'

'He might have fallen.' Jérome looked thoughtful.

'He didn't strike me as much of a walker, let alone a mountaineer!'

The adjutant shook his head. 'It's a mystery.'

'There is one thing,' Pinot said. He took hold of the head and wrenched it around so that the face was visible over the shoulder, a grotesquely unnatural position. 'See this mark here.' He beckoned Jérome closer.

Hamou hung back, not wanting to approach the hideous cadaver. He watched the adjutant pinch his nose and lean in, squinting. 'What am I supposed to be looking at?'

'This mark, on his forehead. It looks... well, it probably occurred naturally, but it's unusual.'

'Doesn't look like anything to me. Could have been caused by a rock, or a tree, as he fell. If he fell.'

The medical examiner shrugged. 'I'm sure you're right.' He sighed and straightened up. 'I'm sorry, I've not been a great deal of use to you.'

'Not at all, not at all. I'm sorry to have called in the favour, Georges. I know you're heading out imminently, but I didn't want some relative crawling out of the woodwork claiming I hadn't done my job.'

The two men moved away from the examination table, and then out of the room. Hamou started to follow them, then turned back and ventured a glance at the hideous corpse. A prickle ran down his spine. The mark was small, just over a centimetre, in the dead centre of the man's forehead, curved, pointed at both ends.

Was it what he thought it was? He blinked, remembering Jérome's words. A rock or a tree... Or was it the mark of the Black Crescent? He chided himself: that was absurd.

It was Friday, so technically his day off, and he was invited for couscous with the family, but seeing Meline's body on the abattoir table had dampened his appetite. He decided to call in on his mother on his way back to beg off lunch.

Arriving at the family home, he found all in hubbub, his sisters running back and forth shrieking excitedly. Lights flashed crazily on and off. Hamou grinned, and went in. There he found Tahir bin Yazid and another man in overalls showing his mother the new magic they had just installed throughout the house: an electric light in every room, electric points in the salon and the kitchen.

Catching sight of her son, Lalla Saïda put her hands to her face. 'What a terrible mother I am! The couscous is not yet cooking: my mind has been bewitched by all this...' She waved wordlessly, taking in the ceiling with its pendant bulb, at the two engineers grinning in the doorway, then made the sign against the evil eye. 'This strange magic.'

'Calm yourself, Yam'mi. It is no trouble to me, no trouble at all. I will come tomorrow when everything is quieter.'

He walked out with Tahir and his electrician and helped them to load their equipment into the truck parked in the square, worrying that he had done the wrong thing in introducing the modern world so precipitously into his mother's life. 'Thank you,' he said quietly. 'She seems a bit...'

'Don't worry, she'll get used to it in no time,' Tahir told him. 'We hooked up your old lady yesterday morning, and when we looked in on her last night, she kissed our hands!'

His old lady? Hamou frowned, then realised they meant Lalla Hasna, whom he had helped with the carpet for her daughter. He thanked them effusively, then caught Tahir's sleeve as he turned away. 'And the bill for the electricity will come to me, yes?'

The engineer gave him a sly smile. 'Don't worry about that, it's all taken care of.' Hamou must have looked alarmed, for he added, 'It's on the same circuit as the administrative offices. All she has is a single light and a socket. Believe me, brother, the administration won't even notice the difference, not even if she runs her little heater day and night.'

'She has a heater?'

Tahir shrugged. 'We had a spare.' He patted Hamou on the shoulder and turned to leave, then turned back. 'And if you come across other poor folk in need, be sure to let me know.'

Hamou smiled warmly. 'I will talk to the caid: perhaps we can establish a fund through the hakam's office.'

He took a short detour on his way home to check in on Lalla Hasna. Her door was ajar, and it was bright beyond so, calling a greeting, he stuck his head around the jamb, and was horrified to find the old woman in tears. 'Lalla, what is it?' He cast a swift glance around her tiny home. The harshness of the single electric bulb hanging from the ceiling made all the more apparent the meanness of the little home. His gaze fell back to the old woman. In her lap lay curled the tabby cat. She raised mournful eyes to him, and he saw that the cat was not moving, and at once he deduced the reason for her sorrow. It seemed the good angel of the world had brought light to her, and the bad angel had taken light away.

'Lalla, I'm so sorry.'

He buried the animal for her in the stony patch of ground outside.

'There are many cats in the world,' he said gently to the old woman, but she shook her head. 'My Mina was special.'

'I have a cat.' Hamou told her about how he had mistaken Madani for a tomcat and come home to find a tangle of kittens suckling at 'his' chest. This raised a smile.

As he was leaving, she caught his hands in her claws. 'Could you bear to part with two of your kittens, when they are weaned?'

Hamou was still grinning as he made his way through the centre of the village, cutting through the square of the artisans to reach the traditional baker on the other side, who made the best bread in Tiziane. He could imagine holding the wide, flat loaf in his hands, the heat from the stone-warmed crust radiating from the paper, the enticing yeasty smell. His mouth ran with water. But as he passed the metalworker's stall, his nose twitched. He peered in as he passed and saw that the man was melting lead over a burner, the molten metal a brooding silver in colour as it swirled sulkily in the pot.

Some deep memory stirred in him, an ancient nostalgia. Then he took off running.

36

Half an hour later he and Houcine were riding for the valley at a fast trot, which made Makouda complain heavily. Both he and the young mokhazni were armed, though he had yet to fill in the paperwork for the guns and ammunition. In retrospect, he should probably have told the adjutant where he was going and why, but it was too late now. Fatima, Houcine's wife, would probably take more placating, since he had dragged the mokhazni away from lunch with the extended family, for which Houcine had thanked him effusively.

There was little life to be seen on the valley road, or on the track up to the villages under the Djebel Kest – everyone was at home eating their Friday couscous – and for this, Hamou was grateful. As they passed the agricultural land outside Tafla, he cast an eye over it and noted with some satisfaction that Azam Tagulla's trees seemed somewhat recovered since the almond-farmer's water supply had been restored.

'Isn't this where you found the Frenchman's body?' Houcine asked as they rode.

'Yes, up there.' Hamou indicated the site high up the terraces, and the mokhazni shaded his eyes.

'Odd sort of spot to find a body. I mean, it's a long way to haul a corpse that size. If he was already dead.' Houcine thought about this for a moment more. 'And if he wasn't, I can't see why Meline would go trampling around there, can you?'

Hamou gave a noncommittal grunt, put his heels to the mule's barrel and encouraged Makouda into a faster trot. They left Tafla behind them, with its picturesque old houses and little white mosque, and started up the zigzagging track that looped up the side of the mountain. By the time they had completed the first great hairpin, the village and its fields already appeared far below them, the valley road further still. Tiziane was barely visible in a heat haze towards the southern horizon, the granite plateau rising beyond the town. Hamou looked down, then rode on a little way, and pulled the mule to a halt. He dismounted, shuffled carefully to the edge, then pulled Makouda a little way further along the track and looked down again.

Here, the rocky jut on which they stood overhung the ground below: beneath lay a sheer drop, broken only by the outstretched limbs of dusty trees and spiny shrubs growing out of the flanks of the mountain. Some of the trees showed pale wounds where branches had recently splintered away. Hamou remembered the one he had picked up to bushwhack a path to the body of Baptiste Meline.

'Come here.' He beckoned to Houcine.

Hakam and mokhazni gazed down at the vertiginous vista. Far below, the agricultural terraces hugged the land, following the contours, areas of green and brownish-red punctuated by undulating drystone walls and concrete irrigation channels. Directly beneath them lay the thick scrubland in which Hamou had found the corpse.

'See that... and there?' He pointed out the damaged vegetation.

Houcine nodded slowly. 'Something large fell down there, and not too long ago.'

'That's what I'm thinking, too.'

Hamou walked slowly around the track in this vicinity, examining the ground, but wind, the passage of feet and hooves and tyres had complexified and obscured the marks in the stony red dust. He remounted Makouda and waited for the mokhazni.

'Is that why we came?' Houcine asked. He sounded disappointed.

Hamou gave a short laugh. 'Partly, but no.'

'I don't know why you're being so mysterious about it.'

'Just testing out a hunch. It could be nonsense.'

Up they went, rounding the next long hairpin, putting yet more yawning space between them and the valley floor. The last time he had been up here, Hamou thought, it had not felt half so remote or gut-tightening. And on the previous occasion when they had come through the village of Tagtout, he had found it charming, with its tall, traditional houses and drifts of multicoloured cats. This time, as they passed through the mountain village, he became aware of a sudden stillness, of inimical stares; of eyes at windows and in doorways, and he remembered what Houcine had said then: *People go missing around here, never to be seen again. You won't get anyone from Tagtout coming to seek your help. They deal with everything themselves, the ancient way. You don't cross a Tagtouti.*

His anxieties must have transferred themselves to Makouda, for the mule started to throw its head and Hamou became suddenly afraid of falling off and finding himself injured and at the mercy of the narrow-faced, silent folk of Tagtout. But, after a bit of sideways dancing and snorting, Makouda settled, and they managed to negotiate the rise out of the village without further incident.

Slimane Chafari's house appeared as they topped the final ridge through the last of the mountain's trees, though this time the approach seemed easier, for some of the wild summer vegetation had either died or been cut back. They dismounted out of sight of the windows and Hamou once more checked the pistol he wore at his side, holstered on a leather bandolier. He watched Houcine check his weapon. They looked at one another.

'I'm coming with you this time,' the mokhazni said. He unslung his rifle. 'Two guns are better than one.'

Hamou nodded. 'I sincerely hope neither will be necessary.'

They tethered the animals and walked purposefully towards the house, knowing the public assassin probably had eyes on them all the way. Hamou knocked, then stood back, surveying the upstairs gunport through which Chafari had stuck the barrel of his bouchfar on the last occasion he was here. It was empty, but a moment later, the door swung open.

'Mohammed ben M'barek, what brings you here once more?' Slimane Chafari leaned against the doorframe, looking amused. At least he appeared to be unarmed.

'I'd rather you call me Hamou Badi.'

'Ah, but I knew your father, so it feels more natural to use the patronymic. And who's your friend with the rather good MAS-36?'

Houcine glanced down at his rifle, as if surprised to hear it praised by such a professional. Hamou had no illusions that if the assassin had wanted them dead, they'd both be lying stretched out on the ground by now. 'Put your weapon down, Houcine,' he told the mokhazni. He turned back to Chafari. 'Aren't you going to invite us in?'

An unreadable expression passed across the man's fine-boned face. 'You'll forgive me for my lack of hospitality, but it's not particularly convenient.'

'I'm afraid I'll have to insist,' Hamou said pleasantly. He watched the assassin's eyebrows shoot up.

'Very well. Just you, though, not the goon.'

Houcine looked affronted, but the hakam made a calming gesture. 'I'll be back out again shortly.' They both knew what this meant; the mokhazni nodded.

There was no offer of tea. Hamou removed his shoes, a surreally domestic gesture when entering a lion's den, he thought, and followed Slimane Chafari down the corridor, surreptitiously sniffing the air, his heightened zouhry senses working overtime. Food, a musky perfume or incense, and under those, something metallic, and something sulphurous. Fortified by his certainty, Hamou followed Chafari into the salon, where he immediately trod on something that made him yelp. He looked down, then picked it up. It was a small red metal car.

Slimane Chafari held his hand out for it and Hamou passed it over without a word, and watched as his long, thin fingers closed over it proprietorially. He reached into his pocket and pulled out the item he carried there, held it out on his outstretched palm.

'One of yours? I smelled molten lead on my last visit.'

The public assassin pursed his lips, then picked up the bullet and weighed it consideringly. The toy car had vanished from his hand as if by magic. 'It might be.' He tossed it up and caught it again. 'But a homemade slug is a homemade slug. A lot of people make their own ammunition.'

'They used to. My uncle Omar used to cast his own bullets. But lead's a lot harder to come by now since the French prohibited the use of it, as I'm sure you know.'

'It's possible to get hold of anything if you know the right people to ask.'

Hamou nodded. 'And what propellant do you use?'

'Now you're asking for all my secrets.'

The hakam regarded him, unsmiling.

Chafari raised his eyebrows. 'I make my own mixture.'

'Does it contain kbrit, as well as gunpowder?'

'Well, well, Mohammed ben M'barek, perhaps you are a magician, too.'

Hamou ignored this. 'That was the bullet that hit the adjutant of Tiziane when he was with the commandant's hunting party out on the plateau last month.'

'Those hunting parties are absurd events. People shooting wildly at anything that moves. It could have been anyone.'

'I already ruled out those who might have been using this sort of ammunition. And it occurred to me that the adjutant was just a little ahead of Baptiste Meline at the time of the shooting. Someone aiming for the *colon* might easily have struck the adjutant in error.'

The public assassin laughed. 'Someone who was not a good shot, maybe.'

'Or someone who was a little unlucky, given the chaos that ensued when the beaters cried the prey.' Hamou took the bullet back from the man, in case it went the same way as the little model car.

'Well, I suppose that is possible.'

'Maybe you finished the job you were paid for more recently?'

The public assassin regarded him sardonically. 'I heard that the man from Imouane with the wayward daughter had the fee he paid returned to him. I am sure if you seek him out, he will confirm that.'

'*Jdih, jdih!* Have you seen my car?' A small child came barrelling into the salon and locked himself onto Slimane Chafari's legs.

The old man tousled his hair, then magicked the toy as if out of his ear, which made the child giggle. 'Go and play quietly, leave the grown-ups to their business.' The assassin smiled indulgently, then met Hamou's stare. 'A young relative. Run along now, *ayao.*'

'I want to stay with you.' The boy looked up adoringly at the man he had called 'grandfather', then turned to regard Hamou. His eyes lit up. 'You're the man who showed me the sultan in the moon!'

'Hello, Sofiane,' Hamou said softly.

The aroma of rose and musk he had initially thought to be incense suddenly became stronger, and there she was in the doorway. Aicha Ghazaal. Aicha the Gazelle.

'Hello, Hamou Badi. I felt sure I'd be seeing you again.'

This time she was not wearing a French cocktail dress and deep red lipstick but a loose Berber kaftan and no make-up at all. She was more stunning than ever, and Hamou felt himself sinking into those green-gold and brown eyes. He had to drag his gaze away. 'He's your father?' Hamou nodded to Slimane Chafari.

Aicha laughed. 'Not precisely, though I'm sure the naughty

old man has children scattered far and wide and high and low across all the Atlas Mountains, don't you, habibi?'

The pair exchanged a fond, conspiratorial glance.

Hamou, who had come semi-prepared for a shoot-out, or for hard words at the least, was flummoxed. He watched as the woman ushered Sofiane out of the room to play with his toy car in another part of the house and tried to dredge up the words he needed, but it was Aicha who took charge.

'What I have to say is not for little ears,' she said, facing Hamou once the child was safely ensconced elsewhere. 'And I would rather we keep it between ourselves than share it with your mokhazni, too.'

'All right,' Hamou said hesitantly. 'But if I don't go out to tell him I'm OK, he's likely to come charging in here.' He went out to find Houcine with his rifle in his hands. 'You can relax, for now.'

Houcine frowned. 'You don't think he did it?'

'Killed Meline? I don't know. But I don't think he's going to kill me.'

When he went back in it was to find the table in the salon covered with small glasses, a bottle of clear liquid and a plate of gazelle horn pastries. Chafari passed him a brimming glass. It smelled strongly of alcohol, but who knew what else might be in it? Hamou put it carefully back on the table. Aicha and the public assassin laughed, and both swallowed the contents of their own glasses in a single gulp.

'It's not every day you discuss murder, is it?' she said, laughing, and refilled her glass. She looked askance at Hamou. 'It's just *mahia*.'

'That's illegal, isn't it?' Hamou said primly, and instantly regretted it.

Aicha laughed. 'Yes, we make fig brandy as well as bullets here. And you know my previous profession. How very brave of you, Hamou Badi, to enter this den of iniquity!'

The teasing stung him into a direct question. 'Were you involved in the death of Baptiste Meline?'

'Are you asking as an officer of the law?' Chafari asked.

'I'm not a policeman any more, only a hakam. I enforce no laws.'

'But you brought an armed mokhazni to our door.'

'He's there for my protection. I'm here as a representative of the community of Tiziane. And, I suppose, out of my own curiosity.'

'It's not an easy question you ask,' Aicha said with a wry smile.

'And it doesn't have an easy answer,' Chafari finished for her.

'Tell me, Hamou,' Aicha said, cocking her head at him. 'Do you believe in justice in this world?'

'Of course.' He felt uneasy.

'Life for life, eye for eye, and wounds equal for equal?'

'I'd rather see justice done under the auspices of the law.' Why did she prompt him into making such pompous statements?

'Sometimes, the law is insufficient. Especially when a crime happened a long time ago. Let me tell you a story. When the French first came to Tiziane there was considerable resistance. The local people did not accept the protectorate easily; some of them fought back and were punished for it. Those that didn't escape into the mountains were sent to prison, the women left to fend for themselves. One Frenchman, newly arrived as a settler, made the most of this situation, offering "help" to women on their own, in exchange for... favours. He had an eye for young women, often very young women. He made a nuisance of himself, but the authorities weren't interested in pursuing complaints against one of their own, and when tribal council members tried to intervene, they were either bribed or ignored.

'One woman refused to let him take her daughter. She went instead to offer herself to him in her place. But she never came home. Her body was found in the oued that runs through the town, shoved in under the bank like so much rubbish. And no one ever did a damned thing about it.'

Hamou's palms started to tingle with sudden deep heat. 'It was me. I found that body. I found... her.' And he related the events of that strange day, how he had stumbled on the wrapped corpse of the woman and, dragging his cousin Moha behind him, had gone running into the town, to report what he had found to the first adult he encountered, the orange seller, who called to the herb seller, who ran for the imam, who brought the mokhazni, who ran to the French commandant's office.

'That woman was my mother, Asir, and I was the one she was trying to protect.'

'I was eleven,' Hamou said miserably.

'And I ten.'

'Was it Meline?' After all he'd heard about the man, he could believe him capable of anything.

Aicha's eyes narrowed to gleaming slits. 'No one ever spoke the man's name. The whole thing was hushed up. I was sent to Casa, to my aunt, and I lived there for a few years. And then she died, and I had somehow to make a living. So, I ended up in the old medina, doing what women have always done when there is no choice left to them.'

'Asir may not have been my wife, but I loved her dearly and if I'd been around when Meline killed her, he would not have lived on this earth for another day, I promise you!' Chafari said fiercely. 'All these years I've made my enquiries. I've heard stories about that creature that would make you vomit. Men like him, they think they're untouchable.' He took Aicha's hand now and folded it between both of his own. 'I wish you had come back to find me rather than staying in the city.'

'You? You were in the Atlas, running with the rebels! Besides, I was sixteen when my aunt died, and bold: I thought I could handle anything. For all its hardships, I loved my life in the medina. Until I didn't. And then, well, fate intervened.' She gave Hamou a knowing smile. 'An angel came out of nowhere and gave me the chance to start anew. So, I reinvented myself, and came back home.'

'You come from Tagtout?' Hamou shivered. *Never cross a Tagtouti…*

'Born and bred. But you knew I came from around here.'

The Valley of the Almonds: he remembered now. 'And Baptiste Meline?'

Slimane Chafari got to his feet. 'It was me. I killed him.'

'Habibi—'

The public assassin cut across her. 'I'm an old man, a dying man. What can they do to me that time won't do more cruelly?' He looked squarely at Hamou. 'I shoved him off the cliff above Tafla after – yes, I admit it – after missing my shot up on the plateau.' He gave Hamou a rueful smile. 'Zakour and I thought it was the perfect diversion, to have him and a couple of his men play the fool, make a lot of noise to create confusion. A shame the French officer got in the way. It would have been the perfect setting for that old pig's death, down in the dust and dirt and boar shit. But...' He shrugged. 'Seems I've lost my touch.'

Hamou nodded as some of the pieces of the puzzle slotted into place. The amghrar of Aflawassif was a better actor than he'd given him credit for. Had the diary entry for their meeting been a backup plan in case the plot failed? 'How did you get him up onto that road above Tafla?' Another thought struck him. 'And where's his car?'

It was Aicha who answered. 'Look, Hamou Badi: a public service has been performed. Meline accumulated a lot of enemies in the years he's been here: fathers, mothers, brothers, cousins, employees, villagers, council members, amghrars.' She counted them off on her fingers. 'Whatever the old man claims, this wasn't a killing performed by a single person: this was justice carried out on behalf of an entire community. But no one will speak out, and there's not much point in trying to persuade them. The French are in disarray: they're not going to pursue a full investigation. And if it goes to the tribal elders? The worst they can do to me is to impose exile, but I'm only visiting, and when I leave you won't be seeing me again.'

'So, what, you're saying *you* killed Meline?' Hamou felt bewildered.

Aicha's lips curled – she was enjoying the drama. 'How do you think we got him up the mountain? I had the old jackal sniffing around me as soon as I arrived. At first he thought I was a rich Frenchwoman, and that kept him respectful for enough time to bait the trap, but he had a good nose, and soon I had him where I wanted him, and suggested a little afternoon sojourn at my dear old uncle's house.' She swept her hands wide. 'We started politely, with mint tea and patisserie.' She slid her gaze to Chafari and they grinned at one another.

'Maybe not just mint,' the public assassin offered with a throaty chuckle.

'And before things got too spicy, he was snoring away on the couch.'

'Merciful god, he weighed a ton,' the assassin complained. 'My back's not been right since.'

'Then we drove him down the mountain in the Chevrolet in the dark of night, and pushed him over the edge.'

'So, the fall killed him?' Hamou asked quietly, taking it all in.

'It's possible the knife in the back he received before he went over may have contributed,' Chafari offered helpfully.

'It was good of the water officer and chieftain of Tafla to lend us their aid in keeping it all quiet. If that old moaner Tagulla hadn't eventually plucked up the courage to come and ask help from the nice hakam, no one would ever have found that pig.' She paused, then added, 'You know the saying that it takes a village to raise a child? Well, maybe it takes a community to despatch a monster.' And Aicha Ghazaal threw back her head and laughed.

Hamou frowned, then asked tentatively, 'And the crescent mark on his forehead?'

The public assassin and his niece exchanged a bewildered look. 'I'm sorry, darling, I have absolutely no idea what you mean,' Aicha said at last.

Hamou's head felt as if it were bursting with too much unwelcome information. He picked up his glass of mahia and downed it in a single swallow, quelling the urge to choke as the liquid burned a passage down his oesophagus. Mastering himself at last, he asked the woman, 'And where will you go?'

'Oh, I don't know. Marrakech? Back to Casa? To start with, anyway. I've acquired a car now, a sweet little 2CV. Sofiane simply adores it. Then maybe on to France? Or even America – I have friends all over.' Aicha turned her dazzling smile on him. 'There's a whole new world out there, waiting for us. And you, darling Hamou, made it all possible. You were the catalyst for all that change, and for the natural justice carried out on Meline. You started everything with that generous gift you gave me in the Bousbir.'

Five minutes later, Hamou was outside again, to find Houcine propped against the garden wall, enjoying a surreptitious Anfa.

'Give me that.'

The mokhazni surrendered the half-smoked cigarette to Hamou at once. 'Sorry. I know I'm on duty.'

But Hamou was already puffing on it energetically. 'Don't worry about that, my friend,' he said after a few long blissful moments which helped to clarify a path through the moral morass. 'We're not on duty. In fact, we were never here.'

37

Baptiste Meline was buried without ceremony in the small Christian cemetery outside Tiziane. Hardly anyone attended: only the adjutant, the hakam, a couple of the clan chiefs Hamou suspected had turned up to be sure he really was dead, and some merchants keen to know the standing of his estate, since he owed them money.

Meline had died without making a will, so the matter of his estate had passed into the hands of Caid Hajj Abdullah, who was minded, he told Hamou, to redistribute the land back to the previous landowners, to pull down the house and split the proceeds from the contents between his household staff. The housekeeper, Jacqueline, however, had left the country burdened by many heavy bags and boxes, it was said, so there was not too much left. The gardener, however, was very happy to be assigned the beautiful Citroën and took to driving it around stuffed with his entire extended family.

Hamou's mother and sisters were fascinated by all the stories circulating. Hamou did his best to change the subject each time Meline's name came up, but there was still one outstanding question that plagued him from his conversation with Slimane Chafari.

One morning when he called at the house on his regular visit to see if the bus had delivered the item he was waiting for,

Hamou at last found his mother alone. Mimouna and Sofia had, he was told, gone to Tiznit for the day to visit the silver market.

'They will come home with all manner of trinkets and adornments unsuitable for single young women.' Lalla Saïda rolled her eyes.

'Well, those can be put away until they're married,' Hamou offered, then wished he'd bitten his tongue.

'And about that!' His mother leapt upon the subject like a cat on a mouse. 'I haven't been idle, even though you've been so uncooperative. Next week I have the representatives of three more young women coming to see me. I have high hopes for these new candidates for your bride, for I've cast my net as far as Taroudant. One of the girls is a teacher. There, I thought that might please you.'

'That was not my pleased face, Yam'mi.' Hamou sighed. The question gnawed at him. If he were to mollify his mother, perhaps she would answer it. He made her a bargain. 'I'll meet one of your candidates if you answer a question I have.'

Lalla Saïda narrowed her eyes at him. What sort of trick was this?

Hamou waited patiently, forming the question in his mind.

'All right then, what do you want to know?'

'I spoke with someone recently who knew my father long ago, when I was still a little boy. He said he'd got his gun from Father.' Hamou paused, watching as his mother tensed. 'He implied that Baab handled a lot of guns in his trade as a merchant.'

Lalla Saïda's expression had become watchful. 'Ask your question,' she said abruptly.

'Was that business, Yam'mi, or political conviction? Did Father really die in a car crash, as you told me?'

'That's two questions, Mohammed.'

She only ever called him that when she was angry with him. He waited.

At last, she sighed. 'Now you will have to meet two of my candidates.'

'You drive a hard bargain, Mother. All right, I'll meet them. But I don't promise to take either of them to wife,' he added warningly.

Lalla Saïda fiddled with the silver ring she always wore that featured two conjoined hands. Beneath those hands, Hamou knew, for he had loved to play with the clever ring when he was a baby, a heart was concealed. He watched now as his mother triggered the mechanism and ran a fingertip over the hidden symbol of love. Then she looked up at her only surviving boy. 'Your father was brave and proud. He loved his family and his country equally. I never lied to you, my son, he did die in a car crash. But it was not a simple accident. The vehicle he was in was fired upon by French troops and crashed off the mountain road from Sidi Ifni. He was bringing in a consignment of weapons for the rebels. There, now you know. He died a hero, but I wish every day that he had lived a coward, for what good did his death do anyone?'

Hamou took her hands in his own. 'I wish you'd told me.' He thought about what she had told him, running the words through his mind. He didn't know how to feel about it. He suspected he'd be taking those words out and turning them over again and again in the days to come. 'How could you bear to see me working for the French?'

His mother shook her head. 'What choice was there? And look at you now. You are Tiziane's hakam, and everyone says good things about you. I'm proud of you, my son. You went away to Casa as a boy and came back as a man.' Her eyes gleamed. 'One who is just about ready to settle down and start his own family.'

Hamou wriggled away to a different area of the conversation. 'It wasn't for nothing, though, was it? His courage, his resistance? The brave acts of those who went before put heart into those who followed. I can't say I agree with some of what the nationalists have done to further the cause but look: next week the sultan is being returned to us and the French are relinquishing the reins of power. Independence is coming to Morocco at last!' He watched as her face lit up. How strong she was, to have borne such a loss, and never spoken of it in all these years. How hard it must have been to raise a family alone and in sorrow, all the while thinking her husband's death had been in vain. He got up and enveloped her in a hug until she beat him off and told him to go away as she had a lot to be getting on with, and he went because he knew she did not want him to see her tears.

It was one of those peaceful November days when the sun was just strong enough to warm without excessive heat and the sky was a serene blue – the shade known as 'king's blue', which seemed apposite. He looked to the Djebel Kest in the distance. How peaceful it looked after all the drama that had subsumed the villages there just a couple of weeks before.

The bus was late, but by now he came more in hope than in expectation. He kicked a stone around with a pair of boys and got dust all over his babouches. They were wearing in nicely now, the acid yellow of the new leather gradually turning a buttery ochre. He was no longer marked out as a newcomer, but beginning to blend in, just as the new order in Tiziane was also beginning to settle. Jérome had formally been put in control of the handover and he and Caid Hajj Abdullah had placed Hamou in charge of the coming celebration of the sultan's return. Women in the villages were busily sewing Moroccan flags and bunting, new dresses and tunics; baking cakes and pastries, the men practising traditional dances. Musicians were arriving from all over, adding their percussive rhythms and high voices to the lively sounds of the town: it was shaping up to be quite a party!

He was thinking over some of the more complex logistics when he heard the bus draw up, groaning under the weight of all the cargo netted on its roof. Hamou saw suitcases and sacks, boxes and bicycles. He went around to the back of the vehicle to wait for cargo to be unloaded, and to keep out of the way of the descending passengers. He was peering up to see if he could spot his delivery, when someone tapped him on the shoulder. Thinking it must be the driver, Hamou turned. And stared. Then he shouted with delight.

'Moha!'

The two cousins embraced, and whooped, dancing a wild caper together. Hamou had never been so happy to see another man in all his life. At last, he held Moha away from him and regarded him in wonder. 'I was so worried about you!'

'I was worried about *you*!'

Moha called to someone, and Hamou saw a young woman approach. He recognised her from that fateful day with the Chadlis in the family apartment in Casa, though her name escaped him.

'My wife, Leila!'

'You're married!' Hamou could hardly believe it. 'You got married and never invited me.'

Moha laughed. 'Don't worry about that: we'll celebrate it again now we've come to live here.'

'You've come to live here?' Hamou echoed stupidly.

'We're all coming, my parents and two of my brothers and their families. I've bought us all building plots out on the Adai road, and for the interim – well, I'm sure the family will provide! I'll be going back and forth to Casa, of course, getting the business running again with the French going, and we'll be handling olives and almonds and argan from Tiziane. I'm going to talk to all the local chiefs: it's a great opportunity for everyone.'

Of course it was. Hamou grinned. He suspected he was going to be making a lot of introductions. 'I thought you were dead!' he said, remembering.

'I thought *you* were!' Moha was grinning so hard that his eyes had become shiny.

'I have your cat.'

'Madani?' Moha was astounded. 'How is that monster?'

'He's a she.'

'I know that!'

'Well, now she has five kittens.'

'What?'

'You'll meet them all.'

Moha shook his head. 'Amazing. It's all amazing. But that's not all. We have something else for you.'

'Ah yes, your washing machine,' Leila said quietly. She had a low, mellifluous voice and a calm presence, in fine counterpoint to the manic energy of her new husband. 'We have it with us.' She gestured towards the roof of the bus.

'Oh, that's wonderful! My mother will be delighted. Well, I hope she will.' It had taken Lalla Saïda a while to get used to the miracle of electricity in the home, and for the first few days she had cursed him, and left little piles of salt around the house, and barley porridge outside, to appease the djinns, whom she thought would be offended by this usurpation of their realm. Then, a thought struck Hamou. His last letter must somehow have found its recipient, otherwise how could there be a washing machine come in with the bus? *Thank you, Didi, my friend*, he offered into the ether. *Thank you!*

'And that's not all.' Moha chuckled. 'Say hello to the new nurse who's answered the call to work at the Tiziane clinic.'

He stepped aside, and there she was, tall and majestic, her mesmeric dark eyes fixed steadily on Hamou's face, an enigmatic smile curving her lips into a sweet crescent moon.

'Hello, Hamou Badi.'

Zina Chadli stepped towards him, and he took her hands in his, and the uncanny horizontal lines that crossed his palms began to sing.

The zouhry had found his own treasure at last.

Author Note

Writing this novel has been a very particular and unusual pleasure. Being a novelist is a solitary job – right up until it becomes an intense joint effort, shared with your publishing team, and then an interactive exercise, shared with your readers. But in this case, the process was different to my usual practice, in which I squirrel myself away with my odd ideas, chasing thoughts down ever-more unlikely rabbit holes as I carry out my research, and then writing the entire story without recourse to anyone else. It can be a lonely business! But *The Black Crescent* came into being out of conversations I had with my husband, Abdellatif. He had a lot of stories to tell – experiences of family and friends in the 1950s, experiences of his own in Casablanca. We would talk and talk, and I would go away and write, and then read each chapter to Abdel. Getting immediate feedback during the course of the writing is a wonderful luxury and spur: sparks fly, imagination ignites.

I had long wanted to write a book set in the mountainous region of south-west Morocco where we live for part of every year, and had been gathering ideas and snippets in a file on my laptop, but the overarching idea to bring them to life had never magically presented itself. Until Abdel and I started talking about the resistance movement in the 1950s, and suddenly a few of those notes in that long-ago file popped into my mind and started to stitch themselves together, and Hamou Badi – Hamou the Marvellous – Amazigh villager turned city policeman, came vividly to life to carry the story from the mountain communities I know so well into the urban heart of Casablanca, and back again to my fictional Tiziane. For Hamou spans two worlds. He has one foot in the traditional Amazigh culture he was born into, with its traditional customs and superstitions, and the other in the world of modern urban politics, just as the figure of the zouhry makes a bridge between the mundane human world and the supernatural land of the spirits.

There is a widely held belief in Morocco that the land hides countless hidden treasures, guarded by the djinns, who live their lives – largely invisibly – among and beside the human population. In the Quran, it is stated that while humans are created from the earth, djinns are smokeless fire, though their origins are probably pagan, as malevolent spirits of place. The legend goes that among humankind there appears from time to time a gifted person known as a zouhry (marked by a clear single horizontal line on their palms and/or their tongues) who has a special connection to the djinns, who carries their luck and can find treasure, and divine water. So prized is the zouhry that even in modern times there have been kidnappings and murders of zouhry children, in the belief that their blood can make the djinns relinquish their treasures. Zouhry children are particularly prized; after they turn ten (the end of the age of innocence), their magic becomes less strong.

Would it be a surprise to hear that Abdel carries the mark of the zouhry on both hands? Somehow it doesn't surprise me at all. I have photos of him in which his eyes shine like those of a djinn. I tease him that he is a treasure finder, and he found me. But in all honesty, I could not have written this book without him. His intimate knowledge of Casablanca, where he worked for a decade, was invaluable. Imagine, if you can, the difficulty of writing about a city which changed the names of nearly all its streets and quarters, bulldozed and rebuilt itself following independence! I tracked down a 1950s A–Z of Casa, but some of the pages were missing or illegible. It was Abdel who walked me through the city, physically and metaphorically, until I knew my way around. We had spent several weeks in Casablanca as we navigated the extraordinary complexities of the bureaucracy required in marrying across two countries and cultures. Visits to government departments there and in Rabat, to consulates and embassies. We walked around the city, took buses and petit taxis to beg favours and gather paperwork. In between we explored the old medina and the bookshop where Abdel used to work, the corniche, and the Great Mosque. Later, when I shipped the entire contents of my London flat by container ship to Casablanca, there to be transferred by road the 700km across the country and over the mountains to Abdel's native village in the Anti-Atlas, I spent a lot of nerve-wracking time in customs' offices and at Casa Port. (If you're interested in the story of how we met and married, it's told in detail on my website www.janejohnsonbooks.com). We've been married nearly eighteen years, and I learn more about Morocco, its rich history and complex cultural nuances with every passing day.

I love to learn when I write fiction, and I hope readers will enjoy learning alongside me. I knew the bare outlines of French imperialisation of North Africa, particularly the more brutal occupation of Algeria (which made a brief appearance in *The Sea Gate*), but little of the detail about how the protectorate, as it was termed, came to an end, and Morocco established its independence. France claimed Morocco in 1912, establishing a wide-ranging bureaucracy and infrastructure (thousands of miles of roads and railways) throughout the country to enable the utilisation of its many rich resources – mineral, agricultural and human. Moroccans were pressed into service on the land, in the cities, and in two world wars. During this time, the Sultan of

Morocco reigned but did not rule; but when the French exiled Mohammed V in 1953, the growing independence movement erupted into action – with demonstrations and protests, strikes, riots and violent direct action – culminating at last in his return in November 1955 and the French eventually relinquishing the protectorate.

Here are some of the resources I turned to in the writing of this novel:

'The significance of blood in religion and magic rituals in Morocco' by Dr Moundir Al Amrani (Department of English Studies and Humanities / National Institute of Posts and Telecommunications, Morocco)

'A Moroccan Political Party: The Istiqlal' – letter from Charles F. Gallagher, Tangier, July 23, 1956 (American Universities Field Staff)

'Urbanisme, hygiénisme et prostitution à Casablanca dans les années 1920' by Christelle Taraud, *French Colonial History* Vol 7, Michigan State University Press (2006)

Morocco: The Islamist Awakening and Other Challenges by Marvine Howe, Oxford University Press (2005)

'Casablanca 1952: Architecture for the anti-colonial struggle or the counter-revolution' by Léopold Lambert, *The Funambulist* magazine (2018)

Interview by Charles Stuart Kennedy with Donald R. Norland, who served as a Political Officer in Morocco from 1952–1956

The works of Mohammed Khair-Eddine and Albert Camus

Berber Village by Bryan Clarke Longman (1959)

Voice of Resistance: Oral Histories of Moroccan Women by Alison Baker, University of New York Press (1998). I cannot thank her enough for interviewing these extraordinarily brave women and letting them tell the stories in their own inimitable voices.

And if you're interested, you will find photos of the city and people of Casablanca in the fifties and of 'Tiziane' and the villages of the valley beneath the Djebel Kest on my website and on my Facebook page – find me at 'Jane Johnson (writer)'.

Jane Johnson
January 2023

Glossary

adhan	Islamic call to prayer
agadir	hilltop grainstore
agulez	wolf
ahwach	a traditional women's dance
alhamdullilah	praise be to God
aman iman	water is life
Amazigh	the Free People, Berbers
amghrar	chieftain
amti	auntie
asrayfi	water official
as salaam aleikum	peace be upon you
ayao	endearment to a child
azul	greetings
baab	father
babouches	leather slippers
badi	marvellous
bahra	beater
balak	make way
baraka	luck
bidonville	shantytown
bismillah	in the name of God
bled	land beyond government control, rural area

bouchfar	blunderbuss
boutagant	wild boar
braani	outsider
brochettes	kebabs
bstilla	savoury-sweet pie
caid	a local administrator
chauf	look
chausch	secretary, assistant
chebakia	sweet pastry
chelb	dog (insult)
chkam	spy
colon	settler
commissariat central	central police station
darija	Moroccan Arabic dialect
derb	quarter, area
djellaba	hooded robe
fantasie	show of horsemanship
fkih	scholar, wise man
gandoura	robe
goumier/goum	soldier, infantryman
guerrab	water-seller
habibi	dear one
haik	woman's robe
hakam	administrative role
hammam	bathhouse
handira	wedding cloak
haram	forbidden
harira	Moroccan soup
hashouma	shame

iftar	Ramadan evening meal
imim	delicious
inshallah	if God wills it
iromaen	settlers
jdih	grandfather
kafir	unbeliever
kbrit	sulphur
khalifa	steward, leader
kif	hashish
la bes	greeting, reassurance
lalla	female honorific, my lady, madam
ma'alem	expert, teacher, craftsman
maf-aman	water diviner
mahia	fig brandy
mahrach	small brown loaf
makouda	spicy potato dumpling
mechaoui	slow roasted lamb
mezian	good
mobilette	scooter
mokhazni	auxiliary, judicial guard
moqqadem	official
muezzin	the person who proclaims the call to the daily prayer
muqarnas	honeycomb plasterwork
na'am	yes
nafar	medina horn-player
niqab	full veil
okhti	sister

oued	wadi, dry riverbed
pasha	a high-ranked official
petit taxi	taxi for short distances
pisé	adobe, clay-and-straw building material
qisas	retaliation in kind
Ramadan Mubarak	Good Ramadan!
shokran	thank you
si, sidi	male honorific, sir
sous le manche	under the sleeve, illicit
tabac jaune	expensive French tobacco
tadgalt	prostitute (pl. tadgalin)
taibouhari	crunchy fried chickpeas
takbilt	tribe
tamelhaft	woman's traditional robe
tamqant	finger pointing
targua	irrigation system
tassanou	liver
timinciwin	good evening
tirrailleurs	skirmishers
triporteur	motorised tricycle
wachha	OK, no problem
yalla	come on
yam'mi	mother
youda	safe, enough
zellij	geometric tilework
zhlih	lost
zouhry	one possessing magical abilities

Acknowledgements

A novel is just a cry in the wilderness until your publishing team swings into action, and I am so lucky in mine. Huge thanks is due to my wonderful editors, Madeleine O'Shea and Nita Pronovost: I love that you work together to give me the best feedback any author could ask for; to Sophie Whitehead for always being there to help; to the extremely talented Emma Rogers and Jessie Price for creating such a striking cover; to Kathryn Colwell and Sophie Ransom for spreading the word; to the sales and marketing team at Head of Zeus for all their hard, innovative work. My global agent, Danny Baror, is an absolute legend.

Thank you to my dear friend Philippa McEwan for dropping everything to read and comment on the rough draft, and to Tahir Shah for his encouragement. Last of all, but always first, my brilliant husband, Abdel, my collaborator and sounding board, researcher and resident zouhry.

About the Author

JANE JOHNSON is a novelist, historian, and publisher. She is the UK publisher of many bestselling authors, including George R.R. Martin. She has written for both adults and children, including the bestselling novels *The Tenth Gift* and *The Salt Road*. Jane is married to a Berber chef she met while climbing in Morocco. She divides her time between London, Cornwall, and the Anti-Atlas Mountains. Connect with her on Twitter @JaneJohnsonBakr, on Facebook @Jane-Johnson-Writer, on Instagram @JaneJohnsonBakrim, or visit her website at JaneJohnsonBooks.com.